The Best
AMERICAN
SHORT
STORIES
1975

The Best AMERICAN SHORT STORIES 1975

And the Yearbook of the American Short Story

Edited by Martha Foley

1975

Houghton Mifflin Company Boston

Printed in the United States of America
C 10 9 8 7 6 5 4 3 2 1

ISBN: 0-395-20719-3
Library of Congress Catalog Card Number: 16-11387

"The Lie" by Russell Banks. First published in *fiction international*, 2/3, edited and published by Joe David Bellamy. Copyright © 1974 by Russell Banks.

"The School" by Donald Barthelme. First published in *The New Yorker*. Copyright © 1974 by The New Yorker Magazine, Inc.

"How to Win" by Rosellen Brown. First published in *The Massachusetts Review*, Vol. XIV, no. 4. Copyright © 1973 by The Massachusetts Review, Inc. From the book *Street Games* by Rosellen Brown. Reprinted by permission of Doubleday & Co., Inc.

"Desert Matinee" by Jerry Bumpus. First published in *fiction international* 2/3, edited and published by Joe David Bellamy. Copyright © 1974 by *fiction international*.

"Bambi Meets the Furies; by Frederick Busch. First published in *The Ohio Review*, Fall 1974. Copyright © 1974 by Frederick Busch.

"Waiting for Astronauts" by Nancy Chaikin. First published in *The Colorado Quarterly*, Autumn 1974. Reprinted by permission of The Colorado Quarterly and Nancy Chaikin. Copyright, 1974, by the University of Colorado, Boulder, Colorado.

"Paths Unto the Dead" by Mary Clearman. First published in *The Georgia Review*, Summer, 1974. Copyright © Summer, 1974, *Georgia Review*, University of Georgia.

"Tyranny" by Lyll Becerra de Jenkins. First published in *The New Yorker*. Copyright © 1974 by The New Yorker Magazine, Inc.

"Cadence" by Andre Dubus. First published in the *Sewanee Review* 82 (Summer 1974). Copyright 1974 by the University of the South. Reprinted by permission of the editor.

"Big Boy" by Jesse Hill Ford. First published in *The Atlantic Monthly*. Copyright © 1973, by The Atlantic Monthly Company, Boston, Mass. Reprinted with permission.

To Leslie Silko
Native American

Acknowledgments

GRATEFUL ACKNOWLEDGMENT for permission to reprint the stories in this volume is made to the following:

The editors of *The Atlantic, The Canadian Fiction Magazine, The Chicago Review, The Colorado Quarterly, Fiction International, The Georgia Review, Harper's Magazine, The Massachusetts Review, The New Yorker, The Ohio Review, Playboy, The Sewanee Review, The Southern Review;* and to Russell Banks, Donald Barthelme, Rosellen Brown, Jerry Bumpus, Frederick Busch, Nancy Chaikin, Mary Clearman, Lyll Becerra de Jenkins, Andre Dubus, Jesse Hill Ford, William Hoffman, Evan Hunter, Paul Kaser, Alistair MacLeod, Jack Matthews, Eugene McNamara, Reynolds Price, Abraham Rothberg, Leslie Silko, Barry Targan, Jose Yglesias.

Foreword

NEVER UNDERESTIMATE the power of a short story! It has been a little remembered but nevertheless historical fact that the first American short story provided literary fuel for the American Revolution. Called "A Pretty Story," it was written by Francis Hopkinson, the artist who designed the American flag. As I wrote in the introduction to *Two Hundred Years of Great American Short Stories, 1774–1974*, published earlier this year, the author's vivid narration of the wrongs inflicted by the British on them was wildly popular with the American colonists. It was published in pamphlet form in September, 1774, while the delegates to the First Continental Congress were assembling at Philadelphia and influenced their deliberations. Two printings were sold out almost immediately, raising the colonists' revolutionary fervor to martial pitch. Thus the story's ending, not in words but in a printed burst of thirteen stars, was prophetic.

What would a historian looking back two hundred years from now find most significant about today's literary scene? We ourselves are too close to it for a real perspective and, if we could acquire such distant hindsight, would undoubtedly be startled by the deductions that will be made. But surely that far-in-the-future chronicler will be impressed by our tremendous, countrywide creative ambition — the thousands of authors, the many literary magazines, the innumerable university courses given over to explication of writings past and present and the abundance of workshops for those eager to write.

Also that future historian is bound to be saddened by the neglect of the good books being published while millions of Americans, all unknowing, remained glued to trashy programs on television and the relentless huckstering interruptions of the commercials, "Buy! Buy! Buy!" In the early days of television, Lee Strasberg, the head of Actors' Studio, told me that just as novels provided much material for film adaptation, so short stories would for televising. Shortly afterward I got into an argument with J. D. Salinger over his refusal to permit television to broadcast his beautiful short stories. "But if every important writer takes the stand you do," I pleaded, "then American television will go the tawdry way of Hollywood movies." He answered only too accurately, "The writing was on the wall before the wall was there."

It has been a curious fact of magazine publishing that, whereas historical novels have been popular with American readers, there have been comparatively few short stories in recent years with both a historical background and literary merit. The imminence of the Bicentennial is undoubtedly responsible for a marked increase in the number of such stories. After many years of being accustomed to only the very modern in short stories, suddenly to be taken back in time is surprisingly relaxing.

The United States has only one indigenous literature, but since it has been oral and not printed its riches have been hidden from us newcomers. It is the literature of the American Indian. Not that hundreds of books by white men have not been written about Indians and most of them, like Western movies, scurrilous. James Fenimore Cooper did irreparable damage with his popular Leatherstocking Tales when, as in *The Last of the Mohicans,* he pictured them as kidnapers and ravishers of white women. Cooper's books are still so popular in Europe that dozens of cheap pulp imitations are ground out to thrill an ignorant reading public. Even liberal Longfellow ended the monotonous singsong of his best-known poem by patronizingly vouchsafing Hiawatha a glorious vision of the coming of the superior white race to his country whose religion he was admonished he should adopt. When I mentioned to a man in Genoa, Italy, a country most flooded with the Cooper imitations, that I was on my way back to the United States he demanded, "Aren't you afraid of the Indians?"

By his vivid and accurate stories of Indian life, Oliver La Farge tried to counter such bigoted prejudice as did Mary Austin and many other writers, historians, and anthropologists. Edmund Wilson in 1959 wrote his book, *Apologies to the Iroquois*, with its self-explanatory title. But we lacked still the veritable voice of the Indians themselves. In my writing classes at Columbia University I first had a chance to hear it from two talented Indian students. One was a Cherokee boy whose great-grandparents had been whipped along "The Trail of Tears" from their fertile green farms in Georgia to segregation on a reservation — polite name for a concentration camp — in an arid section of Oklahoma. The other was a Chinook young woman from the Northwest whose family still has to hide its origin by "passing." Hopefully such inhumanity will end now that Indian writers are emerging as such eloquent spokes men for their people in the stories of Vine Deloria, Thomas Sanchez, and the contributors to "The Man to Send Rain Clouds," an anthology of Indian short stories edited by Kenneth Rosen. *The South Dakota Review* has been a groundbreaker in the use of writing by and about Indians and *The North American Review*, the country's oldest magazine, has just devoted an entire issue to Indians. This is a rather lengthy prologue, I am afraid, to explain why I am so happy to be able to dedicate this year's book to Leslie Silko, a Laguna Pueblo, whose lovely poems and short stories have been appearing in various places. It is meant not only as a heartfelt tribute to her but to the other gifted authors of a race too long unappreciated by my own.

Another anniversary this year but one not marked by marching bands and flying flags has important literary significance. It is the fiftieth anniversary of surrealism. American readers are unaware of how much its influence has permeated our own fiction. Because a modern version of the movement was inaugurated in France, most Americans, when they know of its existence at all, are inclined to dismiss surrealism as some esoteric alien theory about writing. The best brief definition I know is to be found in the American Heritage dictionary: "A literary and artistic movement that attempts to express the workings of the subconscious mind." Joyce's *Ulysses* of course is the most famous example today. But pick up a novel or story of thirty years back and notice how often such expressions interrupt the narration as "he thought," "it seemed to her," "they believed," etcetera, etcetera. Also how it seemed to be some divine law that every time a character spoke it must be announced "he said," "she exclaimed" and a description given of how the words were uttered. Today readers can take all that for granted because we have learned to understand what is called interchangeably "stream of consciousness" or "stream of the unconscious" or "association of ideas."

Coincidentally with surrealism's fiftieth anniversary, there has been more talk going around in literary circles these days about "innovative writing," once called "experimental writing," than I can remember hearing since the old days of *transition,* with which I had the good fortune to be associated. Published by Eugene and Maria Jolas in Paris from 1927 to 1938, *transition* was a focus for the avant garde of American and English writers. Its contributors included Joyce — whose *Finnegan's Wake* it published serially — Gertrude Stein, Hart Crane, William Carlos Williams, Kay Boyle, and translations of French surrealists.

"Jan, actor a airling, beluved Maie. Na ibye a accidieful to tel hir suo. 'Ma bellibone, metels, lowe, delite, bless, ma solance a bewte ik adoure owe.' Te literalist sane a bassed hire."

No, the printer did not pie a lot of type. Those are the opening lines of a short story called "Cokewold Fore Espousage" written in obsolete English, not to be confused with either Old English or Middle English but consisting of words which more recently have fallen by the wayside since 1500. With the brashness of youth I contributed it to *transition* in an effort to out-Joyce Joyce and out-Stein Stein. It is too long, of course to reprint here even if I wanted to be so cruel but I thought it might be fun to resurrect this sample. It was also fun to write. It was fascinating to discover how many words damned as obsolete are still useful and should never have been thrown away. Take *agamist,* for instance, which fits in wonderfully with present mores. One guess! Why, it is someone who doesn't believe in marriage at all!

In going through some early files of *Story* magazine I came across a brilliant 1936 analysis of experimental writing by James Laughlin, then a promising young short story writer just out of Harvard, and now well-known as publisher of New Directions. I laughed when I realized my obsolete story might have been called "Old Words for New" as I saw again the title of Laughlin's essay, "New Words for Old."

There is nothing new about experimental writing, [he begins]. In the Second Century B.C. *'Father' Ennius was making tmeses worthy of our own e e cummings. 'Saxo* cere comminuit brum' *was a good one; a separation of the word itself to show that 'the head is* visibly *split.' Cummings might translate that as 'with a rock (t)he* heSMaSHEd.' *Nashe and Shakespeare were quite as ready to invent a word as James Joyce. Nashe's 'Lenten Stuffe' is a fantastic treasury of neologisms, and the well-remembered 'multitudinous seas* incarnadine' *is only one of the Bard's poetic inventions. Rabelais was a word-maker. So was Jeremy Bentham.*

. . . Throughout the course of every literature are found writers who experimented with language when its conventions suffocated their originality. In terms of his poetical environment Wordsworth was a brash experimenter. His 'Preface to the Lyrical Ballads,' with its demand that poetry return to the common spoken tongue of the common man, compares in spirit with the manifestoes of the transition *group trying in other ways to liberate poetic diction.*

Laughlin goes on to mention a number of other important innovators, such as Dante, Rimbaud, and Eugene Jolas. Surprisingly he omits Laurence Sterne, the literary progenitor of James Joyce and devotee of those one-paragraph chapters which lately have become so popular with short story writers.

Not only is Laughlin's concluding paragraph startlingly apropros of our present national and world situation but it graphically conveys the radical mood of those Depression years.

I have said that I believe that linguistic change must lead the way for social change, or, at least, go hand in hand with it. For when language habits are disintegrated, when the camouflage of verbal superstition is removed, an entrenched oligarchy will find itself marooned on an ever diminishing island of popular support. Thus for me the experimental writer is playing a part as valuable, in its way, as that of the picket or cell organizer. So let us give honor where honor is due: to the shock troops, the fighters in the front line of language, the small intransigeant company of experimental writers.

What Laughlin says about change in language and literature heralding social change is especially significant this year. It was in

the late twenties and in the thirties that innovative writing flour-
ished. My own short story in obsolete words was published by
transition in 1929. That was the year *Variety,* the Broadway theat-
rical weekly, proclaimed in a front page headline WALL STREET LAYS
AN EGG! A year later the Depression was upon us.

A danger confronting the experimental writer is to forget that
style and content should be indivisible. The temptation is to become so preoccupied with form that content is neglected. Rabelais
had a lot of delight in his long word lists just as Joyce did in his
punning, but he never neglected Gargantua and his appetites nor
Pantagruel and his impishness. Nor did Sterne in *Tristram Shandy*
for all his unorthodox literary capers get very far away from
Shandy Hall or the people and places in *Sentimental Journey.* You
know where you are and with whom you are all the way in *Ulysses*
but I feel *Finnegan's Wake* is another matter. There Joyce apparently became so absorbed in what I heard him call while he was
writing it "a mighty synthesis" that I think many of his enthusiastic
admirers, including at least this reader, at times are left out in the
cold.

Often only after they are gone is it fully realized how valuable
such magazines as *transition* and *Story* are. In their time the number
of such magazines was very small. Today this country is blessed
with many more, and good new ones keep coming. Emphasis has
often been placed on the fact that the majority of our most important authors first appeared in the literary magazines. However,
many of our established authors also are proud to appear in those
"little" magazines because of respect for their high editorial standards. Robert Penn Warren, Tennessee Williams, Joyce Carol
Oates are some names that come to mind.

A much larger crop than usual of new literary magazines arrived
on the scene this year, some unfortunately too late to be considered
for this anthology. Among the most intriguing are *Fiction International, Itinerary: Fiction, Ontario Review, Hawaii Review, New Letters, Re: Artes Liberales, Striver's Row,* and the *Capillano Review.* An
unusual project is *The Bicentennial Collection of Texas Short Stories,* the
first in a series to be devoted to the amazing number of good
writers who have come from Texas.

The death of John Crowe Ransom, a fine poet, editor of the
influential *Kenyon Review,* and leader of the New Criticism move-

ment, occurred since the last edition of *The Best American Short Stories,* a collection he once wrote me he would always be glad to help. I was never able to agree with the New Critics' insistence on separating events in an author's life from consideration of their effects on his writing. But Mr. Ransom was a courtly Southern gentleman and our discussions about it the summer we both taught at the University of Utah were always very friendly. His going is a great loss to American letters.

I am grateful to all the editors who have kept this anthology supplied with copies of their magazines and to their authors for generously granting reprint rights. The editor of any new magazine is urged to send copies to me.

The editors and staff of Houghton Mifflin are entitled to gratitude for their help. Finally, tribute is paid to the memory of Edward J. O'Brien who founded this anthology.

Martha Foley

Contents

The Best
AMERICAN
SHORT
STORIES
1975

RUSSELL BANKS

The Lie

(FROM FICTION INTERNATIONAL)

A TEN-YEAR-OLD BOY — maybe eleven maybe nine but no older and certainly no younger — kills his buddy one Alfred Coburn while the two are enemy espionage agents engaged in a life-or-death struggle in the middle of the wide perfectly flat tarred roof of an American owned hotel in Hong Kong. The young killer whose name is Nicholas Lebrun stabs his good buddy in the chest just below the left nipple slicing deftly between two ribs thence through the taut pericardium and plunging unimpeded into the left ventricle of the heart — stabs his friend with an inexpensive penknife manufactured by the Barlow Cutlery Corporation of Springfield, Massachusetts. This knife has a plastic simulated wood grip and a 2½″ steel blade. Also a 1½″ smaller narrower blade.

Alfred poor wide-eyed Alfred squeaks in surprise and falls. Nicholas understands what has happened and runs home.

A distance of approximately one city block separates the Trans-ilex parking lot that has been serving as the roof of an American owned hotel in Hong Kong and the asbestos shingled wood-framed mid-Victorian house that has been serving as the Lebrun home and hearth for over forty years — ever since Nicholas' paternal grandfather was a young newly wedded still childless man. Nicholas' grandfather was named Ernest but he was called Red because of the color of his thick short-cropped hair and mustache. A clockmaker and a good one too Ernest learned his trade (he would have said craft) in his home town of Hartford, Connecticut, and then emigrating to Waltham, Massachusetts, when the time industry shifted to that city shortly before the outbreak of World War II, he went to work for the Waltham Watch Company. A French Protestant and native New Englander, Ernest Lebrun: thrifty, prudent, implacably stable, high-minded and honorable, incorruptible, intelligent, organized, good-humored — all resulting in his having become well-liked and financially secure long before he was forty years old. It might be told that he died in a dreamless sleep shortly after World War II had finally ground to a bewildered halt and sometime during the year that commenced with his grandson Nicholas' birth and winked out with the child's first birthday, a fact surely of considerable moment for Ernest (Red): hanging onto shreds of life until after the birth of his first male grandchild the son of an only son assured finally and at the very end of the continuation of the name, etc.

It is because of the distance between the Transilex parking lot and home and because he ran all the way home that Nicholas is out of breath panting and redfaced when he turns into the scrubby yard and thus arrives safely at what appears to be and what later turns out to be heaven.

Robert Lebrun the boy's middle-ageing auburn haired father a paid-in-full member of the United Association of Plumbers and Pipefitters (AFL-CIO) Local #143 is comfortably swinging on the porch glider smoking an after-supper cigar in the orange summer evening light and from time to time reading from the tabloid newspaper spread on his lap.

Abruptly Nicholas parks himself next to his father upsetting with his momentum the glider's gentle vacillation and the father asks the son his only child heir to his ancient name and lands why is he running? The lad tells his father why he is running. Not of course without considerable encouragement from the father — whose cigar goes slowly out during the telling.

Young Nicholas does not forget to mention the fact that just as he steps off the flat square expanse of tar that has been serving as the Transilex parking lot — now almost innocent of parked automobiles — and onto Brown Street's narrow sidewalk he happens to glance back at his little friend's fallen body, that small heap of summer clothing and inert flesh already used up and thrown out dropped in the middle of the great black square. A little crumpled pile of stuff lying next to the right front tire of a bottle-green British Ford sedan. And in that fraction of a second Nicholas realizes that the owner of the bottle-green sedan — a man who lives in the neighborhood and who unfortunately is notoriously effeminate a practicing pederast in fact mocked to his face by all the neighborhood kids and behind his soft back by all the parents — is strolling blithely across the lot is approaching his little car from the side opposite Nicholas and the car's right front tire. . . .

Now it's possible that the man whose name by the way is Toni Scott does catch a glimpse of Nicholas in flight, but that possibility shall have to remain equivocal and unrealized. The facts which follow shall demonstrate why this is so.

Toni who works as a waiter in an attractively decorated Boston cocktail lounge of socially ambiguous though not inconsiderable fame for several years now has been saving at least five dollars a month by parking his car (illegally to be sure) in the Transilex parking lot always taking care to remove his car well before nine P.M. departure of the Transilex cafeteria second shift and — because of his nighttime working hours — usually managing to slip the innocuous little sedan back into the lot sometime between the four A.M. unlocking and five A.M. arrival of the cafeteria first shift. However this particular summer evening ritual removal of his car from its stolen space definitely even though only partially and from afar *is* observed over young Nicholas Lebrun's fleeing shoulder (fateful damning backward glance!) just before the rigorously bathed meticulously groomed idly smiling Toni Scott filled to the eyes with sweet memories and still sweeter anticipation discovers Alfred Coburn's hard sun-haired body by accidentally smashing its rib cage, sternum and spine with the right front tire of his bottle-green car.

He cuts the wheel hard to the left, revs up the tiny four cylinder motor and spins the car backwards swinging the front of the car around in an arc to the right — so that he can make his exit from the lot by the very gate Nicholas has used just seconds earlier. . . .

It is at this point in the boy's narrative that Robert Lebrun interrupts his son and compels him to insist that no one absolutely no one saw him stab his playmate. He makes the boy reassure him that he (Nicholas) did not extract the penknife from Alfred's chest — an unnecessary reassurance for Toni's right front tire has already torn the knife from its nest of flesh, bone and blood, has ground it against pavement, paint, white pebbles in the tar, has smashed the plastic simulated wood grip and removed all fingerprints. Then Lebrun makes Nicholas repeat several times the part of his narrative that has to do with Toni Scott's arrival on the scene and finally after telling his son in clear exact and step-by-step terms just what he intends to do Lebrun stomps into the house and yelling Emergency Police! to the telephone operator he calls the cops.

In a stage-whisper and speaking rapidly he says that he is Robert Lebrun of number forty-eight Brown Street and his son and another neighborhood kid have just been sexually molested by the neighborhood fag and his son broke away from the guy but the other kid is still with the sonofabitch in his car which is parked in the Transilex parking lot the one that used to be the old Waltham Watch factory lot and he (Lebrun) is leaving right now to kill that filthy sonofabitch with his bare hands so if they want Toni Scott alive they have about three minutes to get to him. He makes one other call — to Alfred Coburn senior over on Ash Street some three blocks further from the parking lot than the Lebrun house is — and using that same rapid whispery voice he tells Alfred Coburn senior what he has just related to the cops.

Then Lebrun lunges for the parking lot and Toni Scott who dials the police department from the public phone booth that stands luminous in a dark corner of the lot hears through the glass walls the rising shrieks of approaching sirens before he has even completed dialing the number . . .

In this story everyone who lies and knows that he lies does so effectively. That is he is believed. Furthermore everyone who lies and yet knows not that he lies — meaning for example Evelyn Lebrun (Nicholas' adoring mother) and poor Alfred Coburn senior and the two or three neighborhood ladies who claim they saw Toni Scott talking to the boys from inside his little green foreign car heard the awful thing call the tykes from their play saw him smilingly offer them candy if they would get into his car — these also manage to lie effectively: they are believed by the police, the rest of the people in the neighborhood, the newspapers, *Time,* the district attorney, the psychiatrists testifying for the prosecution, the psychiatrists testifying for the defense, the defense attorney himself (although he pretends not to believe), the judge, the jury, and the U.S. Court of Appeals.

Everyone who tells the truth — meaning Toni Scott the thirty-eight-year-old fatting balding homosexual — tells the truth stupidly, inconsistently, alternately forgetting and remembering critical details, lying about other unrelated matters and so on into the night. Toni Scott is not believed although now and then he probably is pitied. . . .

Thus the compassionately prompt arrival of the police at the scene of Alfred Coburn's beastly murder — twice-slain savagely by a scorned and therefore enraged deviate — plucks Toni Scott from the huge pipe fitter's hands of Robert Lebrun only to set him down again one year later in Walpole State Prison (life plus ninety-nine years).

It may have been noticed that the original lie originated with Nicholas' dad. It was not mentioned however that once the lie had been designed and manufactured, once it had been released to the interested public, Robert Lebrun began to have certain secret misgivings about the way the lie was being used. The cause of these hesitant shadowy misgivings was not as one might suppose the absurd fate of Toni Scott. Rather it was the consummate skill, the unquestioning grace of movement from blatant truth to absolute falsehood that consistently repeatedly and under the most trying of circumstances was demonstrated by Robert Lebrun's only begotten son the young Nicholas Lebrun. It was almost as if for Nicholas there was no difference between what actually happened and what was said to have happened . . .

"What happened, Nickie?" his father asks. "Why the hell you running in this heat? You never run like that when you're called, only when you're being chased."

"Nobody's chasing me," the kid answers, "but something really awful happened."

"What?"

"I don't know actually. Me and Al was just playing around, see, and he got cut with a knife, only I didn't mean it, it was an accident, honest. You gotta believe me, Pa." The boy uses the same name for his father that Robert Lebrun was taught to use for his.

This probably is the point at which Lebrun begins shuffling fearfully through his memories and imagination for an alibi. The fear of retribution which he now believes to be dominating his son's entire consciousness (even to the boy's physical perceptions, of the scaley white glider, the splintery porch floor catching against the corrugated bottoms of his U.S. Keds, the cooling air laden with the smell of freshly cut grass, the cold zinc-smell of his father's dead cigar, the sounds of his mother's sleek hands washing dishes in warm soapy water) — this fear is in reality now the father's very own.

The father attributes to his son the overwhelming quantity of fear that he knows would have to be his were *he* ten or nine or eleven years old,and faced with "something really awful," "an accident," a wounding that occurs without warning, absolute and in its own terms as well. Right in the middle of the game.

The father's now, the force behind the knife as it buries a 2½″ steel blade in the playmate's bony chest; then comes the realization that the boy is dead absolutely and forever no joke no pretense no foolish vain imitation of the absence of existence; his now, the flight from the body's silent accusation away from this gusty hotel rooftop so deserted and stark in the midst of ragged teeming Oriental architecture; and his, the image seen through tinted wraparound glass of the figure of Toni Scott swishing across the lot towards his bottle-green sedan . . .

✓ And thus Robert Lebrun lies not to save his son but rather to save himself. His own father Ernest (Red) Lebrun would have found the dynamic reversed from the beginning of the lie to the end, and no doubt Robert at some point along the progression was aware of this, knew that his own father were *he* placed in a similar circumstance would not have been able to credit *his* son with possessing an overpowering fear of retribution and thus the child's experience would have remained intact, still his very own, unmolested by the rush of the father's consciousness of himself. And no doubt this awareness of how Ernest Lebrun would have responded to a similar set of circumstance's circumstances in which he Robert Lebrun would have been the lonely unmolested son, was a critical factor in making it impossible even now for Robert to become anything other than the lonely unmolested son. The red-headed Ernest gave to his young son an absolute truth and an absolute falsity and for that reason Robert was forever a child. Robert to his son gave relative truth and relative falsity and for that reason Nicholas was never a child.

The question of responsibility then seems not to have been raised in at least three generations.

DONALD BARTHELME

The School

(FROM THE NEW YORKER)

WELL, WE HAD all these children out planting trees, see, because we figured that . . . that was part of their education, to see how, you know, the root systems . . . and also the sense of responsibility, taking care of things, being individually responsible. You know what I mean. And the trees all died. They were orange trees. I don't know why they died, they just died. Something wrong with the soil possibly or maybe the stuff we got from the nursery . . . wasn't the best. We complained about it. So we've got thirty kids there, each kid had his or her own little tree to plant, and we've got these thirty dead trees. All these kids looking at these little brown sticks, it was depressing.

It wouldn't have been so bad except that . . . Before that, just a couple of weeks before the thing with the trees, the snakes all died. But I think that the snakes — well, the reason that the snakes kicked off was that . . . you remember, the boiler was shut off for four days because of the strike, and that was explicable. It was something you could explain to the kids because of the strike. I mean, none of their parents would let them cross the picket line and they knew there was a strike going on and what it meant. So when things got started up again and we found the snakes they weren't too disturbed.

With the herb gardens it was probably a case of overwatering, and at least now they know not to overwater. The children were very conscientious with the herb gardens and some of them proba-bly . . . you know, slipped them a little extra water when we weren't looking. Or maybe . . . well, I don't like to think about sabotage, although it did occur to us. I mean, it was something that crossed our minds. We were thinking that way probably because before that the gerbils had died, and the white mice had died, and the salamander . . . well, now they know not to carry them around in plastic bags.

Of course we *expected* the tropical fish to die, that was no surprise. Those numbers, you look at them crooked and they're belly-up on the surface. But the lesson plan called for a tropical-fish input at that point, there was nothing we could do, it happens every year, you just have to hurry past it.

We weren't even supposed to have a puppy.

We weren't even supposed to have one, it was just a puppy the Murdoch girl found under a Gristede's truck one day and she was afraid the truck would run over it when the driver had finished making his delivery, so she stuck it in her knapsack and brought it to school with her. So we had this puppy. As soon as I saw the puppy I thought, Oh Christ, I bet it will live for about two weeks and then . . . And that's what it did. It wasn't supposed to be in the classroom at all, there's some kind of regulation about it, but you can't tell them they can't have a puppy when the puppy is already there, right in front of them, running around on the floor and yap yap yapping. They named it Edgar — that is, they named it after me. They had a lot of fun running after it and yelling, "Here, Edgar! Nice Edgar!" Then they'd laugh like hell. They enjoyed the ambiguity. I enjoyed it myself. I don't mind being kidded. They made a little house for it in the supply closet and all that. I don't know what it died of. Distemper, I guess. It probably hadn't had any shots. I got it out of there before the kids got to school. I checked the supply closet each morning, routinely, because I knew what was going to happen. I gave it to the custodian.

And then there was this Korean orphan that the class adopted through the Help the Children program, all the kids brought in a quarter a month, that was the idea. It was an unfortunate thing, the kid's name was Kim and maybe we adopted him too late or something. The cause of death was not stated in the letter we got, they suggested we adopt another child instead and sent us some interesting case histories, but we didn't have the heart. The class took it pretty hard, they began (I think; nobody ever said anything to me directly) to feel that maybe there was something wrong with the school. But I don't think there's anything wrong with the school, particularly, I've seen better and I've seen worse. It was just a run of bad luck. We had an extraordinary number of parents passing away, for instance. There were I think two heart attacks and two suicides, one drowning, and four killed together in a car accident. One stroke. And we had the usual heavy mortality rate among the grandparents, or maybe it was heavier this year, it seemed so. And finally the tragedy.

The tragedy occurred when Matthew Wein and Tony Mavrogordo were playing over where they're excavating for the new federal office building. There were all these big wooden beams stacked, you know, at the edge of the excavation. There's a court case coming out of that, the parents are claiming that the beams were poorly stacked. I don't know what's true and what's not. It's been a strange year.

I forgot to mention Billy Brandt's father, who was knifed fatally when he grappled with a masked intruder in his home.

One day, we had a discussion in class. They asked me, were did they go? The trees, the salamander, the tropical fish, Edgar, the poppas and mommas, Matthew and Tony, where did they go? and I said, I don't know, I don't know. And they said, who knows? and I said, nobody knows. And they said, is death that which gives meaning to life? and I said, no, life is that which gives meaning to life. Then they said, but isn't death, considered as a fundamental datum, the means by which the taken-for-granted mundanity of the everyday may be transcended in the direction of —

I said, yes, maybe.

They said, we don't like it.

I said, that's sound.

They said, it's a bloody shame!

I said, it is.

They said, will you make love now with Helen (our teaching assistant) so that we can see how it is done? We know you like Helen.

I do like Helen but I said that I would not.

We've heard so much about it, they said, but we've never seen it.

I said I would be fired and that it was never, or almost never, done as a demonstration. Helen looked out of the window.

They said, please, please make love with Helen, we require an assertion of value, we are frightened.

I said that they shouldn't be frightened (although I am often frightened) and that there was value everywhere. Helen came and embraced me. I kissed her a few times on the brow. We held each other. The children were excited. Then there was a knock on the door, I opened the door, and the new gerbil walked in. The children cheered wildly.

ROSELLEN BROWN

How to Win

(FROM THE MASSACHUSETTS REVIEW)

ALL THEY NEED AT SCHOOL is permission on a little green card that says *Keep this child at bay. Muffle him, tie his hands, his arms to his ankles, anything at all. Distance, distance. Dose him.* And they gave themselves permission. They never even mentioned a doctor, and their own certified bureaucrat in tweed (does he keep a badge in his pocket like the cops?) drops by the school twice a year for half a day. But I insisted on a doctor. And did and did, had to, because Howard keeps repeating vaguely, that he is "within the normal range of boyish activity."

"But I live with it, all day every day."

"It? Live with *it?*"

Well, Howard can be as holy as he likes, I am his mother and I will not say "him." Him is the part I know, Christopher my first child and first son, the boy who was a helpless warm mound once in a blue nightie tied at the bottom to keep his toes in. ("God, Margaret, you are dramatic and sentimental and sloppy. How about being realistic for a change?") "It" is what races around my room at night, a bat, pulling down the curtain cornice, knocking over the lamps, tearing the petals off the flowers and stomping them, real or fake, to a powder.

Watch Christopher take a room some time; that's the word for it, like an army subduing a deserted plain. He stands in the doorway always for one extra split-split second, straining his shoulders down as though he's hitching himself to some machine, getting into harness. He has no hips, and round little six-year-old shoulders that look frail but are made of welded steel that has no give when you grab them. Then what does he see ahead of him? I'm no good at guessing. The room is an animal asleep, trusting the air, its last mistake. (See, I am sympathetic to the animal.) He leaps on it and leaves it disemboweled, then turns his dark eyes to me where I stand — when I stand, usually I'm dervishing around trying to stop the bloodshed — and they ask me Where did it go? What happened? Who killed this thing, it was just breathing, I wanted to *play* with it. Christopher. When you're not here to look at me I have to laugh at your absurd powers. You are incontinent, you leak energy. As for me, I gave birth to someone else's child.

There is a brochure inside the brown bottle that the doctor assigned us, very gay, full-color, busy with children riding their bicycles right through patches of daffodils, sleeping square in the middle of their pillows, doing their homework with a hazy expression to be attributed to concentration, not medication. NON-ADDICTIVE! NO SIGNIFICANT SIDE EFFECTS! Dosage should decrease by or around puberty. Counter-indications epilepsy, heart and circulatory complications, severe myopia and related eye problems. See Journal of Pediatric Medicine, III 136, F'71; Pharmacology Bulletin, v. 798, 18, pp. 19–26, D'72. CAUTION: DO NOT ALLOW CHILDREN ACCESS TO PILLS! SPECIAL FEATURE: U-LOK-IT CAP! REMEMBER, TEACH YOUR CHILD THE ETIQUETTE OF THE MEDICINE CABINET!

I know how he dreams me. I know because I dream his dreams. He runs to hide in me. Battered by the stick of the old dark he comes fast, hiccoughing terror. By the time I am up, holding him, it has hobbled off, it must be, into his memory. I've pulled on a robe, I spread my arms — do they look winged or webbed? — to pull him out of himself, hide him, swear the witch is nowhere near. He doesn't go to his father. But he won't look at my face.

It was you! He looks up at me finally and says nothing but I see him thinking. So: *I* was the witch, with a club behind my bent back. I the hundred-stalked flower with webbed branches. I with the flayed face held in my two hands like a bloody towel. Then how can I help him?

I whisper to him, wordless; just a music. He answers "Mama." It is a faint knocking, through layers of dirt, through flowers.

His sister Jody will dream those dreams, and all the children who will follow her. I suppose she will, like chicken pox every child can expect them: there's a three o'clock in the dark night of children's souls too, let's not be too arrogant taking our prerogatives. But if she does, she'll dream them alone, no accomplices. I won't meet her halfway, give her my own last fillip, myself in shreds.

I've been keeping a sort of log: a day in the life. For no purpose, since my sense of futility runs deeper than any data can testify to. Still it cools me off.

He is playing with Jacqueline. They are in the Rosenbergs' yard. C. is on his way to the sandbox which belongs to Jackie's baby brother, Brian, so I see trouble ahead. I will not interfere. No, *intervene* is the word they use. Interfere is not as objective, it's the mess that parents make, as opposed to the one the doctors make. As he goes down the long narrow yard at a good clip C. pulls up two peonies, knocks over Brian's big blonde blocky wooden horse (for which he has to stop and plant his feet very deliberately, it's that well-balanced, i.e., expensive). Kicks over short picket fence around tulips, finally gets to sandbox, walks up to Jackie whose back is to him and pushes her hard. She falls against fence and goes crying to her mother with a splinter. She doesn't even bother to retaliate, knowing him too well? Then he leans down into the sand. Turns to me again, that innocent face. It is not conniving, or falsely naive, I swear it's not. He isn't that kind of clever. Nor is he a gruff bully boy who likes to fly from trees and conquer turf: he has a small peaked face, a little French, I think, in need of one of those common Gallic caps with the peak on the front; a narrow forehead on which his dark hair lies flat like a salon haircut. Anything but a bully, this helpless child of mine — he has a weird natural elegance that terrifies me, as though it is true, what I feel, that he was intended to be someone else . . . Now he seems to be saying, Well, take all this stuff away if you don't want me to touch it. Get me out of this goddamn museum. Who says I'm not provoked? *That's what you say to each other.*

Why is *he* not glass? He will break us all without so much as chipping.

The worst thing I can think. I am dozing in the sun, Christopher is in kindergarten, Jody is napping, and I am guiltily trying to coax a little color into my late-fall pallor. It's a depressing bleary sun up there. But I sleep a little, waking in fits and snatches when Migdalia next door lets her kid have it and his whine sails across the yards, and when the bus shakes the earth all the way under the gas mains and water pipes to China. The worst thing is crawling through my head like a stream of red ants: What if he and I, Howie and I, had been somewhere else way back that night we smiled and nodded and made Christopher? If the night had been bone-cracking cold? If we were courting some aloneness, back to back? But it was summer, we were married three months, and the bottom sheet was spread like a picnic cloth. If there is an astrologer's clock, that's what we heard announcing to us the time was propitious; but I rehearse the time again. We lived off Riverside Drive that year and the next, I will float a thundercloud across the river from the Palisades and just as Howie turns to me I will have the most extraordinary burst of rain, sludgy and cold, explode through the open windows everywhere and finish us for the evening. The rugs are soaked, our books on the desk are corrugated with dampness, we snap at each other, Howie breaks a beer glass and blames me. We unmake him . . . Another night we will make a different child. Don't the genes shift daily in their milky medium like lottery tickets in their fishbowl? I unmake Christopher's skin and bone: egg in the water, blind; a single sperm thrusts out of its soft side, retreating. Arrow swimming backwards, tail drags the heavy head away from life. All the probability in the universe cheers. He is unjoined. I wake in a clammy sweat. The sun, such as it was, is caught behind the smokestacks at the far end of Pacific Street. I feel dirty, as though I've sinned in my sleep, and there's that fine perpetual silt on my arms and legs and face, the Con Ed sunburn. I go in and start making lunch for Christopher, who will survive me.

Log: He is sitting at the kitchen table trying to string kidney beans on a needle and thread. They do it in kindergarten. I forgot to ask why. Jody wakes upstairs, way at the back of the house with her door closed, and C. says quietly, without looking up from his string, "Ma, she's up." It's like hearing something happening, I don't know, a mile away. He has the instincts of an Indian guide, except when I stand right next to him to talk. Then it blows right by.

And when she's up. He seems to make a very special effort to be gentle with his little sister. I can see him forcibly subdue himself, tuck his hands inside his pockets or push them into the loops of his pants so that he loses no honor in restraint. But every now and then it gets the better of him. He walked by her just a minute ago and did just what he does to anything that's not nailed down or bigger than he is: gave her a casual but precise push. The way the bathmat slips into the tub without protest, the glass bowl gets smashed, its pieces settling with a resigned tinkle. I am, of course, the one who's resigned: I hear them ring against each other before they hit the ground, in the silence that envelops the shove.

This time Jody chose to lie back on the rug — fortunately it wasn't cement, I am grateful for small favors — and watch him. An amazing, endearing thing for a two-year-old. I think she has all the control that was meant for the two of them, and this is fair to neither. Eyes wide open, untearful, Jody the antidote, was thinking something about her brother. She cannot say what.

When his dosage has been up a while he begins to cringe before her. It is unpredictable and unimaginable but true and I bear witness to it here. As I was writing the above he ran in and hid behind my chair. Along came J., who had just righted herself after the attack on her; she was pulling her corn popper, vaguely humming. For C., an imagined assault? Provoked? Real? Wished-for?

Howard, on his way out of the breakfast chaos, bears his briefcase like a shield, holds it in front of him for lack of space while he winds his way around the table in our little alcove, planting firm kisses on our foreheads. On his way out the door he can be expected to say something cheerful and blind to encourage me through the next unpredictable half hour before I walk Christopher up the block to school. This morning, unlocking the front gate I caught him pondering. "Well, what are other kids like? I mean we've never had any others so how do we know where they fall on the spectrum?"

"We know," I said. "What about Jody?"

"Oh," he said, waving her away like a fly. "I mean boys."

"We also know because we're not knots on logs, some of us, that's how we know. What was it he did to your shaver this morning?"

Smashed it to smithereens is what he did, and left cobweb cracks in the mirror he threw it at.

To which his father shrugged and turned to pull the gate shut
fast.

*

Why did we have Jody. People dare to ask, astonished, though it's
none of their business. They mean, and expect us to forgive them,
how could we take such a martyr's chance. I tell them that when C.
was born I was ready for a large family. You can't be a secretary
forever, no matter how many smash titles your boss edits. Nor an
administrative assistant, nor an indispensable right hand. I've got
my own arms, for which I need all the hands I've got. I like to be
boss, thank you, in my own house. It's a routine by now, canned as
an Alka-Seltzer ad.

But I'll tell you. For a long time I guarded very tensely against
having another baby. C. was hurting me too much, already he was.
Howard would rap with his fist on my nightgowned side, demanding admission. For a while I played virgin. I mean, I didn't try,
I wasn't playing. He just couldn't make any headway. I've heard it
called dys-something; also crossbones, to get right down to what it's
like. (Dys-something put me right in there with my son, doesn't it?
I'll bet there's some drug, some muscle relaxant that bones you
and just lays you out on the knife like a chicken to be stuffed and
trussed . . .) Even though it wasn't his fault I'll never forgive
Howard for using his fists on me, even as gently and facetiously
as he did. Finally I guess he got tired of trying to disarm me one
night at a time, of bringing wine to bed or dancing with me ob-
scenely like a kid at a petting party or otherwise trying to distract
me while he stole up on me. So that's when he convinced me to
have another baby. I guess it seemed easier. "We'll make Christopher our one exceptional child while we surround him with ordinary ones. We'll grow a goddamn garden around him, he'll be
outnumbered."

Well — I bought it. We could make this child matter less. It was
an old and extravagant solution. Black flowers in his brain, what
blight would the next one have, I insisted he *promise* me. He lied,
ah, he lied with his hand between my legs, he swore the next would
be just as beautiful but timid — "Downright phlegmatic, how's
that?" — and would teach Christopher to be human. So I sighed,
desperate to believe, and unlocked my thighs, gone rusty and stiff.

But I'll tell you, right as he turned out, by luck, to be, I think I never trusted him again, one of my two deceitful boys, because whatever abandon I once had is gone, sure as my waist is gone. I feel it now and Howard is punished for it. Starting right then, making Jody, I have dealt myself out in careful proportions, like an unreliable cook bent only on her batter.

Meanwhile I lose one lamp, half the ivory on the piano keys, and all my sewing patterns to my son in a single day. On the same day I lose my temper, lose it so irretrievably that I am tempted to pop one of Christopher's little red pills myself and go quietly. Who's the most frightening, the skimpy six-year-old flying around on the tail of his bird of prey, or his indispensable right hand mama smashing the canned goods into the closet with a sound generally reserved for the shooting range? All the worse, off his habit for a few days, his eyes clear, his own, he is trying to be sweet, he smiles wanly whenever some catastrophe overtakes him, like an actor with no conviction. But someone else controls his muscles. He is not riding it now but lives in the beak of something huge and dark that dangles him just out of my reach.

Our brains are all circuitry; not very imaginative, I tend to see it blue and red and yellow like the wires in phones, easier to sort impulses that way. I want to see inside Christopher's head, I stare viciously though I try to do it when he's involved with something else. (He never is, he would feel me a hundred light years behind him.) I vow never to *study* him again, it's futile anyway, his forehead's not a one-way mirror. Promises, always my promises: they are glass. I knew when they shatter — no, when he shatters them, throwing something of value — there will be edges to draw blood, edges everywhere. He says, "What are you *looking* at all the time? Bad Christopher the dragon?" He looks wilted, pathetic, seen-through. But I haven't seen a thing.

"Chrissie." I put my arms around him. He doesn't want to bruise the air he breathes, maybe we're all jumbled in his sight. He doesn't read yet, I know that's why. It's all upside down or somehow mixed together — cubist sight, is there such a thing? He sees my face and the top of my head, say, at the same time. Or everything looms at him, quivering like a fun-house mirror, swollen, then slowly disappears down to a point. He has to subdue it before

it overtakes him? How would we ever know? Why, if he saw just
what we see — the cool and calm of all the things of the world all
sorted out like laundry ("Oh, Margaret, come off it!") why would
he look so bewildered most of the time like a terrier being dragged
around by his collar, his small face thrust forward into his own
perpetual messes?

He comes to me just for a second, pulling on his tan wind-
breaker, already breathing fast to run away somewhere, and while
I hold him tight a minute, therapeutic hug for both of us, he
pinches my arm until the purple capillaries dance with pain.

"Let me take him with me when I go to D.C. next week." Howard.

I stare at him. "You've got to be kidding."

"No, why would I kid about it? We'll manage, we can go see
some buildings after my conference is out, go to the Smithsonian.
He'd love the giant pendulum." His eyes are already there in the
cool of the great vaulted room where everything echoes and everything can break. I am fascinated by his casualness. "What would
he do all day while you're in your meeting? Friend. My intrepid
friend."

"Oh, we'd manage something. He'd keep busy. Paper and pencil . . ."

"Howie." Am I crazy? Is he? Do we live in the same house?

He comes and takes both my hands. There is that slightly conniving look my husband gets that makes me forget, goddamit, why I
married him. He is all too reasonable and gentle a man most of the
time, but this look is way in the back of his eyes behind a pillar,
peeking out. I feel surrounded. "You can't take him." I wrench
my hands away.

"Maggie —" and he tries to take them again, bungler, as though
they're contested property.

"I forbid it. Insanity. You'll end up crushing him to death to get
a little peace! I know."

He smiles with unbearable patience. "I know how to handle my
son."

But I walk out of the room, thin-lipped, taking a bowl of fruit to
the children who are raging around, both of them, in front of the
grade-A educational television that's raging back.

The next week Howie goes to Washington and we all go to the airport to see him off. I don't know what Howard told him but while Jody sleeps Christopher cries noisily in the back of the car and flings himself around so wildly, like a caged bear, that I have to stop the car on the highway shoulder and buckle him into his seat belt. "You will walk home," I threaten, calm because I can see the battle plan. He's got a little of his father in him; that should make me feel better.

He hisses at me and goes on crying, forcing the tears and walloping the back of my seat with his feet the whole way home.

Log: The long long walk to school. A block and a half. Most of the kids in kindergarten with Christopher walk past our house alone, solidly bearing straight west with the bland eight o'clock sun at their backs. They concentrate, they have been told not to cross heavy traffic alone, not to speak to strangers, not to dawdle. All the major wisdom of motherhood pinned to their jackets like a permission slip. Little orders turning into habits and hardening slowly to super-ego: an amber that holds commands forever. Christopher lacks it the way some children are born without a crucial body chemical. Therefore, I walk him to school every day, rain or shine, awake or asleep.

Jody's in her stroller slouching. She'd rather be home. So would I. It's beginning to get chilly out, edgy, and that means the neighborhood's been stripped of summer and fall, as surely as if a man came by one day confiscating color. What little there is, you wouldn't think it could matter. Blame the mayor. The window-boxes are crowded with brown stringy corpses, like tall crabgrass. Our noble pint-sized trees have shrunk back into themselves, they lose five years in winter. Fontaine, always improving his property, has painted his new brick wall *silver* over the weekend — it has a sepulchral gleam in the vague sunlight, twinkling as placidly as a woman who's come in sequins to a business meeting, *believing* in herself. Bless him. Next door to him the Rosenbergs have bought subtle aged wood shutters, they look like some dissected Vermont barn door, and a big rustic barrel that will stand achingly empty all winter, weighted with a hundred pounds of dirt to exhaust the barrel burglars. I wonder what my illusions look like through the front window.

Christopher's off and running. "Not in the street!" I get so tired
of my voice, especially because I know he doesn't hear it. "Stay on
the curb, Christopher." There's enough damage to be done there.
He is swinging on that new couple's gate, straining the hinges,
trying to fan up a good wind; then, when I look up from attending
to Jody's dropped and splintered Ritz cracker, he's gone — clapping together two garbage can lids across the street. Always under
an old lady's window, though with no particular joy — his job, it's
there to be done. Jody is left with her stroller braked against a tree
for safe keeping while I retrieve him. No one ever told me I'd
grow up to be a shepherdess; and bad at it too — undone by a
single sheep.

We are somehow at the corner, at least I can demand he hold my
hand and drag us across the street where the crossing guard stands
and winks at me daily, as dependably as a blinking light. She is a
good lady, Mrs. Cortes, from a couple of blocks down in the projects, with many matching daughters, one son, Anibal, on the sixth
grade honor roll and another on Riker's Island, a junkie. She is
waving cars and people forward in waves, demonstrating "commu-
nity involvement" to placate the gods who are seeing to Anibal's
future, I know it. I recognize something deep behind her lively
eyes, sunk there: a certain desperate casualness while the world has
its way with her children. Another shepherdess without a chance.
I give her my little salute.

By now, my feet heavy with the monotony of this trip, we are on
the long school block. The barbed wire of the playground breaks
for the entrance halfway down. This street, unlived on, is an unrelenting tangle — no one ever sees the generous souls who
bequeath their dead cars to the children, but there are dozens, in
various stages of decay; they must make regular deliveries. Christopher's castles; creative playthings, and broken already so he
never gets blamed. For some reason he picks the third one. He's
already in there, across a moat of broken windshield glass, reaching
for the steering wheel. The back seat's burned out, the better to
jump on. All the chrome has been cannibalized by the adults —
everything that twists or lifts off, leaving a carcass of flung bones,
its tin flesh dangling.

"Christopher, you are late and I. Am. Not. Waiting." But he
will not come that way. My son demands the laying-on of hands.

Before I can maneuver my way in, feeling middle-aged and worrying about my skirt, hiked up over my rear, he is tussling not with
one boy but with two. They fight over nothing — just lock hands
and wrestle as a kind of greeting. "I break the muh-fuh's head,"
one announces matter-of-factly — second grader maybe. Christopher doesn't fight for stakes like that, though. Whoever wants
his head can have it, he's fighting to get his hands on something,
keep them warm. I am reaching over the jagged door, which is
split in two and full of rain water. The school bell rings, that raspy
grinding, and the two boys, with a whoop, leap over the downed
windshield and are gone. Christopher is grater-scraped along one
cheek but we have arrived more or less in one piece.

I decide I'd better come in with him and see to it his cheek is
washed off. He is, of course, long gone by the time I park the
stroller and take the baby out. He never bothers to say goodbye.
Maybe six-year-olds don't.

I pull open the heavy door to P.S. 193. It comes reluctantly, like
it's in many parts. These doors are not for children. But then,
neither is the school . . . It's a fairly new building but the 1939
World's Fair architecture has just about caught up with the
lobby — those heavy streamlined effects. A ship, that's what it
looks like; a dated ocean liner, or the lobby of Rockefeller Center,
one humble corner of it. What do the kids see, I wonder? Not
grandeur.

There's a big lit-up case to the left that shows off sparse student
pieties, untouchable as seven-layer cakes at the bakery. THIS LAND
IS *Your* LAND, THIS LAND IS *My* LAND. Every figure in the pictures,
brown, black, dead-white (blank), mustard yellow, tulip red and
olive green (who's that?) is connected more or less at the wrist, like
uncut paper dolls (HANDS ACROSS THE SEA). The whole world's
afraid to drop hands, the hell with summit talks, SALT talks, we're
on the buddy system. Well, *they* go up and down the halls irrevocably linked so, their lips sealed, the key thrown over their endless
shoulder, only the teacher nattering on and on about discipline
and respect, wearing heels that must sound like SS boots, though
they are intended merely to mean business. Christopher tells me
only that his teachers are noisy and hurt his ears; he does not
bother to specify how.

And what he sees when he puts his thin shoulder to the door at

8:30 and heaves? He probably catches that glaring unnecessary
shine on the floor, an invitation, and takes it. That worried crease
between big eyes, his face looks back at him out of deep water.
Deeper when he's drugged. So he careens around without ice-
skates, knocks against other kids hard, thumps into closed doors,
nearly cracks open THIS LAND IS YOUR LAND. He is the wise-acre
who dances to hold the door for his class, then when the last dark
pigtail is through skips off in the wrong direction, leaps the steps to
the gym or the auditorium or whatever lives down there in deserted silence most of the morning, the galley of this ship. I don't
blame him, of course I don't, but that isn't the point, is it? I am
deprived of these fashionable rebellious points. We only, madam,
allow those in control to be out of control. As it were. If you
follow. Your son, madam, is not rebelling. He is unable. Is
beyond. Is utterly. Is unthinkable. Catch him before we do.

   We are certainly late, the lines are all gone, the kids settling into
their rooms, their noise dwindling like a cut-back motor. Jody
and I just stand for a minute or two tuning in. Her head is heavy
on my shoulder. Already there's a steady monitor traffic, the offi-
cious kids scurrying to do their teachers' bidding like tailless mice.
I was one of them for years and years, God, faceless and obliging:
official blackboard eraser (which meant a few cool solitary minutes
just before three each day, down in the basement storeroom clapping two erasers together, hard, till they smoked with the day's
vanished lessons). I would hardly have stopped my frantic do-
gooding to give the time of day (off the clocks that jerked forward
with a click every new minute) to the likes of Christopher. I'd
have given him a wide berth, I can see myself going the other
way if I saw him coming towards me in the narrow hall.

   This hall, just like the ones I grew up in except for the "moder-
nistic" shower tile that reaches halfway up, has a muted darkened
feeling, an underwater thrum. Even the tile is like the Queens
Midtown Tunnel, deserted. I will not be particularly welcome in
Christopher's kindergarten room, there is that beleaguered proprietary feeling that any parent is a spy or come to complain. (I, in my
own category, have been forbidden to complain, at least tacitly,
having been told that my son really needs one whole teacher to
himself, if not for his sake, then for the safety of the equipment
and "the consumables," of which he is not one.)

Christopher has disappeared into his class which — I see it
through the little porthole — is neat and earnest and not so terribly
different from a third-grade room, say, with its alphabets and exhor-
tations to patriotism and virtue above eye level. They are allowed
to paint in one color at a time. A few, I see, have graduated
to two; they must be disciplined, promising children in their securely
tied smocks. One spring they will hatch into monitors. Christopher
is undoubtedly banned from the painting corner. (Classroom econ-
omy? Margaret, your kitchen, your bedroom, your bathroom this
morning. Searching for the glass mines hidden between the tiles.)
Mrs. Seabury is inspecting hands. The children turn them, patty-
cake, and step back when she finishes her scrutiny, which is as
grave as a doctor's. Oh Christopher! She has sent him and another
little boy to the sink to scrub; to throw water, that is, and stick
their fingers in the spout in order to shower the children in the
back of the room. I am not going in there to identify myself.

Mrs. Seabury is the kind of teacher who, with all her brown and
black kids on one side of the room (this morning in the back,
getting showered), talks about discrimination and means big from
little, forward from backward, ass from elbow. Now I see she has
made Christopher an honorary Black child, or maybe one of your
more rambunctious Puerto Ricans. They are all massed back there
for the special inattention of the aide, who is one of my least favorite people: she is very young and wears a maxi skirt that the kids
keep stepping on when she bends down. (Therefore she bends
down as little as possible.) The Future Felons of America and their
den mother. I'm caught somewhere between my first flash of
anger and then shame at what I suppose, wearily, is arrogance.
What am I angry at? That he has attained pariah-hood with them,
overcoming his impeccable WASP heritage in a single leap of
adrenalin? Jesus. They are the "unruly characters" he's supposed
to be afraid of: latchkey babies, battered boys and abused girls, or
loved but hungry, scouted by rats while they sleep. Products of
this-and-that converging, social, political, economic, each little
head impaled on a point of the grid. Christopher? My warm,
healthy, nursed and coddled, vitamin-enriched boy, born on Blue
Cross, swaddled in his grandparents' gifts from Lord & Taylor?
What in the hell is our excuse? My pill-popping baby, so sad, so
reduced and taken from himself when he's on, so indescribable,

air-borne, when he's off. This week he is off; I am sneaking him a favor.

I see him now flapping around in a sort of ragged circle with the other unimaginables, under the passive eye of that aide. Crows? Buzzards? Not pigeons, anyway. They make their own rowdy music. Then Christopher clenches his whole body, I see it coming, and stops short, slamming half a dozen kids together, solid rear-end collisions. It looks like the New Jersey Turnpike, everybody whiplashed, tumbling down. No reason, no why's, there is never anything to explain. Was the room taking off, spinning him dizzy? Was he fending something off, or trying to catch hold? The others turn to him, shout so loud I can hear them out here where I'm locked, underwater — and they all pile on. Oh, can they pile! It's a sport in itself. Feet and hands and dark faces deepening a shade. The aide gets out of the way, picking her skirt out of the rubble of children at her feet.

One heavy dark boy with no wrists finally breaks through the victor: his foot is on Christopher's neck. The little pale face jerks up stiffly, like an executed man's. I turn away. When I make myself turn back the crowd is unraveling as Mrs. Seabury approaches. Faces all around are taking on that half-stricken, half-delighted "uh-oh" look. I was always good at that, one of the leaders of censure and shock. It felt good.

*

But Christopher sinks down, quiet. She reaches down roughly and yanks his fresh white collar. Good boy, he doesn't look up at her. But something is broken. The mainspring, the defiant arch of his back that I would recognize, his, mine, I find I am weeping, sound-less as everything around me, I feel it suddenly like blood on my cheeks. This teacher, this stranger and her cohorts have him by his pale limp neck. They are teaching him how to lose; or me how to win. My son is down for the count, breathing comfortably, accommo-dating, only his fingers twitching fiercely at his sides like gill slits puffing, while I stand outside, a baby asleep on my shoulder. I am the traitor, he sees me through my one-way mirror, and he is right. I am the witch. Every day they walk on his neck, I see that now, but he will never tell me about it. I weep but cannot move.

JERRY BUMPUS

Desert Matinee

(FROM FICTION INTERNATIONAL)

THE DUST CLOUD FOLLOWED the arroyo down to the valley and turned when it reached the highway, as Haskel knew it would, fanning wide on both sides of the road and coming straight toward him.

Haskel pulled the truck off the road, cut the motor, and rolling down the window leaned out. He heard far off a buzzing roar like a storm of hornets. He took out his teeth and put them in the breast pocket of his denim jacket. Then rolled up the window and drove on slowly, half-off the road to give them plenty of room.

Still over a mile away he could make them out, thirty or forty abreast so they wouldn't get their own dust. At this distance they were giant insects.

For three days and nights they had been out here, and Haskel had watched them. (Now for the first time they saw him — the flanks of the wide line drew in and they came even faster.) He had watched with binoculars and concluded that above all they were constantly in motion, even at night in their camp, jumping on their motorcycles and riding off as if they all had been stung by the same dire impulse. Or they danced all night, and he saw fights in the yellow light, and they rode round and around the bonfire, though in the distance it appeared they rode into the bonfire and became the fire itself — out of existence on a dare and back again. In the light of day they plunged headlong, whether down the highway, along a trail, or straight across the desert — they didn't need roads. They shot off hills, cutting through the air forward-leaning and furious, as if enraged with the passivity of space.

Five hundred feet ahead of Haskel they slowed. Now they would block the road.

There were even more than he thought — fifty, sixty. Women rode double behind some of them, lean long-legged women in jeans and leather, their faces shrewd as chromium, their eyes rapacious but at the same time paradoxically indifferent — as though their minds were elsewhere, or *they* were in fact elsewhere and these were their souls, fled to the desert. The men were big, long-armed, etched with tattoos. Grinning, their mouths were slashed with the obscene eagerness of wolves. Astraddle their bikes, revving the motors, they tightened a gauntlet down the middle of the road, and as Haskel entered they leaned on the truck and pounded the fenders, grinning in at him.

Then he was through them. In the mirror watched them spread out again in a line. When they were at least two miles down the road Haskel put his teeth back in.

He slowed at the arroyo road. Up there was their camp. After glancing in the mirror, Haskel drove by. If he went up there, they might see his dust and come back.

He went down the highway to the dirt road that led to his place. And nothing beyond, but the canyon rim and, over it, the first of two buttes staring at each other across forty miles. He called them the Big Ideas. Because they looked sure of why they were here.

The truck bounced, tilted on the road, slowly climbing the canyon wall. Then he saw the cabin. A window, crooked chimney, a shed out back. Beyond a narrow meadow, cut with a stream, a forest spread to the rim.

Haskel got out and held his breath, listening. Heard in the woods the crash of hard running. Then the dog, gray-brown, quick and wolflike except it didn't have the absolute, improbable bigness of a wolf, came out of the woods and into the meadow. Haskel squared off to meet it and it lunged against him and banged its jaws in his face, just short of his nose. He choked it, it chewed his shoulder, they stagger-waltzed a big circle and crashed against the truck. Haskel sat on the running board, panting, and the dog stood in front of him, panting too, tongue out, eyes laughing. "The motorcycle people," Haskel announced. The dog shut its mouth, ears pricked. "All of them. We had a parley-vous."

Haskel unloaded the supplies from the cab of the truck and went to the shed to chop wood. The dog wandered off but came back when it saw Haskel walking from the stream toward the cabin with the bucket. They went in and ate.

Later they went out front, watched the valley go down in purple. The sky became night. Abruptly the lights of Lordsburg thirty miles away winked into being.

In the middle of the night the cabin moved. He sat up. The dog, sleeping on the floor beside the bed, stood and yawned in the dark. Haskel went to the door.

Wind — huge and preoccupied, moved down the canyon shaking loose, changing.

Haskel got the binoculars, moved them slowly up the arroyo, looking for the yellow light of the bonfire.

"They're gone," he said. The dog wagged its tail.

He built a fire and put on coffee. The dog curled down and went to sleep.

When the coffee was ready Haskel cooked breakfast. "They're gone for good," he whispered. He ate some and put the rest down for the dog when it woke.

Motor and headlights off, down the long hill the truck rolled, silent except for the creaking of springs and the skee of brakes. Haskel stopped short of the highway, staring at the dim corona above Lordsburg. He turned on the radio and found what he liked — cat music, he called it, coarse and jangling, from Mexico and fading off in miles, laced with static, then coming back louder than before.

An immense breath, change moved over the valley. First light.

He switched off the radio, started the motor, and pulled onto the highway.

He reached the arroyo road as gray dawn opened the sky. The hills were purple-black.

He walked around the bowl where they had camped. The wind had scavenged footprints and tire tracks, everything else it could take. Left behind a ripped-out beercase wedged between two bushes. And some cans scattered here and there, half-buried. Haskel kicked through the remains of the bonfire — the charred carcass of some huge beast they cooked whole and ate on the ground. He moved farther out, circled the camp. Snagged in a bush he found a silk scarf, black and green. He sniffed it but already the desert had taken the smell of the person.

Instead of returning down the arroyo he drove out a trail they had cut with their motorcycles. It forked, then crossed other trails. He turned onto one. And it crossed other trails. These were their streets, a city with no houses or people. He swung a turn, topping a dune, the nose of the truck in the sky, and when it dipped Haskel slammed on the brakes.

Two of them sat in the middle of the trail leaning against each other, a big one and a little one. Long hair, and wore pants but not shirts. Their backs were gray. Maybe the big one was dead, the little one propping him up.

They turned. The big one had a huge sharp chin, making him devilish, self-sure. He stared at Haskel, seemed to already start telling him what to do. The little one got up and helped him to his feet — and the little one was a woman, a girl, her hair hiding her face and partially covering her breasts. The man put his arm over her shoulders, leaned on her, and they came around to the side of the truck. Haskel rolled down his window.

She pushed her hair back with one hand. Her face was small and round. After looking at each other for a moment, she and Haskel spoke at the same time: "What are you doing out here?" — and she said, "Take us."

"To Lordsburg?" he said.

The man lifted his head, his eyes bright black. "No."

"No," the girl said to Haskel, her lips straight, smug.

"We got to stay awake," the man said and swayed back on his heels.

"Away," the girl said, grabbing him with both arms. "Away."

"You're staying out here?" Haskel said.

The girl stepped up on the running board. Leaning in, her face nearly touching Haskel's, she whispered, her eyes gleaming with excitement: "Take Hopalong and me to your place."

"My place?" He nodded. "Okay. Get in."

She went around the truck with Hopalong and opened the door. She stood behind him and pushed to get him up into the truck — and before he was even inside, sprawled knees wide apart, Haskel smelled blood and saw Hopalong's pants were soaked. The girl jumped in after him and slammed the door. "I'm Lily."

Haskel nodded and started the truck. Hopalong's head thunked against the rear window. Lily stared across him at Haskel, her face gray and without expression, her eyes like paraffin.

They helped Hopalong into the cabin and he shoved them away. He sat down at the table and grabbed up the cards with which Haskel played solitaire. His big fingers fumbled with the piece of string tied around the deck, then he shuffled the cards. Grinning fiercely, his bulging cheeks knotting his eyes, he rapped the cards on the table. "Stud," he said slyly and winked at Haskel.

"Come on," Lily said, tugging at his arm. She took the cards from him and pulled harder — "Over here. Come on, Hopalong." He got up and when he looked away from Haskel his mouth fell open, as if discovering the cabin was vast, infinite, with long corridors of light: far away, tiny in the distance, he saw a bed.

He collapsed across it. Haskel was building a fire when he heard a splop and turned to see the bloody trousers in the middle of the floor. With a piece of kindling he carried them out to the shed. When he returned, Hopalong, covered with blankets, lay turned to the wall. Lily wore one of Haskel's shirts, the sleeves rolled up. She was frying bacon and when it was done she took it to Hopalong and whispered too low for Haskel to hear.

"Hopalong won't eat." Haskel looked up. She stood beside him, her hands on her hips. "He used to eat all the time — you know? He was almost famous, he ate so much. Now, nothing. What'll I do?"

Haskel nodded. "You came to the right man: I don't know."

He went outside. The wind was up, rushing down the canyon like a big reckless boy. Haskel ducked around the corner. The sky scooped deep into the valley, a storm moving in. There would be snow, a great wall of snow.

The dog sailed around the corner on a gust of wind. "She kick you out?" Haskel yelled and grabbed its tail. The dog snarled, jerked its head around and snapped at him. When he let go it lunged away and barked. Haskel barked back, and the dog liked that, its eyes gleeful.

The food she cooked for Hopalong was on the table. Haskel sat down and ate it.

Then he built up the fire and got his pipe. He pulled up his chair and almost immediately was lost in the flames' invention. He returned only when, floating up from canyons, he put on another log.

The dog lifted its head, ears pricked. Slowly Haskel turned.

Lily wore only the shirt now, the shirt tail reaching halfway down her thighs. She tiptoed across the room and leaned down to him. Then her face went blank, her eyes faded as if she had forgotten everything.

Hopalong is dead, Haskel thought. That was it. He didn't need to ask her.

"I'll sleep here," Lily whispered.

He heard her making a pallet on the floor behind him. Then she was still, there was nothing but the fire and the wind above the cabin. When he woke, the fire was down and the wind had lain. The sky had the dense silence of snow.

He looked over his shoulder; she lay in a ball under the blankets, her head covered. On the edge of the pallet the dog also lay in a ball, its eyes open, staring at Haskel.

*

Morning. Haskel went out into a gray lull. A great drift buried half the cabin. Below, through thick air, the valley was shallowed with snow and seemed so close Haskel could have climbed to his roof and jumped clear across it. The woods had moved nearer during the storm, the trees immense and dour, shadows deep as caves hunkering under the branches sagging with the weight of the snow.

Haskel tromped out to the shed and got the ax, logs. Scooped off the block and a place to stand, and swung the ax. The log split with a sharp crack that shot down the hill, and Haskel looked up. Air quivered around the cabin. The door slowly opened.

Roaring, Hopalong ran out naked into the snow, his back and shoulders brownish yellow, waxen. The roar hung in the air. He ran hard, then stopped, bent forward, coughing.

Haskel ran down to the cabin, then onto Hopalong's trail. He caught up just short of the woods. "Hold it," Haskel panted. Louder — "Hold it."

Hopalong swung around, reared, rising and opening his arms like a bear turning on dogs, and Haskel saw the huge wide chest, the stomach black with hair wedging down to the bush at the base of the stomach, as if pointing to what Haskel didn't see. For there was not the big thrusting cock Haskel expected. Instead, a gash grinned blood over a white sprig of tendon. Running pumped fresh blood over what had dried on Hopalong's thighs, ringing the snow red around his knees.

Haskel looked up to the man's face and could tell by Hopalong's eyes that he didn't know if Haskel had seen or not, that Hopalong no longer *knew*. Had somehow forgotten what there was about him that another man would find amazing. Hopalong's eyes, large and baffled, hardly paused on Haskel, as if Haskel were just one of a crowd floating before him in the gray light.

"Let's go back," Haskel said.

"Huh?" — and his eyes found Haskel.

"Back to my place. Come on."

Slowly shaking his head, Hopalong made the noise again, the roar that was almost a word but just outside meaning, louder and louder, and he clenched his fists and drew them up. Haskel backed but not fast enough, Hopalong was on him like a falling tree.

Numb deep in snow. Not thinking now. For minutes, maybe longer. Haskel was far away from himself, though now he saw his hands, red with cold. His hands were pushing at the yellow sack of flesh that was the naked man, and with strange easiness (maybe Hopalong was a huge yellow-brown bleeding balloon) Haskel pushed him away.

Haskel sat up, breathing hard, and looked at the sky. His face was blunt numb, maybe he no longer had a face, accepted the possibility that he didn't: Hopalong had lost his cock and was going around taking faces.

Thirty feet away Hopalong and Lily sat side by side in the snow, their backs to Haskel. They were talking low but in the silence Haskel heard them distinctly.

"To Phoenix," she said.

"No. Nothing," Hopalong said.

"Bubba's there. And Nadine."

"Is that Bubba?" Hopalong said and looked over his shoulder at Haskel.

"No," Lily said. "That's just *him*. We can sleep in his house."

Hopalong got to his feet and moved away slowly, Lily calling to him. Haskel rose and started after him, running easily, the snow carrying him on waves.

Hopalong entered the first line of trees and disappeared. Then Haskel saw him again, slipping in and out of view, gliding deeper into the woods. Haskel followed, running hard, but looking over his shoulder he saw the cabin below, a straight line of woodsmoke rising from the chimney.

Ahead, Haskel saw Hopalong down a straight corridor through the woods. Going downhill now, they flew through luminous blue-green silence.

*

It would be a matter of minutes, an hour or two at most. The fire crackled excitedly, the flames danced.

"We can go to Albuquerque," Lily whispered. Hopalong lay flat on his back. Lily leaned down, her hands on his chest, her lips to his ear. Hopalong's eyes were closed and he breathed heavily, his lips flubbering.

Then he was silent. Lily stopped whispering. Haskel turned. She sat on the side of the bed, her legs crossed and her hands in her lap, watching Haskel with the corners of her mouth tucked up primly.

They dragged Hopalong out to the truck; nothing could get him there. Hopalong sat stiffly at the steering wheel, ready to go. Haskel slammed the truck door and he and Lily went into the cabin.

Lily sat at the table and picked up the deck of cards and shuffled them. Haskel rolled her a cigarette and one for himself. "Thanks," she said and dealt.

"My mom says, 'Lily, someday you'll get into something you can't get out of.' I tell her, 'Moms, don't lose any sleep worrying about me.' But maybe she's right.

"Some people just don't care — you know? Bubba don't care. He don't give a shit for anything. When Nadine got busted in

Cruces she called Bubba and Bubba said, 'Tough shit.' " She was silent as they played the hand. She won.

She took the papers and tobacco and rolled another cigarette. Then she shuffled and dealt again.

"Mom says, 'Lily, you're crazy.' She says that because of what happened to Frieda. Frieda's my sister. Not my little sister, her name's Nadine. But Frieda's my big sister that got killed in a crash on Looper Lane in Phoenix. And Mom won't let me forget, like it was my fault. So I tell her if I'm crazy it's because she drove me crazy talking about Frieda. That's what Bubba tells me. Me and Bubba were doing Cunt City when I met Hopalong."

She ground out her cigarette and stood. She pulled the shirt up and over her head as if it were a sweater. With both hands she smoothed back her long hair, her breasts rising and slowly lowering. She came around the table and stepped between Haskel's knees. Putting an arm around his neck, she cupped a breast and put the nipple to his lips. "When Frieda got it she was riding back of Bubba. Bubba swerved to miss a Jag and went up the back of a Mercury and jumped a Pontiac Le Mans and a Chevy van before they came down. Frieda never knew what hit her, but she died with a smile on her face."

Lily took off her trousers and lay naked on the bed. She crossed her legs, resting her ankle on the raised knee of the other leg. "Frankly, I can take it or leave it. Not like Nadine, who has to have it at least every ten hours and if she don't she gets nauseous. But Frieda was just the opposite. Doing it gave her gas, so she quit. She hadn't done it for six days when she racked up on Looper Lane.

"You got a nice one. You should've seen Hopalong's. It was really what you'd call remarkable. That was why the Motor Maniacs cut it off. Bunch of jealous little pricks — that's what I told Hopalong. But it didn't console him enough."

As Haskel lay down, Lily jumped up. She ran across the room, turned, her arms spread wide against the wall behind her. "Ready?" She squatted like a frog, her knees wide apart, and leaped. She sailed through the air and landed on Haskel.

Her hair hung down, framing their faces. She smiled brightly. "There! Gottum Daddy's whanger."

*

Lily got out, slammed the door, and stood beside the road. Haskel scooted down, it would be a long wait.

But then he heard on the silence a flat gray hum. He looked. A dot wavered on the horizon. Then gradually louder, the sound of a motor, tires on concrete. The dot became a car, its windshield glinting. It came fast though by now the driver could see Lily beside the road, thumb out, her other hand on her hip.

The motor cut, there was the strain of brakes and tires, and the car stopped beside Lily. The man at the wheel sat looking straight ahead as Lily got in. The car accelerated, and Lily looked out, but not at Haskel. Her face behind the window disappeared as the car smoothly sped off, two, three miles away, shrinking to a gray speck.

Haskel drove the truck onto the highway and headed the opposite direction, toward Lordsburg.

He hadn't gone far when a caravan of cars pulling horse trailers passed him. When he came to town more cars and trailers were parked along the street.

He parked the truck on a side street. When he walked back, on the main street twenty or thirty women wearing white ten-gallon hats and white leather jackets and pants with long fringe were riding palominos. The women smiled and waved at the people. They rode two blocks down the street, turned, and rode back.

Haskel bought supplies, then headed back out, driving slowly down the straight highway, looking off across the plain widening with afternoon shadows.

He and the dog went to the shed to see how Hopalong was doing. He sat waiting in the corner. In a day or two when the snow was off Haskel would put him in the meadow.

Haskel went into the house and ate supper. He sat at the table awhile, then moved across to the bed and was asleep before sundown.

He woke to the wind, or maybe it was a coyote. But again he heard the dull clomp, snow-muffled. He went to the window.

They came single file, a long procession, more than he had seen in town, all in white leather with fringe and big white hats, all riding palominos shining in the night.

He backed away and stood in the middle of the room with his hands lifted. Then turned, grabbed up a log and threw it on the fire. As he heard the shudder-snort of the horses just outside the door he reached for the coffee pot. He had just banged it on the grate when the door opened wide and he turned to see the first of them leaning forward to clear the doorway as she rode into the cabin. The horse's eyes were huge, dazzled by the light.

FREDERICK BUSCH

Bambi Meets the Furies

(FROM THE OHIO REVIEW)

NOTHING was lighted late in the morning when he wakened in his parents' house and banged in his pajamas and loose laced brogues through its shadows and their smell of scotch. His father's note was typed — the Royal was always uncovered on the tiny imitation Empire secretary in the living room's farthest shadows: too large for the table, it threatened to crush to the floor with a cackling of keys — and it said, all in capitals, GONE TO THEATER TO SET UP REELS FOR MATINEE ETC SEE YOU LATER ON WELCOME BACK

He went to his father's machine, he ratcheted paper in and typed, in capitals, MANY THANKS FOR YOUR FINE TELEGRAM STOP GLAD TO BE HOME WITH YOU STOP SORRY HEAR YOU AND MOM ARE GETTING DIVORCED STOP DELIGHTED YOU WILL SHOW A KIDDIES MATINEE STOP GOOD SHOW STOP

"You're a childish child" he said. Then he said "What else are children good for?" He went to the front (and only) door, he opened it and stood nearly in, nearly out in October, and looked from his father's house that once was his father's and mother's and his. Nobody lived where his father did. Sometimes cows came to graze in the meadows across the road from him; they sheltered in the lee of a fallen powdering elm that was jagged from lightning strikes, and then they swayed their swollen bags away, down the hill, out of sight. He was at the top of it all, in his tiny house of red and white aluminum siding, planted in the center of the hill's broad uppermost field. From his house the road wound down, the hillocks and fields ran away in cinnamon-colored decay, the brush rotted gold, the trees lost their leaves and looked like networks of nerve.

Back inside, then, he went to the small extra bedroom that once had been his, for a year, before he'd gone to work in Philadelphia for a magazine that imitated a magazine in New York that tried to be like *The New Yorker*. He could crop a photo and specify type and proofread pages while the presses turned them out, still wet, and he could watch his parents divorce. "I am very good at my work" he said. "I hate my job at which I'm good." He looked at his suitcase and his socks, the room which had no pictures or prints, cheap muslin curtains, an unframed mirror, no moulding at the ceiling or floor, a scatter rug made out of string. "Now is *this* a job too?"

His father in the bedroom doorway said "What?"

"Huh? Hi, Pop. Hi. What?"

"Is what a job too?"

"Oh."

"Thank you."

"Oh — ah, nothing, I don't know, dreaming out loud."

"Well, enjoy yourself. Enjoy yourself. Welcome home again, Henry. Next time try coming home before four in the morning, and I might even be able to do more than stagger around in circles when you get here, huh?"

"Nothing wrong with circles, Pop. I'm sorry I came so late."

"Just a spur-of-the-moment coming home, was it?"

"Just a little coming home."

"Yes. Well: welcome home."

"Yes. Yes, thank you, Pop."

"Yes. How come you locked the door?"

"What door?"

"The door to the house."

"Did I lock it?"

"Yes, you locked the door to the house, Henry."

"What do you know? I didn't know I was doing that, Pop — city living, I guess. I'm used to protecting myself all the time, you know?"

His father, walking to the other rooms, said "Nothing to defend from in here, Henry. You relax. Feel safe."

He followed, in shoes and pajamas, and watched his father put ice in a glass in the milky light of the kitchenette. "How's business, Pop?"

"Trash."

"Excuse me?"

His father poured in scotch and carried the low wide glass to the darkness of the living room. "Trash, I said. Distributors in Utica send me trash. Crap. I wouldn't pay fifty cents to see one of what I've been showing this year — blowjobs in living color, gang rapes, fifteen murders per children's featurette. Garbage. I'm ashamed to go to village board meetings, I'm scared lest someone say 'Hank, what in Christ are you *showing* us?" I wouldn't know how to an-swer. Listen." He sat and sighed and moved the glass back and forth in his hand as if it were a pendulum. "Listen, today I'm doing a matinee and you know what I'm showing? *Bambi*. Again! And you know what? It's the cleanest — it's the best movie bar nothing that I've showed all year."

Henry said "Sex all over the place, huh?"

"Listen," his father said, "if that's what sex is supposed to be now — and *I* never knew it in what *I've* done all my life — then you can keep it, keep the goddam entire business."

"And the distributor doesn't give you any choice? Is it —"

"The same as always, yeah, and no he won't give me a choice. Like Rollo over to the smoke shop: you think he gets a choice of what paperback books he can sell? No way, boy. He stocks what they send. And he stocks *trash*, let me tell you: absolute smut and filth and garbage, it could make you sick. Well, I don't know if it could make *you* sick, you haven't told me what you're up to in Philly."

"Fine, fine."

"What?"

"Ah, everything's fine, Pop, business going good, I'm doing fine. Yeah. I guess I'll get to be a managing editor some time, or produc-tion chief, something like that, probably, then managing editor some year or other."

"No kidding."

"No, really, it's going real good."

"Good."

"Yeah, no kidding, really good."

"That's good, Henry, good. Have a drink."

"No, Pop, I don't think so. Thanks."

"I think you can use it, maybe."

He walked to the small window that looked on the dooryard and the barren top of the hill and stood still. "Pop, I probably could. But not now, thanks a lot anyway."

"You could use it, you mean, on account of Mother?"

"I *am* having a little difficulty being quite this casual about it, yes, now that you mention your coming divorce. Yes, as a matter of fact. Uh-huh. See, I'm not sure what I should do, Pop. Sort of, '*Say:* how's your divorce with my mother coming?' Something like that? Say, Pop, how's your divorce with my mother coming? That all right?"

"Slowly, boy, slowly. No need being hysterical. You're old enough, aren't you? Can't you really take this at all? Listen: You're old enough now for your *own* divorce."

"Ha ha."

"Oh, have a drink, Henry. Sit down and relax."

"No, I don't want a drink."

"You don't mind if I drink, do you?"

"No."

"Then what are you after, Henry? You're standing there like a kid waiting for something to be handed to him. You think — you think you deserve something? What do you think you deserve?"

"I don't know."

"But you do want something from me, don't you, Henry?"

"Pop, I don't know what I want. You're right, I want — I just don't know *what*." He moved his feet on the nylon rug and looked out the window at the wind carrying pieces of leaf and whole leaves past the house; the stubby autumn grass which looked like an animal's hide didn't move. He turned, he looked at Sears, Roebuck furniture — veneers and plastics, washable fibers, replaceable parts. His father sat in a low broad chair someone had probably sold him as Spanish Coast Moderne, and his drip-dry shirt was large on him, his thin fibrous neck looked too small, his skin too tight. The long brown hair, uncombed, looked artificial, like a store-window manikin's wig. His father looked at his scotch, which cost more than his shirt for a fifth — much of which he had drunk since Henry had left his car on the road and walked along the lane to say hello, my mother called to say you're getting divorced after thirty-two years.

"And what did Mother say?" his father said.

"She said you're getting divorced, Pop. She said it's a real good idea."

"Did she? Yes. Well, judging things — catastrophes, accidents, earthquakes, government decisions, Congresses — that was always her forte. Or do you say for*tay?* I can't ever remember. But she could always tell you how things are, couldn't she. They'd start a little unimportant war in Chile, capture the radio station in Santiago, broadcast some declaration of victory that somebody here would pick up and mention on the six o'clock news, and *wham:* 'Disgusting' she'd say. Just like that. You could always count on her. And don't look away from me like that! Henry — I didn't mean to shout, but don't look away, Henry, all right? That judges me as fast as she judged Chile, understand? I didn't mean to be mean."

"Well you are, Pop. I think you're being mean."

His father said "Sure. Yes, I am, I am being mean." Then he said "Because to tell you the truth —"

"Yes? Yes? What, Pop?"

"Because I don't know what to do."

He looked at his father and said "Are you as confused as *I* am?"

His father said "Would you like to drink a drink of Cutty Sark with me?"

He shook his head. His father was watching the ice cubes drift. "No thank you. Not yet, later on."

"Better get some soon. You know, it doesn't feel better."

"No?"

"No. It feels worse. You might as well grab some comfort now."

"Are you comforted?"

"No."

"Then what are you doing?"

"Well, the more you grab, the less you know you're not comforted." He laughed to his drink, then stared down into the glass while Henry watched him from the window and then looked out again, to where the winds continued to strip the trees and draw the sky closer down.

Henry said "Would you like me to turn some lights on?"

"You feel dark?"

"There's light enough, I guess."

"I can see."

"Okay. I won't turn any lights on."

"All right, Henry. You suit yourself. It's not the house you grew up in, but it's yours as much as you want it."

He said "Thanks." Then: "Thank you, Pop." Then: "I'm glad I came."

His father said "Good." Lower in his throat, he said "Me too. I'm pleased you came home."

"Except — "

Except *now* what the hell do we do?" He laughed to the drink and Henry laughed at the window and then they both stopped, said nothing, while his father ticked the whisky back and forth.

Henry said "You know, I must have seen this house a lot of times. A really huge number of times, I must have walked back and forth on the lane so many times — you know, I never noticed the telephone poles? Or maybe I saw them and never remembered. But it's like I never saw one two three four *five* thirty-foot poles with all those cables on them, can you believe it?"

"Don't you know why?" his father said. "Because of your age, I'll bet you. You were too old when we came here. You were living alone in your life by then is why. Listen, Henry, if you had been a kid and living here, you would've been *up* those poles. I know about kids, I show them their movies. Kids see things to climb on. But you were a man by then."

"I wish you — "

"But I have to admit it: I thought about it. Sometimes I'd walk down to the road and on my way I'd see those big goddam things and think about you climbing up them and Mother hollering out the door for you to come down, or be careful, or stay put where you were until the volunteer fire people could huff and puff out of the village and come up the hill at five miles an hour in lowest gear and put a ladder up and bring you back down. I have to admit it. I used to wish you were here."

He said "I never even saw them, Pop." And then he said "I wonder why you never told me that."

"Well."

"Yeah — "

"Well, godammit, it's hard to say things. That's all."

"Yeah, listen, no: I understand that, Pop. I always had this — hard time saying things I wanted you to —"

"What, Henry?"

"Ah: that."

"That?"

"What we said."

"Good. Okay with me."

"You understand me, Pop?"

"Okay."

"Pop?"

"I understand it, yes."

"No, I wanted to tell you: Mom and I talked for a long time on the telephone."

"She still in New York?"

"She's in Boston, Pop."

"Well, I'll be damned. Her brother?"

"He's representing her, she said."

"Well, I'll be damned. Or maybe fleeced, with that shyster working on me."

"She was really upset."

"Yes, well divorce at fifty-five can be unnerving. So I'm told. Being fifty-seven, of course, there's a dif —"

"I talked to her about coming here."

The ice cubes rang on the glass like a bell. His father whistled, and Henry pulled the hem of his pajamas down, leaned his forehead on the window's chilly pane. His father said "You had a right to."

"You don't sound like you believe that."

"No. I don't. I mean, I believe it all right, I hate it, though, is all."

He said "I think I did have a right to do that, Pop."

"Yes. Maybe so. Maybe it's more like you had a right to *want* to."

"But my father and my mother, for Godsakes!"

"Listen, boy: my *wife*."

"You mean we have to compete for this terrible horrible stupid —"

"My wife! Henry, my wife wanted to leave me here and I had to let her leave me here because she wanted to *do* it! Talking about rights. *Her* right. Henry, do you love me? Do you think you love me a lot?"

He looked out the window and said "Yes. I love you a lot."

"Isn't that why you very politely don't say anything about your old man drinking whisky and sitting here trying to work up a drunk when he didn't used to be able to drink two *beers* without sitting down?"

"Yes."

"Because you love me?"

"Yes."

"Then why can't you love me good enough to let me do this thing myself? This murder she's committing on me?"

"Because I love you both! I want to *help!*"

"You."

"What? *What?*"

"Help yourself, you're helping yourself, Henry. That's who you're loving."

"Me?"

"You."

"All I'm doing is helping *me?*"

"Uh-huh. Why not? You're a kid some ways is all."

"Is that what I am."

"Running up and down the telephone poles, Henry."

"And — you *let* her go. The same as sending her off, is that what you mean? You let her go away?"

"Yes."

"And that's what I don't understand because I'm still a kid? You let her go and that's called loving?"

For a time there was nothing, then: "Yes. It was all I had left that she wanted, then."

Henry said "Tell her!"

"Come on. That would be taking it back."

"Yeah. Well from this telephone pole here *I* could tell her, Pop. I mean, I don't know what the hell to tell anyone about anything anymore, but I could tell her, I could figure it out and I —"

"You bleeding goddam well could not."

"Not."

"No."

"No."

"Henry, would you like a drink?"

"I told her to come here, Pop."

"Then tell her not to come here, Henry. *She* can say when she'll come. Don't you know *any*thing? What in Christ's name do you have to know in your business? What in the name of Christ do they require of people who spend their little lives on words? Don't you see it at *all*? When she does it for *me*, boy. When she comes here for me and for her — not for you. Don't you see a little bit of anything at all? Henry, you are out of this picture, Henry: this is me and her. *We* decide what happens, boy. Don't you see? You're *out!*"

"I'm very sorry."

"Oh — *I'm* sorry. I'm a little sorry too."

"Pop, but she's coming."

The ice cube rang and rang. "Well, you did a job, boy."

"She calling from the airport and I'm supposed to go and pick her up and bring her home."

"I'll bet you are."

"I didn't know, Pop. Honestly, you can't —"

"No, I can't. Did the plane take off yet?"

"Coming down now, nearly. Very soon."

"Henry, I'll forgive you for this. Understand? I will finally forgive you for this."

The glass came down on a table and the ice cubes rang. He walked to the kitchenette, rattled the knob on the cellar door, thumped down the wooden steps. Henry stayed at the window, looking out, watching the black wires wave in the wind, waiting for the little electrical cry to come in from the first pole to the second to the third to the fourth to the fifth and into the house, into him.

Then his father was back in the room and going past him, to the door. He carried the large red sign in one hand, a clawhammer in the other. Nails were a shadow in the pocket of his flimsy shirt. His neck was rigid and too thin. He said "I'll be back."

"Where are you going?"

"I'll be right back" he said.

"Pop — let's have a drink now."

"Later."

"Pop? What if the phone rings?"

"Answer," his father said.

He went outside and Henry stood at the window and watched him move on the lane to the road. Henry closed his eyes and squeezed at his skull with his hands, and ran the reel in reverse: had his father backing from his white-painted doorframe, jerking backward down his narrow bouldery lane to stand — cut-out picture of a man, propped straight — before the sign that stood before the road that, now, went backward from his house. NO TRESPASSING, bordered vermilion like the red of leaves that fell — with golden leaves, green and yellow leaves, brown leaves curling early from their fibers — up through the air and onto their trees in the backward-blowing wind. And then the sign was down and in his hand as the hammer jerked, and he stood before the tree he hadn't nailed NO TRESPASSING to, and then he marched backward with his sign and hammer — animated woeful marionette — into his dooryard where he waited, his back facing the door, shoulders slumped, head nearly nodding, and then the door flew open and he jerked himself (was hauled, invisibly) back inside, the door hurled shut, the house was alone on its hill, in silence flying backward as the leaves sailed up to naked trees and brought that bareness back to dying bloom.

NANCY CHAIKIN

Waiting for Astronauts

(FROM THE COLORADO QUARTERLY)

WE WAIT in the parking lot. Inside the motel, early, early in this April morning, other people (Daniel, my husband, among them) sleep soundly, unobsessed, or turn, or shower and dress. Perhaps at this moment the astronauts themselves prepare to leave. We cannot be sure; we know only, since the kind desk-clerk has so informed my son, that they are here, today, in rooms just off this parking lot. When they leave for the Space Center, she has told us, it may be possible to see and speak to them; they will be wearing their coveralls. But there is no question that Adam would recognize them anyway.

I feel his great apprehension beneath the calm. His trench coat, a dark green poplin from which he seems to have bled the smudges beneath his eyes, conceals only underwear, since he has learned from his friends that it is unmanly, even at thirteen, to sleep in pajamas. (Do the astronauts? I wonder now.) And though he shivers slightly, he is not uncomfortable, warmed as he is with the vitality of this devotion, his beautiful obsession with Space; it lights and informs his eyes, the chiseled soberness of his serious mouth, his stubborn, cleft chin.

I think: they will see a small, dark-eyed boy, fringed about the ears and neckline, like some young Roman, and holding a large sketch pad. When he extends that Saturn V sketch for their signatures, as he intended when he drew it on the plane, will they look at it? Will they sense for how many of his years he has, like them, been pointed toward the moon?

As for myself, very much earthbound, I am a creature of mundane requirements — chilled in the slight wind blowing in from the Cape, grainy gray in my eyes and mouth from lack of sleep, instinctively fearful for my child's hopes — and I vow that I shall never tell him of how I longed to return to my bed, sleep through his dream and my role in it. I am not a good waiter.

It is nineteen sixty-nine; no one has yet touched the surface of the moon (though soon, very soon, we shall glimpse its fine gray powder on our midnight screens and marvel briefly at its sifting through a human hand); but to me the bleak sunrise hours in this graveled lot are as alien as the dunes and craters of my son's secret life.

Inside our room, Adam's father sleeps the sleep of the exonerated: his face, in repose, round, like the face of the moon, the corners of his mouth upturned, as they usually are, the mouth of a pleasant man, a mild man, my husband. He is close to this child, strangely connected, through points of difference rather than through what they share; for where Daniel is precise, certain, all reliability and balance with his gifts of science, Adam rebels and gets away: erratic, quixotic, even flamboyant with those same gifts. Still, in their genes precision has bound them together, leaving me, the mother body, shut outside in wonder.

Adam has taken those genes, as he takes all offerings, with dispassionate acceptance and mutated them to his own uses. With his father's tools, he will defy the disciplines of our gravity, he will walk on the moon, on Mars, in landscapes of which neither poet nor science has yet dreamed. Then Daniel, too, will lose him in a new way, a certainty I find strangely reassuring. For they communicate only on the most abstract level, while I, so sharply excluded from that mathematical sphere, so blind in their sunlight, I, alone, can *feel* this child at times as though I carried him still inside of me. Might his father, so confident of, so devoted to his laws of science (and who sleeps now, I think uncharitably, while I shiver beside his son), cherish or even apprehend such excitement as stirs in my fatigue? Would it occur to that sleeping Daniel to worry, as I do now, sunlight seeping through my weariness, lest the astronauts *never* arrive, *never* open their doors and greet our son in his waiting, in his brightening day?

"Soon, soon!" he reassures me now; Adam needs my company as though, left alone, without witness, he might lose the meaning of what he does. I nod, agreeably; sometimes it is important to remember that he is still a child. The difficulty of this, I think, is what makes contact with him, sometimes, so tenuous, so fragile, so frequently endangered.

Nevertheless, I retreat to the rented car, now, no longer willing to support this emerging image: the indefatigable stage mother, standing in the wings. It has been less than an hour, actually, but Adam seems to shrink in the waiting, his raincoat fading lighter, the matching circles growing darker in the change of time and light. My own fatigue resembles a bad morning-after; but I am amazed by his stoic patience and reminded of how, waiting just before his fifth Christmas for the holiday show at our Planetarium, I had tried to pass the time by indicating the planets which hung, in a colorful but accurate mobile, over the doorway. It was then that I discovered that he knew them; he knew them all! By name and distance from the sun, his small finger and eager voice had pointed them out while around him, for the first time, those who listened (I among them) imagined what he might some day be.

"I hear something!" he calls over to me, perhaps only to keep me awake and undiscouraged. "Pretty soon, now!" He revives and warms to his human prey. How stubborn he is! How he gratifies and gets away from me! I think: I shall never catch him again.

At last the air seems sweeter, balmier, though the time is still awesome, still missing the horns which will soon blare into our silence, the sounds of early risers. Even the sunrise has somehow seemed to be missing a sound track, perhaps because we know how soon we shall reach toward heaven, how soon even grasp it!

Only fifteen miles from our motel, the Vehicle Assembly Building glows on the eastern horizon. It is a stunning structure, solid, impenetrable, appropriate to the way in which the men who sleep in its rocket-wombs shall soon be dwarfed by them. Still, Adam, who turns only occasionally to glance its way, stands, equally solid, between the building and its astronauts, preserving the two distances, those opposing perspectives of worship and intensely personal love.

"I hear them!" he confirms. And, only seconds later, the first door opens, the first of the mighty men steps out and spies him there. Clutching his sketch pad, Adam goes forward to greet his astronaut. So, I think, it has started; we are in labor with joy. And I make a silent prayer for their mercy.

He is a tall man, this first of them, and is closely followed by two smaller colleagues, all of them agreeably flattered to be stopped at this hour by an admirer. It is early in the program for them to be recognized in public, and the eager attention has not yet begun to cloy. So the broad Texas-tanned face, still creased by sleep, relaxes into a genuine grin: the benevolent rancher, the leathery cowboy, the athlete, the pilot — all are in the posture he shows my boy.

"Captain Duffy!" Adam's voice surprises me with its easy camaraderie. "Will you and your friends sign my sketch for me?" Only the slight tremble of his thin, long-fingered hand gives my boy away in his excitement. I would give my soul to touch him now.

"Sure thing, Tiger!" the grin wider, the inflection so John-Wayne. Even the unfortunate choice of epithet cannot tarnish him; he glows in the gathering sunlight like something turning to gold. He reaches for the pad, "Say, what's your name, Boy?" Behind him, his friends push their hands further into their pockets, not wishing to steal from his glory. They are his crew, and he will one day walk, with one of them, upon the silent surface of the moon, while below, in our own darkness, we shall watch with wonder.

"Adam," the child says, without his usual hesitation before a name he has not enjoyed. "My name is Adam, Captain."

The wide, white-toothed Baptist smile is genuine, now. "That's a pretty special name," he says. And, "Adam!" he adds aloud, as he scrawls the name above his message. Behind him, the others nod vigorously. But as if they sense that this radar is as efficient as theirs, they allow no condescension into their approval; quite suddently, I love them all!

Now, as the other two sign, Adam asks his questions, prattles technically in his bliss. I lean back into the car again, well out of their range; the day has begun. Before it ends he will have collected signatures and answers from more than a dozen of these men. By their names and nicknames, he knows them all! Chipmunk Saunders, Bull Betowski, the formidable Anderson whose razor intellect and cold mid-western image will so soon be obscured by glory and a first, fateful step — each of them instantly identified and signed into the treasured sketch pad. For years afterward, this sketch will hang, hallowed and isolated, on the wall above Adam's bed, in the shrine he will make of his room.

And it is a great burden he places upon them, though we cannot yet know for how many human failures they will ultimately be held

accountable. Already he complains of Duffy's crewcut, Saunders'
humorlessness, Anderson's glacial composure. I, too, have my com-
plaints as, one by one, or in twos or threes (sometimes too quickly
even for Adam's vigilance), they leave their rooms and approach
us. For their jargon grates, and each of them reflects, in his own
way, the bland, Bond-Bread image of the Eisenhower years:
smooth, tanned, impassive faces, all of them from cereal-land. It is
only long afterward, when we see them on our home screens, when
their expensive violations of the atmosphere have already begun to
bore or inflame their countrymen, that I hear the humanity under
the jargon and sense the depth which informs their incredible,
machine-like performance.

Indeed, had they been merely superhuman, extra-terrestrial
creatures (catapulted as they were into the spatial wilderness), it
would have been enough. But they are so much more than that,
imprisoned in their strange interplanetary ambience, accountable
to computers as often as to men; they are men of faith who dare to
tamper with natural limits, cerebral men who dare to survive.

Though I have many times wanted to say to them, as someone
may some day wish to say it to my son: "Watch out! Oh, watch out!
You are going too far!"; though this has seemed, of all ways, the most
frightening way in which we might lose our children, our men;
though their lunar and global thrusts have seemed to cause even
floods and earthquakes, unnatural turns of every variety, the
equanimity, the cool serenity of these men has defied us all.
Armed with statistics, with data, with the power of those infernal,
awesome explosions which propel them through Space, they simply exceed our ken. And my son, who senses this, forbears to laugh
at us; he knows that, already, he goes with them. He can afford
this charity.

"Actually, you know," he tells me now, as we rest in the room
while his father dresses for breakfast, "it's a very primitive craft,
that Saturn."

"Of course." I am tentatively sardonic. Primitive! How, primitive? I close my eyes and lean back upon the pillow, while, on the
other bed, Adam inspects his autographs.

"Almost as primitive," he continues, seeming almost to be running down, like an old phonograph, "almost as primitive as the
automobile."

"Oh, well," I manage, half asleep, myself, "surely not all *that* primitive!" Who can grapple with such things, anyway? But he does not answer. Perhaps he is too tired, in any case, to deal with my doubt.

But at breakfast, revived, we review for Daniel our windfall. A covey of astronauts! a gaggle! a pride! Ye gods! an awful lot of them, anyway. We are in high, ridiculous spirits. Coming out of the woodwork, they are! Daniel says it in his English accent for us, and Adam, on cue, doubles up laughing and then, predictably, tries to top it with an English accent of his own; and suddenly, we are all laughing helplessly and when my hiccups start, as they always do, Adam all but falls off his chair laughing.

Outside again! "Just look at that VAB! Just grab that baby!" Adam is stiff with excitement as he and his father leave for the Center, on tour, and I for the beach. His weariness has really got him hopped-up now, the adrenaline pumping through and animating his joy. Perhaps he will sag and give out too soon, I think. But such days, as I remind myself and Daniel, are not subject to the application of judgment. Old rules do not apply. He has been shot from a cannon, our son! And I, wandering alone toward the white sands of Cocoa Beach, I am pleased to be alone and to be making my slow and solitary advance toward sleep, blessed, sun-baked sleep.

The shore is still cool and completely deserted. How marvelous to be the single human creature on this long white strip! How clever to have escaped the depressing, unmade motel room and the unhappy-looking local woman who will clean it superficially while we are out.

Dozing only intermittently, I wake to watch the sandpipers, those burbling, skinny-limbed, hyperkinetic ladies of the beach, as they skitter to the water's edge and then, crying their terror and delight, lift their skirts and skitter back toward safety. Their tireless, joyful game with the surf enchants me; they have no fear of me, only of the water, if that is what sends them ambivalently to and fro in a matchstick-legged dance! I sit alone on Cocoa Beach, shading my eyes against the climbing sun, and love those innocent, chattering, ambivalent creatures as they define the curious pleasure of this solitude, this day. At last, lying back upon my towel, under the rosy cover of my eyelids, I fall into a brief but perfect sleep.

"You're going to burn, you know." The shadow across my face

awakens me even before the unmistakably Texas-female voice. She is tall, quite young, and was probably once one of those long-legged beauties in cowboy hats who kick their way through southwestern football. She is all tan and health inside her simple tank suit, and I am instantly embarrassed by my bright Lastex (my Joseph-suit! its many colors seem to vibrate in the sunlight) and my white-skinned northernness.

"I'm sure," I say, trying to keep my voice unsectional. "But I was tired. I guess I just fell asleep."

She is right, of course; my arms are already blotchy and the sun stings on my shoulders.

"Ah," she smiles, "you must be a space mother." A space mother! Are we already a national phenomenon? Am I merely part of a burgeoning group: tired, slightly superfluous women who, like camp followers, trail their children while they follow their dreams?

"How could you tell?" I am rueful, wry, just short of impolite; I can feel the telling fatigue as it pulls at my face. Besides, her earnestness and her youth are irritating to me.

"Only by the circles under your eyes," still smiling. There is nothing remotely bitchy or oblique here; *her* eyes are clear, direct, Texas-beauty bright. I must get away from her!

"Are you one, too?" But, of course, I know that she isn't.

"Heavens, no!" she is ingenuously thankful. I cannot really blame her for that, either. But "I have a husband in the Program," she goes on. "Sometimes we come down together while he checks things out." And, "Space hardware," she adds.

Space hardware! I nod, though I grow slightly apprehensive now. Space hardware; the Program; space mothers! A whole world spawned secretly by that great rocket, less than twenty miles away! A new world, an industry, mysterious to me as some vast, dark underground city in which, small and insignificant, my boy has already begun to get away. Hundreds upon thousands of men who have discarded language for the dry lingo of technology: their hearts cold planets, like the moon; their jargon bloodless; their faces bland. Already Adam moves among them with his father; it is I, alone, who am the tourist here.

I start to gather up my things; without intending it, she has spoiled my time. We had no intention, Adam and Daniel and I, of giving up, so soon, the proprietary nature of our claim; time enough when the first foot set down in lunar dust, to lose this old obsession to the world. But now, I resent this premature forfeit; we are not ready to share our astronauts. Not yet!

Mildly depressed, hoping not to appear rude (as though I might mean to avenge her intrusion), I carefully say goodbye, blaming the sun, the hour, the weariness in my bones. And when I leave her there, honeying in the sunlight, I wonder whether there is not something almost ominous in the darkness which now, so suddenly, tugs at my holiday-heart.

But I find no answering harmonic in the excitement of my husband and son when they return; they are all discovery, all energy and elation! My depression, discordant in such a climate, mercifully diffuses and disappears. For they have come within feet of the wonders which so diminish them, man-made wonders which speak, nevertheless, more of computers than of men. Whether it is science, or pseudo-science, miracle or man, operating inside that great building, behind its ponderous door — it has a wondrous creature in its maw: Saturn, our huge, self-amputating friend, borne, in its deceptive sleeping stage, by tractors with cleats weighing more than a ton, to the pad where it shall rise in violent beauty from its sleep. They have watched and wondered at it, Daniel and Adam. As if to celebrate further their own insignificance, they have stopped briefly, thoughtfully, at that commemorative site where three men incinerated in their alien womb are mourned, their vulnerability memorialized forever. The intimations of heaven and hell have sobered them there; they acknowledge, as though superstitiously, the reflection of their own diminishment. For, even in their world of numbers, they are no longer safe.

"My God!" they exclaim with one voice. "Good God! It's big!" And, of course, I make the appropriate gestures and sounds of astonishment. But as in the world of mathematics, I prefer not to contemplate such frightening certainties; like the door of the building in which they wandered, some panel slides impenetrably closed in my mind. Irrevocable changes, dislodged limits, contingencies, computers: all frighten me, as does the slipping away of my child, through darkness, to another planet.

"I saw Commander Brant again," he tells me now. "You remember him, the big one?" Indeed I do! A giant of a man, dazzling,

magnetic, seeming, of all of them, too big for the capsule in which
he trains to travel.

"He said to come to his room tonight and rap about things."
Adam quivers with expectation. "It's just down the row there."
And he points toward where that morning's wait (eons ago!) chilled
our bones. I share his pleasure; but unlike him, I worry lest the
promise be forgotten.

As, indeed, it is. For that night, an exhausted Adam, listening
tentatively at that door down the line, hears what he takes to be the
sounds of a party coming from Brant's room. He does not even
knock; forestalled but undiscouraged, he returns to us with his
plans. They do not seem unreasonable. "After all," he reassures
us, as well as himself, "it *is* a Saturday night. And I figure to catch
him in the morning, before we leave. I'm tired, anway."

"Why don't we try just once again?" It is not so much disappointment as a premonitory unease which prompts my peris-
tence. A nagging, stirring uneasiness, it is, like some slender poi-
sonous creature slithering along the surface of my thoughts; still, it
is a ridiculous idea and I quickly abandon it. Adam is far beyond
anything but an early bedtime.

We all retire soon afterward, he to his own room, almost eagerly,
we to ours, after a short walk under a thickening sky. "Don't worry,"
Daniel pats my neck comfortingly, "he'll catch his boy in the morning, all right. He's a stubborn little son of a gun when he wants
something." He laughs appreciatively.

But in my head disappointment still stirs, implying danger, and
mixes crazily at last with a sleep which is broken by the discomforts
of sunburn. I toss like a fevered patient under the fragmented
images and strangely erotic dreams of a giant astronaut. Even
years later, after Brant has landed a golden a LEM-spider upon
moon-dust, I shall feel the echoes of these powerful, unpleasant
dreams.

It is raining, a harbinger, or so it seems to me, of our departure.
I glance across at Daniel, still sleeping (though through the night,
I now recall, through my dreams, I felt his tentative cooling touch
upon my back), and I marvel again at the unconsciously benign
curvatures of his face: the mouth, the cheeks, even the outside
curve of closed lids, all upward as in pleasure. A man of good
will.

It has little to do with me, I must acknowledge ruefully, this optimism of his. I am all frets and anxious requirements, while he, a morning person, whistles at the bathroom mirror, all full of resilience and hope. What would I give to be like him! I know his equanimity to be the implacable maturity of the man of science; sometimes, watching Adam, I prayerfully tell, like sacred beads, the plainly Daniel-facets of him. I comfort myself that he is like him already. I assure myself that he could never be like me.

Now, with the closing of a nearby door, I am shut off, finally, from the last traces of sleep. It is Adam, loose on the early morning.

"It's much too early!" I cry aloud. Beside me, Daniel stirs irritably; a disturbance of sleep is the single unforgivable conjugal sin. I must admit to being secretly pleased, however, to have him conscious, even alerted, during the onset of what I see now to be a forthcoming crisis of unknown dimensions. If Adam is to confront his astronaut and find him human, outside the door of that room, it is his father who shall be obliged to confront Adam.

Is he married, this Brant? I wonder wildly. I reach for my clothes, eking painful motion from under the sandpaper sting of my sunburn. And does it matter, really, in terms of how he will greet that boy, what charity he will manage in the rain outside that room? For I have no doubt that Adam will stand there, stolid and implacable, to collect on an unkept promise from a man whose glitter may well turn to pyrite. If Brant is a married man, infidelity to his wife will matter less to Adam, should he apprehend it, than infidelity to his word; I pray for Brant's compassion, for his insight, for his empathy. With a kind of irrational, fragmented fear, a powerful if misplaced need to protect, I propose to deter Adam before it is too late. "I'm going after him," I say now. "Daniel, wake up!" But Daniel, with his own powerful need to protect, has rewrapped himself in the safety of sleep. I am alone with my fears.

Daniel stirs again, but does not wake, as I open the door of our room. Lucky Daniel! Nevertheless, I take care to shut it noiselessly, feeling myself, suddenly, rather foolish, overzealous in this essentially small drama; breathing more calmly, I make my way down the walk, toward Brant's room. It is not difficult to make out, from Adam's distant posture, that he has, again, been listening hopefully at that other door. Again I start to hurry, hoping to reach the door before it opens, prescience, like some early symptom, aching in my skull.

But I am too late. My child, so single-minded, so enviably insulated from the qualms which limit most of us, is still there, poised to pounce, when Brant, with a precipitous flinging open of the fatal door, brushes past him, his long arm shielding (as though from a hostile press) a lovely, nubile creature — all blonde and honey-skinned — whom he now stashes in the back seat of his car, almost out of the range of Adam's frankly curious regard. Then, slamming that door, he just as quickly brushes past again, returning to his room. Indomitable, Adam peers through the partially closed entrance into the darkness of Brant's hiding place, only barely respectful in his distance. Oh Lord! I could strangle the child!

"I came last night," he calls, "but you sounded busy. Then, suddenly self-conscious, he grinds his toe into a crack near the door. "Commander Brant?" he recovers, calls again to the emptiness. Oh Lord! Will there soon, someday, be humor in this? I cannot see the point in stopping him now.

And Brant, hitching up his pants, tucking a shirt tail in against his magnificent, flat belly, still putting himself together, comes to the door, at last, to acknowledge the boy. I manage to shrink away from his line of sight, as though to deny even a peripheral connection to that faithful, fortified creature at his threshold. "Yes, well, sorry about that, Son." Brant manages a weary grin, his face, no longer so young, creasing into small inroads of sleeplessness and late drinking. He is, nevertheless, in blunt size, still stunning, still a giant, albeit a crumpled one, looming there over our Adam.

"Oh it's okay, Sir." But of course it isn't; the stubborn chin should have told Brant that in the first place; it is never okay to renege on Adam. Still, the child manages to dredge up some uncommon respect: "You had no obligation." Pause; instinct, no doubt, advising caution. But not long enough! "Still, Sir, I was wondering about that P.R. memo from the Center —."

And before I can cry "Too fast, Adam!" or somehow place myself between the boy and failure, he is abruptly stopped by the man, himself, who crowds harshly past him out into the rain. After all, I remind myself, he is only a man. His forbearance has been impressive. "Next time, Son. Write me a letter about it." Brant's face dissembles, now, into earnest apology; but he continues to back defensively away, toward the car, holding up one huge hand as though to fend him off.

Later, Daniel will say: "You had no business cornering the guy." And Adam will concede as much. But now, at this moment, I am enraged, not by the sullied magnetism of this man, not even by the bland obtuseness of our child, but simply by having to bear witness to this ludicrous charade: the hero backs away from the persistent child, mildly embarrassed, mildly naughty, hero in a jam. The worst Saturday-afternoon-selected-short-subject scene is to conclude our weekend. I cannot laugh at it; but later, telling it to friends, Daniel and I, with all the treachery of raconteur-parents, will turn it into a farce.

How has that been possible, after such a moment, with its fleeting, excruciating sadness for Adam, the human failure, the gold gone to tarnish? I am still haunted by the image of him, spluttering in the rain, still reaching, when that giant Brant backs his way to perfidy, opens the door of his car, and speeds away.

"Goddam reckless driving," is all that Adam mutters. It is only months later, when we read of Brant's divorce, that I think he must understand the oblique way in which he has suffered from human miscalculation. Still, he never says; even today, I do not know how much Adam knows. I can only wonder whether he feels, as I did, that for one moment, at least, Brant had to hate him; that would be the worst of all.

MARY CLEARMAN

Paths Unto the Dead

(FROM THE GEORGIA REVIEW)

SUCCESSIVE ICE AGES had shaped the land, as though a careless sweep of clawed fingers had gouged the still malleable plains into plateau and valley. Thus cruelly torn, the land became harsher. The hills lay bare under the sweep of the galaxy, waiting from the beginning of time until the end. These years, wheatfields rolled their seasonal gold across the prarie, a momentary phenomenon that would soon be gone. Already the fine dust of the hot season filtered over fields, fences, and the fragile tracks of men.

The river bottom offered some protection. Here, at the foot of a narrow road through the bluffs, willows grew along the water. The milk cow and her heifer had found shade at the foot of their pasture, where they waited, switching flies and watching the house for signs of milking time. Nearer the buildings the hens clucked their concerns of the moment from their dust nests under the chokecherries.

The white frame house and its little patch of lawn were overhung by a seventy-year-old maple. The tree was one of several saplings that had been brought hundreds of miles by buggy; only this one had survived the first killing winter, but now it spread patterned green shade over the porch where the women sat, and had sprouts of its own around the base. Like the women who sat in its shade and rocked, the tree had settled into a bitter world for the course of its span.

Two of the women on the porch were white-haired. They resembled each other, though in fact they were related only by marriage. Both were physically strong women; they both had light blue eyes — childlike eyes, the young woman thought — and wore starched homemade dresses. Years of chores in garden and barnyard had left their arms and faces as brown and seamed as walnuts.

The thinner of the two old women jumped to her feet with surprising ease, and shaded her gaze with her hand.

"That cat's got kittens hidden somewhere. Look at her, there she goes to the barn with another mouse."

The other old woman, her sister-in-law, continued to rock. "I expect the place can hold another batch of kittens, Dorothy."

"They'll grow up wild and bother the hens."

"Jeff's little girls will tame them when they come to visit."

"They'll be too much for the little girls. They'll be wild and spry by the time the girls get here," Dorothy countered, but her arguments had the lack of conviction of a spinster in the presence of a woman who has been married.

"Jeff's little girls have grown. I hardly knew little Peggy when I saw her at the funeral." The rocking chair's gentle motion continued. "So many of Lavinia's friends there, and so many flowers."

"It was the first funeral I ever went to where they didn't have the obituary read," objected Dorothy. "That surprised me. I wonder whose idea that was."

The young woman, Jean, who sat on the porch steps, was familiar enough with her great-aunts' patterns of response that she could have predicted every word, though it had been three years since she had last listened to them. The limitations of their conversation, the sunbaked barnyard, and the dark little house with its oilcloth and spotty floors depressed her as much as the desultory talk of her grandmother's funeral, only a week past. The visit with the two old ladies was paid out of duty and the memory of past affection; but already she toyed with ways to escape ahead of time.

"Jean begins to look like Lavinia, doesn't she?" her Aunt Emily observed unexpectedly. Her rocking chair continued its unhurried rhythm.

Aunt Dorothy turned from her observation of the gray barncat's doings, and gave Jean a sharp, considering look. "I never thought of it before, Emily."

Emily laid her knitting in her lap and rocked on. Her blue eyes were faraway. "I was thinking about Lavinia and how she looked at

the time she taught at the Bally-Dome. She was about the age Jean
is now."

Dorothy looked critically at her great-niece. "The way you girls
wear your hair now, all skinned back, and those steel-rimmed
glasses! You'd be right in style for my day, Jean."

Jean smiled politely and tucked a wisp of brown hair behind her
ear, but inwardly she felt familiar resentment rising that anyone
could think that she, Jean, was what these old women once had
been. Her own supple brown hands lay loosely in the lap of her
short cotton dress; her aunts' hands, always filled with knitting or
sewing or food or tools, were gnarled, stiffened with too much
heavy work and scarred by work that was too dangerous. Aunt
Emily had a deep mark on her wrist that Jean knew was a rope
burn, and both old women could display nicks and troughs on their
fingers that had been left by knives, mowing-machine teeth, or
barbed wire. Any prettiness that they might have had, they had
used up right away, Jean thought with resentment. It was as
though prettiness were something to be left behind as soon as
possible; and she looked with protectiveness at her own smooth
fingers.

Emily resumed her knitting. "I always thought Lavinia was the
prettiest of Edward's sisters."

"Pretty is as pretty does," said Dorothy sharply, but she was ready
to yield to the pleasure of reminiscence. "I was ten years old when
you married Edward and came here to live. We all had new dresses
for the wedding, and all the neighbors came — I remember the
buggies coming across the ford. Alice was fourteen then, and Lavinia was eighteen."

And now there were only Emily and Dorothy, Jean supplied to
herself. Alice dead in young womanhood, Edward in middle age.
And Lavinia, her grandmother, buried last week. And yet the
voices of the two old women were as undisturbed and light, dropping off into the sunlight as inconsequentially as the clicks of the
knitting needles or the unruffled sounds of the hens in the heat of
the day.

"Doesn't it bother you to talk about them?" she demanded without thinking, and bit her lip the next moment; but the old ladies
exchanged indulgent looks over her head.

"Now, Jean, what will be, will be," said Emily gently, and Dorothy nodded her small white head from her seat on the porch railing. Jean again felt the resentment rise, but her aunts' voices pattered on.

"Hard to believe Lavinia was ever as skinny as Jean."

"She wasn't," Dorothy objected. "None of us ran to skin and bones the way the girls do today. We all had flesh."

Aunt Emily knitted on decisively. "Dorothy, you don't remember. Lavinia had an elegant slim figure as a young woman. It was after she was married and the babies came, and things were so hard out there on the homestead that she went to flesh."

Dorothy looked mulish. Then she slid off her perch on the porch railing and crossed to the door with her surprisingly easy steps. "I'll just get Mama's album."

Aunt Emily knitted on, but her mouth twitched. It was the closest she every came to a smile. "My mother-in-law — that was your great-grandmother, Jean — used to say that Dorothy could never sit still long enough to get married."

Dorothy came back through the screen door, carrying the large plush-covered album. She looked suspiciously at her sister-in-law. "Guess I can sit still. Doesn't mean I wanted to get married, though."

Jean knew the album from childhood. The dusty blue plush under her fingertips recalled sticky afternoons on Aunt Emily's porch with her cousins, eating fried chicken and giggling over the clothes and stiff postures of their elders, while the originals of many of the photographs drowsed in the parlor after their Sunday dinner. Some of the faces in the album she could still name, not because she could associate these youthful lines and planes with the people she had known (in almost every case the known face seemed to Jean to be so changed as to be completely unconnected with the early likeness), but from summer afternoons of clamoring, "Who's that, Aunt Emily? Who's that in the buggy? On the fence?" It was inconceivable, for example, that her own grandmother, whom Jean had known as a broad, silent old woman with painfully misshapen feet and joints, could ever have been the startled child whose high woolen collar seemed to be throttling her. Or that her grandfather, that mysterious suspendered mountain wheezing in his chair, had a counterpart in the narrow-chinned youth peering slyly at the camera from beneath his greased wings of hair.

To the child, there had simply been no connection between the fading likenesses and the known flesh; that Aunt Emily always replied to the constantly reiterated "Who's that?" with "That's your Aunt Dorothy when she started school in town," or "That's my father with his buggy horse, and the boy holding the halter went away to Cuba and was killed," or "That's your grandfather when he first filed on the homestead," was only a game in which Aunt Emily always managed to parry the child's unbelieving questions with an outlandish but unassailable answer.

The young woman, however, began to see remembered likenesses as her aunts turned the crumbling black pages. Here a tilt of a head, there a scowl. Recognizing these faces of the dead, somehow caught here for a little while in fading photographs pasted to album leaves that after seventy years were beginning to decompose, with names and histories remembered by the two old women (how long before the names went to the grave and the photographs became dust?) made her uneasy, and she looked off across the sunbaked barnyard with distaste.

Dorothy, who had forgotten her purpose in fetching the album, called Jean's attention to a posed studio portrait of four small children.

"Do you know which is your father?"

"The second one," Jean answered automatically. *Who's that, Aunt Emily?* But looking more carefully at the six-year-old boy in the constricting collar, she could see the line of eyebrows and nose, the set of the eyes, that would become the besieged outlook of the man.

Emily looked over from her rocker. "That picture was taken in March, just before they moved out to the homestead."

"The spring of the diphtheria epidemic."

"And Jeff was born that summer."

After the little girls died of diphtheria, Jean added to herself. The children stared out at the photographer, pale above their unnaturally confining clothing.

"How did she stand it?" she cried. "She had eight children and lost five. Two of diphtheria, two of influenza, one drowned. Living out there on the homestead for days and days without seeing anybody, and there isn't even a tree in sight. Carrying all her water a quarter of mile, and Grandfather never ever talked, to her or anybody else —"

The old ladies looked at each other again, and Emily knitted carefully to the end of her row. "Things come to us, and we meet them. Your grandmother did her duty, same as we all did." She seemed to recognize that her words were untranslatable to her great-niece, and laid down her needles. She sat for a moment, turning her stiffened hands palm upward, and Jean remembered that Emily had also lost a child in the diphtheria epidemic.

"Things pass," said Emily at last.

Jean looked away. The sun beat on the little board walk, wilting the grass and Aunt Dorothy's row of sweet peas. Heat shimmered over the bare road and the dusty chokecherries beyond it. One chicken chased another with a ruffling of white feathers through the weeds on the other side of the fence, and the gray cat emerged from the barn, looking carefully in all directions before disappearing into the weeds on her own business. The dusty little circle seemed all at once not merely tedious, but suffocating. Of course, things passed. Their lives had passed with no more disturbance and less comfort than the lives of the chickens that Aunt Dorothy fed and that Aunt Emily would stew for Sunday dinner, one by one, or the existence of the cautious barncat, who would watch for field mice until a hawk sighted her and plummeted successfully.

Jean took a deep breath. Her own life would pass, the days would dawn and fade, but at least she had *had* something. She plucked at the hem of her expensive cotton dress, noting again the flexibility of her tapering brown fingers, the glint of the sun on her handcrafted bracelet. Unlike her grandmother and her great-aunts, she had her job and her clothes, her records and books and her glimpses of what she still thought of as the "outside world," if not at first hand, at least through foreign films. She had lived in the city and visited coffee houses and discotheques, and she had slept with three men. All this Jean offered up as a shield between herself and the smothering energy of the sun. At least she had had experiences.

Aunt Dorothy looked from her sister-in-law's face to her niece, and turned a leaf in the album. "That's Jesse MacGregor," she said. "He came over here from Scotland, and herded sheep for my father. Your great-grandfather's sheepherder, Jean."

Jean had seen the picture before, but she looked obediently, squinting as sunlight fell over the page. The man leading a horse in the picture wore the drab clothing and heavy mustache that the child remembered. To the child, the unfamiliar face had been no-age, a face out of the undifferentiated limbo of grownupness. The young woman saw, as if through an overlay of memory, that Jesse MacGregor had an energetic cock of his head and high spirit in his face that turned, not toward the horse he led, but toward the photographer. Jesse MacGregor had been a young man on the day someone with a complicated camera had troubled to go through the ritual of recording the face of a hired sheepherder from Scotland.

"Lavinia took that picture," Emily said. "She bought the camera in the late fall, with the first of her school money from the Bally-Dome."

Dorothy looked sharply at her sister-in-law. "Jesse MacGregor was an awful man for the drink. Papa used to say that Jesse was a dependable man until he had the first wee drink. And then nothing could keep him until he'd finished his spree."

Emily pursed her lips. "Yes, he drank."

"Why, Emily! No one ever liked to speak in front of us girls, but I can remember as clear as yesterday, Jesse riding in after dark and singing out by the water tank, and Papa would get up from the supper table without saying anything, and go out —" Dorothy's voice dwindled. "Anyway, I don't think Lavinia ever *thought* about Jesse MacGregor —"

Emily started another row. "Jesse MacGregor was a dependable man, sober. I remember —"

Jean looked up to see that Emily had let her knitting fall into her lap again, and was looking out at the bend of the river that could be seen through the willows.

"It was after I'd married Edward. Lavinia had to file on her homestead — the place on the benchland where your father lives, Jean. It was a thirty-mile ride to the county seat, too far for her to go alone, and the men were gone, Edward and his father — but Lavinia had to get in to the courthouse, and she was getting ready for the ride, and her mother was nearly beside herself. And then Jesse rode in from the sheep camp that morning. It was time for his spree.

"So Jesse said he'd ride in to town with Lavinia, and then her mother *was* wild. But Lavinia said nonsense, she had to go to town, and if Jesse MacGregor rode one way with her, she might be able to find someone who'd ride back with her. Jesse caught a fresh horse, and they started out.

"Mother worried all afternoon, and all evening, and all the next morning. But late on the second day, Lavinia and Jesse rode in. Jesse stopped at the corral, changed horses, and left again. Lavinia turned her horse out and came up to the house. We were all waiting in the kitchen."

Emily plucked at her ball of yarn with her thickened fingertips. "Lavinia said they'd ridden to town, and that she had filed her claim. Then she went to her aunt's house for the night, wondering what would happen in the morning. But in the morning, Jesse MacGregor was at the door with her horse, cold sober. He rode all the way home with her, saw that she was safe, and turned around and rode thirty miles back to town for his spree."

"That's what drink can do to a man," said Dorothy.

"What happened to him?" asked Jean. She had never heard the story of Jesse MacGregor, or recalled anything attached to his picture but his name.

Her aunts did not answer. Dorothy turned her birdlike white head from side to side; Emily sat quietly, withdrawn into her own thoughts.

"He was shot," Emily said at last, rousing herself. "He was shot while watching your great-grandfather's sheep, and no one ever knew who did it."

"Lavinia never gave him a thought," Dorothy insisted jealously.

"No," said Emily thoughtfully, "I don't think she ever did. Certainly not from the day she met Jefferson Evers. But it was right after that —"

"Now, Emily, you've got no business to think he did it deliberately, especially after all these years."

"Did what?" demanded Jean. "Who? My grandfather?"

"No, no," said Emily. "Jesse MacGregor. He went on a spree the day Lavinia got her engagement ring, and when he sobered up, he went up in the hills to the sheep. When they found his body, he was fifteen miles north, clear over on the Blackwell range."

"Now, Emily —"

"He knew that country well," Emily went on, as if Dorothy had not spoken. "And he knew how touchy things were getting about grazing rights. None of the men liked to discuss it in front of us, but it was rumored that the Blackwells had threatened to have any man shot who tried to steal grass."

Dorothy opened her mouth, but Emily went on, her words falling as lightly, her voice as inconsequential, as when she had talked of Lavinia's funeral or the barncat's kittens. "Jesse knew what would happen from the minute he turned those sheep north, and all the days it would have taken to drive them into strange grazing land."

Jean looked down at the picture. Jesse MacGregor's face had faded after sixty years, but the outlines of his body still expressed vigorous life.

"He was quite good-looking, wasn't he?" she asked.

"He was considered a very handsome man," Aunt Dorothy answered, crimping her mouth. "But Lavinia never looked at another man after she met Jefferson Evers."

Rays of sunlight fell through the maple leaves and whitened the picture of Jesse MacGregor, but Jean could see the lines of the young man's shoulders, the angle of his hat, with her eyes shut. She wished suddenly that she could not.

"Did Grandma know — how he felt?" she asked, uncomfortable with a vocabulary that she knew had far different connotations for her aunts.

Emily sighed. "I suppose she must have. We didn't talk of such things."

"She couldn't have married him," put in Dorothy. "All he had were the clothes he wore. And his sprees —"

"He was always a man who liked being alive," said Emily.

It was late afternoon, and Jean could leave now, get away from the scent of mildew and dust and the infirmities of old women. Tomorrow she would take the plane back home, to her own apartment and her own concerns, her own life that she protected so carefully from the decay that had found her grandmother and her aunts.

The sun was still hot, but Jean shuddered with an unfamiliar feeling of the cold. She would take back with her the story of her grandmother and Jesse MacGregor, and how Jesse MacGregor, a man who liked being alive, had deliberately turned his sheep north to unfriendly grazing land on the day her grandmother had become engaged to another man. Jean stood up and brushed off her skirt. The story of Jesse MacGregor seemed to her the first sign of the decay she feared.

"Lavinia never *thought* of Jesse MacGregor," Dorothy crooned. Jean looked up at the new note in her aunt's voice, but Dorothy was looking at Emily.

Emily rocked once, twice. The ball of yarn rolled out of her lap. "It was a long time ago," she said.

"Lavinia never thought —"

"No, no." Emily's knitting lay abandoned, a stitch or two pulled out from the unwinding ball of yarn. "Never Lavinia. I was the one who thought of Jesse MacGregor."

"Emily!" warned Dorothy.

But Jean ran the step or two down the path and picked up the escaping ball of yarn. The story of Jesse MacGregor had unwound farther already than she had ever wanted to hear.

LYLL BECERRA DE JENKINS

Tyranny

(FROM THE NEW YORKER)

I WAS SEVENTEEN when my father published his first editorial attacking the general who ruled our country — a man who had been one of his closest friends. The editorial appeared in October, near the end of my junior year of high school. Later the same week, Mother Andrea, the principal of the convent, told me that my father did not have to attend the school's commencement exercises. "Señor Maldonado must be bored with these ceremonies," she said. "Please tell him, Marta, that this time we are excusing him." For the first graduation I could remember my father would not be sitting on the dais with Bishop Vargas and the other dignitaries.

When I got home that day, I told my father what Mother Andrea had said. He was amused. "So Bishop Vargas is already coaching the good nuns, eh?" he said.

"Oh, God, what will happen to us!" my mother said, with a terror that at the time did not seem warranted.

Then a few nights later she said to Papa, "Did you really believe, Miguel, that your friend the General was different from other politicians?"

"I believed in him, yes, and made others believe in him," Papa said. "Now that the man has turned into a tyrant I cannot remain silent."

"Always your beliefs," Mama said. "And this time at your family's expense!"

Discussions like this soon took place in the presence of my brother and me almost every night.

As my father's attacks on the General increased, my schoolmates began to avoid me. With the nuns the change was also gradual. At first they continued to laugh and joke with me, but checked to be sure that no one close to the government was watching. Then they started ignoring my questions in class. "I'm glad you asked, Martica" and "Maybe your father will come give us a talk on the subject" gave way to "Can't you see you're interrupting, Marta?" Finally, like my friends, the nuns avoided me entirely.

The convent — an old castle, built by a Spanish viceroy of the sixteenth century for his mulatto mistress — was my second home. As a young girl I had run through its long, narrow corridors, searching for secret passages and imagining I saw the ghosts of the conquistadors. Now, as I walked the corridors of the convent, the nuns scattered from my path like crows taking flight.

Had they made me their favorite because I was the daughter of the General's friend, I wondered. Had the nuns truly admired my father and his editorials, or had their compliments been inspired by his influence with the government?

I would ask my brother, Ricardo, who was fourteen, "At your school are the teachers and boys still speaking to you?" and he would shrug his shoulders. The last week in November, at the very end of the school year, Ricardo announced with an air of indifference that he was not going to carry the school standard in the commencement-day parade. "Brother Juan says that the standard is too heavy for me."

"That's interesting," my father said. "You were strong enough to carry it last year and the year before. Perhaps by some miracle of Heaven the standard has grown heavier during the past months." Ricardo was the only one who laughed at this remark.

For the holidays, we drove, as we did every year, to my mother's family's country house. Father did not come along. Seeing the streams and weeping willows along the road and the peasants in their colorful ponchos and sombreros — and everything so exactly the way it always was — I began to hope that while we were away we might receive word that my father and the General had settled their differences.

In the country, we learned from our relatives that Papa had refused a position in a European embassy. "What a mistake!" my uncles said. "It is selfish of Miguel to deprive his children of the cultural advantages of Europe." Even worse in their eyes was Papa's disloyalty to the General, his friend. In the past my uncles had congratulated Mother on her husband's editorial position, saying that it was men with Papa's integrity our country needed.

For the first time, Ricardo and I felt ill at ease around our cousins. "You're such a *tonto*, Ricardo!" they would say. Or "Come on, Marta, don't you have anything clever to add?"   In our eagerness to please, we bored them.

I was telling our cousins a joke one afternoon when one of my aunts passed through the room with a pitcher of lemonade and stopped to listen. As I paused before the punch line, she said, shaking her head, "Goodness, Marta, you're looking more like your father every day!" Everyone burst out laughing. To look like my father was to have a bulldog's face. Whereas on Papa, with his prematurely silver hair and charming manners, such a face was attractive, it could only be lamentable on a girl. "But Ricardo," my aunt said as she walked away, "Ricardo is like our family; he looks like his mother."

Ricardo and I began spending our days playing dominoes alone on the veranda. We were glad when Mama cut the vacation short.

Back in the city we saw police patrols and jeeps everywhere. Papa explained that there was now a midnight curfew. Then he said,"I received an official ultimatum. I was told that if I don't agree to a public reconciliation with the General, my paper will be closed. You might as well know it. The paper is now being printed on a small private press. As of last week, it's circulating underground."

"Ah, we have returned to a nightmare," Mama said.

"I am sorry." Papa said. "To remain silent is to become an accomplice to the crimes — the abuses. If you only knew! But let's not talk about this. I'm glad you're back."

Later, Ricardo said to me, "Marta, how can Papa be so selfish? Can't he see what Mama is going through?"

One thing that Papa had not told us was that in our absence he and a few of his friends from the newspaper had begun holding nighttime meetings at our house. We learned of these meetings from our maid. "Ay, Señora, I'm so frightened," she said to Mama the following morning. "I don't know how much longer I'll be able to work in this house." She told Mama that the neighbors were all furious with Papa because they felt that they and their property were endangered; anonymous bomb threats had been made against Papa.

"See, Marta, see?" Ricardo whispered. "Everyone is against Papa."

Ricardo and I stayed close to the house for the rest of our vacation. After the maid stopped coming, I helped Mama with the housework, but my friends did not call or visit and I had much free time in which to think.

Was it possible, I asked myself, that our teachers and friends, Mama's family, and the neighbors could all be wrong? It was only from Papa that we heard any mention of crimes and abuses. Where were these things happening, and to whom? Mama had begged Papa not to bring his underground paper into our home. In the remaining daily paper there were pictures of the General attending banquets and church functions, and pictures of beauty queens and soccer stars. Nothing else.

"Everyone is against Papa because everyone is afraid to speak the truth," I said to Ricardo, but without much conviction.

"Papa *likes* to be different from everyone else," Ricardo said.

I remembered the time Papa had been invited to lay the cornerstone for a new social club and we had watched while the speakers competed with one another in praising the project. But, in a short speech, my father had said that a new club was not only unneccessary but an affront in a city where children slept in the streets and beggars crowded the aisles of churches. "We are obsessed with monuments and social clubs," he had said. "Our city is like a woman who throws a garish dress over underwear that is soiled and ragged."

"We must ask Papa to explain what's really going on," I finally said to Ricardo.

We never asked. It was as if we were afraid that his answers might make our going back to school in the fall more difficult. "I'm going to pretend I'm sick," Ricardo said. And then, "But if I don't go to school everybody will say that I am afraid and will call me a coward."

And I said — hoping that this might be true — "I think that by now our teachers and friends have realized that whatever is going on between Papa and the General is not our fault."

*

School began the first week in February. The day before school opened, Papa said to me, half joking, "Let me know, Marta, if the General's picture has been enshrined in the chapel." Mama was calm as she served Ricardo and me our breakfast the next morning. But, when we were leaving the house, she gave us each a desperate, long embrace.

Ricardo and I walked close to one another on our way to school. At several of the houses, the women stood at their doors, sending their children off. *"Buenos dias,"* I shouted to them as in the past. They stared, barely moving their lips to answer. At the end of the block I burst out, "But why, Ricardo, why? What have we done?"

Ricardo said, "Marta, *please!"*

At school, the first thing I noticed was a huge picture of the General hanging in the vestibule next to the portrait of St. Cecilia, the patroness of the convent. Then I noticed the fear in the nuns' faces at the sight of me and the speed with which my former friends ran off down the corridor. I might have been Satan, complete with horns and tail, coming into the convent with his books under his arm. It seems strange, as I look back now, that at no time during that day or during the days that followed did I consider staying home. And I continued to believe that Papa's falling-out with the General was temporary.

There was no comfort in the fact that I was not alone in being ostracized. The man who had owned our country's most important radio station, a man Papa greatly admired, had two daughters in the school. Instinctively, we ignored one another. Rather than submit to the General's censorship, their father had surrendered his station to the government and was now broadcasting from a hidden transmitter. The Julian sisters were younger — Ricardo's age — and with their long necks and delicate features they had the fragile appearance of lilies. Always inseparable, the sisters stood together in dark alcoves, hid behind pillars, and disappeared into the bathroom during recreation periods. "Come on, girls," the nuns would call in exasperation. "Come here, in front! What do you think — that you're invisible?" I also longed to make myself invisible.

The daughters of high-ranking military men had become dictators within the convent. Even the nuns feared them. There were three in my class. Early in the term one of them said to me, "Marta,

you get A's on your compositions; here, write mine," and shortly
thereafter I was writing compositions for all three. Mother Tekla
assigned us the same subject week after week with small vari-
ations — Our General. "Write a brief biography describing his
outstanding qualities," she would tell us. Or "In two pages point
out the similarities between Our General and Simón Bolívar."

"Our General," I would write, and then my pen would stop.
"Our General . . ." I sat staring at the blank page for hours, until I
hit upon a trick. Copying from editorials in the official press, I was
able to fill pages by changing the language slightly. "Our General is
ahead of his time," one editorial said. I wrote, "Our General is a
man with vision." Ricardo joined in the game. Imitating the handwriting of the girl whose homework I was doing, he wrote, "Our
General is infallible, like God!" We giggled and then laughed as we
imagined the reaction of the nuns.

"In an exemplary gesture of democracy Our General invited
some university students to participate in an open dialogue," another editorial said. Papa had told us the truth about this event.
"It was the usual," he had said. "The usual dialogue between students and bayonets." "In a gesture of generosity," I wrote for one
of the three girls, "Our General invited the university students to
join him in a frank conversation. It's too bad the students didn't
appreciate this privilege. They were disrespectful to Our General.
Five students are dead, several lie wounded in the hospital. It's
expected that other students will learn from this lesson." After that
the requests for compositions stopped. My submissiveness to the
three dictators continued, however. I laughed at their jokes; I
picked up their books; I complimented them on their clothes.

And yet none of this was as hateful to me as a new class in
Contemporary Events which the nuns had added to the daily schedule. After lunch, the entire school would march to the auditorium
to listen to a broadcast from the government radio station. The
audience on the air and in the school auditorium was informed that
rebellion was cropping up here and there — acts incited by irres-
ponsible agitators. We would hear — this part I listened to with
terror — the names of those who had been imprisoned in the past
hours, and of those who had disobeyed the orders of the General
and whom the military authorities had been forced to shoot. The
nuns listened in silence, shaking their heads at the mention of
agitators. "It is the sacred duty of our country's leader to repel the

conspiracies against our fatherland," Mother Petronila, the nun in charge of Contemporary Events, said once, but she was only repeating what Bishop Vargas had said at Sunday Mass. At the close of the broadcast we would sing patriotic hymns like "Marchemos a la Libertad" and "Justicia Vencerá." "Come on, loud! I want to hear everyone!" Mother Petronila would urge, clapping her chubby hands. And we sang, *"Libertaaaaaad . . . Justiciaaaaa!"*

As we were walking home together one afternoon, Ricardo said, "At recess today the boys were all calling me *'hijo de traidor.'* " *"Hijo de traidor,"* he repeated. To cover the tremor in his voice he tried to laugh. "Son of a traitor" was as insulting as "son of a whore." There were days that year when I would leave the convent rehearsing to myself what I planned to say to my father: "Papa, I admire your courage; I believe in what you're doing. Papa, I'm proud of you." But then I would see Ricardo waiting for me at the corner near his school and the impulse died.

We were hardly speaking to Papa by June. Weekends, Ricardo and I played cards with Mama in the glass-enclosed patio that adjoined the study where Papa was forever typing. Even now I can hear the silence at that card table, and in the background the loud music of a neighbor's radio, the shouts of Ricardo's friends playing soccer, and the tireless rat-tat-tat of the typewriter. I see my father in the shabby gray poncho he wore around the house, dragging his feet like an old man, and I see my mother's hands as she dealt the cards. I see my brother and myself as we slouched at the table. What's happening to us, I would wonder.

The only times when Ricardo and I seemed to resemble our former selves were the nights when Papa's friends from the paper came to our house for their meetings. Mama would leave coffee and pastries on a small table in a corner of the dining room; then she would rush to her bedroom and, with the lights out, watch the street from her window.

From where we sat at the landing of the stairs, Ricardo and I could see the men arriving separately, wearing hats and bulky overcoats, and whispering as they removed the folders and papers that they had hidden inside their coats. There was one — a dark young man, with curly black hair — whom they called Alfonso. I could not take my eyes off him.

Some nights my father and his friends spoke rapidly, slapping each other's backs, interrupting one another as they went into the dining room.

"Marta, I think it will happen soon — maybe tomorrow, this week," Ricardo would whisper.

"What, Ricardo?"

"He'll be overthrown. The General."

We would go to our rooms believing that an event that would change our lives was about to take place. One night I dreamed that dressed in long white gowns my classmates and I were marching into the auditorium to the music of Mother Petronila's piano. My father rose from his chair on the dais and came toward me, my diploma in his hand.

In September, the General ordered an eight-o'clock curfew, and my father's friends were forced to remain at our house all night. They made a sombre group in the morning as they stood by our door, shrouded in cigarette smoke, waiting in silence for the last patrol car to pass. When the meetings couldn't be held with safety at our house, they still took place, in the houses of one or another of my father's political friends. The nights that he was away, Mama would go from room to room switching the lights on and then off, muttering her prayers. We would hear police whistles and shooting in the distance and the sound of jeeps approaching and the sirens of the police cars. "Do you hear, Marta, Ricardo?" Mama would ask. "Do you hear it?"

Then the meetings stopped entirely. My father and his friends no longer dared to be out on the streets at night. People were disappearing on their way home from work. Others were dragged from their beds. A few had been shot by the military police right on the street. Papa typed at all hours, hardly ever leaving the house. "He is afraid, Marta," Ricardo said.

"Oh, God, what will happen to you — to us?" Mama kept asking.

"We'll leave immediately after Marta's graduation. I'm taking steps, making provisions. Leave things to me; don't worry," Papa would say.

We had only one visitor now. On certain afternoons Señor Hernandez, a lawyer and close friend of my father, would bring proofs of the newspaper to the house and pick up my father's typed copy, which he then hid in the lining of his coat. As the two men lingered by our door, they would gaze at the floor in silence. Looking down at them from the landing one day — Hernandez in his bulky overcoat, my father in his gray poncho — I had the feeling that they were growing smaller, that they were shrinking.

A month before graduation, Mother Andrea called me out of the convent dining room. At the words "Marta, please come. I'd like to speak to you," I felt panic. With the same words, the week before, she had summoned the Julian sisters when relatives of the girls brought the news that their father had been shot down by the military police. I thought first of Papa. Had the police forced their way into our house? Had they arrested Papa? Ricardo was at home, in bed with a stomach upset. Had he and Mama been arrested, too? I followed Mother Andrea into an empty classroom, with my heart beating wildly. She walked past the desks and went up to stand on the teacher's platform. Behind her, on the blackboard, was a note asking the seniors to stay after class to discuss the graduation ceremony. I wondered why Mother Tekla, whose handwriting I recognized, had bothered to list all of the names. Only one name was missing — mine. I looked up at Mother Andrea. She seemed absorbed in reading a paper that she held in one hand, while her other hand kept touching the crucifix that hung from her waist.

She finally spoke. "Marta, this is a graduation certification. You'll be leaving with your family soon. The graduation should not be an obstacle to your departure." She looked away from me and spoke hurriedly. "We think about your mother often, and pray for all of you — for your father especially. Fanaticism is a form of madness that destroys all that is noble in man. We trust we've given you spiritual resources sufficient to share with your family and to sustain you through whatever tribulations may lie ahead." Her voice went on and on. "This, Marta" — she was showing me the neatly typed page with my name at the top — "is equivalent to your diploma. It's as if you were graduating, as if you were receiving the diploma with your classmates, but your physical presence is — how should I say it —"

"Invisible," I said.

"That's it. I'm sending this to your parents. Go now; don't let your lunch get cold."

I did not go back to the convent. Papa had to hurry his plans for leaving. The building that had housed the newspaper was rented out as storage space, the proceeds from which Señor Hernandez would send us in monthly checks. Mama packed round the clock. The living room was full of suitcases with bedclothes and linens. But where were we going, Ricardo and I wanted to know.

Papa finally told us. Getting visas was out of the question. We were going to go south, to the border, and then across it. "It's a matter of days now," he said. "I'm trying to establish a new press. I will not abandon my struggle or my friends." A few days later he announced, "We are leaving this weekend." But the decision was not Papa's to make.

Thursday night, after Mama and Ricardo had gone upstairs to bed, Papa and I were talking in the living room when we heard a knock at the door. Papa frowned. He patted my head, took off his reading glasses, and slowly walked to the foyer door. I heard men's voices, then silence. Presently my father came into the room with two Army officers — a major with a thin mustache and a captain. The major removed his cap when he saw me. My father held a paper in his hand. He explained that the officers had instructions to escort us out of the city. "Tonight, Marta," he added, and thrust the paper in his pocket.

"It is the policy of our General to treat his enemies with honor and benevolence," said the captain.

"Is it also the policy of your General to intrude on a family's privacy and to frighten children and women at midnight?" my father asked.

Mama was standing in the doorway, her dark eyes immense. Papa went to her and they stood whispering. "I'm all right," she said. "I'll go wake Ricardo." But she did not move. Her eyes were on the captain, who was trying to open the case of my father's typewriter.

"There's no need to inspect!" the major said sharply, and then, to Mama, "We'll take the suitcases out while you get ready." He left the room and returned immediately with two soldiers.

We moved about the house in silence, trying not to look at each other, picking up books, toilet articles, Ricardo's medicines. Then Mama stood at the foot of the stairs, gazing around her. "Ready?" Papa asked. Out on the street, I saw that the two soldiers were gone. The officers were waiting for us in a limousine. The captain was at the wheel. As the four of us got in the back, I could sense the neighbors watching us from behind their doors and windows.

It was a clear night. The streets were deserted except for military vehicles and jeeps carrying men who saluted the two officers as we drove by. We passed Ricardo's school. Ahead I saw the belfry light of the convent chapel. I thought I saw the white of a nun's nightdress.

We had to stop several times for Ricardo to vomit. In the darkness we could make out pastures, huts, rows of eucalyptus, and the shadows of the light poles thrown across the road. At one point, the major took over the driving. While the other man slept, he talked to Papa. "You've probably guessed where we are going, Señor Maldonado," he said. Then he told us that we were on our way to an isolated town with a small military base where a house was waiting for us. We were to remain there indefinitely, under close military surveillance. "You're among the luckier ones, Señor Maldonado," the major said.

"*Gracias a Dios*," Mama muttered. Papa took out his handkerchief and blew his nose. "We'll be back," he whispered to me. "Maybe not as soon as we'd like, but you'll see. All this has not been in vain. Everything will be the way it was before."

The sky was growing light. We began to meet peasants and burros on the road. Before us lay a hillside with modest houses, a small church tower, and an old fort, all enclosed by a high brick wall. Inside the wall was a whitewashed house with a tile roof — our home for the next sixteen months, my father's honorable prison.

ANDRE DUBUS

Cadence

(FROM THE SEWANEE REVIEW)

HE STOOD in the summer Virginia twilight, an officer candidate, nineteen years old, wearing Marine utilities and helmet, an M1 rifle in one hand, its butt resting on the earth, a pack high on his back, the straps buckled too tightly around his shoulders; because he was short he was the last man in the rank. He stood in the front rank and watched Gunnery Sergeant Hathaway and Lieutenant Swenson in front of the platoon, talking quietly to each other, the lieutenant tall and confident, the sergeant short, squat, with a beer gut; at night, he had told them, he went home and drank beer with his old lady. He could walk the entire platoon into the ground. Or so he made them believe. He had small, brown, murderous eyes; he scowled when he was quiet or thinking; and, at rest, his narrow lips tended downward at the corners. Now he turned from the lieutenant and faced the platoon. They stood on the crest of a low hill; beyond Hathaway the earth sloped down to a darkened meadow and then rose again, a wooded hill whose black trees touched the gray sky.

"We're going back over the Hill Trail," he said, and someone groaned and at first Paul fixed on that sound as a source of strength: someone else dreaded the hills as much as he did. Around him he could sense a fearful gathering of resolve, and now the groan he had first clung to became something else: a harbinger of his own failure. He knew that, except for Hugh Munson standing beside him, he was the least durable of all; and since these men, a good half of them varsity athletes, were afraid, his own fear became nearly unbearable. It became physical: it

took a penetrating fall into his legs and weakened his knees so
he felt he was not supported by muscle and bone but by faint
nerves alone.

"We'll put the little men up front," Hathaway said, "so you long-
legged pacesetters'll know what it's like to bring up the rear."

They moved in two files, down a sloping trail flanked by black
trees. Hugh was directly behind him. To his left, leading the other
file, was Whalen; he was wide as a door. He was a wrestler from
Purdue. They moved down past trees and thick underbrush into
the dark of the woods, and behind him he heard the sounds of
blindness: a thumping body and clattering rifle as someone tripped
and fell; there were curses, and voices warned those coming behind
them, told of a branch reaching across the trail; from the rear
Hathaway called: "Close it up close it up, don't lose sight of the man
in front of you." Paul walked step for step beside Whalen and
watched tall Lieutenant Swenson setting the pace, watched his pack
and helmet as he started to climb and, looking up and past the
lieutenant, up the wide corridor between the trees, he saw against
the sky the crest of the first hill.

Then he was climbing, his legs and lungs already screaming at
him that they could not, and he saw himself at home in his room
last winter and spring, getting ready for this: push-ups and sit-ups,
leg lifts and squat jumps and deep kneebends, exercises which
made his body feel good but did little for it, and as he climbed and
the muscles of his thighs bulged and tightened and his lungs demanded more and more of the humid air, he despised that memory of himself, despised himself for being so far removed from the
world of men that he had believed in calisthenics, had not even
considered running, though he had six months to get in condition
after signing the contract with the Marine captain who had come
one day like salvation into the student union, wearing the blue
uniform and the manly beauty that would fulfill Paul's dreams.
Now those dreams were an illusion: he was close to the top of the
first hill, his calf and thigh muscles burning, his lungs gasping, and
his face, near sobbing, was fixed in pain. His one desire that he felt
with each breath, each step up the hard face of the hill, was not
endurance: it was deliverance. He wanted to go home, and to have
this done for him in some magical or lucky way that would give
him honor in his father's eyes. So as he moved over the top of

the hill, Whalen panting beside him, and followed Lieutenant
Swenson steeply down, he wished and then prayed that he would
break his leg.

He descended: away from the moonlight, down into the shadows
and toward the black at the foot of the hill. His strides were short
now and quick, his body leaned backward so he wouldn't fall, and
once again his instincts and his wishes were at odds: wanting a
broken leg, he did not want to fall and break it; wanting to go
home, he did not want to quit and pack his seabag and suitcase, and
go. For there was that too: they would let him quit. That was the
provision which had seemed harmless enough, even congenial, as
he lifted his pen in the student union. He could stop and sit or lean
against a tree and wait for the platoon to pass and Sergeant Hathaway's bulk to appear like an apparition of fortitude and conscience out of the dark, strong and harsh and hoarse, and he could
then say: "Sir, I want to go home." It would be over then, he would
drift onto the train tomorrow and then to the airport and fly home
in a nimbus of shame to face his father's blue and humiliated eyes,
which he had last seen beaming at him before the embrace that,
four and a half weeks ago, sent him crossing the asphalt to the
plane.

It was a Sunday. Sergeants met the planes in Washington and
put the men on buses that were green and waxed, and drove them
through the last of the warm setting sun to Quantico. The conversations aboard the bus were apprehensive and friendly. They all
wore civilian clothes except Paul. At home he had joined the reserve and his captain had told him to wear his uniform and he had:
starched cotton khaki, and it was wrinkled from his flight. The
sergeants did not look at the uniform or at him either; or, if they
did, they had a way of looking that was not looking at him. By the
time he reached the barracks he felt that he existed solely in his
own interior voice. Then he started up the stairs, carrying seabag
and suitcase, guided up by the press of his companions, and as he
went down a corridor toward the squad bay he passed an open
office and Sergeant Hathaway entered his life: not a voice but a
roar, and he turned and stood at attention, seabag and suitcase
heavy in each hand, seeing now with vision narrowed and dimmed
by fear the raging face, the pointing finger; and he tried for the
voice to say Me, sir? but already Hathaway was coming toward him

and with both fists struck his chest one short hard blow, the fists
then opening to grip his shirt and jerk him forward into the office;
he heard the shirt tear; somewhere outside the door he dropped
his luggage; perhaps they hit the doorjamb as he was going
through, and he stood at attention in the office; other men were
there, his eyes were aware of them but he was not, for in the
cascade of curses from that red and raging face he could feel and
know only his fear: his body was trembling, he knew as though he
could see it that his face was drained white, and now he had to form
answers because the curses were changing to questions, Hathaway's
voice still at a roar, his dark loathing eyes close to Paul's and at the
same height; Paul told him his name.

"Where did it happen?"

"Sir?"

"Where did she do it. Where the fuck were you born."

"Lake Charles, Louisiana, sir."

"Well no shit Lake Charles Louisiana sir, you college idiot, you
think I know where that is? Where is it?"

"South of New Orleans sir."

"South of New Orleans. How far south."

"About two hundred miles sir."

"Well no shit. Are you a fucking fish? Answer me, candidate
shitbird. Are you a fucking fish?"

"No sir."

"No sir. Why aren't you a fish?"

"I don't know sir."

"You don't know. Well you better be a goddamn fish because
two hundred miles south of New Orleans is in the Gulf of fucking
Mexico."

"West sir."

"You said south. Are you calling me a liar, fartbreath? I'll break
your jaw. You know that? Do you know that?"

"Sir?"

"Do you know I can break your goddamn jaw?"

"Yes sir."

"Do you want me to?"

"No sir."

"Why not? You can't use it. You can't goddamn talk. If I had a
piece of gear that wasn't worth a shit and I didn't know how to use

it anyway I wouldn't give a good rat's ass if somebody broke it.
Stop shaking. Who told you to wear that uniform? I said stop
shaking."

"My captain sir."

"My *cap*tain. Who the fuck is your captain."

"My reserve captain sir."

"Is he a ragpicker?"

"Sir?"

"Is he a *rag*picker. How does he *eat*."

"He has a hardware store, sir."

"He's a ragpicker. Say it."

"He's a ragpicker, sir."

"I told you to stop shaking. Say my reserve captain is a ragpicker."

"My reserve captain is a ragpicker, sir."

Then the two fists came up again and struck his chest and
gripped the shirt, shaking him back and forth, and stiff and quivering and with legs like weeds he had no balance, and when Hathaway shoved and released him he fell backward and crashed
against a steel wall locker; then Hathaway had him pressed against
it, holding the shirt again, banging him against the locker, yelling:
"You can't wear that uniform you shit you don't even know how to
wear that uniform you wore it on the goddamn plane playing
Marine goddamnit — Well you're not a Marine and you'll never
be a Marine, you won't make it here one week, you will not be here
for chow next Sunday, because you are a shit and I will break your
ass in five days, I will break it so hard that for the rest of your
miserable fucking life every time you see a man you'll crawl under
a table and piss in you skivvies. Give me those emblems. Give
them to me! Take them off, take them off, take them off —"
Paul's hands rising first to the left collar, the hands trembling so
that he could not hold the emblem and collar still, his right hand
trying to remove the emblem while Hathaway's fists squeezed the
shirt tight across his chest and slowly rocked him back and forth,
the hands trembling; he was watching them and they couldn't do
it, the fingers would not stop, they would not hold; then with
a jerk and a shove Hathaway flung him against the locker, screaming at him; and he felt tears in his eyes, seemed to be watching
the tears in his eyes, pleading with them to at least stay there
and not stain his cheeks; somewhere behind Hathaway the other

men were still watching but they were a blur of khaki and flesh: he was enveloped and penetrated by Hathaway's screaming and he could see nothing in the world except his fingers working at the emblems.

Then it was over. The emblems were off, they were in Hathaway's hand, and he was out in the corridor, propelled to the door and thrown to the opposite wall with such speed that he did not even feel the movement: he only knew Hathaway's two hands, one at the back of his collar, one at the seat of his pants. He picked up his suitcase and seabag, and feeling bodiless as a cloud, he moved down the hall and into the lighted squad bay where the others were making bunks and hanging clothes in wall lockers and folding them into foot lockers, and he stood violated and stunned in the light. Then someone was helping him. Someone short and muscular and calm (it was Whalen), a quiet midwestern voice whose hand took the seabag and suitcase, whose head nodded for him to follow the quick athletic strides that led him to his bunk. Later that night he lay in the bunk and prayed dear please God please dear God may I have sugar in my blood. The next day the doctors would look at them and he must fail, he must go home; in his life he had been humiliated, but never never had anyone made his own flesh so uninhabitable. He must go home.

But his body failed him. It was healthy enough for them to keep it and torment it, but not strong enough, and each day he woke tired and rushed to the head where men crowded two or three deep at the mirrors to shave and others, already shaved, waited outside toilet stalls; then back to the squad bay to make his bunk, the blanket taut and without wrinkle, then running down the stairs and into the cool first light of day and, in formation with the others, he marched to chow where he ate huge meals because on the second day of training Hathaway had said: "Little man, I want you to eat everything but the table cloth;" so on those mornings, not yet hungry, his stomach in fact near-queasy at the early morning smell of hot grease that reached him a block from the chow hall, he ate cereal and eggs and pancakes and toast and potatoes and milk, and the day began. Calisthenics and running in formation around the drill field, long runs whose distances and pace were at the whim of Lieutenant Swenson, or the obstacle course, or assaulting hills or climbing the Hill Trail, and each day there came a point when his body gave out, became a witch's curse of one hundred and forty-five pounds of pain that he had to bear, and he would look over at Hugh Munson trying to do a push-up, his back arching, his belly drawn to the earth as though gravity had chosen him for an extra, jesting pull; at Hugh hanging from the chinning bar, his face contorted, his legs jerking, a man on a gibbet; at Hugh climbing the. Hill Trail, his face pale and open-mouthed and dripping, the eyes showing pain and nothing more, his body swaying like a fighter senseless on his feet; at Hugh's arms taking him halfway up the rope and no more so he hung suspended like an exclamation point at the end of Hathaway's bellowing scorn.

In the squad bay they helped each other. Every Saturday morning there was a battalion inspection and on Friday nights, sometimes until three or four in the morning, Paul and Hugh worked together, rolling and unrolling and rolling again their shelter halves until, folded in a U, they fit perfectly on the haversacks which they had packed so neatly and squarely they resembled canvas boxes. They took apart their rifles and cleaned each part; in the head they scrubbed their cartridge belts with stiff brushes, then put them in the dryer in the laundry room downstairs; and they worked on shoes and boots, spit-shining the shoes and one pair of boots, and saddle-soaping a second pair of boots which they wore to the field; they washed their utility caps and sprayed them with starch and fitted them over tin cans so they would shape as they dried. And, while they worked, they drilled each other on the sort of questions they expected the battalion commander to ask. What *is* enfilade fire, candidate Hugh? Why that, colonel, is when the axis of fire coincides with the axis of the enemy. And can you name the chain of command as well? I can, my colonel, and, sorry to say, it begins with Ike. At night during the week and on Saturday afternoons they studied for exams. Hugh learned quickly to read maps and use the compass, and he helped Paul with these, spreading the map on his foot locker, talking, pointing, as Paul chewed his lip and frowned at the brown contour lines which were supposed to become, in his mind, hills and draws and ridges and cliffs. On Sunday afternoons they walked to the town of Quantico and, dressed in civilian clothes, drank beer incognito in bars filled with sergeants. Once they took the train to Washington and saw the Lincoln Memorial and pretended not to weep; then, proud of their legs and wind, they climbed the Washington Monument. One Saturday night they got happily and absolutely drunk in Quantico and walked home singing love songs.

Hugh slept in the bunk above Paul's. His father was dead, he lived with his mother and a younger sister, and at night in the squad bay he liked talking about his girl in Bronxville; on summer afternoons he and Molly took the train into New York.

"What do you do?" Paul said. He stood next to their bunk; Hugh sat on his, looking down at Paul; he wore a T-shirt, his bare arms were thin, and high on his cheekbones were sparse freckles.

"She takes me to museums a lot."

"What kind of museums?"

"Art."

"I've never been to one."

"That's because you're from the south. I can see her now, standing in front of a painting. Oh Hugh, she'll say, and she'll grab my arm. Jesus."

"Are you going to marry her?"

"In two years. She's a snapper like you, but hell I don't care. Sometimes I go to mass with her. She says I'll have to sign an agreement; I mean it's not *her* making me, and she's not bitchy about it; there's nothing she can do about it, that's all. You know, agree to raise the kids Catholics. That Nazi crap your Pope cooked up."

"You don't mind?"

"Naw, it's *Mol*ly I want. *Her,* man —"

Now in his mind Paul was miles and months away from the squad bay and the smells of men and canvas and leather polish and gun oil, he was back in those nights last fall and winter and spring, showing her the stories he wrote, buying for her Hemingway's books, one at a time, chronologically, in hardcover; the books were for their library, his and Tommie's, after they were married; he did not tell her that. Because for a long time he did not know if she loved him. Her eyes said it, the glow in her cheeks said it, her voice said it. But she never did; not with her controlled embraces and kisses, and not with words. It was the words he wanted. It became an obsession: they drank and danced in night clubs, they saw movies, they spent hours parked in front of her house, and he told her his dreams and believed he was the only young man who had ever had such dreams and had ever told them to such a tender girl; but all this seemed incomplete because she didn't give him the words. Then one night in early summer she told him she loved him. She was a practical and headstrong girl; the next week she went to see a priest. He was young, supercilious, and sometimes snide. She spent an hour with him, most of it in anger, and that night she told Paul she must not see him again. She must not love him. She would not sign contracts. She spoke bitterly of incense and hocus-pocus and graven images. Standing at Hugh's bunk, remembering that long year of nights with Tommie, yearning again for the sound of his own voice, gently received, and the swelling of his heart as he told Tommie what he had to and wanted to be, he felt divided and perplexed; he looked at Hugh's face and thought of Molly's hand reaching out for that arm, holding it, drawing Hugh close to her as she gazed at a painting. He blinked his eyes, scratched his crew-cut head, returned to the squad bay with an exorcising wrench and a weary sigh.

"— Sometimes she lets me touch her, just the breasts you see, and that's fine, I don't push it. When she lets me I'm goddamn *grateful*. Jesus, you got to get a girl again. There's nothing like it. You know that? *Nothing.* It's another world, man."

On a hot gray afternoon he faced Hugh on the athletic field, both of them wearing gold football helmets, holding pugil sticks at the ready, as if they were rifles with fixed bayonets. Paul's fists gripped and encircled the smooth round wood; on either end of it was a large stuffed canvas cylinder; he looked into Hugh's eyes, felt the eyes of the circled platoon around him, and waited for Hathaway's signal to begin. When it came he slashed at Hugh's shoulder and neck but Hugh parried with the stick, then he jabbed twice at Hugh's face, backing him up, and swung the lower end of the stick around in a butt stroke that landed hard on Hugh's ribs; then with speed he didn't know he had he was jabbing Hugh's chest, Hathaway shouting now: "That's it, little man: keep him going, keep him going; Munson get your balance, use your feet, goddamnit —" driving Hugh back in a circle, smacking him hard on the helmeted ear; Hugh's face was flushed, his eyes betrayed, angry; Paul jabbing at those eyes, slashing at the head and neck, butt stroking hip and ribs, charging, keeping Hugh off balance so he could not hit back, could only hold his stick diagonally across his body, Paul feinting and working over and under and around the stick, his hands tingling with the blows he landed until Hathaway stopped him: "All right, little man, that's enough; Carmichael and Vought, put on the headgear."

Paul took off the helmet and handed it and the pugil stick to Carmichael. He picked up his cap from the grass; it lay next to Hugh's, and as he rose with it Hugh was beside him, stooping for his cap, murmuring: "Jesus, you really like this shit, don't you."

Paul watched Carmichael and Vought fighting, and pretended he hadn't heard. He felt Hugh standing beside him. Then he glanced at Hathaway, across the circle. Hathaway was watching him.

In the dark he was climbing the sixth and final hill, even the moon was gone, either hidden by trees or clouds or out of his vision because he was in such pain that he could see only that: his pain; the air was gray and heavy and humid, and he could not get enough of it; even as he inhaled his lungs demanded more and he exhaled with a rush and again drew in air, his mouth open, his throat and tongue dry, haunting his mind with images he could not escape: cold oranges, iced tea, lemonade, his canteen of water — He was falling back. He wasn't abreast of Whalen anymore, he was next to the man behind Whalen and then back to the third man, and he moaned and strove and achieved a semblance of a job, a tottering climb away from the third man and past the second and up with Whalen again, then from behind people were yelling at him, or trying to, their voices diminished, choked off by their own demanding lungs: they were cursing him for lagging and then running to catch up, causing a gap which they had to close with their burning legs. Behind him Hugh was silent and Paul wondered if that silence was because of empathy or because Hugh was too tired to curse him aloud; he decided it was empathy and wished it were not.

And now Lieutenant Swenson reached the top, a tall helmeted silhouette halted and waiting against the oppressive and mindless sky, and Paul's heart leaped in victory and resilience, he crested the hill, went happily past Swenson's panting and sweating face, plunged downward, leaning back, hard thighs and calves bouncing on the earth, then Swenson jogged past him, into the lead again and, walking now, brought them slowly down the hill and out of the trees, onto the wide quiet gravel road and again stepped aside and watched them go past, telling them quietly to close it up, close it up, you people, and Paul's stride was long and light and drunk with fatigue; he tried to punch Whalen's arm but couldn't reach him and didn't have the strength to veer from his course and do it — Then Swenson's voice high and clear: " 'tawn: ten*hugh*," and he straightened his back and with shoulders so tired and aching that he barely felt the cutting packstraps, he marched to Swenson's tenor cadence, loving now the triumphant rhythm of boots in loose gravel, cooling in his drying sweat, able now to think of water as a promise the night would keep. Then Swenson called out: "Are you ready, Gunny?" and, from the rear, Hathaway's answering growl: "Aye, Lieutenant —" and Paul's heart chilled, he had heard the mischievous threat in Swenson's voice and now it came: "Double time —" a pause: crunching boots: groans, and then "— *huhn*."

Swenson ran past him on long legs, swerved to the front of the two files, and slowed to a pace that already Paul knew he couldn't keep. For perhaps a quarter of a mile he ran step for step with Whalen, and then he was finished. His stride shortened and slowed. Whalen was ahead of him and he tried once to catch up, but as he lifted his legs they refused him, they came down slower, shorter, and falling back now he moved to his left so the men behind him could go on. For a moment he ran beside Hugh. Hugh jerked his pale face to the left, looked at him, tried to say something; then he was gone. Paul was running alone between the two files, they were moving past him, some spoke encouragement as they went — hang in there, man — then he was among the tall ones at the rear and still he was dropping back, then a strong hand extended from a gasping shadowed face and took his rifle and went on.

He did not look behind him but he knew: he could feel at his back the empty road, and he was dropping back into it when the last two men, flanking him, each took an arm and held him up. "You can do it," they said. "Keep going," they said. He ran with them. Vaguely above the sounds of his breathing he could hear the pain of others: the desperate breathing and always the sound of boots, not rhythmic now, for each man ran in step with his own struggle, but anyway steady, and that is what finally did him in: the endlessness of that sound. Hands were still holding his arms; he was held up and pulled forward, his head lolled, he felt his legs giving way, his arms, his shoulders, he was sinking, they were pulling him forward but he was sinking, his eyes closed, he saw red-laced black and then it was over, he was falling forward to the gravel, and then he struck it but not with his face: with his knees and arms and hands. Then his face settled forward onto the gravel. He was not unconscious, and he lay in a shameful moment of knowledge that he would remember for the rest of his life: he had quit before his body failed; the legs which now lay in the gravel still had strength which he could feel; and already, within this short respite, his lungs were ready again. They hurt, they labored, but they were ready.

"He passed out, sir."

They were standing above him. The platoon was running up the road.

"Who is it?" Hathaway said.

"It's Clement, sir."

"Leave his rifle here and you men catch up with the platoon."

"Aye-aye, sir."

There were two of them. They went up the road, running hard to catch up, and he wanted to tell them he was sorry he had lied, but he knew he never would. Then he heard or felt Hathaway squat beside him, the small strong hands took his shoulders and turned him over on his back and unbuckled his chin strap. He blinked up at Hawthaway's eyes: they were concerned, interested yet distant, as though he were disassembling a weapon whose parts were new to him; and they were knowing too, as if he were not appraising the condition of Paul's body alone but the lack of will that had allowed it to fall behind, to give up a rifle, to crap out.

"What happened, Clement?"

"I don't know, sir. I blacked out."

Hathaway's hands reached under Paul's hip, lifted him enough to twist the canteen around, open the flaps, pull it from the cover. The crunching of the platoon receded and was gone up the road in the dark. Hathaway handed him the canteen.

"Take two swallows."

Paul lifted his head and drank.

"Now stand up."

He stood, replaced the canteen on his hip, and buckled his chin strap. His shirt was soaked; under it the T-shirt clung to his back and chest.

"Here's your weapon."

He took the M1 and slung it on his shoulder.

"Let's go," Hathaway said, and started jogging up the road, Paul moving beside him, the fear starting again, touching his heart like a feather and draining his legs of their strength. But it didn't last. Within the first hundred yards it was gone, replaced by the quick-lunged leg-aching knowledge that there was no use being afraid because he knew, as he had known the instant his knees and hands and arms hit the gravel, that he was strong enough to make it; that Hathaway would not let him do anything but make it; and so his fear was impotent, it offered no chance of escape, and he ran now with Hathaway, mesmerized by his own despair. He tried to remember the road, how many bends there were, so he could look forward to that last curve which would disclose the lighted streets of what now felt like home. He could not remember how many curves there were. Then they rounded one and Hathaway said, "Hold it," and walked toward the edge of the road. Paul wiped sweat from his eyes, blinked them, and peered beyond Hathaway's back and shoulders at the black trees. He followed Hathaway and then he saw, at the side of the road, a man on his hands and knees. As he got closer he breathed the smell.

"Who is it?" Hathaway said.

"Munson." His voice rose weakly from the smell. Paul moved closer and stood beside Hathaway, looking down at Hugh.

"Are you finished?"Hathaway said.

"I think so."

"Then stand up." His voice was low, near coaxing in its demand.

Hugh pushed himself up, stood, then retched again and leaned over the ditch and dry-heaved. When he was done he remained bent over the ditch, waiting. Then he picked up his rifle and stood straight, but he did not turn to face them. He took off his helmet and held it in front of him, down at his waist, took something from it, then one hand rose to his face. He was wiping it with a piece of toilet paper. He dropped the paper into the ditch, then turned

and looked at Hathaway. Then he saw Paul, who was looking at
Hugh's drained face and feeling it as if it were his own: the cool
sweat, the raw sour throat.

"Man—" Hugh said, looking at Paul, his voice and eyes petulant;
then he closed his eyes and shook his head.

"We'll run it in now," Hathaway said.

Hugh opened his eyes.

"I threw up," he said.

"And you're done." Hathaway pointed up the road. "And the
barracks is that way."

"I'll walk."

"When you get back to New York you can do that, Munson. You
can diddle your girl and puke on a six-pack and walk back to the
frat house all you want. But here you run. Put on your helmet."

Hugh slung his rifle on his shoulder and put his helmet on his
head.

"Buckle it."

He buckled it under his chin, then looked at Hathaway.

"I can't run. I threw up." He gave Paul a weary glance, and
looked up the road. "It's not that I won't. I just can't, that's all."

He stood looking at them. Then he reached back for his canteen, it rose pale in the moonlight, and he drank.

"All right, Munson: two swallows, then start walking; Clement,
let's go."

He looked at Hugh lowering the canteen, his head back gargling,
then his eyes were on the road directly in front of him as he ran up
a long stretch then rounded a curve and looked ahead and saw
more of the road, the trees, and the black sky at the horizon; he was
too tired to lift his head and see the moon and stars and this made
him feel trapped on a road that would never end. Before the next
curve he reached the point of fatigue he had surrendered to when
he fell, and he moved through it into a new plane of struggle where
he was certain that now his body would truly fail him, would fold
and topple in spite of the volition Hathaway gave him. And then
something else happened, something he had never experienced.
Suddenly his legs told him they could go as far as he wanted them
to. They did not care for his heat-aching head, for his thirst; they
did not care for his pain. They told him this so strongly that he was
frightened, as though his legs would force him to hang on as they

spent the night jogging over Virginia hills; then he regained possession of them. They were his, they were running beside a man who had walked out of the Chosin Reservoir, and they were going to make it. When Paul turned the last bend and saw the street lights and brick buildings and the platoon, which had reached the blacktop road by the athletic field and was marching now, he felt both triumphant and disappointed: he wanted to show Hathaway he could keep going.

They left the gravel and now his feet pounded on the gift of smooth blacktop. They approached the platoon, then ran alongside it, and as they came abreast of Lieutenant Swenson, Hathaway said: "Lieutenant, you better send a jeep back for Munson. Me and Clement's going to hit the grinder; we had a long rest up the road." The lieutenant nodded. Paul and Hathaway passed the platoon and turned onto the blacktop parade field and started to circle it. It was a half-mile run. For a while Paul could hear Swenson's fading cadence, then it stopped and he knew Swenson was dismissing the platoon. In the silence of the night he ran alongside Hathaway, listened to Hathaway's breath and pounding feet, glanced at him, and looked up at the full moon over the woods. They left the parade field and jogged up the road between brick barracks until they reached Bravo Company and Hathaway stopped. Paul faced him and stood at attention. His legs felt like they were still running. He was breathing fast and deep, his face dripping and red. Hathaway's eyes were not glaring, not even studying Paul; they seemed fixed instead on his own weariness.

"You get in the barracks, you get some salt tablets and you take 'em. I don't care if you've been drinking goddamn Gulf water all your life. Dismissed."

The rest of the platoon were in the showers. As he climbed the stairs he heard the spraying water, the tired, exultant, and ironic voices. In the corridor at the top of the stairs he stopped and looked at the full-length mirror, looked at his short lean body standing straight, the helmet on his head, the pack with a protruding bayonet handle, the rifle slung on his shoulder. His shirt and patches on his thighs were dark green with sweat. Then he moved on to the water fountain and took four salt tablets from the dispenser and swallowed them one at a time, tilting his head back to swallow, remembering the salt tablets on the construction job when he was sixteen and his father got him the job and drove him to work on the first day and introduced him to the foreman and said: "Work him, Jesse; make a man of him." Jesse was a quiet wiry Cajun; he nodded, told Paul to stow his lunch in the toolshed and get a pick and a spade. All morning he worked bare-headed under the hot June sun; he worked with the Negroes, digging a trench for the foundation, and at noon he was weak and nauseated and could not eat. He went behind the shed and lay in the shade. The Negroes watched him and asked him wasn't he going to eat. He told them he didn't feel like it. At one o'clock he was back in the trench, and thirty minutes later he looked up and saw his father in seersucker and straw hat standing with Jesse at the trench's edge. "Come on up, son," his father said. "I'm all right," and he lifted the pick and dropped more than drove it into the clay at his feet. "You just need a hat, that's all," his father said. "Come on up, I'll buy you one and bring you back to work." He laid the pick beside the trench, turned to the Negro working behind him, and said, "I'll be right back." "Sure," the Negro said. "You get that hat." He climbed out of the trench and walked quietly beside his father to the car. "Jesse called me," his father said in the car. "He said the nigras told him you didn't eat lunch. It's just the sun, that's all. We'll get you a hat. Did you take salt tablets?" Paul said yes, he had. His father bought him a pith helmet and, at the soda fountain, a Seven-Up and a sandwich. "Jesse said you didn't tell anybody you felt bad." "No," Paul said. "I didn't." His father stirred his coffee, looked away. Paul could feel his father's shy pride and he loved it, but he was ashamed too, for when he had looked up and seen his father on the job, he had had a moment of hope when he thought his father had come to tenderly take him home.

By the time he got out of his gear and hung his wet uniform by the window and wiped his rifle clean and lightly oiled it, the rest of the platoon were out of the showers, most were in their bunks, and the lights would go out in five minutes. Paul went to the shower and stayed long under the hot spray, feeling the sweat and dirt leave him, and sleep rising through his aching legs, to his arms and shoulders, to all save his quick heart. He was drying himself when Whalen came in, wearing shorts, and stood at the urinal and looked over his shoulder at Paul.

"You and Hathaway run all the way in?"

"Yeah."

"Then the grinder?"

Paul nodded.

"Good," Whalen said, and turned back to the urinal. Paul looked at his strong, muscled wrestler's back and shoulders. When Whalen passed him going out, Paul swung lightly and punched his arm.

"See you in the morning," he said.

The squad bay was dark when Paul entered with a towel around his waist. Already most of them were asleep, their breath shallow and slow. There was enough light from the corridor so he could see the rifle rack in the middle of the room, and the double bunks on either side, and the wall lockers against the walls. He went to his bunk. Hugh was sitting on the edge of it, his elbows on his knees, his forehead resting on his palms. His helmet and rifle and pack and cartridge belt were on the floor in front of his feet. He looked up, and Paul moved closer to him in the dark.

"How's it going," he said softly.

"I threw *up,* man. You see what I mean? That's stupid, goddamnit. For *what.* What's the point of doing something that makes you puke. I was going to keep running till the goddamn stuff came up all over me. Is that smart, man?" Hugh stood; someone farther down stirred on his bunk; Hugh took Paul's arm and squeezed it; he smelled of sweat, his breath was sour, and he leaned close, lowering his voice. "Then you crapped out and I thought good. *Good,* goddamnit. And man I peeled off and went to the side of the road and waited for it to come up. Then I was going to find you and walk in and drink goddamn water and piss in the road and piss on all of them." He released Paul's arm. "But that goddamn Doberman pinscher made you run in. Jesus Christ what am I *do*ing here. What am I *do*ing here," and he turned and struck his mattress, stood looking at his fist on the bed, then raised it and struck again. Paul's hand went up to touch Hugh's shoulder, but stopped in the space between them and fell back to his side. He did not speak either. He looked at Hugh's profiled staring face, then turned away and bent over his foot locker at the head of the bunk and took out a T-shirt and a pair of shorts, neatly folded. He put them on and sat on his locker while Hugh dropped his clothes to the floor and walked out of the squad bay, to the showers.

He got into the lower bunk and lay on his back, waiting for his muscles to relax and sleep to come. But he was still awake when Hugh came back and stepped over the gear on the floor and climbed into his bunk. He wanted to ask Hugh if he'd like him to clean his rifle, but he could not. He lay with aching legs and shoulders and back and arms, and gazed up at Hugh's bunk and listened to his shifting weight. Soon Hugh settled and breathed softly, in sleep. Paul lay awake, among silhouettes of bunks and wall lockers and rifle racks. They and the walls and the pale windows all seemed to breathe, and to exude the smells of men. Farther down the squad bay someone snored. Hugh murmured in his sleep, then was quiet again.

When the lights went on he exploded frightened out of sleep, swung his legs to the floor, and his foot landed on the stock of Hugh's rifle. He stepped over it and trotted to the head, shaved at a lavatory with Whalen, waited outside a toilet stall but the line was too long and with tightening bowels he returned to the squad bay. Hugh was lying on his bunk. Going past it to the wall locker he said: "Hey Hugh. Hugh, reveille." He opened his locker and then looked back; Hugh was awake, blinking, looking at the ceiling.

"Hugh —" Hugh did not look at him. "Your *gear,* Hugh; what about your *gear.*"

He didn't move. Paul put on utilities and spit-shined boots and ran past him. At the door he stopped and looked back. The others were coming, tucking in shirts, putting on caps. Hugh was sitting on the edge of his bunk, watching them move toward the door. Outside the morning was still cool and Hathaway waited, his boots shining in the sunlight. The platoon formed in front of him and his head snapped toward the space beside Paul.

"Clement, did Munson goddamn puke and die on the road last night?"

"He's coming, sir."

"He's coming. Well no shit he's coming. What do you people think this is — goddamn civilian life where everybody crosses the streets on his own time? A platoon is not out of the barracks until every member of that platoon is out of the barracks, and you people are not out of the barracks yet. You are still *in* there with — o-ho —" He was looking beyond them, at the barracks to their rear. "Well now here he is. You people are here now. Munson, you asshole, come up here." Paul heard Munson to his left, coming around the platoon; he walked slowly. He entered Paul's vision and Paul watched him going up to Hathaway and standing at attention.

"Well no shit Munson." His voice was low. "Well no shit now. Mr. Munson has joined us for chow. He slept a little late this morning. I understand, Munson. It tires a man out, riding home in a jeep. It gets a man tired, when he knows he's the only one who can't hack it. It sometimes gets him so tired he *doesn't even fucking shave!* Who do you think you are that you don't shave! I'll tell you who you are: you are *noth*ing you are *noth*ing you are *noth*ing. The best part of you dripped down your old man's *leg!*" Paul watched Hugh's flushed open-mouthed face; Hathaway's voice was lower now: "Munson, do you know about the goddamn elephants. Answer me Munson or I'll have you puking every piece of chow the Marine Corps feeds your ugly face. Elephants, Munson. Those big gray fuckers that live in the boondocks. They are like Marines, Munson. They stick with the herd. And if one of that herd fucks up in such a way as to piss off the rest of the herd, you know what they do to him? They exile that son of a bitch. They kick his ass out. You know what he does then? Son of a bitch gets lonesome. So everywhere the herd goes he is sure to follow. But they won't let him back in, Munson. So pretty soon he gets so lonesome he goes crazy and he starts running around the boondocks pulling up trees and stepping on troops and you have to go in and shoot him. Munson, you have fucked up my herd and I don't want your scrawny ass in it, so you are going to march thirty paces to the rear of this platoon. Now move out."

"I'm going home."

He left Hathaway and walked past the platoon.

"Munson!"

He stopped and turned around.

"I'm going home. I'm going to chow and then I'm going to see the chaplain and I'm going home."

He turned and walked down the road, toward the chow hall.

"Mun*son!*"

He did not look back. His hands were in his pockets, his head down; then he lifted it. He seemed to be sniffing the morning air.

Hathaway's mouth was open, as though to yell again; then he turned to the platoon. He called them to attention and marched them down the road. Paul could see Hugh ahead of them, until he turned a corner around a building and was gone. Then Hathaway, in the rhythm of cadence, called again and again: "You won't *talk* to Mun-son talk talk *talk* to Mun-son you won't *look* at Mun-son look look *look* at Mun-son —"

And, in the chow hall, no one did. Paul sat with the platoon, listened to them talking in low voices about Hugh and, because he couldn't see him, Hugh seemed to be everywhere, filling the chow hall.

Later that morning, at close order drill, the platoon was not balanced. Hugh had left a hole in the file, and Paul moved up to fill it, leaving the file one man short in the rear. Marching in fresh starched utilities, his cartridge belt brushed clean, his oiled rifle on his shoulder, and his boot heels jarring on the blacktop, he dissolved into unity with the rest of the platoon. Under the sun they sweated and drilled. The other three platoons of Bravo Company were drilling too, sergeants' voices lilted in the humid air, and Paul strode and pivoted and ignored the tickling sweat on his nose. Hathaway's cadence enveloped him within the clomping boots. His body flowed with the sounds. "March from the waist down, people. Dig in your heels. That's it, people. Lean back. Swing your arms. That's it, people —" With squared shoulders and sucked-in gut, his right elbow and bicep pressed tight against his ribs, his sweaty right palm gripping the rifle butt, Paul leaned back and marched, his eyes on the clipped hair and cap in front of him; certainty descended on him; warmly, like the morning sun.

JESSE HILL FORD

Big Boy

(FROM THE ATLANTIC)

HAKE MORRIS married a big-boned woman. Hake was a low-built white man and the woman he married stood taller than Hake and she was part Cherokee Indian. Hake was in no shape or condition to do better.

He was a poor man. He cropped in Sligo County first on one place and then on another. He seemed always to be saving enough old plowline to tie what little he and his Indian woman had to a wagon — borrowed wagon, borrowed mules — for the next move to the next place.

Children came along. Hake paid them little nevermind. Then along came Big Boy. And he was the last.

By now Hake had landed east of Somerton on a sizable farm owned by Mr. Jefferson Purser. Seven families lived on the farm and each had its own parcel of acreage to tend and plant, till and harvest.

Big Boy grew up on that farm and because the authorities had got strict, Big Boy had to board the school bus of a morning and be gone all day sometimes until after dark nine months of the year. Thus he was little use to Hake except in the summers when he did good work until the corn was laid by.

It was during this time that tractors started coming on strong in West Tennessee and Mr. Purser took in mind to buy a cotton picker and a bean combine and a corn sheller — three expensive machines. It changed Hake's luck. When the other hands had been turned off the place Hake Morris remained. Mr. Jefferson Purser had kept Hake because Hake knew what a clutch was and could shift gears and never left any machinery out in the weather.

Thus Hake, who always was a bad hand with mules and never could work them properly nor speak to them so they wouldn't kick him now and again and try to break his bones, Hake was just fine and could stay where he was, once the tractors and the machines came on, for Hake Morris was a wonder with machines.

And Big Boy came fifteen. He was big too. He was three of Hake and two of his mother. Big Boy seemed like he ate more than all the rest of the Morris family put together.

Big Boy was fifteen and it was cotton-picking time and Hake was running the picker night and day, getting the crop out while he had a chance during a dry spell. Experience had taught lessons to Hake and Mr. Jefferson Purser. They knew never to let wet weather close in and be depending on something that weighs several tons and has to go about on wheels. Come wet weather and you could leave your cotton in the field or take the chance of bogging down your picker. So when it came a dry spell during picking season it was night and day . . .

Just in the midst of this here came Lawyer Hedgepath from Somerton wanting to see Hake. Lawyer Hedgepath drove the biggest car made and was not somebody anybody ever told the word "no."

When Hake came in for dinner it was already after dark. There sat Lawyer Hedgepath before the teevee in the one stuffed easy chair. Hake had seen the big gleaming automobile outside. He had guessed it might be trouble.

Lawyer Hedgepath stood up. He was a good bit taller than Hake and didn't offer to shake hands. He wanted to know how the cotton was.

"Yessir. OK if the weather holds," says Hake.

"For some years, as you may know, I've had more than a passing interest in our Somerton High School," says Lawyer Hedgepath. "I try to help the football coach. I've been president of the Quarterback Club. Take a ball team, one that wins, and it's a source of pride, Hake. So like my daddy who was a lawyer before me I try to maintain an interest in our high school football."

"Yessir," says Hake.

"I want your boy to play for Somerton, Hake. The coach wants him. He's got the makings of a fine football player."

"I've disallowed for him to play ball," says Hake. And not knowing what else to do or say he sat down to his supper then. His woman brought his food. Hake commenced eating and was more at his ease for knowing it was not trouble but football the lawyer had in mind. Big Boy had mentioned to Hake about Lawyer Hedgepath and the coach talking to him about playing ball. Hake had merely told the boy: "That's disallowed, as you know."

Uninvited, Lawyer Hedgepath came to where Hake was and took a chair at the table. He was big and he was finely dressed. He had brown eyes and a level look about him and he started talking. He said what a chance it was if a boy got the right start with a big high school where football was liked. The coaches would train him. Scouts from the big colleges would come watch him play. Here was a way a boy could get himself a big expensive education and help Somerton at the same time. If he was the right boy.

"Yessir," says Hake. "But he is needed here. He has spoke to me once about it already but I have disallowed him, as I already said just now. Just like I have disallowed him to hunt. Can't afford license nor gun nor shotgun shells. Disallowed him a dog. Can't feed a dog. Hereabout this place in my condition everything mighty nigh has to be disallowed. Take a rich man, he would not understand it. That I know, a rich man. Could he understand it he would not be rich."

"My daddy farmed. My granddaddy farmed," says Oman Hedgepath. "My great-granddaddy farmed before them. Back as far as the history of my family goes, we have farmed. So be sure, Mr. Morris, that I appreciate the problems. I know the obstacles, the hardships, and all the disappointments of farming. I know them at first hand because I grew up on the farm myself, sir."

Hake was near about to believing. Even though he knew the truth. Big money wasn't made by farming. Farm money hadn't bought the lawyer's car standing outside in the early frost just falling. That car was the biggest thing made. Even if Oman Hedgepath lived on a farm, which he did, that didn't make him a farmer. Hake knew what he knew. And he knew that Oman Hedgepath had servants to wait on him and servants to drive him about when he didn't feel like driving himself. And more servants worked in Lawyer Hedgepath's flower beds and weeded his shrubs than lived on this whole place. And this place measured some fifteen hundred acres.

Still, just listening, Hake gradually came to feel he knew this man and he felt something close to pride at having Oman Hedgepath here visiting him, Hake Morris, in a personal way. All this did something for Hake that he was glad for, such that far from jumping up from the table when he was finished eating he accepted one of Lawyer Hedgepath's cigars. And they sat smoking as though they had all the time there was in the world, and didn't have several acres of cotton out there waiting to be picked while the ground was yet dry.

And while they sat thus smoking and visiting, Big Boy pulled into the company, right up to the table like a full-grown man. His cheeks were chapped by the cold. He wore a faded denim jacket that was too small for him and had on the big old Army GI shoes Hake had found for him in the surplus store at Pinoak. It's said those shoes come from battlefields, pulled from the feet of dead soldiers. Hake paid no attention to that. He found the shoes, they were big enough, and he had reached straight down into his overalls and bought them for Big Boy.

"We'd arrange things so Big Boy could work on the weekends and pick up a little money." Oman Hedgepath was saying. "Somerton Warriors need a linesman. Big Boy needs a good education."

"How much money?" says Hake. "On the weekends."

Oman Hedgepath named sixty dollars a month. Hake let his cigar lie so long in the coffee can lid ashtray that it went out and Oman — he insisted on being called Oman now — went on about the call of a man's patriotic duty, and the call of a man to football, and likened both to the call men get when it comes to them that God has chosen them to preach. "Tell you, Hake, I b'lieve this boy has a *call* to play football for the Warriors. Wouldn't surprise me next year to see him make twenty dollars a week during school and move up to twice that or more during the summer."

"I can't *hardly* stand in his way, on that," Hake heard himself saying. And he looked at Big Boy. "What about it, son? How you feel about going and moving to Somerton and playing for the — ah —"

"The Warriors," says Oman. "Need a light there, Hake?" The

lawyer brought a kitchen match out of his pocket and struck it on his thumbnail with a swift, businesslike movement. He held the flame across the table and Hake puffed hard to relight his cigar.

"Strong, but it's good. Kind is it?"

"Cuban," says Oman Hedgepath. "Friends smuggle 'em in for me when they come from Europe. Can't get 'em anymore in this country."

"Can't?" says Hake, puffing the big, black, strong cigar. "Ever now and then I might buy me a King Edward. Give you a King Edward sometime, how about that — ah — Oman?" Hake didn't want to seem like a man who would remain beholden.

"You let Big Boy move to town and wouldn't surprise me if somebody didn't lay down a full box of King Edwards on this table," says Oman. "Plus maybe a *bottle* of something!"

The way Oman said it was so funny Hake had to laugh in spite of himself. Then he heard himself asking Big Boy again what about it and Big Boy just nodded *yes,* that he wanted to move into Somerton.

"About when would he go, then?" says Hake. "If I was to say *yes,* I mean."

"Take him in tonight," says Oman Hedgepath. "Let him ride in town with me."

"Tonight?"

"Wait here a minute. Something in the car I forgot — wait a minute." And the lawyer left the table and went outdoors.

Hake looked at the boy. "What about it? You willing? You want to go?"

Big Boy looked down at his hands.

"Looks like a fine chance to me, son," says Hake. "Go call your mama and tell her I said to come in here."

Big Boy went into the next room and came back with her. One thing about her she was shy about talking to strangers. It was easy to see how close the boy favored her. He had her same high cheekbones and her same proud black eyes. His teeth were good like hers and his skin was that same dark golden color. And he was big and he'd grow bigger still and he was part her and part Hake. And Hake, being the age he was, would never hope to have more children. Hake Morris would die without a purebred white child to his name and credit and all his descendants would henceforth and forever be off-brand sort of folks. But he'd had no choice. It had been her or nothing and besides all that he loved her. She could saw wood and swing an axe like a man, and she was tough so that if anything bothered her or hurt her she never let on and whined. She stood silent, waiting.

"Boy wants to go live in Somerton. Wants to play ball."

"Ball," she said.

"Football," says Hake. "Warriors need him real bad. Want to get his clothes together?"

The outside door opened. It was Oman Hedgepath. He had a bottle in his hand. He shut the door. "Mrs. Morris? I thought so. I'd know in a minute you were Big Boy's mother. How are you?"

"Fine." Almost a whisper.

"How you feel about Big Boy coming to play football for Somerton?"

"Fine." The same near whisper.

"She needs to get his clothes together," says Hake. "Go on now and get him ready. Lawyer Hedgepath can't wait all night on him. This is busy times."

"Don't hurry on my account," says Oman. "Take your time, Mrs. Morris."

She and the boy have gone into the tacked-on shed room where he sleeps. The two of them move back and forth in the room, getting him ready.

"Wouldn't have a couple of glasses, would you, Hake?" says Oman. He opens the bottle.

"Some old jelly glasses here somewheres," says Hake, getting up and fetching two glasses from the shelf over the kitchen sink. "You like yours with R.C., Oman?"

"Straight, thanks," says Oman.

"I seen some of the highway patrol take theirs with R.C.," says Hake, bringing the glasses. "We keep R.C. for Big Boy. I take mine straight. Always did. But I don't but rarely take a drink."

"Now's a good time," Oman says. He pours a drink into each glass. "Big Boy's success."

"I'll go for that," says Hake. He empties his glass in a swallow. Oman pours him another. Hake takes a closer look at the bottle. "Good stuff," he says.

The liquor has started to stir Hake's blood when his woman

walks out with Big Boy's things rolled in a bed blanket. She's tied
up both ends with a piece of binder twine. Big Boy comes behind
her with some things in a grocery sack.

"You could have took my suitcase," says Hake.

"This is fine," says Big Boy.

"Wouldn't of minded you taking my suitcase. You're welcome to
it. Old suitcase ain't worth much. But — if you're satisfied with a
bed blanket, Big Boy, then I guess that satisfies me."

"It's OK," says Big Boy.

Oman Hedgepath stands up. "Well," he says. "We ready — are
we?"

"Sit and stay a spell. You don't have to rush off," says Hake.
"Don't forget your bottle, Oman."

"That stays here," says Oman. "Handy for cold weather like
tonight."

Hake stands up then. He wants to hug Big Boy but he can't
bring himself to do it. They've long since got beyond all that.
"Y'all better get on the road, then, I guess," says Hake.

"You'll come watch him play, Hake," says Oman Hedgepath.
"We'll take good care of him. You'll be proud of him."

"Sure will. That'll be just fine," says Hake. "Bye now and Big
Boy you mind and do what they tell you and . . ." But he could not
think what else. The woman stood in beside him. Big Boy and
Oman went out the door into the cold. The car doors slammed.
The big car's engine turned over and started. The lights flashed on
bright and the car moved slowly away down between the fences
dividing the fields.

Hake watched until the car reached the main road and swung left
and went purring softly away on the gravel. When he finally shut
the door the woman was already sitting down at the table in her
usual chair. Hake got her a jelly glass from the shelf. Without
saying anything she took the glass in her big, blunt hand and
looked at it.

"Fine bourbon," says Hake. "Early Times and they don't make
no finer. I bet they don't make no whiskey in the world the equal
of Early Times."

"Good spirits."

"Huh?" Hake poured her a little drink.

"My grandmother took about this much four or five times a day. Said it made good spirits."

"Injun?"

The woman nodded. "I never tasted it but I remember the smell. This has the same smell."

"Drink up," says Hake. "Try it."

"I don't want to waste it. How much does it cost?"

Hake sighed. "It's a gift. Lawyer Hedgepath is known for one of the richest men around here anywhere. You heard of him, ain't you? Well, that's who that was. Know where this cigar come from — I swear if it's not gone out again. The Cubans could take a page out of King Edward's book to make a cigar that will stay lit. Where's a match?"

She went to the cupboard and brought him the kitchen matches. When she sat down she pulled her blue cotton dress close and held it gathered at her throat.

Hake lit the cigar. For the third time he puffed to get it started. It had a dark taste and was too strong to be inhaled. Nor was it in any way sweet-tasting like cigars Hake now and then bought at the grocery in Pinoak where he traded. He sat then and smoked doggedly, determined to enjoy the cigar.

"You ain't gonna even try it?" says Hake. One hand still held her dress gathered at the throat as though she were cold. She held the jelly glass in the other hand. Hake felt thick about the mouth.

"Don't know what my grandmother saw in it," she says.

"Just forget about her."

"Why?"

"Well — she's been dead a long time, ain't she?"

"Whiskey reminds me of her, that's all."

"But you ain't all total Injun. You got a deal of white blood. Couldn't tell you from a white women myself didn't I know what you really was. Take some horses, or even now and then you find a dog and you can't look at him to tell if he wasn't a registered animal. Same with cattle. I seen whiteface cows you'd never know had a wild drop of blood in 'em if you didn't just happen to have the inside dope on it what their breeding was."

He saw that her glass was empty and poured her another drink. Heck fire, he was thinking. He thought of the lawyer's big automobile and how it had moved off so comfortable like and the exhaust had fanned around real slow like a white peacock tail and the big machine had whirred. Big Boy riding in that automobile. Big Boy gone to live in town somewhere. Big Boy a grown-up, educated man. Big Boy, with buttonholes in his shirt collars like Oman Hedgepath's.

"She sang the rain song."

"Sang what? How's that?"

"The rain song." Her glass was empty again. The woman sure could pour it down, Hake was thinking.

"*Who?*" says Hake. His mind was on that big car, a Lincoln Continental at least, if not something larger. Could of been a Cadillac. It had got so lately a man couldn't tell one from another whereas in his youth he might have known them all by sight, by year and brand.

"My grandmother."

"Aw?" says Hake. "Had a singin' voice? Never knew Injuns sang. Never seen no Injun perform a song on teevee," he said thoughtfully. And as though to reward himself for this discovery he poured himself another nip — but a little one this time. Whiskey must be saved. Maybe just one nip on Christmas Day. A nip each for him and the woman.

"She sang to me. Took me on her lap and sang."

"Sang what? Hymns or regular songs?"

"Just the rain song." Her fingers began to move up and down on the table. She was singing something in a low voice and it made him nervous. She was showing a side of herself he hadn't glimpsed before, never in all the years of their life together. And something was dawning on him. He felt the start of a feeling he sometimes had the next day after a bad trade, a trade done in haste, whereas a little waiting, a little deliberation might have saved him fifty dollars. He was glad when she hushed and couldn't seem to remember any more of whatever it was she had been singing. "Good spirits," she said, and looked at her glass.

"Listen," he said. "You know that Big Boy is the last —?"

"Yes."

"We got no more kids. It never come to me Big Boy was the last. Yet I knew he was the youngest. This leaves me alone. Nothing but me. No kin of mine in the house or on the place. They are all gone. The baby's gone."

She was not listening, though. She was singing again. She reminded him of a gosh damned tomtom. Almost in spite of himself he poured some more whiskey in her glass.

She stopped singing and took a drink. "Big Boy will be famous," she said. "The night before the day he was born I dreamed it. Big Boy Morris. Wait and watch and see if he won't be famous." It wasn't like her. She was talking so much her tongue was loose as a wiggling snake.

Hake gave her a look. She had picked up Oman Hedgepath's abandoned cigar. She struck a match and lit it, putting her mouth where another's mouth had been. She drew the smoke down into her lungs and breathed it out again like a creature of steel.

"Big Boy's gonna be on teevee," she said, "Cherokee Indian on teevee, Big Boy Morris. Um!"

"Doing what?" says Hake.

"Football. Um," she inhaled again.

The remembrance of that stuff she had been singing rose to the back of his mind. Rain! It hit him and made his scalp move. He sprang up. She didn't move. While he piled into his coat and readied himself to rush outside she sat very still. He went out and pulled the door shut and ran to the cotton picker. Frost was on the windshield. He made a turn in close to the house and had a glimpse of her through the window sitting in the same place she had been sitting when he had jumped up. He was still frightened by that dreadful thought — rain. Seeing the woman was like looking at a dummy in a store window. He completed the turn and headed through the gate into the field past the picked-over rows. Shreds and scraps of cotton hung from the brown, aging bolls. With a sigh he swung into the white gleam of the fresh locks. He seemed to feel in his own hands the steel work of those chattering spindles.

He was cold. But by the time he had made his first pass to the rows' end the cab had begun to warm up and when he felt the warmth Hake wondered where C.B., his Negro helper, was, for C.B. was supposed to follow him. Was the man waiting here somewhere in the field? Had he been too shy to approach the house to see why Hake did not come back right away after supper? Hake wondered if the Negro had stayed in the cold all this time or if he had given up on Hake and gone home.

Then, beginning the second pass, he saw C.B. and pulled the picker to a halt, put it in neutral, and climbed down out of the cab.

C.B.'s head was wrapped in a thick, bulging scarf — an old sweater, perhaps.

"What kept me was Big Boy he left and went in town to live and play football," Hake said in a loud voice.

"Say he sick?"

"Naw, got him a job in Somerton. Left home. Now mind and follow me."

C.B. nodded. Hake climbed back into the warm cab and engaged the gears. Big Boy — gone. And well, Hake didn't even know where the boy was staying. Gone, all that quick. It was like death and Hake was still pondering it when they finally shut down for the night. Big Boy was still on his mind when he crawled into bed beside the woman. She lay snoring, dead asleep. Hake pondered what it could mean and he wondered where his own life had gone. And while he lay awake, knowing that Big Boy's bed was empty, another part of him was listening and fearful lest something hit the windows or strike the roof. A part of him was listening to make sure rain didn't come up and catch him. It was the way of rain to sneak up on a man unawares. Hake lay thus, for what seemed a long time, staring into darkness and feeling the abandoned shed room, feeling the emptiness where Big Boy had been.

WILLIAM HOFFMAN

The Spirit in Me

(FROM THE SEWANEE REVIEW)

I LOOK ACROSS PALE CORN to the dusty road between wooded mountains and see the dust itself rising behind the blue car moving too
fast. She, the lady of the manor, comes again in early summer when
heat of city rasps her flesh and her flatlands turn hard and red
brown like dried blood.

She comes from Virginia west to ancestral acres, a jagged
country of rock outcroppings and mountains gutted and scarred.
She rests in deep shade at the mansion her great-grandfather
built, three stories of dungeonlike stone topped by a copper roof
which glints in noon sun. She comes with sin.

Her blue car passes my church, a board-and-batten building hammered together by my father, the roughness of new lumber first
against his hands and then against my own. As a boy I labor with
him evenings, carrying buckets of water from the stream which
wrinkles over mossy rocks. I hoe the mortar, my blade furrowing
the gray. As a young man I hammer on the new roof after a north
wind curls off the old tin. In the beginning there are brethren to
help.

"She's back," they say each summer. "She's returned."

"Cast your eyes down," I say.

"She lets us fish in her lake," LeRoy Ackers says. He is an elec-
trician at the mine. I've seen him with sparks falling around him
like a fiery rain.

"In Beelzebub's pond," I say.

She wears green, yellow, and lavender, her summer dresses
bright around pampered flesh of her neck and arms. She has

green, yellow, and lavender shoes, and perhaps underneath she wears those colors too, if she wears anything at all.

When she drives into our dusty town, she passes the granite courthouse and iron cannon splotched by pigeons. Men stand on narrow buckled sidewalks which are mountain shaded, their bodies stilled, the skin taunt across their faces. They watch the brace of her shoulders and the swing of her silken calves as she walks into the stone post office. They breathe the air after her, their nostrils searching out her perfume.

"She lets us hunt her woods," Perry Henry says. Perry's bulldozer blade carves chunks from the mountains.

"She is the huntress," I say.

As a boy, before I become an instrument, I watch her. I climb from the cabin in my father's hollow, the cabin held level on the mountainside by smooth flat rocks hauled from the creek. I hide in sycamores to look over the stone wall beyond which she and her girl friends play croquet on the grass. Her black hair is tied with a white ribbon.

A black man catches me up the sycamore. His name is Darce. He circles the tree and yells, but I don't move. I lie wound about a limb, my face down into leaves.

"I'll get me an ax!" he threatens.

The girls, holding their striped mallets, stand watching, and the mother, a fair woman wearing a white sun hat, hurries from the mansion, her fingers pinching up the white dress in front of her thighs. The girls point at me and laugh — only not the girl, who speaks for me.

"He's not hurting anything," she says.

"But he shouldn't be there," the mother says.

"It isn't wrong to climb a tree," the girl says.

I believe then she knows me as I know her, that she's seen me in town when she's driven through by Darce. I am already dreaming, dreams in which there are dirtiness and blood. She floats up from flowers of her mother's garden, from among the yellow blooms, her skirt belled. I fall on grass among the croquet wickets. She leaps and drifts down on me, the black heels of her shoes lighting on my chest, sinking red into my chest, while she smiles, until I am covered by her perfumed and gently lowering skirt.

Then in me pumping begins, the terrible pumping. I wake soiled and afraid. The night around me, I wash in the cold creek.

I believe she must cause my dreams. I stand on the sidewalk waiting for her to pass. An afternoon she sits in the car while her mother mails packages at the post office. I walk close, but the girl goes on talking to Darce who waits to open the car door for the mother.

"What you staring at, big-feet?" Darce asks me.

"Who is it?" the girl asks.

"The boy with big feet who was up the tree," Darce says.

"Oh," she says and only glances at me. "I thought he had red hair."

I walk away, climb the side of the mountain, and roll rocks down, watching them smash through laurel and bounce across the black highway. I almost hit a silver gasoline truck. The driver gets out and shouts curses up the mountain. I hate her but I still have dreams.

"They was common once," my father rages when they arrest him because of snakes. "The old man didn't have a pisspot when he first come to these mountains. My grandfather fed him. He'd have starved the winter withouten my grandfather's hog and hominy."

I am afraid of dreams and the stains on myself. No water washes me clean. That summer I go into the mountain, into the wet blackness of the mine which has the sulphuric smell of the pit. The first day as I work setting locust props to hold the roof, a blue light flashes before me and cracks like a thousand whips. All the hair is singed from my body. I am thrown on the haulway floor among gobbets of coal. The whips crack through the mine, and a voice says, "You are my instrument."

My eyes ablaze with thunderbolts, I am carried from the mountain and laid on cinders where I am born again. The sun in my face is not as searing as the flame I've seen. Fire damp they call it — methane — but I know Whose terrible power has rent the darkness.

"Glory!" my mother says, already dying, already shrunk so her toadstool skin drapes her bones like cloth worn thin. When she coughs, part of her insides come up and are spat on the ground.

"I heard the whirlwind," I say.

"O glory!" she says. "You done blessed this house like your father."

My father has died in a roof fall and lies on the mountain among crooked tombstones and purple thistle. My mother and I go to our knees. We hold each other and sway against the patched quilt on the bed.

"Take my boy and use him!" she calls. She is crying.

I dream no more.

During winters they keep Darce and his black wife at the manor above the town. In summer green comes to cover earth scars, and the mansion is so planted with trees and shrubs that only the copper roof and part of the walls show, but winters the earth opens its sores, and the wind shrills off the mountain like hounds of a frozen Hell. The mansion stands alone in the wind, the stones like a tomb over us. Neither crow nor hawk dares fly into the blast.

"It was built on our blood," the union man says. "Every lump of coal hauled out has our blood on it."

"Yet they send baskets at Christmas," my sister Renna says. She is a thin lorn woman who plays a golden cornet for the Salvation Army.

"It's food spiced with sulphur," I say.

I am a man, and the girl becomes the lady who, like her mother, returns in summers, after a time with a husband, an army officer who brings horses on a railroad car and rides the ridges, he in brown boots and a campaign hat, cantering along trails made by timbering crews, among stumps, hoofs thumping the earth like drumming.

He rides horses into town too, past the muddy Fords and Chevrolets, past the motionless men who stand like burned timber in front of the courthouse. At the post office boys fight to hold his horse. He gives them shiny dimes.

There are again children at the mansion, hers, two girls, small and quick as she was. They play croquet on the lawn or go to the lake where the father teaches them to pull the green boat with green oars over water shadowed by spruce pines. He teaches them to draw up bass from the deep, from so deep the fish are as white of belly as coal grubbers who gnaw inside the darkness of the mountain.

"She gives books to our library," Fazio, principal of the high school, says.

"There is only one Book," I say.

I study that Book at the Only Jehovah Bible College in Charleston. I ride the bus each Friday after I come out of the mountain.

The city has a river which is a brown gash among smoking chemical plants, and the college is in a building which was once a tannery. It shakes with the power of our voices.

On Sunday night going home a tipsy woman sits beside me in the bus. She has bluish eyelids and a painted mouth. Her pink skirt is short, her lap smooth and satiny. In the sweeping darkness of the bus she smells of wine.

Before we reach my hollow, she laughs and touches me. With her small strong hand she does a thing. With my hand I too do a thing. When I leave the bus to step down onto the weedlashed shoulder of the road, she sits rigid in her seat, her eyes closed, spit running from her mouth. The bus drives into blackness of the mountains, its red lights hazy through exhaust.

In blackness I go to the mountain river and strip off my clothes to wash in the healing water. I beat my flesh with stones until I bleed. I lie face up on a rock and wind flogs me. "I shall be clean," I promise the night.

Now I have children of my own, not from a wife, but from the Spirit. I feed and treat them tenderly. They lie among clean curls of wood shavings which rustle slightly. During spring and summer I harvest young rabbits hanging in my snares.

My children know me, the heat of my hand, and they raise their heads when I lower meals to them. They know my fingers when I lift them from their box. I hold them as gently as wafers.

There is a time, a day in summer. Wild flowers bloom in fields. The scars of my rocky land are hidden by the yellow of weltering daisies. She and her daughters are picking flowers. They come across a field in their colored dresses, bright like flowers themselves. I stand at the edge, in shadows of locust trees.

"Oh!" she says, noticing me. She is afraid. "You're Mr. . . . ?"

"Gormer," I say.

"Of course. I've heard about your lay ministry at the church."

"Yes," I say.

There is a breeze off mountains that afternoon, from the south, off sunny ridges, and the breeze bends flowers and wild grass toward her, as if all those blooms are worshiping her. It is a vision I have of grass and flowers bending before her.

"Well, the church has needed a minister," she says.

Her daughters run among flowers of the field. They are hidden by blooms. Her lavender dress is blowing against her, flat against her body and curved around her legs. Along with sweetness of flowers, the breeze carries perfume off her skin to me.

"What is it?" she asks, staring at me.

Because there is a terrible bending in me too, a darkness forcing me down among flowers, my knees crushing flowers, the juice of them on my pants. Bees fly into my face. I can't lift myself but am pressed against the hot moist ground, a black hand mashing my back, my breath smothering in blooms. I raise a hand to her.

"Don't do that," she says, causing flowers to drag against her dress. "I'll have you arrested."

My hand toward her, I crawl, the blooms and stalks of yellow flowers scratching my face. She gathers her running daughters from among the blooms and hurries them before her across the field. Among them bees spiral.

I lower my face to wild grass. I clutch stalks of flowers and hear bees. I weep into the yielding earth until shadows of the mountain slide over me.

"She helped with the town water," Capito says. Capito operates a Joy machine whose whirling steel teeth chew the shiny seam.

"It is not the water of life," I say.

I am an ugly man, my trunk short, my legs thick and bowed, but I've been given blessings and power. I know there will be judgment. There is always judgment.

First her husband, the army officer, goes to war. There are photographs of him in newspapers, wearing his uniform, and there is a picture of him on his black horse jumping a fence, but now he lies in the darkness where no man bounds until the clangor of the last golden trumpet.

"He was a good fellow," Beasley, a super at the mine, says. "He talked funny, but he came to fire company meetings."

"He would like fire," I say.

For many summers she doesn't return. She keeps Darce, the black man, up there to clean, cut hedges, and turn on the big furnace when fields grow jagged again as they shed grass and flowers. Ice scabs the mountain. Nights a light is seen — Darce and his toothless arthritic wife living in a third-floor room. The light is blackened by snow.

"She allows the children to skate on her lake," Miss Bozack, the public health nurse, says. "She sent her permission."

"She will need ice," I say.

For many summers she doesn't come until the warming after-noon when she speeds along the dusty road between the pale corn, she and her daughters, and more baggage in a second car which her secretary drives. The daughters are young ladies now, with bare arms and thin tan legs. They open windows of the mansion. That evening there are many lights.

During the summer she hires workmen and painters. She has the boathouse and bathhouse at the lake repaired, new shutters hung. Weeds are burned from the tennis court, and freshly-laun-dered lines are nailed into clay. Squeaking sprinklers coil water over the lawn. On mown grass she has a party with music. People drive from Beckley and Bluefield to dance under oaks.

"Like old times," Puckett says, Puckett a shriveled coal grubber who, trapped in the mine, axed off his own arm to be screaming free of coal. He sits on a bottle crate and looks at colored lights among oaks on the mountain

"You liked old times, did you?" I aks.

"They bled us," he says. "Before the union they bled us, and now the union bleeds us, but the family had style. The old man smoked dollar cigars and drove a black Packard coupe." Puckett nods. "She still has style."

"Pleasing is the face of evil," I say.

The daughters, the young ladies, do not stay long, though she invites people from cities — young men who come in toy cars. She has the stable fixed and a new float put on the lake, but it is not enough for the daughters. They want to be in places where there are always music, laughter, and the parading of flesh. Except for servants, she is often alone in the mansion.

"What does she do?" Ross asks. Ross owns a tin-roof store which tilts among cinders and weeds, a single peeling gas pump in front.

"She picks her flowers and sits in shade to sew," Benita, his wife, says. Benita has helped wash windows of the mansion and with the cleaning of the heavy yellow curtains in the parlor.

"Sews?" Ross asks. "Why would she sew when she can have that and everything else done for her?"

"She likes to keep busy," Benita says. "Just like her mister would repair leather."

"Toil of Satan," I say.

I know she will come, and I wait her visit. I too am alone. My vision has set me apart. In haulways of the mine men do not set their lunch pails near me. When I walk into the cafe of the bus station, they quiet. Sundays, standing at the altar of my church, I lift my children, and the hush is so whole that I hear willow branches dragging in the stream.

I know she will not be alone. I am at the church on a July morning painting eaves which rain has rotted. The air is still, though dust devils stir the corn. Crows caw over the hot land. From my ladder I look toward the mansion, dark in oak shade. I watch the blue car sliding from shade.

I climb down and go inside. Through the pointed doorway I see that Darce is driving. He is old now, white-headed, but he still struts. He wears a black tie and billed cap. The car, the blue Lincoln, stops, yet dust rolls past it and settles on grass and thistle.

I wipe sweat from my face and wait before the altar. They honk their horn as if I will leave the sanctuary at their command, as if I am a servant to run for them instead of possessing the true Word from the mouth of the Only Jehovah.

Twice more they honk, but I stand in stillness of my church, seeing dust twist in sun shafts and seeing the golden grain of oak pews I have wiped clean and laid black hymnbooks on. I see the empty oak cross.

There are footsteps and a shadow in the doorway. Darce comes. He scowls, full of pride of that family, as if he shares their blood.

"She is in the car," he says.

"She's welcome here," I say. I smile, knowing she will not come in, that holy places are forbidden her.

"She don't have to be welcome," Darce says. "She's waiting for you."

I am tempted to wrath and chastisement of this black man who swaggers in a white man's country. But I understand he too is an instrument.

Smiling, I walk along the aisle and beneath the pointed doorway to the steps and the disturbed dust under sycamores. I hear crows caw and water running among willows.

She sits in the rear of her blue car, no hat on her darkly tinted hair. The window is up to keep her cool. She rolls it down, but

only part way. I smell her perfume. Darce stops beside me. He is
watchdog over her. She tries to be haughty like her mother.

"My grandfather put aside land for this church," she says. "He
wanted it used as do I."

"It is being used," I say.

"But not for that," she says. "They tell me —" She stops speaking. Her face creases its powder, and her hands move on her
lavender lap. "I've heard —"

"What?" I ask.

"You're using the snakes," Darce says. "People talk in town."

"This church was never meant for that," she says.

She is agitated, and her hands rub on her lavender lap. Her
white, bejeweled fingers tremble. Her knees rise under her summer dress. She is afraid of me.

"In this church everything's sanctified by the Book," I say.

"Everybody knows you're using snakes," Darce says. "Somebody's going to get hurt."

"The righteous can't be hurt," I say.

"I won't have it," she says and balls her fingers. "You must stop
or —"

"Or?" I ask.

"You must stop."

I smile. She has never been in the church. On Sundays she is
driven more than forty miles to Bluefield to a heathen church with
spires, candles, and jeweled harlots. She is forbidden a truly holy
place.

She rolls up her window and rolls it down again.

"I don't want to interfere," she says. "But you must stop."

"Come in and see," I say.

"She don't have to come in," Darce says.

"I hope you'll take to heart what I tell you," she says.

"You better," Darce says.

I stand in dust while Darce gets in the car and drives her away.
There is no breeze, and the shadows are hot. Dust palls my skin. I
climb my ladder to finish painting eaves.

That night I lie awake on my cot and her perfume seeps to me. I
pray, my head against the floor. I raise my eyes to see lightning
flash among black mountains. The thunder talks to me.

Sunday I carry my sleek children to church in their wooden box.

Cars park beneath the sycamores. Men stand in shade to smoke while women enter with their children to sit in the oak pews. When they see the box beside the altar, their faces tighten and gloss.

"We'll sing," I say. "We'll raise voices to the Lord."

I lead the singing. My baritone is loud and strong. Their mouths move, but they watch the box.

> *Nail me to Thy cross,*
> *Spill Thy blood on me,*
> *Lower Thy thorns to cut my brow,*
> *Seize my soul to Thee.*

After the singing, I preach. I feel myself fill with Spirit, swell with It. Heat comes into me. The people's faces are like white soil to be planted by my words.

"Believing is trust," I say. "Believing is knowing the mighty arm of Jehovah covers and protects you."

The congregation is afraid of me and my power. Their eyes keep moving to the box. Women hold their children close.

"I want to see your belief," I tell them. "I want you to prove you have it. If you have it, all the dynamite and bombs in the world can't make a dent in you. You can feed with lions and tigers. Show God the proof by standing and coming forward to this altar!"

As I know, they do not come. They stare with shiny, unblinking eyes. I cross to the box, unlatch it, and lift a child in each hand. I hold them at the centers of their waxy pimpled bodies so their tails dangle and their heads sway.

"If you have belief, you can do these things," I say and drape my white-stitched, flickering children around my neck. I hang them over my shoulders and let them slide inside my shirt. I kiss them on their coarse drifting heads.

"O ye of little faith!" I cry.

I know she will hear. Perhaps she walks through her garden to the gate in the stone wall and listens to my voice on the breeze. I burn the Sabbath with my words. I raise my face to her mountain.

"Those in the faith cannot be bruised!" I shout.

Monday evening when I drive to the church from the mine I find a padlock. A hasp has been screwed into the door, the screws bright in the violated wood. I see Darce's footsteps in dust.

I drive my Ford into town where I walk past the bus station and the closed movie theater with its boarded windows and lacy posters. I pass the barber shop, the post office, and the granite courthouse. I wait for people to speak, to take my side in righteousness, but though they know of the padlock, they will not look at me. They act as if they do not see me. She has won them.

Only Giles Hooper, the deputy, standing in uniform by the cannon on the courthouse lawn, speaks. His hands hang from the black cartridge belt which divides his stomach.

"Stay away from the church," he says. "Next time she'll have a warrant."

"It is my church," I say.

"You may think it's yours, but the law says the land and building still belong to the company. She's hired a preacher. You stay away."

"I am an instrument, and the Holy Spirit works through me," I say.

He would not look into my eyes.

"I do what the law makes me do," he says.

And so do I do what the law makes me do, the eternal law of the Only Living God. I walk to my car. People back in shadows watch. I drive from town and among corn to the stone gateposts and along the gravel which is laid white between dogwoods. I pass stone benches and red flowers growing from stone urns.

In front of the manor I stop. I walk across grass which stripes my black shoes. The guests are at the side of the house, on a flagstone terrace where a table has been set with food, bottles, silver dishes, and ice in bowls. Silver horses' heads decorate glasses stuck in white knitted holders.

People from cities hold glasses and talk. They pluck food from the table and spear shrimp with silver toothpicks. Their mouths are red with sauce. When they see me, they are silent.

"Mr. Gormer, leave this place," she says.

"You are damned," I tell her.

"I'll throw him out," Darce says. He wears a white coat and carries a tray.

"Who is it?" a man asks, her man. He has graying brown hair and a brown mustache on a tanned face. He has been coming from Bluefield to play tennis and swim with her. I have seen them walking in the woods.

"Mr. Gormer's leaving," she says.

"Have you ever?" a young woman, the secretary, asks. When I stare, she whitens.

"You are all damned," I say.

"I'm throwing him out," Darce says.

"I'll help," her man says.

They walk toward me, but I back across grass. On the terrace hands are motionless, and mouths are closed over words. In fright the young secretary has touched her breasts.

"You are all judged," I say.

Darce and her man come after me. I bump an oak. They grab me. The man's fingers are strong. I feel his strength in the ache of my arm.

"Just make him leave," she says.

There is a sound rising. Giles Hooper drives through the gateway. Lights of the police car flash red. They shove me into the cage of the rear seat where the handles have been removed. Giles drives me into the valley, but I look back to see people on the terrace talking now, excited. With them I leave fear.

"I'll see about your car," Giles says. "You bother her again and I'll drop the jail on you."

"Do you believe you can stop the working of divine leaven?" I ask.

"Don't put your tongue on me," Giles says. "I'll lower the jail on you if I have to send you to Beckley."

I smile because I can call down fire to smite him, but he is not the evil. He is only her agent and is so frightened of me he twitches yellowish fingers near his bone-handled Smith and Wesson.

He takes me to my hollow and cabin where I live with my children. At night I hear them glide among clean wood shavings. I listen to them, the dry wind, and the stream, and I remember my mother keening, a sound like wind.

I do not again drive into town. I do not go to the church or the mine. I walk in the forest to collect game from my snares. I squat among ferns in damp shadows.

From shadows I see her walking with her man. She wears a red blouse which bares her arms. Her bracelets and earrings flash. She holds his hand. Under tree dusk I watch them kiss.

On a night I lie in laurel near the lake her grandfather built. His crews dynamited hemlocks and dammed a valley below the manor.

He set iron deer upon planted grass. The mountain water lies still and deep.

She and her man have eaten among terrace candles and stroll to the lake, she holding to his arm. There is a breeze but no ripple on the water. I watch the smoldering of fireflies and cigarettes.

She and the man switch on lights to enter the white bathhouse. They come out wearing bathing suits. Her flesh is glazed by moon. Silverish they move into dark water.

I listen to laughter and splashing. They climb the ladder onto the float where they lie under moon. I run into the forest. I run so fast I make my own wind.

I return with the box. Biting my breath, I kneel among laurel. She and her man swim in from the float. They rise from the dark water. She starts away, but he reaches after her and draws her. In moon I see him put his mouth on her. She holds to him as he unties the top of her bathing suit. He kisses her, and I whimper. Her hands are splayed over his temples. He lifts and carries her into the bathhouse. A click causes lights to die.

I slip to the door and hear them inside. The black shutters are already closed. Silently I tie them with line from the boathouse. I shut off power by screwing out fuses. Kneeling on the steps, I lovingly feed my children through the doorway. They flow off my palms into darkness. I pull the door closed and drop the heavy lock into the hasp.

She and her man hear and try to switch on lights. They rattle the door. The man asks about the circuit breaker. The switch keeps clicking.

As I walk into the forest I hear her gasp. I do not turn even at the first scream.

EVAN HUNTER

The Analyst

(FROM PLAYBOY)

I HAD THE BARREL of the gun in my mouth and my finger on the trigger when he appeared suddenly in the woods. He stopped in the clearing some 50 feet away and stared at me mutely. He was wearing a long brown overcoat and a brown woolen watch cap pulled down over his ears. It was still mild for November, but a long, soiled yellow muffler was wrapped around his neck and trailing down the front of his coat. A parcel wrapped in brown paper was tucked under his arm. The man was the town idiot, the end product of four generations of inbreeding. He lived in one of the ramshackle tin-and-wooden structures his family had thrown together on a hillside near the abandoned hat factory. His name was Virgil. I had seen him shambling along the back roads often, invariably carrying the parcel wrapped in brown paper tied with string. He would lift his head whenever an automobile went past, and grin widely, and raise the forefinger and middle finger of his right hand in the V-for-victory sign. There were people who said his father had been killed in the Bulge during World War Two. I had no idea how old he was. His chin and cheeks were virtually beardless, his skin unwrinkled, his blue eyes twinkling with secret merriment each time he flashed the V. He grinned and flashed it at me now. It had taken every ounce of courage I could muster to bring myself into these woods and take the gun from my pocket and shove the barrel into my mouth. I pocketed the gun now and turned my back to him and began walking up toward the road where I had parked my car.

"Hello!" he called. "Nice day."

I heard him walking toward me through the fallen leaves.

"Nice day," he said again, and I turned to face him. He was still grinning. He had put his hands into the pockets of the long coat, his head was cocked to the side, his eyebrows raised in expectation of an answer.

"Yes," I said.

"Hope it don't rain," he said.

"I don't think it will."

"I'm Virgil," he said.

"Yes, I know."

"Everybody knows me," he said, and he nodded in self-acknowledgment of his celebrity. "That your car up there?" he asked.

"Yes."

"Nice car."

"Thank you."

"Nice day, too," he said. He seemed to have run out of conversation. He nodded his head and smiled at me. "Hope it don't rain. Did they say rain?"

"I don't know."

"Sure hope it don't. That your car?"

"Yes."

"Could you give me a ride?"

"Where to?"

"The post office. Got to mail this. See?" he said, and he took a soiled and crumpled envelope from his coat pocket. "Is that enough of a stamp on it?"

"Yes," I said.

"It's to Hattie. My sister. Her birthday's Saturday. Will it get there?"

"Where does she live?"

"Same place I do. Is that too far?"

"No, she'll get it in time."

"Sure hope so," he said. "Sure hope it don't rain, too."

We walked up to the car in silence.

"Fender's all bent," he said.

"Yes."

"Tch!" he said, and he opened the door and climbed in. "Well," he said cheerfully, "you can fix it, don't worry."

At the post office, he got out of the car, grinned and flashed the V sign at me.

I drove back home.

I did not see him again till the following Wednesday.

I had been in the city looking for a job — it is not easy for an aging unemployed executive to find work. I still could not believe I'd been fired two months before.

"I've been with the company twelve years," I told Ralph. We looked at each other across the polished width of his desk, never any papers on that desk, pencils always sharpened and at the ready, but never a scrap of paper on it. I sometimes wondered what he *did* with all those sharpened pencils.

"It's not my decision," he said. "It came from upstairs."

"Well, can't you go upstairs and tell them you disagree? Ralph, I've been working here for twelve years."

"Andrew," he said, "what can I tell you?"

"You can tell me you'll go to bat for me."

"I can't do that."

"Ralph," I said, "I've got a fifty-thousand-dollar mortgage and two sons in college; the tuition comes to twenty-five hundred a semester for each of them; they cost me five thousand bucks before I bat an eyelash. I bought the Mercedes on time, that's another four hundred a month to meet the payments —"

"Trade it in for a Volks," Ralph said.

"Ralph, listen to me for a minute, will you? I'm forty-eight years old, I don't know any other line of work; who the hell is going to hire me at the salary I'm getting here? For Christ's sake, Ralph, can't you *please* go upstairs and tell them I need another chance is all?"

"Andrew," he said, "you blew the McGregor deal. You blew a two-hundred-and-fifty-thousand-dollar deal because you were dead drunk at one o'clock in the afternoon. We're not in business for our health here."

"Ralph," I said, "please."

"Andrew," he said, and he shrugged.

Through the windshield, I saw Virgil lift his hand in the V sign. In his other hand, he was carrying the customary parcel, clutched tightly to his chest. I pulled to the side of the road and rolled down the window.

"Want a lift?" I said.

"Hello there," he said, and he climbed in. "Nice day," he said.

"Yeah, just beautiful," I said.

"Just beautiful," he said, completely missing my tone. "Sure hope it don't rain. Did they say rain?"

"No, they didn't say rain."

"Sure hope not," he said.

"Did your sister get her card in time?"

"What card?"

"The birthday card."

"My birthday's June," he said. "June twelfth. Sure hope it's a nice day."

"Where are you coming from?" I asked.

"Oh, just walking," he said. "I walk."

"What's in the package?" I asked.

"A sweater. Case it rains and gets cold. I don't like to get cold. Where *you* coming from?"

"The city."

"Oh, yeah, the city. I been to the city. I don't like it there, it's noisy. You like it there?"

"Not today, I didn't."

"Was it raining in the city?"

"It *seemed* like it was raining."

"Oh, yeah, it rains a lot in the city."

"I was looking for a job," I said. "I'm out of work."

"Oh, well, that's all right," he said cheerfully. "You should carry a sweater, like I do. Then, if it rains, you won't get cold. But I don't think it'll rain today. Did they say rain?"

"Where do you want me to drop you, Virgil?"

"That's OK. Anyplace is fine. I walk, you know."

"How about the post office?"

"Fine," he said. "Maybe there's some mail."

I dropped him off at the post office and then parked the car and went into the bank. Peter Capoletti, the manager, signaled to me as I was filling out a withdrawal slip. I went over to his desk.

"How's it going?" he asked.

"Fine," I said.

"Andrew," he said, "the checking account is overdrawn."

"Is it? My wife," I said, and smiled. "She never has learned how to balance that thing."

"Andrew, it's overdrawn by more than two thousand dollars."

"Yeah," I said. "Well, Pete, why don't you just transfer the necessary funds from the savings account ——"

"There's only fifteen hundred dollars in the savings account," he said.

"Well . . ."

"What do you want me to do, Andrew?"

"Well, let me see, maybe I can — let me talk it over with Beth, OK? I'll stop in tomorrow morning, OK?"

"Andrew, I either have to pay those checks or stamp them 'Insufficient Funds' and return them. I can't pay them, because there isn't enough money in either of your accounts to cover them. Now, Andrew, if I stamp them 'Insufficient Funds,' those people you wrote the checks to are within their rights to bring charges against you. *Criminal* charges, Andrew. Now, I'm not saying anybody's going to be that rotten, but there's the chance somebody will, and it's a serious offense, Andrew, so please don't let this go longer than tomorrow morning, OK? Please talk it over with Beth and see what you can do and come in early tomorrow morning, OK? I'm talking to you like a brother, Andrew."

"I appreciate it."

"But I'm also an officer of this bank."

"Yes, I know."

"OK, Andrew?"

"Yes, Peter. Thanks."

I called my father long-distance. His wife answered the phone. He had divorced my mother ten years before and she had slowly drunk herself to death, or rather, had finally drunk herself into a stupor that caused her to crash her automobile into an oncoming milk truck. "Hello, Andrew," his wife said without enthusiasm, "I'll get him."

When he came onto the line, I told him I'd lost my job and needed at least $3000 right away.

"Where am I supposed to get three thousand dollars?" he said.

"Just to tide me over till I find another job," I said.

"I don't have three thousand dollars," he said.

"Dad," I said, "I *know* you've got three thousand dollars. I'm desperate, Dad."

"You've always been a pain in the ass," he said wearily.

"Dad, I tried to kill myself last week."

"I don't believe you."

"I had the gun in my mouth."

"You're not that stupid," he said. "You're not stupid enough to do a thing like that."

"Dad, please, can you wire me three thousand dollars? Can you send it right away?"

"When the hell are you going to grow up, Andrew?"

"Dad?"

"I can manage five hundred," he said.

"Thank you. Thank you, Dad."

"And this is the last time," he said, and he hung up.

It was four o'clock in the afternoon, one P.M. on the Coast. He had probably taken the call outside, at the swimming pool. But all he could manage was $500. The gun had been his. He had given it to me when he moved to California. "I won't be needing a pistol in Beverly Hills," he'd told me. I thought of the gun as I went through the house looking for things I could hock. I was a Smith & Wesson .32-caliber revolver. The barrel was short, but the sight had bruised the roof of my mouth that day last week when I was about to take my own life. I thought of the gun and I thought of Virgil coming through the woods and flashing the V sign at me and grinning. I mixed myself a double Scotch and soda and then went into the kitchen.

"Beth," I said, "I want to sell the station wagon."

She turned from the sink. We had fired the housekeeper a month ago, when it had begun to look as though I wouldn't find another job too easily. Beth looked tired. It was a big house and she was having difficulty running it alone.

"Why the station wagon?" she asked. "The station wagon is *my* car."

"The station wagon is paid for."

"You can still get more for the Mercedes."

"Beth," I said, "I *need* the Mercedes."

"Why?"

"If I look like I'm down and out, they'll know it."

"Who will? Your ladyfriends?"

"I don't have any ladyfriends, Beth. I'm talking about prospective employers."

"Do you take prospective employers for rides in your Mercedes?"

"Some of the places I've been going to are in industrial parks. The people I talk to can look out their windows and see what kind of car I'm driving."

"Do they also come outside and leave lipsticked cigarette butts in your ashtray?"

"Beth, I'm going to sell the station wagon, and that's that."

"Do whatever the hell you want," she said, and she went back to rinsing the salad greens.

I sold the station wagon that afternoon. I got $3300 for it. The next morning, I went to the bank and deposited the money in the checking account.

Then I tried phoning Alison.

She was just leaving the house when I got there. She was wearing dungarees and a Navy pea jacket. This was the middle of November, but she still wore sandals on her feet.

"You shouldn't have come here," she said. "I told you never to come here."

"I tried calling you. Your phone was busy."

"What do you want, Andrew?"

"I want to make love to you."

"I told you no," she said. "I told you we were finished."

"And do you know what I did that day? I tried to kill myself. I went into the woods with my father's pistol ——"

"Andrew," she said, "that's a lot of crap, and you know it."

"It's true. I almost did it."

"What stopped you?" she said. "Andrew, your car's right out there in the driveway; if anybody should see it and mention to my husband ——"

"The *hell* with your husband!"

"Sure, the hell with him, I agree. I'm not worrying about *him,* I'm worrying about myself. I don't want to make waves, Andrew. I've got a very nice life here. I don't want you or anybody else upsetting it."

"You told me you loved me."

"I did. I don't anymore."

"You can't just stop loving somebody."

"Can't I?"

"Alison, look, let's go get a drink someplace, OK? I just want to talk to you, OK?"

"You can talk to me here. You've got five minutes to talk to me." She looked at her watch.

"I love you, Alison."

"You don't love anyone but yourself, Andrew. Anyway, *I* don't love *you*, so that's that."

"Is there someone else? Is that it? Have you taken up with another man?"

"That's none of your business."

"That means yes."

"It means it's none of your business."

"Alison, just come for a drink, OK?"

"I don't want to come for a drink; it's only eleven o'clock in the morning. Besides, coming for a drink means ending up in a motel. I don't want to go to bed with you, Andrew. Can you understand that? Do you think you can understand that?"

"You said it was better with me than with anyone in your life. You said that, Alison."

"It was."

"Then how can ——"

"It isn't anymore." She looked at her watch again. "I've got to go," she said.

"Who are you meeting? The man who was on the phone with you?"

"Andrew," she said, "get the hell out of here before I call the police, huh?"

I looked for Virgil; I don't know why I looked for him. I drove all over the back roads of the town, looking for him. I found him at close to two o'clock. There's a place where the road becomes a wooden bridge that crosses the river. He was standing there, looking down at the water. The collar of his long brown coat was pulled up over his ears, the soiled yellow muffler wrapped tight around his throat, trailing. He was holding the paper parcel against his chest. He grinned and flashed the V sign as soon as he heard the car. I rolled down the window.

"Want a lift?" I said.

"OK," he said, and he got in. "Nice day," he said.

"How have you been?" I asked.

"Fine. You don't think it'll rain, do you?"

"No."

"You been to the city again?"

"No," I said, "not today."

And then, suddenly, I was telling him everything. I told him how I'd registered with an agency that specialized in placing high-salaried executives, but so far I'd struck out each and every time they'd arranged an interview for me. I told him I was beginning to think Ralph was bad-mouthing me around the field, can you imagine that son of a bitch firing me after 12 years, sitting there behind his spotless desk and passing down orders from on high, just obeying orders, chum, that's all, sorry, chum, you drink too much. I told Virgil I honestly didn't believe I drank more than most men with the kind of pressures I had to live with, told him that on the afternoon I'd taken old man McGregor to lunch, *he'd* been the one who started tossing down double martinis as if they were going out of style, *he'd* been the one who'd got *me* drunk, for Christ's sake, and then had had the gall to phone that same afternoon and tell the company he no longer wished to do business with us.

"Well, that's OK," Virgil said.

Because, what the hell, I told him, a man isn't an alcoholic just because he has a few social drinks every now and then; you'd think I was a goddamn alco*hol*ic the way Ralph was talking, firing me after 12 years with the company, can you imagine that, not even a gold watch, I said, and laughed, and Virgil laughed with me, how do you like that, Virgil, not even a gold watch. And my father, you know, the rotten bastard left my mother when she was 43 years old, can you imagine that, she never was a raving beauty, well, who the hell knows, I'm her son, how can a son judge his own mother? But at 43, her chances of ever finding another man were nil, though *he* didn't have any trouble finding himself a young floozy, oh, no. She used to be a dancer in a show, Virgil, he took her out to California, bought a big house for her in Beverly Hills, swimming pool, tennis courts, the works, offered to send me $500, would you believe it? Probably pays his goddamn Japanese gardener more than that in a week. Five hundred dollars; I should have told him what he could do with his measly $500.

"Well, yeah," Virgil said, still laughing about the gold watch.

And my wife, I told him, you know, Virgil, you're a wise man never to have gotten married, you're not married, are you, Virgil? I mean, what have I done for her over the years except bust my ass

for her? You know how much that house cost, Virgil? A hundred
and fifty thousand dollars, I *still* owe fifty to the bank, you think
that doesn't bite into a man's salary each month? And sending the
kids to college? Lots of men, when their kids go off to school, they
tell the kids they're on their own, no more tuition, fellows, no more
expenses, you're on your own. I mean, what the hell, Virgil, I paid
their way through private school, both of them, but does my wife
consider that when she's yelling about other women as if I've had a
lot of them? Three women, in all the years we've been married,
Virgil, that's not a lot. I'm not promiscuous, Virgil, I wouldn't call
myself promiscuous. I enjoy it as much as any other man, but I
don't go looking around for it, if it comes my way, it comes my way,
I'm not a chaser, Virgil. I met Alison at a cocktail party here in
town, and if you want to know the truth, *she was* the one who made
all the advances, I'm not kidding, Virgil. Started dancing close
right off and, well, you know, generally getting me very excited,
and practically to the point of being *forced* to ask her if she'd like
to meet me for lunch one day, it was either that or get arrested,
you know what I mean, Virgil?
   Virgil laughed. "Oh, yeah," he said. "Yeah."
   So today she tells me it's all over, second time she's told me that,
as if the first time wasn't bad enough. I don't have to take that kind
of crap from anybody, Virgil, especially not a woman, I just don't
have to. You know what I did the first time she told me? We were
in the motel, same motel we'd been going to for the past two years,
yes. *Yes,* Virgil, two *years* it was going on, this wasn't a casual thing,
we *loved* each other, or at least *I* loved her, who the hell knows *what*
she was doing all those years, except screwing her stupid brains
out. Tells me while we're in the shower together, tells me she
thinks maybe it's time we stopped seeing each other, soaping my
back while she tells me, says it's time we moved on, time we experienced new things. I said What the hell are you talking about?
She said I'm trying to tell you we're finished, Andrew, through,
over and done with, I'm trying to say goodbye, Andrew.
   I went home that day, I dropped her off where her car was
parked first, and then I drove home and went upstairs to the bedroom where I keep my father's pistol in the top drawer of the
dresser, Beth was downstairs, my wife, Beth, she was downstairs.
And I loaded the gun, I put six cartridges into the gun, though I

knew I'd need only one, six cartridges, and I carried it downstairs tucked into my belt, and I had three Scotches neat before I left the house. The barrel fit easily in my mouth, I was ready to pull the trigger, I had my finger around the trigger when you came into the woods, that's what I was about to do that day, Virgil, I was about to kill myself, can you understand that, I was ready to take my own life, and then you stepped into the clearing and grinned and flashed the V sign.

"Yeah," Virgil said, and he grinned and flashed the V sign now.

Ahh, Jesus, I said, I don't know what I'm going to do next. If I don't get a job soon, I just don't know what the hell I'm going to do. You may find me out there in the woods one day, just lying dead in the leaves, I swear to God, Virgil, I just don't know what I'm going to do next. The whole damn thing has collapsed, the whole damn house of cards has fallen in on my head.

"Well, don't worry," Virgil said. "It don't look like rain."

I dropped him off in front of the post office. He grinned and flashed the V sign at me and then closed the door. I looked at the dashboard clock. We had been driving around for close to an hour.

Fifty minutes, to be exact.

I began looking for him regularly after that.

I didn't know his exact walking route, but I did know I could find him at the wooden bridge at about two o'clock every day, and I looked for him sometimes two, sometimes three times a week, depending on how much I felt like talking. I didn't know why I was talking to *him,* of all people. I still don't know. Maybe I just wanted somebody . . . neutral. Someone who wouldn't criticize me for drinking too much and blowing important company deals, someone who wouldn't tell me I ought to grow up, who wouldn't always accuse me of running around with other women, who wouldn't drop me for a new lover — someone who'd just listen and say, "Well, that's OK, don't worry." I talked to him a lot and he listened, or at least I thought he was listening. His responses never varied, though as the weeks wore on, he seemed to talk less and less, seemed never to laugh at the little jokes I made, just sat in silence as I drove the back roads for close to an hour each time.

I had been telling him that things were no better, I still hadn't found a job, Beth was threatening to leave me if I didn't stop fooling around with other women, which warning might have been amusing if it wasn't so goddamn serious; I hadn't been to bed with anyone else since that day at the beginning of November when Alison had soaped my back and told me we were through. Virgil listened in silence as I told him I was afraid I might try to take my own life again. I glanced at him, his face looked drawn, his mouth was tight, his shoulders were slumped, he seemed to cling more fiercely to the paper parcel tied with string. I stopped the car. I pulled up the hand brake.

"Virgil," I said, "you'd be doing me a very big favor if you took the gun and kept it for me. I've got it in the glove compartment; I'd appreciate it if you took it home with you and hid it someplace. And don't tell me where you've put it, because, Virgil, if things don't change in a little while, I'm going to be tempted to take that gun and stick it in my mouth again and blow out my brains, and I just don't want to know where it is. Will you do me that favor, Virgil?"

He began to whimper and shake his head.

"Virgil," I said, "you've been a better friend to me in these past weeks than you can possibly know. You probably won't understand this, but being able to talk to you has made me feel a lot better; it's been a tremendous relief just to get some of this burden off my shoulders. Talking to you has done that for me, Virgil. And maybe you don't consider yourself my friend, maybe you don't even know what the word friendship means, but I'd appreciate it, I'd sincerely appreciate it if you took this gun and hid it away from me, because I'll sure as hell use it on myself if you don't."

Virgil was still whimpering. I opened the glove compartment.

"Here," I said. "It's loaded, so be careful with it. Just put it someplace, bury it in the woods, for all I care, just so I won't be able to get my hands on it. OK, Virgil? Will you do that for me?"

Virgil shook his head and backed away from me. I thrust the gun into his hands.

"Take it," I said.

He took the gun. In a small frightened voice, he said, "Will it rain? Do you think it'll rain?"

It was raining the next day when they found him in the woods. A torn piece of brown wrapping paper and a broken piece of string were lying by his side. He was wearing two sweaters under the long brown overcoat. The rain fell steadily on the sodden leaves around him, washing away his blood. The pistol was still in his mouth. Nobody could figure out why he'd done it. He'd always seemed so happy-go-lucky.

I found a job the very next week. I also met a girl on the train. She is 22 years old and I see her every Friday afternoon, when we spend two or three hours together in a motel near my office. I don't drink anymore. But I don't drink any less, either. That's a joke Virgil might have appreciated, he always used to chuckle at my jokes — in the beginning, anyway. He always used to chuckle and say, "Well, that's OK, don't worry."

He was right.

There'd really been nothing to worry about all along.

PAUL KASER

How Jerem Came Home

(FROM THE COLORADO QUARTERLY)

WINTER CAME IN EARLY that year. One night it came in while I slept, a black dog wandering over the hills, licking the ringing fence wires with frost, howling down from the northeast. A week after that first snow we got word by telegram that my brother would not be coming back from Korea. No one told me he was dead. My father said only that Jerem would not be coming back from that cold place where he had been for the last eight months. I believed he had been to the place where winter comes from. I asked why he didn't want to come back down to West Virginia. My father walked away. The sun began to come weakly through the gray of the kitchen windows. Mother's houseplants, lining the sills, drew back into themselves to wait for resurrection Sunday. My mother stopped watering them and they disappeared, sleeping in the shriveled yellow stocks.

The memorial service was held at the Presbyterian Church in Glenville. It was a cold sunny day. There were flags inside and out. Someone said the flag on the altar had been sent by the president himself.

After the service my grandmother walked with me to her little house on the street behind the church. She was not crying as my mother and sister were. She walked steadily, seemed almost to be smiling.

"Why did they make Jerem dead?" I asked her.

"Good ones only die for three days. Then they rise and walk in glory."

"Three days? Why did they kill him then? What was the good?"

"The heathen die forever. They don't understand how the good ones come back in glory."

"Will he come back here, you mean?"

"I imagine so. You'll often know when they are back if you know how to listen proper and to see what you're looking at. But never mind that."

"Grandma, are you touched?"

"Who said that? Where'd you hear such a lie? From your Aunt Ada? Family's been talking again, behind my back."

"No. Just some folks at the church. They wondered why you looked so happy. They allowed as how you were touched a little, but I said no, that couldn't be."

"Talking that way around children. They never listen to me any more. Jerem wouldn't have gone if I'd had my way. I studied. I watched how them birds moved last spring. I knew from that and some other things, too, the hand of death would be on him if they let that boy go off north. I told them all, but they wouldn't let me hide poor Jerem in the cellar, the way your great-grandma Tanner done her man in the sixties. He'd been with us today, your brother, if they'd listened to me."

"But he's coming back?"

"To the Beulah Land."

"Is that in Gilmer County?" We had reached the door of the little house.

"You won't tell them what I say. Can you keep our secret?"

"Yes."

Grandma lifted her hand toward the hills. "It's just yonder, beyond Middle Creek. Now we'll go in and have some raisin pie."

One day when the snow still lay clean over the slopes of worn-out farmland around us, my uncle came down from Wheeling. He asked if he could buy the Plymouth. It had belonged to Jerem and waited for him now, jacked up on wood blocks in the snow behind the house. When my father showed he didn't want to talk about selling it, my uncle shook his head and said he was just trying to help out some. Mother said to go ahead and sell it, but Father would not talk about it any more.

When my uncle had gone north again, Father went out and taped some cardboard over the car's broken window. He ran his hand along the door frame where a lace of rust was growing. Then he brushed the snow off the front seat, slammed the door shut, and wiped the ice and snow from the windshield as though someone were inside and going to drive. The interior cast rivulets of light back to the disappearing winter sun.

Because they were not calling the men to the mines regularly that fall or winter, my father was often free to bring me home early from school and take me with him on hunting trips. When it was too late in the season for coon and squirrel, we went after rabbits with the beagles. Whenever my father left the yard with the shotgun and the beagles, the big blueticks moaned at him. They dragged their muddy chains back and forth, trembling at the high warm voice of the beagle pack. On these trips it was my job to carry the extra shells for my father's twenty gauge in my jacket pockets. I liked to go on the rabbit hunts because it wasn't necessary to sit in the cold dark waiting for the hounds to tree a coon or bring around a fox. With rabbits you could keep moving and didn't have to worry about making noise. Mother said a six-year-old boy was too young to be out on any kind of a hunt, but my father didn't like to go out alone. When we went out to the fields, he would remind me that when I had enough experience, he would take Jerem's old four-ten shotgun down from the attic and let me see if I could handle it.

One day in midwinter we were out and the sugar-glaze snow broke in plates beneath our boots. Only a few wet brown weeds could be seen above the fenceline drifts. I was wondering how Jerem would feel about my using his shotgun when a rabbit burst from a clump of brambles in front of us. Father sighted on it as it angled away from us and shot off its hind legs. Then the oldest beagle, a tawny bitch, came out of the brush and was on the rabbit before I could reach it. She had waited, as we had, for the others to drive the rabbit up the valley. Now she had it to herself, gnawing its back. The rabbit's eyes were iced with blood. It screamed like a human baby from its contorted pink throat. I picked it up by its ears and kicked the bitch aside. When my father came near, I turned my face away and pretended to be watching for the rest of the pack to come up the valley. I didn't want him to think I was crying because of the death of the rabbit. It wasn't that. For a moment the rabbit squirming to death in my hands, the beagle leaping against my leg, my father's voice over the broken face of the snow were lost in a deepening shadow. When I turned at last to look back, I saw my father snapping the rabbit's neck with his cold-spotted hands.

As we walked home, I asked him if next spring we could clean and paint the Plymouth; drawn by that and the warm weather Jerem might decide to come back. My father grabbed me by the shoulder and shook me. "You can forget that. I'm telling you he's not coming back. Didn't you understand when we got that tele-gram? Didn't I tell you plain? He can't come back. Forget about him, won't you?"

I ran home ahead of him and threw the rabbit onto the back porch. Then I crossed the yard and went into the crib shed. For a long time I sat on the stained gray padding of the tractor seat. I heard the hounds greeting my father, chains rattling, then the slam of the kitchen screen door. Through the crib slats on my left, wind came to sift the snow dust over the red, broken corn. A dry rattle came from the shucks along the floor, mice burrowing deeper into papery nests. I envied the summer blacksnake, coiled in the black-est warmth beneath the stone foundation of the shed. The mice and hounds quieted, and I looked out to see the new snow set-tling dimly over outbuildings and abandoned harrow plates. The cracked rubber of the steering wheel tasted black against my tongue. I was cold and getting hungry, but I did not want to see my father. I was afraid of what it was he couldn't say. I was afraid he was as confused as I was, that only the rabbit, stiffening on the porch, knew more than we, the thing to be known only in that final moment.

From the house my mother was calling my name. She banged a pan against the door handle and the hounds answered out of their dreams. Through harsh persistent music I found my way back into the yellow light of the kitchen.

Two days later my father announced after dinner that in the spring we would be moving north to one of the Ohio cities. My uncle, who had made a lot of money managing a pulp mill near Wheeling, was buying our farm. No one said anything when my father told us this, but the next day my sister, who was just begin-ning high school, ran away to my grandmother's house in town.

She sent word that she couldn't leave her whole life behind that way, even if we could. In a week she was back, just to get her scrapbook, she said, but she didn't leave us again.

I saw that it would not do any good. My mother said to think how much better the schools and stores would be up there. My father said I could take my pick of the new beagle litter in the barn to take along north. While I was kneeling at the box making my choice, he loaded all the other hounds into the pickup and took them off to give away or sell to hunters whose lands bordered ours. Then he came back and told me about the great Ohio River. He told me it was bigger than all the rivers in West Virginia put together. It carried barges as big as our house, and when it flooded, it washed away whole counties from Ohio and Kentucky and carried them and all their people down to New Orleans. But he didn't talk much about what was beyond the river. He said only that it would be better there; there would be more money and he could buy a brand new shotgun for me in no time.

It had been a long time then since I had thought of Jerem, but one day I decided that we must be going north to meet him. I didn't dare mention this to anyone. I thought it might be a surprise they were keeping for me.

On a Saturday late in February some high school boys came from town and knocked the last of the ice away from Jerem's old Plymouth. They gave my father some money, put the wheels back on the car, and worked for a while on the motor. I stayed inside all afternoon and watched them from my bedroom window. When they had driven out of sight on the muddy road to town, I came downstairs. My mother was in the kitchen. She didn't notice me so I scraped a chair up to the table and sat down. "I hate him."

She turned to me. "I've told you not to use that word, that's an ugly word."

"But I do. I hate him."

"Now, who do you mean? I'm sure if you think about it, you don't really hate anyone."

"He sold Jerem's car. Just for the money. What's Jerem going to say about that when we see him up north? He'll want to know what happened to his car and I'll tell him. I'll tell him what father did. I hate him. He can't tell the truth and all he wants is money . . ."

My throat pinched off the last words. I put my head down breathing hot against my fists.

My mother was standing above me. When I tried to run out of the kitchen, she held my arm. I thought she would strike me, but she took my hand and held it under her apron against her stomach. Her strength surprised me then. I could not move. "Jerem is not up north. He is dead and you can't find him ever again on this earth. I thought you understood. But this, do you feel it move? A baby. Maybe a new brother." Then she let me go and I ran out of the kitchen.

Just before we left the farm, grandmother came up from town to find out about the baby my mother was carrying. My mother lay on the sofa and grandmother held a silver coin on a silver chain over my mother's stomach. Slowly the coin began to swing back and forth in the damp spring air. The old woman laughed and slipped the coin into her pocket. "A boy, sure as you live. If it'd gone in a circle, t'would have been a girl. Well, you're almost too old, dear, but it's been done plenty times before. You're still strong and you've the peace of having another boy to make up for your loss."

My mother sat up shaking her head. "I don't believe a word of it. And your own father was a doctor. Grandma, you should be ashamed."

My grandmother sat back serenely on the rocker. "I've not been wrong with this but once and that when the weather was acting up back in forty-three. Believe as you will, I know the facts."

In front of the house my father was loading boxes of clothing and dishes into the pickup. Suddenly I wanted to go out to him and tell him that now, with winter gone, I wouldn't be looking for Jerem to come home anymore. I moved abruptly toward the light and noticed that my grandmother had stopped rocking, that she was watching my movement, tensed and transfixed as a hunting cat. She seemed surprised that she could not stop me that way, but she said nothing as I turned.

Before we left her for the last time, the old woman put her face close to mine as I sat in the bed of the pickup. The sugar pines were shimmering black needles in her eyes. "Jerem's come home, boy. I saw him yesterday at the creek. No, don't tell them. He's with me for good now and I'll never let the fools send him off to die again. What are you frowning at? You, too? You think I'm touched like those church folks, now? Go on then. Once you cross that river you'll forget. There's water that can make you forget, grow, too; so I won't begrudge you that. Men and women, there's always betrayal between them of one kind or another, I suppose. But me and Jerem, we're okay here, even if it's not for you or them." She pointed to the cab of the truck where my parents and sister were sitting. "Don't let them bring you back, son. For all the power of spring it's still a dead land for some . . ." She wanted to say more to me, the most important of all by the look on her face, but the pickup motor interrupted and began to pull me away. She didn't move but her form seemed to break apart in the light and shadow, dissolving by its own volition. Only the line of morning trees remained, to dim and then disappear behind the hill.

ALISTAIR MacLEOD

The Lost Salt Gift of Blood

(FROM THE SOUTHERN REVIEW)

NOW IN THE EARLY evening the sun is flashing everything in gold. It bathes the blunt gray rocks that loom yearningly out toward Europe and it touches upon the stunted spruce and the low-lying lichens and the delicate hardy ferns and the ganglia rooted moss and the tiny tough rock cranberries. The gray and slanting rain squalls have swept in from the sea and then departed with all the suddenness of surprise marauders. Everything before them and beneath them has been rapidly, briefly, and thoroughly drenched and now the wet droplets catch and hold the sun's infusion in a myriad of rainbow colors. For beyond the harbor's mouth more tiny squalls seem to be forming, moving rapidly across the surface of the sea out there beyond land's end where the blue ocean turns to gray in rain and distance and the strain of eyes. Even farther out, somewhere beyond Cape Spear lies Dublin and the Irish coast; far away but still the nearest land and closer now than is Toronto or Detroit to say nothing of North America's more western cities; seeming almost hazily visible now in imagination's mist.

Overhead the ivory white gulls wheel and cry, flashing also in the purity of the sun and the clean, freshly washed air. Sometimes they glide to the blue green surface of the harbor, squawking and garbling; at times almost standing on their pink webbed feet as if they would walk on water, flapping their wings pompously against their breasts like over-conditioned he-men who have successfully passed their body-building courses. At other times they gather in lazy groups on the rocks above the harbor's entrance murmuring softly to themselves or looking also quietly out toward what must be Ireland and the vastness of the sea.

The harbor itself is very small and softly curving, seeming like a tiny, peaceful womb nurturing the life that now lies within it but which originated from without; came from without and through the narrow, rock-tight channel that admits the entering and withdrawing sea. That sea is entering again now, forcing itself gently but inevitably between the tightness of the opening and laving the rocky walls and rising and rolling into the harbor's inner cove. The dories rise at their moorings and the tide laps higher on the piles and advances upward toward the high-water marks upon the land; the running moon-drawn tides of spring.

Around the edges of the harbor brightly colored houses dot the wet and glistening rocks. In some ways they seem almost like defiantly optimistic horseshoe nails; yellow and scarlet and green and pink; buoyantly yet firmly permanent in the gray unsundered rock.

At the harbor's entrance the small boys are jigging for the beautifully speckled salmon-pink sea trout. Barefootedly they stand on the tide-wet rocks flicking their wrists and sending their glistening lines in shimmering golden arcs out into the rising tide. Their voices mount excitedly as they shout to one another encouragement, advice, consolation. The trout fleck dazzlingly on their sides as they are drawn toward the rocks, turning to seeming silver as they flash within the sea.

It is all of this that I see now, standing at the final road's end of my twenty-five hundred mile journey. The road ends here — quite literally ends at the door of a now abandoned fishing shanty some six brief yards in front of where I stand. The shanty is gray and weatherbeaten with two boarded up windows, vanishing, wind-whipped shingles and a heavy rusted padlock chained fast to a twisted door. Piled before the twisted door and its equally twisted frame are some marker buoys, a small pile of rotted rope, a broken oar and an old and rust-flaked anchor.

The option of driving my small rented Volkswagen the remaining six yards and then negotiating a tight many twists of the steering wheel turn still exists. I would be then facing toward the west and could simply retrace the manner of my coming. I could easily drive away before anything might begin.

Instead I walk beyond the road's end and the fishing shanty and begin to descend the rocky path that winds tortuously and nar-

rowly along and down the cliff's edge to the sea. The small stones
roll and turn and scrape beside and beneath my shoes and after
only a few steps the leather is nicked and scratched. My toes press
hard against its straining surface.

As I approach the actual water's edge four small boys are jumping excitedly upon the glistening rocks. One of them has made a
strike and is attempting to reel in his silver, turning prize. The
other three have laid down their rods in their enthusiasm and are
shouting encouragement and giving almost physical moral support: "Don't let him get away, John," they say. "Keep the line
steady." "Hold the end of the rod up." "Reel in the slack."
"Good." "What a dandy!"

Across the harbor's clear water another six or seven shout the
same delirious messages. The silver, turning fish is drawn toward
the rock. In the shallows he flips and arcs, his flashing body breaking the water's surface as he walks upon his tail. The small fisherman has now his rod almost completely vertical. Its tip sings and
vibrates high above his head while at his feet the trout spins and
curves. Both of his hands are clenched around the rod and his
knuckles strain white through the water-roughened redness of
small boy hands. He does not know whether he should relinquish
the rod and grasp at the lurching trout or merely heave the rod
backward and flip the fish behind him. Suddenly he decides upon
the latter but even as he heaves his bare feet slide out from beneath
him on the smooth wetness of the rock and he slips down into the
water. With a pirouetting leap the trout turns glisteningly and
tears itself free. In a darting flash of darkened greenness it rights
itself within the regained water and is gone. "Oh damn!" says the
small fisherman, struggling upright onto his rock. He bites his
lower lip to hold back the tears welling within his eyes. There is a
small trickle of blood coursing down from a tiny scratch on the
inside of his wrist and he is wet up to his knees. I reach down to
retrieve the rod and return it to him.

Suddenly a shout rises from the opposite shore. Another line
zings tautly through the water throwing off fine showers of iri-
descent droplets. The shouts and contagious excitement spread
anew. "Don't let him get away!" "Good for you." "Hang on!"
"Hang on!"

I am caught up in it myself and wish also to shout some enthusiastic advice but I do not know what to say. The trout curves up

from the water in a wriggling arch and lands behind the boys in the moss and lichen that grow down to the sea-washed rocks. They race to free it from the line and proclaim about its size.

On our side of the harbor the boys begin to talk. "Where do you live?" they ask and is it far away and is it bigger than St. John's? Awkwardly I try to tell them the nature of the North American midwest. In turn I ask them if they go to school. "Yes," they say. Some of them go to St. Bonaventure's which is the Catholic school and others go to Twilling Memorial. They are all in either grades four or five. All of them say that they like school and that they like their teachers.

The fishing is good they say and they come here almost every evening. "Yesterday I caught me a nine pounder," says John. Eagerly they show me all of their simple equipment. The rods are of all varieties as are the lines. At the lines' ends the leaders are thin transparencies terminating in grotesque three-clustered hooks. A foot or so from each hook there is a silver spike knotted into the leader. Some of the boys say the trout are attracted by the flashing of the spike; others say that it acts only as a weight or sinker. No line is without one.

"Here, sir," says John, "have a go. Don't get your shoes wet." Standing on the slippery rocks in my smooth-soled shoes I twice attempt awkward casts. Both times the line loops up too highly and the spike splashes down far short of the running, rising life of the channel.

"Just a flick of the wrist, sir," he says, "just a flick of the wrist. You'll soon get the hang of it." His hair is red and curly and his face is splashed with freckles and his eyes are clear and blue. I attempt three or four more casts and then pass the rod back to the hands where it belongs.

And now it is time for supper. The calls float down from the women standing in the doorways of the multi-colored houses and obediently the small fishermen gather up their equipment and their catches and prepare to ascend the narrow upward-winding paths. The sun has descended deeper into the sea and the evening has become quite cool. I recognize this with surprise and a slight shiver. In spite of the advice given to me and my own precautions my feet are wet and chilled within my shoes. No place to be unless barefooted or in rubber boots. Perhaps for me no place at all.

As we lean into the steepness of the path my young companions continue to talk; their accents broad and Irish. One of them used to have a tame sea gull at his house, had it for seven years. His older brother found it on the rocks and brought it home. His grandfather called it Joey. "Because it talked so much," explained John. It died last week and they held a funeral about a mile away from the shore where there was enough soil to dig a grave. Along the shore itself it is almost solid rock and there is no ground for a grave. It's the same with people they say. All week they have been hopefully looking along the base of the cliffs for another sea gull but have not found one. You cannot kill a sea gull they say, the government protects them because they are scavengers and keep the harbors clean.

The path is narrow and we walk in single file. By the time we reach the shanty and my rented car I am wheezing and badly out of breath. So badly out of shape for a man of thirty-three; sauna baths do nothing for your wind. The boys walk easily, laughing and talking beside me. With polite enthusiasm they comment upon my car. Again there exists the possibility of restarting the car's engine and driving back the road that I have come. After all, I have not seen a single adult except for the women calling down the news of supper. I stand and fiddle with my keys.

The appearance of the man and the dog is sudden and unexpected. We have been so casual and unaware in front of the small automobile that we have neither seen nor heard their approach along the rock-worn road. The dog is short, stocky and black and white. White hair floats and feathers freely from his sturdy legs and paws as he trots along the rock looking expectantly out into the harbor. He takes no notice of me. The man is short and stocky as well and he also appears as black and white. His rubber boots are black and his dark heavy worsted trousers are supported by a broadly scarred and blackened belt. The buckle is shaped like a dory with a fisherman standing in the bow. Above the belt there is a dark navy woolen jersey and upon his head a toque of the same material. His hair beneath the toque is white as is the three-or-four-day stubble on his face. His eyes are blue and his hands heavy, gnarled, and misshapen. It is hard to tell from looking at him whether he is in his sixties, seventies, or eighties.

"Well, it is a nice evening tonight," he says looking first at John and then to me. "The barometer has not dropped so perhaps fair weather will continue for a day or two. It will be good for the fishing."

He picks a piece of gnarled, gray driftwood from the roadside and swings it slowly back and forth in his right hand. With desperate anticipation the dog dances back and forth before him, his intense eyes glittering at the stick. When it is thrown into the harbor he barks joyously and disappears, hurling himself down the bank in a scrambling avalanche of small stones. In seconds he reappears with only his head visible, cutting a silent but rapidly advancing *V* through the quiet serenity of the harbor. The boys run to the bank's edge and shout encouragement to him — much as they had been doing earlier for one another. "It's farther out," they cry, "to the right, to the right." Almost totally submerged, he cannot see the stick he swims to find. The boys toss stones in its general direction and he raises himself out of the water to see their landing splashdowns and to change his wide-waked course.

"How have you been?" asks the old man, reaching for a pipe and a pouch of tobacco and then without waiting for an answer, "perhaps you'll stay for supper. There are just the three of us now."

We begin to walk along the road in the direction that he has come. Before long the boys rejoin us accompanied by the dripping dog with the recovered stick. He waits for the old man to take it from him and then showers us all with a spray of water from his shaggy coat. The man pats and scratches the damp head and the dripping ears. He keeps the returned stick and thwacks it against his rubber boots as we continue to walk along the rocky road I have so recently traveled in my Volkswagen.

Within a few yards the houses begin to appear upon our left. Frame and flat-roofed, they cling to the rocks looking down into the harbor. In storms their windows are splashed by the sea but now their bright colors are buoyantly brave in the shadows of the descending dusk. At the third gate, John, the man, and the dog turn in. I follow them. The remaining boys continue on; they wave and say, "So long."

The path that leads through the narrow whitewashed gate has had its stone worn smooth by the passing of countless feet. On either side there is a row of small, smooth stones, also neatly whitewashed, and seeming like a procession of large white eggs or tiny unbaked loaves of bread. Beyond these stones and also on either side, there are some castoff tires also whitewashed and serving as flower beds. Within each whitened circumference the colorful low-flying flowers nod; some hardy strain of pansies or perhaps marigolds. The path leads on to the square, green house, with its white borders and shutters. On one side of the wooden doorstep a skate blade has been nailed — for the wiping off of feet and beyond the swinging screen door there is a porch which smells saltily of the sea. A variety of sou'westers and rubber boots and mitts and caps hang from the driven nails or lie at the base of the wooden walls.

Beyond the porch there is the kitchen where the woman is at work. All of us enter. The dog walks across the linoleum covered floor, his nails clacking, and flings himself with a contented sigh beneath the wooden table. Almost instantly he is asleep, his coat still wet from his swim within the sea.

The kitchen is small. It has an iron cook stove, a table against one wall and three or four handmade chairs of wood. There is also a wooden rocking chair covered by a cushion. The rockers are so thin from years of use that it is hard to believe they still function. Close by the table there is a wash stand with two pails of water upon it. A wash basin hangs from a driven nail in its side and above it is an old-fashioned mirrored medicine cabinet. There is also a large cupboard, a low-lying couch, and a window facing upon the sea. On the walls a barometer hangs as well as two pictures, one of a rather jaunty young couple taken many years ago. It is yellowed and rather indistinct; the woman in a long dress with her hair done up in ringlets, the man with a serge suit that is slightly too large for him and with a tweed cap pulled rakishly over his right eye. He has an accordion strapped over his shoulders and his hands are fanned out on the buttons and keys. The other is one of the Christ-child. Beneath it is written, "Sweet Heart of Jesus Pray for Us."

The woman at the stove is tall and fine featured. Her gray hair is combed briskly back from her forehead and neatly coiled with a large pin at the base of her neck. Her eyes are as gray as the storm scud of the sea. Like her husband it is difficult to define her age other than that it is past sixty. She wears a blue print dress, a plain blue apron and low-heeled brown shoes. She is turning fish within a frying pan when we enter.

Her eyes contain only mild surprise as she first regards me. Then with recognition they glow in open hostility which in turn

subsides and yields to self-control. She continues at the stove while
the rest of us sit upon the chairs.

During the meal that follows we are reserved and shy in our
lonely adult ways; groping for and protecting what perhaps may be
the only awful dignity we possess. John, unheedingly, talks on and
on. He is in the fifth grade and is doing well. They are learning
percentages and the mysteries of decimals; to change a percent to a
decimal fraction you move the decimal point two places to the left
and drop the percent sign. You always, always do so. They are
learning the different breeds of domestic animals: the four main
breeds of dairy cattle are Holstein, Ayrshire, Guernsey, and Jersey. He can play the mouth organ and will demonstrate after
supper. He has twelve lobster traps of his own. They were originally broken ones thrown up on the rocky shore by storms. Ira, he
says nodding toward the old man, helped him fix them, nailing on
new lathes and knitting new headings. Now they are set along the
rocks near the harbor's entrance. He is averaging a pound a trap
and the "big" fishermen say that that is better than some of them
are doing. He is saving his money in a little imitation keg that was
also washed up on the shore. He would like to buy an outboard
motor for the small reconditioned skiff he now uses to visit his
traps. At present he has only oars.

"John here has the makings of a good fisherman," says the old
man. "He's up at five most every morning when I am putting on
the fire. He and the dog are already out along the shore and back
before I've made tea."

"When I was in Toronto," says John, "no one was ever up before
seven. I would make my own tea and wait. It was wonderful sad.
There were gulls there though, flying over Toronto harbor. We
went to see them on two Sundays."

After the supper we move the chairs back from the table. The
woman clears away the dishes and the old man turns on the radio.
First he listens to the weather forecast and then turns to short wave
where he picks up the conversations from the offshore fishing
boats. They are conversations of catches and winds and tides and
of the women left behind on the rocky shores. John appears with
his mouth organ, standing at a respectful distance. The old man
notices him, nods, and shuts off the radio. Rising, he goes upstairs, the sound of his feet echoing down to us. Returning he

carries an old and battered accordion. "My fingers have so much rheumatism," he says, "that I find it hard to play anymore."

Seated, he slips his arms through the straps and begins the squeezing accordion motions. His wife takes off her apron and stands behind him with one hand upon his shoulder. For a moment they take on the essence of the once young people in the photograph. They begin to sing:

> *Come all ye fair and tender ladies*
> *Take warning how you court your men*
> *They're like the stars on a summer's morning*
> *First they'll appear and then they're gone.*
>
> *I wish I were a tiny sparrow*
> *And I had wings and I could fly*
> *I'd fly away to my own true lover*
> *And all he'd ask I would deny.*
>
> *Alas I'm not a tiny sparrow*
> *I have not wings nor can fly*
> *And on this earth in grief and sorrow*
> *I am bound until I die.*

John sits on one of the homemade chairs playing his mouth organ. He seems as all mouth organ players the world over: his right foot tapping out the measures and his small shoulders now round and hunched above the cupped hand instrument.

"Come now and sing with us, John," says the old man.

Obediently he takes the mouth organ from his mouth and shakes the moisture drops upon his sleeve. All three of them begin to sing, spanning easily the half century of time that touches their extremes. The old and the young singing now their songs of loss in different comprehensions. Stranded here, alien of my middle generation, I tap my leather foot self-consciously upon the linoleum. The words sweep up and swirl about my head. Fog does not touch like snow yet it is more heavy and more dense. Oh moisture comes in many forms!

> *All alone as I strayed by the banks of the river*
> *Watching the moonbeams at evening of day*

All alone as I wandered I spied a young stranger
Weeping and wailing with many a sigh.

Weeping for one who is now lying lonely
Weeping for one who no mortal can save
As the foaming dark waters flow silently past him
Onward they flow over young Jenny's grave.

Oh Jenny my darling come tarry here with me
Don't leave me alone, love, distracted in pain
For as death is the dagger that plied us asunder
Wide is the gulf love between you and I.

After the singing stops we all sit rather uncomfortably for a moment. The mood seeming to hang heavily upon our shoulders. Then with my single exception all come suddenly to action. John gets up and takes his battered school books to the kitchen table. The dog jumps up on a chair beside him and watches solemnly in a supervisory manner. The woman takes some navy yarn, the color of her husband's jersey and begins to knit. She is making another jersey and is working on the sleeve. The old man rises and beckons me to follow him into the tiny parlor. The stuffed furniture is old and worn. There is a tiny woodburning heater in the center of the room. It stands on a square of galvanized metal which protects the floor from falling, burning coals. The stove pipe rises and vanishes into the wall on its way to the upstairs. There is an old-fashioned mantlepiece on the wall behind the stove. It is covered with odd shapes of driftwood from the shore and a variety of exotically shaped bottles, blue and green and red which are from the shore as well. There are pictures here too: of the couple in the other picture; and one of them with their five daughters; and one of the five daughters by themselves. In that far-off picture time all of the daughters seem roughly between the ages of ten and eighteen. The youngest has the reddest hair of all. So red that it seems to triumph over the nonphotographic colors of lonely black and white. The pictures are in standard wooden frames.

From behind the ancient chesterfield the old man pulls a collapsible card table and pulls down its warped and shaky legs. Also from behind the chesterfield he takes a faded checkerboard and a large old-fashioned matchbox of rattling wooden checkers. The spine of the board is almost cracked through and is strengthened by layers of adhesive tape. The checkers are circumferences of wood sawed from a length of broom handle. They are about three quarters of an inch thick. Half of them are painted a very bright blue and the other half an equally eye-catching red. "John made these," says the old man, "all of them are not really the same thickness but they are good enough. He gave it a good try."

We begin to play checkers. He takes the blue and I the red. The house is silent with only the click-clack of the knitting needles sounding through the quiet rooms. From time to time the old man lights his pipe, digging out the old ashes with a flattened nail and tamping in the fresh tobacco with the same nail's head. The blue smoke winds lazily and haphazardly toward the low-beamed ceiling. The game is solemn as is the next and then the next. Neither of us loses all of the time.

"It is time for some of us to be in bed," says the old woman after awhile. She gathers up her knitting and rises from her chair. In the kitchen John neatly stacks his school books on one corner of the table in anticipation of the morning. He goes outside for a moment and then returns. Saying goodnight very formally he goes up the stairs to bed. In a short while the old woman follows, her footsteps traveling the same route.

We continue to play our checkers, wreathed in smoke and only partially aware of the muffled footfalls sounding softly above our heads.

When the old man gets up to go outside I am not really surprised, any more than I am when he returns with the brown, ostensible vinegar jug. Poking at the declining kitchen fire, he moves the kettle about seeking the warmest spot on the cooling stove. He takes two glasses from the cupboard, a sugar bowl and two spoons. The kettle begins to boil.

Even before tasting it, I know the rum to be strong and overproof. It comes at night and in fog from the French islands of St. Pierre and Miquelon. Coming over in the low-throttled fishing boats, riding in imitation gas cans. He mixes the rum and the sugar first, watching them marry and dissolve. Then to prevent the breakage of the glasses he places a teaspoon in each and adds the boiling water. The odor rises richly, its sweetness hung in steam.

He brings the glasses to the table, holding them by their tops so that his fingers will not burn.

We do not say anything for some time, sitting upon the chairs, while the sweetened, heated richness moves warmly through and from our stomachs and spreads upward to our brains. Outside the wind begins to blow, moaning and faintly rattling the window's whitened shutters. He rises and brings refills. We are warm within the dark and still within the wind. A clock strikes regularly the strokes of ten.

It is difficult to talk at times with or without liquor; difficult to achieve the actual act of saying. Sitting still we listen further to the rattle of the wind; not knowing where nor how we should begin. Again the glasses are refilled.

"When she married in Toronto," he says at last, "we figured that maybe John should be with her and with her husband. That maybe he would be having more of a chance there in the city. But we would be putting it off and it weren't until nigh on two years ago that he went. Went with a woman from down the cove going to visit her daughter. Well, what was wrong was that we missed him wonderful awful. More fearful than we ever thought. Even the dog. Just pacing the floor and looking out the window and walking along the rocks of the shore. Like us had no moorings, lost in the fog or on the ice floes in a snow squall. Nigh sick unto our hearts we was. Even the grandmother who before that was maybe thinking small to herself that he was trouble in her old age. Ourselves having never had no sons only daughters."

He pauses, then rising goes upstairs and returns with an envelope. From it he takes a picture which shows two young people standing self-consciously before a half-ton pickup with a wooden extension ladder fastened to its side. They appear to be in their middle twenties. The door of the truck has the information: "Jim Farrell, Toronto: Housepainting, Eavestroughing, Aluminum Siding, Phone 481-3484," lettered on its surface.

"This was in the last letter," he says. "That Farrell I guess was a nice enough fellow, from Heartsick Bay he was.

"Anyway they could have no more peace with John than we could without him. Like I says he was here too long before his going and it all took ahold of us the way it will. They sent word that he was coming on the plane to St. John's with a woman they'd met through a Newfoundland club. I was to go to St. John's to meet him. Well, it was all wrong the night before the going. The signs all bad; the grandmother knocked off the lampshade and it broke in a hunnerd pieces — the sign of death; and the window blind fell and clattered there on the floor and then lied still. And the dog runned around like he was crazy, moanen and cryen worse than the swiles does out on the ice, and throwen hisself against the walls and jumpen on the table and at the window where the blind fell until we would have to be letten him out. But it be no better for he runned and throwed hisself in the sea and then come back and howled outside the same window and jumped against the wall, splashen the water from his coat all over it. Then he be runnen back to the sea again. All the neighbors heard him and said I should bide at home and not go to St. John's at all. We be all wonderful scared and not know what to do and the next mornen, first thing I drops me knife.

"But still I feels I has to go. It be foggy all the day and everyone be thinken the plane won't come or be able to land. And I says, small to myself, now here in the fog be the bad luck and the death but then there the plane be, almost like a ghost ship comen out the fog with all its lights shinen. I think maybe he won't be on it but soon he comen through the fog, first with the woman and then seeen me and starten to run, closer and closer till I can feel him in me arms and the tears on both our cheeks. Powerful strange how things will take one. That night they be killed."

From the envelope that contained the picture he draws forth a tattered clipping:

Jennifer Farrell of Roncevalles Avenue was instantly killed early this morning and her husband James died later in emergency at St. Joseph's Hospital. The accident occurred about 2 A.M. when the pickup truck in which they were traveling went out of control on Queen St. W. and struck a utility pole. It is thought that bad visibility caused by a heavy fog may have contributed to the accident. The Farrells were originally from Newfoundland.

Again he moves to refill the glasses. "We be all alone," he says. "All our other daughters married and far away in Montreal, Toronto, or the States. Hard for them to come back here, even to visit; they comes only every three years or so for perhaps a week. So we be haven only him."

And now my head begins to reel even as I move to the filling of my own glass. Not waiting this time for the courtesy of his offer. Making myself perhaps too much at home with this man's glass and this man's rum and this man's house and all the feelings of his love. Even as I did before. Still locked again for words.

Outside we stand and urinate, turning our backs to the seeming gale so as not to splash our wind snapped trousers. We are almost driven forward to rock upon our toes and settle on our heels, so blow the gusts. Yet in spite of all, the stars shine clearly down. It will indeed be a good day for the fishing and this wind eventually will calm. The salt hangs heavy in the air and the water booms against the rugged rocks. I take a stone and throw it against the wind into the sea.

Going up the stairs we clutch the wooden bannister unsteadily and say goodnight.

The room has changed very little. The window rattles in the wind and the unfinished beams sway and creak. The room is full of sound. Like a foolish Lockwood I approach the window although I hear no voice. There is no Catherine who cries to be let in. Standing unsteadily on one foot when required I manage to undress, draping my trousers across the wooden chair. The bed is clean. It makes no sound. It is plain and wooden, its mattress stuffed with hay or kelp. I feel it with my hand and pull back the heavy patchwork quilts. Still I do not go into it. Instead I go back to the door which has no knob but only an ingenious latch formed from a twisted nail. Turning it, I go out into the hallway. All is dark and the house seems even more inclined to creak where there is no window. Feeling along the wall with my outstretched hand I find the door quite easily. It is closed with the same kind of latch and not difficult to open. But no one waits on the other side. I stand and bend my ear to hear the even sound of my one son's sleeping. He does not beckon anymore than the nonexistent voice in the outside wind. I hesitate to touch the latch for fear that I may waken him and disturb his dreams. And if I did what would I say? Yet I would like to see him in his sleep this once and see the room with the quiet bed once more and the wooden chair beside it from off an old wrecked trawler. There is no boiled egg or shaker of salt or glass of water waiting on the chair within this closed room's darkness.

Once though there was a belief held in the outports, that if a girl would see her own true lover she should boil an egg and scoop out half the shell and fill it with salt. Then she should take it to bed with her and eat it leaving a glass of water by her bedside. In the night her future husband or a vision of him would appear and offer her the glass. But she must only do it once.

It is the type of belief that bright young graduate students were collecting eleven years ago for the theses and archives of North America and also, they hoped, for their own fame. Even as they sought the near-Elizabethan songs and ballads that had sailed from County Kerry and from Devon and Cornwall. All about the wild, wide sea and the flashing silver dagger and the lost and faithless lover. Echoes to and from the lovely, lonely hills and glens of West Virginia and the standing stones of Tennessee.

Across the hall the old people are asleep. The old man's snoring rattles as do the windows; except that now and then there are catching gasps within his breath. In three or four short hours he will be awake and will go down to light his fire. I turn and walk back softly to my room.

Within the bed the warm sweetness of the rum is heavy and intense. The darkness presses down upon me but still it brings no sleep. There are no voices and no shadows that are real. There are only walls of memory touched restlessly by flickers of imagination.

Oh I would like to see my way more clearly. I, who have never understood the mystery of fog. I would perhaps like to capture it in a jar like the beautiful childhood butterflies that always die in spite of the airholes punched with nails in the covers of their captivity — leaving behind the vapors of their lives and deaths; or perhaps as the unknowing child who collects the gray moist condoms from the lover's lanes only to have them taken from him and to be told to wash his hands. Oh I have collected many things I did not understand.

And perhaps now I should go and say, oh son of my *summa cum laude* loins, come away from the lonely gulls and the silver trout and I will take you to the land of the Tastee Freeze where

you may sleep till ten of nine. And I will show you the elevator
to the apartment on the sixteenth floor and introduce you to the
buzzer system and the yards of the wrought iron fences where
the Doberman pinscher runs silently at night. Or may I offer you
the money that is the fruit of my collecting and my most success-
ful life? Or shall I wait to meet you in some known or unknown
bitterness like Yeats's Cuchulain by the wind-whipped sea or as
Sohrab and Rustum by the future flowing river?

Again I collect dreams. For I do not know enough of the fog on
Toronto's Queen St. West and the grinding crash of the pickup
and of lost and misplaced love.

I am up early in the morning as the man kindles the fire from
the driftwood splinters. The outside light is breaking and the
wind is calm. John tumbles down the stairs. Scarcely stopping
to splash his face and pull on his jacket, he is gone accompanied
by the dog. The old man smokes his pipe and waits for the water
to boil. When it does he pours some into the teapot then passes
the kettle to me. I take it to the washstand and fill the small, tin
basin in readiness for my shaving. My face looks back from the
mirrored cabinet. The woman softly descends the stairs.

"I think I will go back today," I say while looking into the
mirror at my face and at those in the room behind me. I try to
emphasize the "I." "I just thought I would like to make this
trip — again. I think I can leave the car in St. John's and fly back
directly." The woman begins to move about the table, setting
out the round white plates. The man quietly tamps his pipe.

The door opens and John and the dog return. They have been
down along the shore to see what has happened throughout the
night. "Well, John," says the old man, "what did you find?"

He opens his hand to reveal a smooth round stone. It is of the
deepest green inlaid with veins of darkest ebony. It has been
worn and polished by the unrelenting restlessness of the sea and
buffed and burnished by the graveled sand. All of its inade-
quacies have been removed and it glows with the luster of near
perfection.

"It is very beautiful," I say.

"Yes," he says, "I like to collect them." Suddenly he looks up
to my eyes and thrusts the stone toward me. "Here," he says,
"would you like to have it?"

Even as I reach out my hand I turn my head to the others in the room. They are both looking out through the window to the sea.

"Why thank you," I say. "Thank you very much. Yes, I would. Thank you. Thanks." I take it from his outstretched hand and place it in my pocket.

We eat our breakfast in near silence. After it is finished the boy and dog go out once more. I prepare to leave.

"Well, I must go," I say, hesitating at the door. "It will take me awhile to get to St. John's." I offer my hand to the man. He takes it in his strong fingers and shakes it firmly.

"Thank you," says the woman. "I don't know if you know what I mean but thank you."

"I think I do," I say. I stand and fiddle with the keys. "I would somehow like to help or keep in touch but . . ."

"But there is no phone," he says, "and both of us can hardly write. Perhaps that's why we never told you. John is getting to be a pretty good hand at it though."

"Good-bye," we say again, "good-bye, good-bye."

The sun is shining clearly now and the small boats are putt-putting about the harbor. I enter my unlocked car and start its engine. The gravel turns beneath the wheels. I pass the house and wave to the man and woman standing in the yard.

On a distant cliff the children are shouting. Their voices carol down through the sun-washed air and the dogs are curving and dancing about them in excited circles. They are carrying something that looks like a crippled gull. Perhaps they will make it well. I toot the horn. "Good-bye," they shout and wave, "good-bye, good-bye."

The airport terminal is strangely familiar. A symbol of impermanence, it is itself glisteningly permanent. Its formica surfaces have been designed to stay. At the counter a middle-aged man in mock exasperation is explaining to the girl that it is Newark he wishes to go to *not* New York.

There are not many of us and soon we are ticketed and lifting through and above the sun-shot fog. The meals are served in tinfoil and in plastic. We eat above the clouds looking at the tips of wings.

The man beside me is a heavy equipment salesman who has been trying to make a sale to the developers of Labrador's re-

sources. He has been away a week and is returning to his wife
and children.

Later in the day we land in the middle of the continent. Because of the changing time zones the distance we have come
seems eerily unreal. The heat shimmers in little waves upon the
runway. This is the equipment salesman's final destination
while for me it is but the place where I must change flights to
continue even farther into the heartland. Still we go down the
wheeled-up stairs together, donning our sunglasses, and stepping across the heated concrete and through the terminal's
pneumatic doors. The salesman's wife stands waiting along with
two small children who are the first to see him. They race toward
him with their arms outstretched "Daddy, Daddy," they cry, "what
did you bring me? What did you bring me?"

JACK MATTHEWS

The Burial

(FROM THE GEORGIA REVIEW)

Moses Beno

It come to me right away, like a smell or a far-off sound you been hearing for a long time, and all of a sudden there it is. Like thunder over the hills or a wind picking up from off the river or a coming out of the woods up north. It was just a hour or two before supper.

Only this, it come from the river. I was out there a hoeing corn, with my head down and my back straight, but not thinking of nothing but them little wild pea vines and such that grow like spider webs around the young corn stalks. And then it was I straightened up, just to rest my back a second and maybe wipe the sweat out of my eyes and from offn my forehead; and there it was, silent as a snake, a coming straight for the little landing where I keep my rowboat, but where they ain't room for nothing bigger.

But it was a coming, anyway. The air was so still that the smoke didn't hardly lift at all from the river, but just kind of laid there on the water downstream, where the boat was a coming from.

And then, right after I look, I could hear the chug of the engines, and it was like that chugging sound, it made me realize that they was headed straight for my little dock, like they meant to ram it right up into the bank. They wasn't nobody on the deck, even though it was a hot evening, like I said, and right in the middle of July.

Yes, I knew it then. They was something wrong. And I laid my hoe down and went into my house, where my wife said, "Why are they coming here?" and I said, "That is what I mean to find out."

And then she said, "Why are you taking down your gun?" And I told her I meant to have it in my hand in case I needed it. Then she just looked at our infant child in the crib, the way a woman will do, because it is the nearest thing to their heart. And right away after that, she looked at our boy, and said, "You keep your self right here inside," and he was just a staring at her with his eyes wide open, and he said, "I will."

They was both scared. I could tell. Because it was not right for a steamboat, a big riverboat like that, to turn from its course in the channel and head toward that little dock I made eight or ten years ago out of locust posts and whipsawed walnut boards. It was not right to see no body at all a standing on the deck and a waving their hand, the way they will sometimes do way out in the channel, even, if they see you a hoeing corn or slopping the hogs.

No, it was something else, and I knew it from the start, like I have been saying. And maybe my wife and boy, they knew it too.

They did not do anything as crazy as I thought they was going to do. They did not come right up to my dock and they did not get theirselves stuck in the mud bottom.

What they did was stop about sixty or seventy feet from shore, and then it was I saw the first sign of life. It was the Captain, with his Captain hat on, but otherwise in shirtsleeves. He come out on the deck and he just looked at me a minute, where I was standing in the path with my gun cradled in my arm.

He didn't say nothing, but went back inside; in a minute they was four men that come out with him on to the deck. They was river boat men, you could tell that. They wasn't gentlemen and they wasn't passengers. You could tell that. It didn't look like they was any sign of passengers at all, but then you couldn't really say, because whoever was on board that steamboat, why they was keeping theirselves inside. Whatever the reason was.

Then one of the crew members, he pulled a tarpaulin off something that was a laying there on the deck in front of the wheelhouse, and they was no mistaking what *it* was. It was a coffin. Somebody had hammered it together with some kind of cheap wood. It looked like yellow poplar from where I was a standing, there up the bank a ways.

The four of them got busy and lifted it up and carried it to the edge of the deck, and then they unlatched the side of the boat, what they call the gunnel, and I saw what they was a planning to do. They was a planning to bring that coffin a shore. And when I saw that, I knew what else they had in mind. They had it in mind to bring that coffin up the path, right on past my house, and take it to a little graveyard that lies about a quarter mile up the path, where it meets the road. I don't know how he knew it, but that Captain knew they was a graveyard there, and he knew this was where they had to land if they was a going to bury some body in it.

I did not move. I stood there and just looked at them while they unloaded that coffin into a rowboat, and then got in the rowboat and rowed theirselves to my dock. After they had first looked at me, they didn't wave or nothing, and they didn't look at me again. Now, you know that is not right. That is not the way people are supposed to act, unless they is something wrong.

While they was a rowing up to my dock, I just moved slow and quiet down toward them a little bit and the minute the Captain put his hand on one of them locust posts at the end of the dock, I said, "Take your hand off that post."

The Captain, he didn't move. He just lifted his face and looked at me. He was younger than I expected, with little bitty eyes that looked like he was tired to death.

"Get yourself back to the boat, and take that thing with you," I said.

The four crew members just sat there and looked at me, like they didn't care one way or another, even if I shot them dead, one by one. The Captain, he looked a little bit that way, too. He cleared his throat, like he was getting set to say something, but he didn't. And now he wasn't a looking at me. He was staring at his hand that was still holding on to that locust post at the end of my dock, and keeping the boat from drifting off. He was studying that hand, like he did not understand it.

"You heard what I told you," I said. "Get your hand off that post and take that thing back to the steamboat with you, and get yourself out of here."

The Captain, he did not move his eyes. He was still a looking at his hand, and he said, "We have got to bury this man. He died last night. He was one of my crew."

"You will not bury him here," I said.

Then he looked at me and said, "We don't want to bury him here. We want to bury him in the graveyard."

I lied to him and said, "They ain't no graveyard here."

"Well," the Captain said, "I happen to know that they *is*. I have been to it, and I know."

"They ain't no graveyard within five miles of this place," I said, lying once again.

"I know they is," the Captain said.

"Are you calling me a liar?" I said.

"No, but I am saying they is a graveyard up that path, up there by the road. Because I have see it."

"I could blow your head off for calling me a liar," I said.

The Captain nodded and said, "Yes, you could do that, but then there would be two bodies to bury in that graveyard up there."

For a minute, I just looked at him, and he looked back at me, and then I nodded, deciding to let it drop.

"Well, you still can't land," I told him.

"We don't want to bury him on your property," the Captain said. "I think you should understand that."

"I do understand," I told him. "And I understand something else. I understand what it is you have got in that coffin."

"It's only the body of a man," the Captain said. "Surely, they ain't nothing wrong with that."

"No, they is more than the body of a man that you have in there," I said. Because now I was sure what it was. I had heard the talk up and down the river, and every body was afeared that it was a coming back, any day now. I don't mind saying that I was afeared too. And had been for a long time at the thought it was coming.

"Nothing but a dead body," the Captain said with a tired look on his face and shaking his head.

"No, they is more than that," I said. "And I am not going to let you bring it ashore and carry it past my house to the graveyard. Because my wife and two children are in that house, and I will not let that thing get near them, because I know what it is."

"Aren't you a Christian?" the Captain cried suddenly. "Don't you understand that you can't refuse to bury the dead?"

"You take him on up the river," I said. "You can bury him at Hockingport, or even Parkersburg. But you can't bury him here, because I am not going to let you."

The Captain had let go of the post, and I had not even noticed. Now, the boat was floating free of the dock, but not one of them was making a move to row back to the steamboat.

"You know," the Captain said, "that if we wanted to do it that way, we could go on back to the boat and get ourselves some guns, and we could by God bring this coffin ashore and bury it the way it should be buried."

"You would have to bury more than one," I said. "if they was any of you left to bury the others."

The Captain, he stood up in the boat and pointed his finger at me like he was a preacher, and he cried out in a loud voice, "Do you know what you are doing? Do you?"

"I know what is in that coffin," I said. "And I intend to protect my own."

"It is a dead man, and that is all," the Captain said.

"It is a dead man, but that *ain't* all," I said. "Are you ready to swear that the body in that coffin is the body of a man who died in a knife fight? Are you? Are you prepared to swear he was killed with a pistol? A rifle? Was he hit over the head? Did he die of old age? Did he die of a cough? Did he?"

The Captain, he was sitting down again, and the boat was just drifting a little to the side, almost to where it would go into the weeds and mud of the shore. The crew members had not moved a muscle since we had started arguing. They might as well have been dead theirselves.

"At least, you are not a liar," I said. "At least, you are not ready to swear he died of anything but what you and me both *know* he died of. I will tell you something, I almost knew it the minute I saw you coming to the shore. They is talk all up and down the river, and people are afeared. So you take that thing and put it back on your boat where it belongs, and you take it up river to

Hockingport or Parkersburg or even Pittsburgh or hell, for all I give a damn. But you are not going to bury it on my land, and you are not a going to carry it up past my house with my wife and children in it on the way to that graveyard."

When I said this, I lowered my gun so that it was pointing right at the Captain's face.

For a minute he sat there, looking up the barrel of my gun, like maybe he wouldn't care a lot whether he died or not. Then he just nodded and said a few words to his men, and before long, they was a rowing back to the steamboat, as slow and sad as they had left it only a little while before.

I don't care. A man has the right to protect what is his. A man has the right to protect his home and his family.

They wasn't about to bring that thing, with what I knew was inside it, up past my house. Never. Not as long as I could hold a gun and keep them away.

Edward Clark

The first case along the river was at Chester. They was a Dr. Hibbard who come and looked at him. He was a steamboatman that took sick and they brought him into Chester, and they called this Dr. Hibbard, who come and examined him, and said the words that no body wanted to hear. Yes, it was cholera.

Dr. Hibbard, he started home through the woods on his horse after doctoring that steamboatman. In the middle of the woods, he took sick his self all of a sudden, so that he could hardly move. But he got off his horse and took a dose of calomel, and laid right down beside the road and went to sleep. When he woke up, he felt better, so that he could climb back up on his horse and return to his home. This was in July. The doctor recovered.

Yes, they was several other people in Chester who took ill, and most of them died. Fear rode on the wind and it walked in the summer heat. Van Weldon, a coffin maker, went every where and helped out, but he never got sick. John Ware, a harness maker, died of it; and so did William Torrence and a boy named Bosworth and a man by the name of Horton.

This was in 1834, the year of the great epidemic along the

river. But what I have to tell you happened the year before, and it has to do with a man named Moses Beno, up the river some twenty to thirty miles, in Meigs County, who I never actually met, but who I know about and still dream about ever now and then. I will never forget him and what he did and the way he did it, as long as I live. No, I never met this man Beno, but I listened to him talk, just that one time, and I will never forget it.

I was a crew member of a steamboat that plied its way up and down the river in them days. Oh, it was early, and a long time ago. Mad Ann Bailey had been dead only seven or eight years. They used to talk about seeing her on the porch of her cabin, smoking her pipe and telling about the Indians she had killed. And they was still Indians around, too. Some was married to niggers, and some was married to white people. Why, they wasn't no telling who them people up in the little valleys was, or who they come from. Some people talked about a clan up the Hocking Valley a ways that come from Thomas Jefferson's black maid, and carried Thomas Jefferson's blood in their veins.

But it is not them I wish to tell about. It is the man named Moses Beno, and what I seen one evening in the summer, when the cholera talk was just a starting, and people was afraid like it was the Devil after their souls.

Back in them days, if you saw smoke a coming out of the woods, it was almost as likely smoke from a campfire as from a cabin. Oh, this was a wild valley, at that time. And I was still a pup, just barely a year on the river, and I couldn't have steered that boat down the deep channel past Gallipolis without running it aground.

One of the boys on the boat got sick one night. He was a drinker, oh, about seventeen or eighteen year old. Not much older than me. I think his name was Jenkins or Tompkins. Something like that. I hardly had nothing to do with him, and when he didn't show up for his watch, why we just thought maybe he was sick from drinking. But it wasn't that.

And when they found him dead in his bunk, ever body on board that boat knew what it was. There was no mistake. And no body said nothing to no body else. And no body stepped out on the deck, even, unless you had to keep the old boat a going and you was a crew member.

The Captain, he got all of us who wasn't a standing watch

together, and he said, "Boys, I think you all know what this is
that has struck down one of our members. I think there is no
doubt in any body's mind. But I am not going to say the word,
and I am going to ask you not to speak that word, neither. If
any body on this boat finds out that a crew member died last
night, you tell them it was delirium tremens, because every body
knowed that boy was a bad drinker."

Then the Captain just stood there a looking at us, and not
saying a word, until we all felt sort of uncomfortable, like we was
thinking evil thoughts, or something.

But the Captain, he hadn't finished with us. And what he said
was that we was going to land at a place only five or six mile up
river, where he knowed they was a graveyard near by, so we
could bury the corpse right away, the sooner the better, and yet
give it a decent burial in a real Christian graveyard, instead of
just digging a hole and dropping it in the ground like a dead dog
or cat.

Well, we didn't none of us say nothing to no body. I am right
certain. But do you know, we didn't have to. Because every
body knowed what it was, but they didn't say nothing neither.
No sir! There wasn't no questions asked because no body had
any doubts. What they did was all stay inside their cabins, where
some of them prayed and some of them quietly wept and some
quietly got drunk. Some did all three, but there wasn't no body
left to care one way or the other, because the hand of Death, it
had been laid on our hearts, and each man was left a wondering if
he would be next to catch it and die. The truth was, the cholera
was some thing awful to behold and terrible to contemplate,
because a strong man could catch it and die in a few hours,
whereas a little infant might catch it and not die at all. There was
no telling one way or the other, and that was one thing that made
it seem even worse, because it was beyond human understanding, like the judgment of God Hisself, or maybe even the
Devil.

Whatever awaited us, we did not know. Like he said, the
Captain turned toward the shore a few miles up the river, and we
could see a little log cabin there on a knoll and a man standing at
the top of the bank, a holding a rifle cradled in his arms.

We anchored a little ways off the bank, and loaded that coffin
into a rowboat. I was one of them that rowed it right up to the

little dock there, and I saw every thing that happened, and heard every word that was spoke.

Yes, this was the man named Moses Beno, and he was a spectacle to behold. Why, he must have been seven feet tall and as skinny and knobby as a thorn tree. He was hairy and bearded, like he had been stranded on some desert island some place but had never been found. One eye was bleached like a fish scale, and the other was black. The afternoon sun was almost exactly behind his head so that he looked like he was wearing a halo of wickedness while he stood there on the bank and defied us with a rifle in his hands.

Yes, this was the man Moses Beno, and he was crazy. You could tell. It showed all over. He was dressed like a river rat, but he talked like a preacher, and he talked about that little log cabin like it was a palace, and about his family like they was all dressed in robes and wearing crowns, while he stood out there and protected them.

Nothing the Captain said would move Beno. He was liable to shoot the first man that set foot on the dock. That's what he said. "The first man that sets foot on that dock will get his damned head blowed off." He said it calm and steady, like he was talking about the weather. His voice, it was low and quiet, like he was almost a hoping you would not hear, so he could go ahead and shoot you dead if you disobeyed his orders.

They was nothing to do. We turned around and took that corpse about half a mile up the river, where we landed again and just dug a grave on the bank and dumped the corpse in it.

By now, the Captain was drunk, and so was one of the boys who dug that grave with me. I was not drunk, because I did not believe in whiskey and such.

Yes, the Captain read the service above that fresh grave, and he cursed as much as he prayed. Some body had told him Beno's name, and he spoke it like he was a speaking of a snake or the Devil hisself.

And it is true, Moses Beno was an evil, uncharitable, and un-Christian man.

Next year, the cholera epidemic hit the river for sure, and whether you believe it or not, I am going to tell you something: Moses Beno was the only one who come down with it in all that long stretch between Gallipolis and Hockingport, and he died like he was plucked by the hand of God.

I can't help it, whether you believe it or not.

But such is the Judgment of God, and don't you forget.

Calvin Beno

To the best of my memory, he never once spoke my name. And I don't think he ever looked at me, either. At least, I can't remember the way *he* looked, exactly.

But then he was the tallest man in the county, people said. He was so tall he was almost a freak. He was blind in one eye, and as skinny as a flag pole. So all them early memories have to do with him moving around so far above me, I can't hardly believe he saw the ground.

I do remember his smell, though. His clothes, they smelled sour all the time, from sweat and the sawdust of green wood, I suspect. He did not trust people. My Momma said if he went to town, why people would point at him when he walked past, and little children would sometimes cry. He had a long beard and long hair, and people said he was a mad man. Momma said he bought this land way back from the road, down on the river, to get away from other people. The only one he trusted was Momma. Maybe because she was scared half to death of just about every body, including him. All her life she walked with her hands folded in her apron, a staring at the ground like she didn't deserve to rise above it. And he never noticed me at all, like I just said.

Yes, I remember that day well. It was hot, and I was in the cabin, which was most always cool, because it was under two great big beech trees that would sometimes drop their little nuts a pattering down on the shake roof when the wind blowed at night.

Momma saw the steamboat first. Daddy was out in the garden, a hoeing the sweet corn.

Some times the river boats would blow their horns out there in the channel when they come by. Daddy never lifted his hand to wave, but some times he would stop and watch them, to be sure they went on by. I never had no body to play with, and Momma said I would talk to myself in whispers all day long.

She didn't talk, and neither did he. My infant brother, Ned, was too young to know any thing at all. This was in 1833. It had to be, because it was just one year before the cholera struck. I remember it pretty well. It is maybe not the first memory I have of life on this earth, but it is the first memory with almost all the details of a picture. It is the first memory that happened to me in a way that I was part of it. So that what happened that day, or what *begun* to happen, was about me, in a way.

That was the first time ever that a river boat turned around and started to come right toward us. Momma said, "Oh, Lord!" and I was so excited that I wet my pants, right there in the cool house where I stood a looking through the doorway and watching what Momma was a watching.

"Oh, Lord!" she whispered, and I was so scared at seeing that boat turn around and start toward us that I was peeing down my pant leg before I even knowed I had to pee. I remember that terrible sweet warm feeling down my leg even today, and the thought makes me want to roar like a wild beast.

When Daddy come in, I was afraid he would see what I had done, and I was afraid he would maybe kill me. Like they said he done a tanner up river before he come down here and built our place all alone by itself.

But he didn't look at me no more than he ever did. He just went up to the fire place and he got his gun. Momma, she asked him what he was doing, and he said something. I don't remember what, exactly.

And then he went outside and stood on the bank above the little dock, a waiting for the river boat as it got nearer and nearer.

Momma told me, "You keep your self right here inside," and I said, "I will."

Both of us stood there and watched him. The Captain of the river boat put up an argument, but Daddy would not let him bring the coffin ashore. It was the coffin of a man who had died of cholera, right there on the boat. They wanted to bury him right away, because they knew what it was, and they were afraid.

Yes, he knew what it was, too. He knew danger when he saw it. Because he had spent his life distrusting strangers and other people, and he could sense when danger come near, the way it did that day.

You could tell them river boat men was mad. But they could not get past Daddy, because he kept on a saying, "What was I supposed to do? Was I supposed to let them come ashore and poison us?"

He read the Bible after that. Most people thought he could not read, but it was just that he could not write anything, except for his name, of course.

But he sat there a reading the Bible, moving his lips with the words, for hours at a time, it seemed. All that winter, sitting by the fire, he read and read, while Momma sewed or cooked or carded wool. She did not hum or sing. There was no music of any kind in our house. It was as silent as the grave. That is the way I remember it always was.

Yes, I remember it all. I remember what he said it was, that he was out there coming between the poison of the world and us. He said it with his glazed eye fixed on Momma, and his mind lying somewhere behind that eye, fixed on the truth of what he was saying.

"Do you think it could be any thing else," he said, "that would make me keep you here where it is safe?"

No body said, safe from what. No body asked. Mother would not have crossed him with a word, not even a question. I would not have said any thing, for I was as afraid of him as of the world he talked about.

The next summer he died of the cholera. He did not say it, but he might have thought he was coming between it and us again. Standing somewhere off in his mind, like it was as real as a corn field, and they was this steamboat that come ashore like death, and he held up his gun and said, "No, damn it, you can not pass."

Mother, she has been dead almost a half century now.

But Ned, he is still alive, and so am I.

I sit on the front porch of a summer evening, and I look out and I think of that old time. It would be good if there was a place, like they say Heaven is, where I might see him again and watch him a while, and try to figure him out.

Or maybe it would be hell. Who could know? I surely do not.

Yes, some think his death was a judgment. Nobody could rightly argue against such a thought. But by God, you do not have to believe it either. Such an idea is too handy. I have learned that things just don't work out that easy and clear. Do you say I can't bear witness, because of the love a child naturally has for his father? Why, I didn't hardly know that man; and as for love, why, when I try to remember him, I realize that you might as well try to love a tree or a river.

No, love don't have nothing to do with it. Truth don't either. And God doesn't have nothing to do with it. None of the things you can name.

What it was, and maybe this is all you can say, is that there was this man who stood up there on that day and kept the steamboatmen from carrying a diseased corpse past our house. Then he died a year later, from the very disease he was afraid of.

All you can say is he come between something out there and the three of us, Mother and Ned and me. What he saw from inside his head, no body can say. What he was thinking when he was a laying there dying, no body can imagine.

Something was buried and festering in his memory already, when it first started. He learned to fear some thing, yes, and no body will see it like he did. But you can hold the world off only so long, and then it will come a knocking at your door.

He stood up there and held them off with his gun. For a little while, at least. Hell, he probably wasn't even *thinking* of *us* at the time.

That is all you can say.

Samuel Reed

My grandfather Beno had an older brother named Moses. There is a story that I have heard my father tell about him many a time. It is sort of a family legend.

What it is, there was a terrible cholera plague that hit along the river one time, way long before the Civil War. Great Uncle Moses lived right on the bank of the river with his wife and three children. Two girls and a boy. They say he was a big man, six and a half feet tall and wide as a barn.

Anyway, there was a steamboat coming up the river one day,

and he looked up from whatever it was he was doing and saw that they were coming out of the channel, headed right toward his place.

It was like right away he knew what they had in mind. He'd gotten the word from somebody that the steamboats were just full of the plague. Just crawling with it. In fact, people believed they were carrying it up river from the Mississippi, all the way from Memphis and New Orleans. And maybe they were right. Who can tell?

Whatever the truth of the matter, Great Uncle Moses wasn't having any of it. Several people had died during the night on the steamboat, and the Captain wanted to land and bury them on his property, right there on the bank, as soon as possible, so the damned stuff wouldn't spread any further. You can understand how he felt.

But like I say, Moses Beno wasn't having any of it. No sir, not for one minute. He picked up his gun and held them all off, alone. The story is, he didn't actually fire at any of them when they tried to bring the first coffin ashore, but he discharged a shot and put a dimple in the water right beside one of the oars, and that was enough to discourage them from coming any closer.

I imagine he could reload about as fast as you or I could take a shell out of our pocket and slide it in the chamber of a single shot. Well, maybe not quite that fast, but almost.

Anyway, the interesting thing was that the cholera came back next year, just as bad, and he was the only one in the whole area who came down with it and died. They say it hit pretty bad down river toward Cincinnati, and various other places. But not in Meigs County.

Great Uncle Moses had only one eye. I think Dad told me that he'd lost the other one when an old musket blew up in his hands while he was still a boy. That old black powder was treacherous stuff, and sometimes they'd make guns that *nobody* would know how strong the breech on it was.

That was years ago. They buried the corpses from the steamboat just upriver a piece, out of sight around the bend.

I suppose the old man thought he was in the right.

Funny, my calling him an old man. Because according to the genealogical research I've been doing, he couldn't have been over twenty-eight or twenty-nine years old when he died.

But people grew up fast in those days, and aged fast.

At the time, people naturally considered his death a retribution. You can see how they would.

Ted Adams

Somewhere over there on that knoll, there used to be an old log house. Grady Weldon told me the story when he was in his nineties, about a year before he died. His memory was sharp as a tack, and when he'd look out at you from those little blue eyes of his, you knew you were in the presence of a smart old man who had a lot of good stories to tell.

Like I say, he's the one who told me about the man who lived in that old log house. It was way back in the days before the Civil War, when they had cholera plagues along the river. One day, a steamboat tried to land to bury some passengers that had just died.

But this old farmer went out there on the bank with his rifle and held them off, made them take their corpses and bury them downriver near Gallipolis, in a regular graveyard.

The story is that the plague hit anyway, and in another month he was dead, along with his whole family. Wiped out.

I've often thought of that story. I've often stood here and gazed at that spot and tried to imagine what the cabin looked like then, and the river beyond.

Several people knew about it, and it's even included in one of the local histories, I forget which one. George Trice says it didn't happen here, but upriver a couple of miles, at the big bend. But I'll take Grady's word for it; that old man knew his local history, and of course he was nearer to the time it happened. Probably he had even known some of the people who could remember the event first hand. Even though it was a long time ago: about 1840 or 1845.

Like I say, I often think about that story and about the kind of man it would take to hold off a whole steamboat full of frightened, hysterical people. Obviously, he had a lot of courage, and thought he was in the right. Maybe he was.

At the time, people thought he got what was coming to him,

refusing Christian burial to so many people. God, they must have died like flies when that damned business started!

I don't remember whether Grady ever did mention the name of that man or not. If he did, I've forgotten.

But it's quite a story, if you think about it. And I'm convinced that's exactly where he lived, right over there. You can sort of make out where there was a clearing at one time. Grady said there was even a dock down there on the river, where the steamboat tied up that day.

Yes, there are a lot of stories hereabouts. Many of them forgotten. A lot of life has been lived in this valley, and sometimes you can almost feel it, like a gentle breeze you hardly notice, and wonder about all the strange things that have happened through the years, right here, right in this place.

EUGENE McNAMARA

The Howard Parker
Montcrief Hoax

(FROM THE CANADIAN FICTION MAGAZINE)

THE FACULTY LUNCHROOM was filled with hazards. It was a snide of whispers, a drone of bores, a fang of tired wit. In order to survive, Clyde had to move swiftly, find safety in numbers, say, *God, I'm glad you people are here. I almost had to sit with Them.* And that would put him safely with, and of, that table. Most of the bores had tenure, which meant that they had accepted this third-rate excuse for a college as the end of their careers. For the most part, they were aging in grade (never never never to make Full Professor) and bitter, sullenly looking back to the mediocre graduate school record, perhaps one or two cramped articles mined out of their drab dissertations, and certainly ahead to an abyss of freshman compositions.

Some of the younger instructors were bores too, but their boring quality lacked the earnest, existential quality that experience had given to the older bores. The younger bores had yet to develop style. There was O'Hara for example, who had gone through graduate school with Clyde. For two years, summer and winter, he had worn what looked like the same shirt. Clyde wondered if he had shellacked it so that he could simply dust it once a week and save on laundry bills. Now, he habitually skipped haircuts, wore tattered-collar shirts (*maybe it was the same one*) and neglected to remove the cleaning label from his suit. He and Clyde shared an office, and his presence daily filled Clyde with despair. How often had he seen him, tapping a paper on his desk with a red pencil stub, face uplifted in agony to some petulant student, the stapled yellow ticket glaring from his wrinkled suit sleeve. Such qualities had to be inbred.

The older bores usually sat together, pooling their pettiness. There was Max Garson, Chairman of the Department, an elderly Hoosier, hunter, fisherman, anti-Semite, anti-intellectual, and Dolly Elliot, a faded Southern belle who more properly should have been named Amanda. There was Edna Stefanson, a big, booming woman who looked like the late John L. Lewis, but without his dramatic eyebrows. Asa Kelly held that Edna was secretly in love with Dolly, but that Dolly was hopelessly and irrevocably bound to Max, who knew not of her devotion. Gerald Peters, an agonizing young man who was engaged in writing yet another draft of his dissertation, was one of them. Clyde posed to Asa that the reason the Drafts were *de facto* unacceptable to Peters' committee was that they were written out in violet ink. Asa theorized that Peters suffered from an unformulated lust for Garson and a consequent hatred for Dolly, which he masked by treating her with syrupy gallantry.

There were others to avoid as well; Richard Jaspar, the Complete Administrator, who possibly kept a frequency list at home of his smiles, cordial nods, casual hellos, and stopped functioning when his quota for the month had passed its mean, and Milton Warren, a white-haired ass, who very early in life had yielded to the small lust of wanting to see his name in annual bibliographies.

One day Clyde had to sit with them. Max had seen him enter, had caught his eye and called out loudly:

"Here's a place, Clyde."

Clyde was trapped. With a half-rueful smile, he joined them.

"Oh Gerald," Dolly was saying, "We're all dying to hear 'bout your organ."

Dolly's remark fell in one of those interstices in time when there is a simultaneous pause in every conversation in a room and there is a pulse of silence and whatever is said then echoes naked and alone. Gerald had recently installed a small electric organ in his apartment and was teaching himself how to play it. It was to this that Dolly referred, though the listeners at other tables may not have known this.

"I suppose you are all wondering," Gerald said with a tremulous smile, "how I was able to fit my organ into my small apartment."

"They do make them small these days, don't they?" said Max.

"My organ is smaller than the kind you'd find in a cathedral or a theatre, but it *is* as large as a piano —"

"Your place isn't *small,* Gerald," said Dolly, "You might call it *compact.* And it does have such an air!"

Gerald smiled again.

"You must all come over to see my organ," he said.

"And to see you play on it," cried Dolly.

Clyde reflected on the time when the conversation had gotten around the Great Houses in a certain town. Dolly had spoken then of having seen the residence of one of the last nineteenth century Captains of Industry, one Robert Catt. *The Catt House,* she had said reverently, *is the largest in town.*

Clyde and Asa regarded the scene about them with wry detachment. Asa was using the school as a way-station while he bombarded department heads, old friends, and chance acquaintances met at conventions with old off-prints and new vita sheets, constantly probing for the opportunity to get out. Clyde's case was more complicated. He was stuck. For some demonic reason, or perhaps simply because of a chance slack moment of inattention and lack of foresight at a crucial moment in his past, he had elected to write his dissertation on George Crabbe.

This, of course, damned him forever to the lower regions of academic life. What department head, possessed of whatever undreamed of depths of charity, could give a man preference, rank, promotion, if he had constantly to think of him as Our Crabbe Man? Think of having to introduce him to visitors! Yes, this is Clyde Griffin, our Crabbe man. One could imagine the swift look of incomprehension, of incredulity. Crabman? Why, it sounded like a Flash Gordon character. Who could ever take him seriously?

Clyde was in luck today, and made it safely to a good table. Asa was there, and Esther Goode, and Mary Stange. The peril of democracy was evinced by the presence of O'Hara and Clement Paul. Clyde thought of Paul as the archetype of his eternal adversary: a mover, a comer, an academic hustler, on all the impor-

tant committees, writing and publishing — competent, sound read-
able stuff too — all over the place. He would not stay here
much longer. Asa was leaning over the table, talking earnestly to
Mary Stange. Clyde sat down next to Esther, nodded quickly to
everyone, and arranged his food in front of him.

"I understand," Asa called down to him, "That the juvenilia
has just been edited."

Clyde supressed a smile. He and Asa had a running joke,
which unwound lazily like a bright thread through the dull fabric
of their days. They had made up a man: Howard Parker Montcrief, and a biography to fit. He was, they decided, a transitional
figure, living at the end of the nineteenth and into the twentieth
century. He had thus been privy to the councils of Wilde, Ruskin, Pater, indeed, any of the late Victorians they wanted him to
know. But he also knew and was intimate with Yeats, Pound,
Eliot, Hemingway, Fitzgerald, Wolfe —

"Even on the edges of the major movements," Asa would in-
tone as if perparing an article for *Literature in Transition,* "Montcrief remains an important figure if only because of the wide
range of his intellectual and artistic involvements."

The idea was to test the depths of duplicity and guile in their
fellows. One of them would begin in the manner Asa just had —
an open, casual reference to the latest letter uncovered, a fugi-
tive poem re-edited, the juvenilia — and the juvenilia — and the
other would pick it up, just as casually as Clyde did now returning
it, neatly, over the net:

"Yes, but I should have thought that nothing definitive could
be done until the Huntley Papers are released."

The idea was to see how far an anxious academic could be
pushed before he'd fall and nod and say Oh yes! *Parker Montcrief! Why I haven't read him in years.*

"Those Papers," Asa put in grimly, "won't be released until
Auden dies."

"*Long* after," Clyde nodded. "I shouldn't wonder if old Huntley himself hadn't had a hand in supressing the *Soho Sonnets.*"

"I wonder if Montcrief weren't the man in the macintosh in
Ulysses," Asa said. "That might explain Eliot's fit of pique when
Huntley brought out a limited and signed edition of the Cheap-
side version."

"I am afraid," said Clement Paul, quietly but distinctly, "That I don't know who you are talking about."

This was it. The crucial moment. Asa glanced quickly down the table at Clyde. Clyde caught just the glimmer of acquiescence: his turn.

"Howard Parker Montcrief."

There was a pause, the tennis ball, big, white, furry, floated over the net, bounced once, cleanly.

"I am afraid that I don't know the man."

There was just the suggestion of another pause, as if perhaps Clyde waited for a cock to crow, and then Asa closed in for the final volley.

"*Parker* Montcrief? Surely you're familiar with the Yeats correspondence. Around 1913, I think, just after he had met Pound."

"I often think of that great, gangling lout arriving in France with his precious letter from Pater clutched in his fist," Asa laughed, he looked and sounded exactly like Errol Flynn playing Robin Hood.

There was another delicate pause. Clement's face was set, masklike. Then he shook his head decisively.

"No. Absolutely a blank to me."

Asa nodded, as if in affirmation.

"Not too surprising, Clement. Most of his stuff's in manuscript, some of it in letters to friends."

"Only recently uncovered," said Clyde. "His sister was sitting on a good deal of the correspondence with Ruskin."

Esther Goode, who read Ayn Rand, and who showed absolutely no interest at all in the Montcrief ploy, turned sideways, her legs still crossed, her dress pulling tight across her thigh. Clyde stifled an almost overwheming desire to put his hand up her skirt and kiss her drooping wet lips.

"He spent most of his life on the Continent," Clyde said gloomily.

"Self-exiled," added Asa.

"I doubt if the whole story will ever be told about his relationship with Joyce's daughter," Clyde said in a thoughtful, judicious voice. "At least, not in our lifetime."

"I'm afraid the man's a mystery to me," Clement said flatly.

Clyde felt a grudging admiration for him. Given his kind of

character, it must have been excruciating to sit through a conversation like this and know absolutely nothing about it. Still, he had carried it off well, suggesting by the very flatness of his tone that what there was to know couldn't be too important, since *he* didn't know about it. The lunch conversation subsided into private murmurs again, Asa talking, or *rather* listening, to Mary, O'Hara boring Clement. Clyde tried to keep his eyes off Esther's thigh.

The first time he had seen Esther, three years ago, when they both started as instructors, she had been fatter than she was now. Still, he had noticed her. And now she was in full bloom, hips like jugs, full legs. They weren't the kind that seemed to be in fashion among the girls in his classes. Stick legs. Oh no. Esther's were like a ballet dancer's: strong, but smooth, with no ugly bunches of muscle. When she crossed them, her skirt pulled tight around them and the bottom of her thigh showed. Clyde liked that. When he had first seen her, her hair had been a wild blonde bush. Since then, she had cut it in Ayn Rand style.

"How is your seminar coming along" he asked her.

"All right," she said frowning down at her empty salad bowl. "I just don't have the time to give to it. With all these — *damn!* —"

She looked down at her knee, pulled the skirt back, twisting her leg up to the side. Clyde felt dizzy.

"Another run! Excuse me, Clyde."

She left. Clyde watched her leave. His eyes grew thoughtful. He saw them having a sinful late supper in the private dining room at Delmonico's, dark red velvet hangings, the rich wood panels gleaming in the candlelight, the champagne chilling in the chased silver bucket, her lying back, half-*couchant,* on the sofa, her breasts heaving against the plunging *décolletage,* her delicious dress en *dishabille,* her air totally *degagé,* both of them *in flagrante delicto,* he resplendent in evening dress, he does not remove his gloves, she slowly crosses her legs with a whisper of silk against silk, his glittering eye gloats on her exposed ankle.

"One of my students," Asa called to him, pulling him back, "went on a pilgrimage to Toronto last weekend. He's a McLuhanatic. Hovered outside the great man's office for an hour and couldn't get up the courage to knock."

"Hoping to touch the hem of his garment?" Mary asked.

"No, seriously, the boy is really hooked. He skulked over to McLuhan's house and took some water from the garden hose. Keeps it in his room now in an old Bromo bottle. Calls it holy water."

"Could he have known Montcrief," Clyde put in, more out of habit than anything else. Mary would never bite, since she wasn't interested in anything that happened after 1798, with the possible exceptions of the Dreyfus Affair, the McCarthy-Army hearings, and Watergate.

"It's probable," Asa frowned thoughtfully, "Wyndham Lewis was in Windsor in the early 'Forties at the same time Kenner and McLuhan were. And during the last American journey, in 1942, Montcrief spent a few days in Detroit —"

"Right across the river," Clyde cried. "It's unthinkable that he wouldn't have called on Lewis."

"Of course McLuhan was just a young instructor at the time," Asa pondered, "But one can't help wondering how Montcrief's keen eye could have overlooked him."

Mary stubbed out her cigarette and got up. After she left, for a few moments, Asa and Clyde were silent. Asa was staring thoughtfully at the wall.

"It is time, I think, Griffin, to go a step further in our research," he said. "I believe that the time is now ripe to show some of the manuscript to our colleagues. That bastard Clement for instance."

Asa's head snapped around.

"I have a whole batch of poems I wrote when I was an undergraduate. It's not bad stuff, but it's out of date — allusive, romantic, Yeatsian — *just the sort of stuff Montcrief would have been writing in his transitional period.*"

Asa's eyes glowed.

"You, Griffin, are going to do the definitive edition of these poems. To get into Esther's pants — don't look so shocked, your passion is transparent — you can't be the Crabbe man. You must become a Howard Roark type success. The Montcrief man!"

As they left, Asa gripped Clyde's elbow.

"And I shall help you," he whispered. Clyde was never sure when Asa was and was not serious.

Mary Stange caught Clyde by the arm as he was coming out of the lunchroom.

"How are you voting on this office hours thing, Griffin?"

Her tone, if not downright unfriendly, was chilling and formal. Clyde was caught off-balance. His usual response to such a question would have been to pass it off as a joke, or finally, still with humor, say that it was against his principles to tell. But Mary's blitzkreig approach so unnerved him that he had no time for dissimulation. "Why *for* the damn thing, of course!"

She nodded abruptly, still looking at him in an appraising manner.

"Fine, Clyde. I was sure that we could count on you."

They stood in the crowded hall, facing each other. Even though the noise in the hall was quite loud, he heard every word,

"If you betray us. We'll get you."

Then she was gone into the crowd without a backward glance. Could he have heard right? Who the hell was "we"? Clyde stood there for a long moment.

A fourteen-page mimeographed Philosophy of Office Hours had been prepared and circulated by the *Ad Hoc* Department Committee on Office Hours early in the week as preparation for the meeting. Garson had convened the committee in October to study the always nagging question of regulating the staff's consultations with the students. He had packed the committee with Peters and Stefanson, thinking to move things in the direction he had in mind from the beginning.

But something seemed to happen to the committee once they began to meet. For one thing, it took them quite a long time to come up with a report, and they had gone to a great deal of trouble to prepare this Philosophy of Office Hours which had a bibliography attached to it including articles from the *New York Times* and *College English*. For another, word was leaked that the report was going to be quite liberal. Garson had retired grimly into his office from whence he called them, severally, for little heart-to-heart talks about their respective Futures. But, as the time for the meeting to consider the report drew near, no one could quite add up the variables in the department and comfortably predict the outcome.

Asa came over that evening with the poems. While he worked

gleefully on them, adding a gloss, interpolating a few obscure Persian deities here and there, Clyde rewrote some papers he had done on Crabbe just after finishing his dissertation. They had been sent out to several journals and rejected. Now he substituted Montcrief's name for Crabbe's, changed dates and freely put in Joyce, Pound and Eliot whenever any of Crabbe's contemporaries appeared, adding Ibsen once or twice for variety. He also added *alienation, crisis, impending catastrophe, existential disaffiliation, loss of value* and *inability to love* as frequently as his old syntax would allow. Within two hours, they were ready for the composition of the Introduction.

"The important thing," said Asa, "Is to establish something in print as soon as possible. We'll send each exegesis off separately to different journals, *multiple submission!* And at the same time, the whole bundle to a publisher. If we can make it a book, then the acknowledgments will help establish the study as one that's been going on for a long time."

"I wish we could get into *Fuck You: A Magazine of the Arts*," he added. "Think how striking that would look in the acknowledgments."

Clyde looked troubled.

"I don't know, Asa. To fool around at lunch is one thing. But to try to trick the whole academic world —"

Asa leaned over the table towards him.

"You don't have any choice," he said in a dead voice. "Your days are numbered at this place."

"What? Say, do you mean Mary Stange?"

"Mary Stange? No, what has she got to do with it? Never mind her — she has no power — but Jasper does. He's bucking for Dean. And he'll get it."

"Jasper! What has he got against me?" Clyde looked puzzled.

"Edna Stefanson went in to complain to Garson and him that you were terrorizing her with obscene phone calls."

"Me? Obscene phone —"

"That's right," Asa nodded. "She was positive that she could identify your voice. But Garson told her she was crazy and threw her out of the office."

"I didn't know Garson had it in him," Clyde said.

"He doesn't. He just doesn't want any public upset before the office hours vote is over. He wouldn't listen when O'Hara told

him that he had seen you and Esther kissing behind the Fine
Arts laboratory and that he knew that you had spent all night in
her apartment."

"What *is* this," Clyde threw down his pen, "A dammed plot?"

"My theory is that the two were quite independent of each
other. But the point is, even though Garson won't do anything
right now, Jasper has his fishy eye on you. Whether you're guilty
or not, you're a controversial character. That makes you expen-
dable."

Asa paused.

"Besides, you're a Crabbe man. That alone makes you expend-
able."

"Why do they hate me? I don't understand."

Asa leaned back, rolled his eyes at the ceiling.

"Clyde, your contempt for Garson and O'Hara is obvious. You
aren't as clever at hiding your feelings as you think you are
Look: Edna is infatuated with Dolly, who in turn loves Max.
You despise Garson. If Edna can discredit you with Garson, this
will (a) make Dolly notice her as a moral heroine, and (b) at the
same time draw Dolly's attention to her as a sexually desirable
object — someone to whom people would want to talk dirty on
the phone."

"If I ever did want to talk dirty on the phone," Clyde said,
"She would be the last woman in the world I'd call It all sounds
too complicated for me."

"Don't forget O'Hara. He can see how infatuated you are with
Esther. Everyone can. He didn't know about Edna's complaint.
All he did was to put a few guesses together and come up with a
story which he was fairly certain was true anyway. I wonder if
he has a Jesuit background — But the upshot was to cancel out
Edna's story. If *one* were true, the other couldn't be."

"If I could get Gerald to run in and tell Max that I made an
indecent proposal in the washroom, I'd be home free," Clyde
tried to smile.

"No," Asa said seriously, as if the suggestion were really to be
considered. "That would only convince Jasper that you were
either a sexual monster or somebody too disliked by too many
people — he wouldn't care which — In either case he'd have to
convince Garson to get rid of you."

"Asa, what the hell am I going to do?"

"Just what you are doing," Asa said quietly. "Making a name for yourself as a scholar so you can get a better job."

They began to make up a list of smaller, newer, less prestigious journals which would not have an immense backlog of material, and hence could possibly bring out the stuff sooner.

"Say!" Clyde looked up, "How do *you* know all this?"

Asa chuckled.

"Milton Warren confides in me. *He* heard it all from Jasper's secretary."

Clyde groaned.

"Does everybody know?"

They went back to work.

Later, as Asa left, Clyde said somberly:

"I feel as if I were about to embark on a hazardous journey."

Asa looked at him.

"That was a quotation," Clyde recited, "From a letter Montcrief wrote to his brother just before he left England for the Continent in 1913. He was never to return permanently."

Asa nodded in satisfaction.

"You *are* the Montcrief man."

Report of the English Department Ad Hoc Committee on Office Hours. Respectfully submitted May 19, 1972.

Mr. Gerald Peters
Miss Edna Stefanson
Dr. Clement Paul (Chairman)
Dr. Asa Kelly
Dr. Milton Warren

1. This committee recommends that it be considered a major duty of each instructor to meet with his students for the purpose of individual consultation.
2. This committee recommends that it is desirable for these meetings to take place at mutually convenient times and places.
3. This committee recommends that each instructor should announce and post his office hours in a prominent place as early in the semester as possible. The department secretary should be given a copy of this schedule.

Minutes of English Department meeting May 19, 1972.

The meeting was called to order at 3:30 P.M. by Dr. Garson. The absence of quorum was suggested by Miss Stange. Dr. Garson said there was a quorum present. After some discussion, the report of the *Ad Hoc* Committee on Office Hours was accepted for discussion. It was MOVED by Mr. Peters, SECONDED by Dr. Garson that the report be taken up *seriatum*: CARRIED. It was MOVED by Dr. Griffen, SECONDED by Dr. Kelly that the "important" be substituted for "major" in recommendation one. After some discussion, Miss Stange MOVED THE QUESTION: CARRIED (as amended, "important" substituted for "major.") After some discussion on recommendation two, Dr. Garson proposed an amendment: That the Department Chairman give final approval to the times and places suggested by the individual instructors. Dr. Garson felt that it would be inappropriate for him to make this amendment himself and suggested that someone else make it in his place. After some discussion, it was felt that it would not be improper for Dr. Garson to make the amendment himself. It was MOVED by Dr. Garson, SECONDED by Mr. Peters to add the phrase "with final approval of such times and places be given by the Department Chairman." After some discussion, Mr. Peters MOVED THE QUESTION: DEFEATED. Dr. Garson pointed out to the members the vital importance of some kind of uniformity in the office hours, otherwise some people would be meeting far too many hours while others might shirk their duty. Miss Stange MOVED and Miss Goode SECONDED an amendment: that the phrase "It is strongly recommended that instructors schedule at least three hours per week for such conferences" be added to recommendation two. After some discussion Mr. Peters MOVED, and Miss Stefanson SECONDED an amendment to the amendment: that "three" be changed to "four" and that the words "on at least four different days" be added. After some discussion, Dr. Garson put the Question on the amendment to the amendment: DEFEATED. After some discussion, the Question on the amendment was put: CARRIED. The amended recommendation two was put: CARRIED. Dr. Garson pointed out to the department members that their duty lay in developing the whole student and that certain people in the administration were very much aware of how this duty was performed by the various members of the department. After some discussion of recommendation three, Miss Stefanson MOVED and Mr. Peters SECONDED an amendment to change "should" to "shall" in both places. After some discussion, the recommendation, as amended was CARRIED.

Miss Stange MOVED and Dr. Griffin SECONDED a vote of thanks to the committee for their hard work and dedication. CARRIED (Unanimous)

Mr. Peters MOVED and Dr. Warren SECONDED a motion to adjourn. CARRIED.

The meeting was adjourned, *sine die,* at 6:45 P.M.

THE INFLUENCE OF LA BELLE EPOQUE ON HOWARD PARKER MONTCRIEF

by Clyde Griffin

Henry James had referred to Montcrief as "our poor friend" when he had first met him at an afternoon of Lady Elcho's. Certain references in the Journals *from this period make it obvious that Montcrief was, for James, the embodiment of American vulgarism. He was Weymarsh personified. But for a time shortly after this meeting, Montcrief held a position as music critic on the nonconformist weekly,* The Clarion. *It was in that capacity that he attended the premiere of Strauss's* Elektra *at Dresden in 1909. A letter to Joyce dated Feb. 1st of that year reveals the profound effect the music had on him. The polyrhythms, the dissonances, and above all "a deep sense of the decadent and cruel hidden in [human] nature" were never to leave him. In a sense, Montcreif was born — spiritually — at Dresden in 1909 . . .*

Clyde read over what he had written with satisfaction. It hit just the right note. He had practiced it in the bathroom, searching for the proper blend of resonant seriousness, appropriate allusion, and an over-all tone of thoroughness. He had even provided potential nit-pickers among his future readers and reviewers with a minor error *(The Clarion* had not been a nonconformist weekly) which he knew would give them great joy to seize upon, and bend them to think more favorably of the book as a whole once they had established a psychic superiority over it.

He slipped a postal coupon under the paper clip and put the manuscript into a large envelope. This was the final step: the submission of a paper to be considered for next year's MLA convention. Two other papers had been accepted and were pending publication by journals in the middle rank of prestige. The edition of the poems was being read at a university press. Asa was busy creating a bundle of correspondence between Pound and Montcrief (c. 1915) with appropriate references to the works he was also in the process of composing.

Meanwhile, Clyde had gotten up enough courage to ask Esther out to dinner. It came off badly, since he had always been cowed by haughty waiters. The evening ended with Esther giving him a lecture on how terribly altruistic he was, how warped and hampered this made him.

Her interest in him, however negative, was thus established, and they went on a picnic one Sunday late in May. There was a slight sharpness in the air that day, as if winter instead of the impending summer was poised to strike. Clyde, ever open to premonitions, felt a foreboding of another fiasco. A brilliant yellow bird flew out of a bush near them, across a long slope of hill, to light in a tree near the bottom.

"What kind of bird is that, Esther?"

"I don't know. It was yellow, wasn't it?"

They saw several more birds during the course of the day. Neither of them could identify any of them. Esther stood for a moment on a little rise, looking up into the sun, the wind blowing her dress taut against her body. Clyde's desire gorged in him, even though he recognized the pose as literary, even filmic (Patricia Neal in *The Fountainhead*). His concept of the picnic was more in the mode of a nineteenth century bohemian artist's *déjeuner,* with him dressed in a soft alpaca coat, a flowing cravat, even a bowler, a white napkin spread on the lawn, Esther in the nude, posing casually in the background. Towards this end, he brought along a bottle of red wine and loaf of Italian bread.

They had a great deal of trouble getting the cork out of the bottle, as he had neglected to bring a corkscrew. They had no knife for the bread, so they had to tear chunks off of it, which, Clyde hoped, offset the cork *gaffe* and did add a touch of heavy gusto, perhaps a necessary tone of ruralism which the occasion demanded. There were bits of cork in the wine. There was no white napkin.

He tried to kiss her. There were bread crumbs all over, the bottle was in the way and got knocked over and spilled on his pant leg and had to be retrieved, and both of them were awkwardly propped up on one elbow on the grass. She allowed the kiss, however, returning it with some interest and fevor. But she wouldn't lie back, which was absolutely essential for stage two of Clyde's plan. So, after a few hot minutes of kissing, they cleaned up the remains of the lunch and walked back to the parking lot, holding hands, not saying much.

How would Howard Roark have handled it? Probably kick her in the belly first, then fling himself on her, never mind the damn wine bottle, warding off her attempt to knee him in the groin with a side-turned thigh. Clyde flicked a glance at Esther who seemed deep in thought. How committed to Rand was she?

Would it work?

Asa had once, in graduate school, tried to seduce the woman who taught a course in Medieval Romance. She was a beautiful woman, in her early thirties, warm and friendly, up to a certain point where all intimacy halted. She seemed to have no interest at all in life outside her subject. Asa hit on the device of using all the courtly love conventions in her presence. Since she knew all the conventions, knew them, in fact, better than anyone else in the world save an eighty-year-old scholar in Stockholm, how could she resist? And, in the Romances, the devices always, eventually, worked.

Asa took to sighing deeply in her presence, throwing agonized amorous expressions around when she was near by, contrived to look pale and wan, left awful sonnets lying on the table in the department common room, even groaned audibly when she passed him on campus, falling into a Pre-Raphaelite pose: Dante on the Ponte Vecchio seeing Beatrice for the first time, she surrounded by voluptuous women in flowing draperies, who flaunt their full figures at him, but she, all oblivious of his presence, floats along, the essense of spirituality. The impact on Dante is immediate: his right hand gropes out to the stone railing of the bridge for support as his step falters, his left hand is clutching at his breast as if to stifle his heart's wild leap. He stares, transfixed, taken, forever enthralled.

Asa perfected this pose, wore his clothing in artful disarray, brooded openly in selected settings on campus where she usually walked on her way to the library, waiting for her discovery of him and for her inevitable pity. Asa kept it up for over a month. Nothing. Not even the flick of an eyelash. He gave it up as a futile job. Obviously she was not as dedicated to her subject as she pretended to be.

Would the same sort of device work on Esther? Clyde stayed up that night reading *Atlas Shrugged*. He tried to copy the mannerisms of speech, and practiced poses of authority, strength, and brutal honesty in front of the mirror. No use. It all came off like a cartoon of Charles Atlas. It would have to be his coming debut as the Montcrief man or nothing. He had, at all costs, to get away from this insane school.

That summer, Clyde stayed in town, shut up in his apartment, correcting galley proofs for the Montcrief edition, which had been accepted by the first publisher they tried. All the articles were eventually placed too, along with two new ones, "Irony and Ambiguity in the *Soho Sonnets*," and "The Rhetoric of *Hobson's Choice:* Montcrief's Middle Period." But the most gratifying of all, he was invited to give his paper to the Literature in Transition Section at the MLA convention.

Even Paul was impressed when he heard the news in September. Esther came back from her family home in upstate New York with a tan, Peters returned from Cape Cod with another draft of his dissertation, and Mary Stange had left for another job at a school which was constantly hovering close to CAUT censure because its repeated threatening gestures towards the little academic freedom which precariously existed there.

"Do you suppose," Asa said to Clyde, "That Mary is a CIA agent?"

Otherwise, nothing had changed. Dolly smelled more strongly of lavender and seemed more desperately antimated when Garson was near by. Edna Stefanson glared at him in the halls, Jasper's smiles were frosty.

Clyde was so involved with his new classes and with finishing three more articles that fall that he had little opportunity to continue his pursuit of Esther. He was also engaged in negotiating a Montcrief casebook, tentatively to be titled *The Montcrief Di-*

lemma: Materials for Analysis, and a *Montcrief Reader,* as soon
as Asa could finish writing it. But when he would return from
MLA in triumph, a one-man industry, how could she resist him?
Already he was carrying on a steadily growing correspondence
with editors and scholars all over the country. A small denomi-
national school in Michigan invited him to give a guest lecture
and apologized that the token fee they were able to offer, but
hoped — *Three hundred plus expenses!* If this were tokenism, it
looked as if he would have a busy schedule of guest lecturing
this year.

Possibly too, there would be job offers at MLA — not certainly,
at the slave market, where gross bargaining went on in an atmosphere compounded of sweat and naked despair — but urbanely,
over cocktails, all couched in genteel tones, quietly dropping the
terms in front of him: full professorial rank, of course, immediate
tenure, a light load, perhaps a graduate seminar and shall we say
fifteen thousand to start? With an offer like that in his pocket, he
could play Roark for her all right, roar his defiance at Garson, quit
in fine style, tearing off with her hanging onto him.

It was the year when all the young instructors at the MLA
convention looked like the young Faulkner, with full drooping
moustaches, and wore thick-waled corduroy suits. It was the
year after full beards were fashionable, two years after the Year
of Frye. As soon as Clyde arrived and checked in, he went off
to see his publisher's booth. There was supposed to be an advance display of the Montcrief edition.

"Clyde!" A voice called to him as he pushed through the
crowd. "Over here!"

It was Asa, who was standing next to a booth which demonstrated a filmstrip machine, talking to a girl. As Clyde pushed
towards them he could see that the filmstrip was a production of
Dr. Faustus. The girl's badge proclaimed her as MARY FAL-
LON MOUNT ST MARY COLLEGE CHICAGO, ILL.

"I want you to meet a friend of mine, Mary." said Asa. "He's
an important critic in contemporary literature. The foremost authority on Montcrief in North America. Maybe even the world."

"Who's Montcrief," Mary Fallon asked. "How do you do. My
name is MARY."

"I know," said Clyde.

Asa's voice grew serious.

"Listen, Clyde. Did you hear?"

"What?" asked Clyde, craning his neck to see if he could spot the publisher's booth. "Listen, Asa, why don't we meet . . ."

"No *Listen,* Clyde," Asa leaned in close to him. "Just before I left for the convention I heard about it. Dolly was taking up a collection for a gift. Clyde, Esther is engaged."

Clyde's head stopped moving.

"What. Who?"

"Milton Warren."

The three of them went out for a drink. Asa had a meeting with a department chairman from Texas who seemed promising, so he left after the first drink. Clyde and Mary Fallon had several more.

"Miss Fallon, the taste of success is as ashes in my mouth. Tell me about life in Chicago, Illinois."

Clyde noticed that Miss Fallon had very kind and concerned eyes and an old-fashioned mouth — the kind that used to be called "bee-stung." But her legs were 1970's. Too bad. Boyish. Straight. You could run a two by four between her femurs and she wouldn't get a sliver.

"Who is this Montcrief, Clyde?"

Ah the sly hussy. Get a man to talking about his specialty and he would forget his hurt.

"I'd rather talk about George Crabbe," he said.

"I started out in this business as a Crabbe man."

"All right," Mary said agreeably, slipping her arm comfortably through his. "Let's have another drink and you tell me about George Grab. I'm in structural linguistics myself. I don't fool around too much with literature."

"Crabbe, Miss Fallon, was born in 1754 — His name is spelled with an 'e' at the end, which differentiates him from the George Crabb who was born some twenty-four years later anyhow and who died nineteen years *after* my man, and who was a philologist anyway — the one without the 'e' — Maybe you've heard of *him?*"

Miss Fallon was trying to get the olive out from under her ice cube. Clyde helped her.

"No. We ran an Eliot poem through the computer once."

Clyde gave her his olive.

"We seem to need more drinks, Miss Fallon."

"Call me Mary, No. I never heard of either Crab. Montcrief neither. Tell me about them."

"Mary. Is there much of a future in linguistics? I'm getting tired of Montcrief."

He ordered two more drinks.

"There's a great future in it, really great," the last word drawled, low, like honey. Then she sat upright and pulled slightly away from him. "I remember now! I saw your name in the program. Don't you give your paper tonight?"

"Uh. I don't think so. Where's my program? Listen, should we have dinner here or at Delmonico's? *Is* there a Delmonico's?"

"I'm not sure. I don't think so. But your *paper*. We'd better check. I'll go borrow a program from those people over there —"

She slipped out of the booth. Clyde sighed, and looked around at his colleagues who crowded the room, who were laughing, talking, confident, sleek, full of assurances. He watched Mary walking back. He decided that her legs weren't as skinny as he had too hastily thought they were.

"It's tomorrow morning. In Banquet Room B," Mary smiled.

"I'm just an old fashioned guy, Mary. Just a slow Crabbe man to the core. And I'm certainly glad that you're here. I almost had to sit with Them."

She sat down next to him again, put her hand down on the cushion between them.

Anyhow.

REYNOLDS PRICE

Night and Day at Panacea

(FROM HARPER'S MAGAZINE)

— AUGUST 1904

HE SCARED THE OLD NEGRO, not by intention but because the
path was wet and silent from the hard rain shower toward four
o'clock and because — soaked himself and tired from the long
walk — he looked more harmful than in fact he was.

The old man dropped the plank he had loudly wrenched from
the shed (there were three more at his feet, good dry heart-pine)
and said, "Who you after?"

Forrest smiled — "Nobody" — and knew it was the first lie
he'd told in months.

"They ain't here then. They ain't been here. I'm the man here
and the white man give me permission for this." He pointed to
the shed's south wall — half stripped of siding, the uprights exposed to day. Green light slotted to the dry earth floor.

Forrest looked to the floor. The white flint circles of masonry
were there, apparently unchanged. He walked forward to
them — and found the center of the room to be dark.

The old man said, "Who are you?"

Forrest bent to see. Both springs were there — far down in the
shade, clogged with the trash of years, spider silk, but visibly
running, their overflow absorbed by buried piping that, miracu-
lously open, carried the water outdoors, downhill. A chained
enamel cup stood on the rim of the closer spring. Forrest
reached to take it (seeing, as he reached, that its mate was gone,
ripped from its chain and nowhere in sight).

"Drink a drop of that, you'll die before night."

Forrest looked up, smiling. "I may anyhow."

"You sick?"

Forrest nodded and extended his soaked arms. "Pneumonia."

"Not in August," the Negro said.

"Then exhaustion. I have walked fourteen miles since break-fast. I have not eaten since. I am tired, wet, hungry: and my wife and boy have left me. I'm a lonesome ghost." He intended fun.

"You a man. What your name?"

"Forrest Mayfield."

"Where from?"

"Up north. Near Bracey, Virginia."

"That's a *hundred* miles."

"You been there?" Forrest said.

The Negro said, "Near it."

"Who are you?" Forrest said.

"Eighty-some years old."

"How long you lived here?"

"Most of my life — last forty years." The old eyes, yellow as piano keys, met Forrest's, unblinking.

"Where were you in April a year ago then?"

The Negro thought. "Bound to been here," he said.

"You were hiding then."

"What you aiming at?"

"I was here that April with twenty schoolchildren, a dozen mothers, three or four teachers besides myself, buggies and horses — there was nobody here."

The man said, "What's the name of this place?"

"Panacea Springs."

He pointed at the springs with a black hand folded and dry as Forrest's grip. "You think that's one of them healing springs?"

Forrest said, "The old folks did, awhile back." He squatted by the circles.

"They all dead, ain't they?"

"Who?"

"Them folks, and what they thought."

Forrest looked at the old face. It was almost surely smiling. "Dead and gone," he said.

The Negro said, "I know what I'm talking about. I worked at one of them places in Virginia, when I was a boy. Weren't noth-

ing but water. Make your pecker work. Like anybody's water."
He stood while the words worked over to Forrest through cool
damp dimness. Then he also squatted and faced Forrest, eye
level, eight feet away. Then he broke into high continuous
laughter — a boy's voice, young.

Helpless, Forrest joined him.

By seven o'clock they had cooked a supper of side meat and
hominy and kettle coffee on the smallest stove in the kitchen of
the abandoned Springs Hotel, using the boards from the springhouse as fuel. Then — the Negro leading — they climbed the
back stairs and walked the long hall to the front of the house, the
second-story porch. The old man carried the hot iron pan with
their mutual food; Forrest carried the kettle and the two spring
cups, having wrenched off the last one at the Negro's instructions. The porch floor was thick with branches, dead leaves,
fallen hornets' nests, a child's shoe; but a space had been cleared
at the breezy north end. The Negro headed there and, with his
free hand, motioned Forrest to sit in the better place — on the
floor with his back to the wall of the house, looking out at the top
of the thick undergrowth which had reached that high. The man
himself sat — as easy as a boy — with his back to the posts of the
lovely railing; he brought out his long folding knife, halved the
meat, and pushed the pan toward Forrest. "Half of it yours."

"Thank you," Forrest said and reached out his hand.

"Forgot your spoon." The Negro felt himself on both breast
pockets, reached into one, and drew out a tin spoon and held it to
Forrest.

"Where's yours?" Forrest said.

"Just one," he said. "Just one, for company. I got good
fingers." He flexed his long fingers — the spoon still in them.

So Forrest took the spoon; and they ate in silence — each con-
suming exactly half of all the pan held and hot cups of coffee. By
then, with the thickness of leaves around them, they were nearly
in darkness. Lightning bugs had started their signaling. The old
man searched himself again, found a plug of tobacco, and again
with his knife cut two equal chews and offered one to Forrest.
He took it, though he did not normally chew; and the silence
continued while they both made starts on the rich dark cud. The
quiet, the general peace was so heavy — despite the presence

three feet away of a strange old Negro, maybe wild, with a
knife — that it calmed whatever pain or fear had survived Forrest's day, the long hot walk. Or not so much calmed as pressed
it down by a greater force — his need for rest having found perfect harbor in this place like a happy afterworld for heroes de-
stroyed in the war of love, an Elysium promised in no religion
palpably here, tonight, and his.

At last the Negro rose, spat over the rail, and said, "Mayfield —
that your truthful name?"

"Yes," Forrest said.

"That name I told you — that won't my truthful name."

Forrest was certain he had heard no name — its absence was
part of the peace he'd felt — but he said, "All right."

"I don't tell my truthful name to nobody."

"That's all right with me. I'm obliged to you for kindness. I'll
be leaving at daylight."

"What you doing here?" the Negro said.

"You invited me to supper."

"In that shed, I mean — by them dirty springs." He spat
again.

Forrest also stood and quietly turned out the contents of his
mouth to the dark leaves below. Then he swallowed two mouth-
fuls of bitter spit in the effort to cleanse his tongue and teeth.
His back was turned to both the Negro and the springhouse, but
his voice was clear and firm. "This is where a young lady and I
made a promise some time ago. I came back to see it."

"You seen it, ain't you?"

"What was left of it," Forrest said. "The little you had left."
He wanted to laugh but his head turned instead; and he begged
the Negro, "Who are you? What are you doing here?"

"Don't blame me," the Negro said. "I never knew you, never
heard you was coming. All I thought was, nobody here for thirty,
forty years; nobody coming; I'm keeping me warm." Though the
heat of the day had barely lifted, he cradled his arms on himself,
rubbed his shoulders.

Calm again, Forrest said, "Tell me something to call you."

The Negro thought. "You need to call me, you call me Gid."

"Thank you," Forrest said. Then he sat again by the cold iron
pan and looked up to meet the Negro's eyes — hardly possible

now, with the progress of evening. "Beg your pardon," he said.
"I'd have blamed whoever I spoke to today. I'm in serious
trouble."

Gid nodded. "Who you kill?"

"That girl that loved me." Forrest felt that his answer was in
fact the truth, though he also knew it would throw this old man
into some incalculable response. He knew he wanted that —
strike, counterstrike.

"And you come back here to the place you found her?"

"Yes."

"They looking for you?"

"No," Forrest said.

"They starting tomorrow?"

"No," Forrest said.

"They already found her? and they ain't hunting you?"

"They got her. They don't care where I go."

"She white?"

"Yes," Forrest said.

"You crazy, ain't you?"

Forrest laughed a little and nodded. "But safe."

"Where you going tomorrow?"

"Back home. Virginia."

"Who waiting for you?"

"Kin-people, my job."

"That's one more thing than waits on me."

"What's that?" Forrest said.

"Dying. Sickness. That do make two." He was smiling apparently; his voice seemed filtered through a broad smile.

"No people at all?" Forrest said. "On earth?"

"Oh, I've got people, I'm fairly sure — two questions about
them: where they at? they waiting for *me?*"

Forrest said, "Who are you?" He waited a little. "I'm perfectly safe. Never hurt a fly. That's half my problem."

"Just killed your woman?"

Forrest nodded. The lie seemed a handsome gift, return for
shelter.

"Banky Patterson," the Negro said, "born what they called a
slave, around here — somewhere around here, some eighty

years past. A good while past, leastways, anyhow — this place won't built when I was born, not as I recall. What I recall — you seen I'm in my good mind, ain't you?"

Forrest nodded, all dark.

"What I recall — my mama belonged to a man named Fitts that owned this land through here, three hundred acres. His own house stood where we at now — we on his foundation; his house done burned — and my mama had a little place near your springs. They was there, same as now — no shed to roof them but dirty as now. Everybody round here cleaned them out once at least, as a child, and drank a cold handful — bitter as alum, tasted like a fart, a month-old egg — but nobody ever took a second drink and, sure God, nobody ever thought the world would *pay* to drink it. They did for a while — so it look like, don't it? So word got to me — but I never had to watch it: dances and sick folks, sick folks dancing. I got out of here." He stopped as if at the sudden end of a stock of generosity he'd thought was larger.

"When was that?" Forrest said.

"You tell me," he said. "That's most of my study — when things happen; how they got away from me." He stopped again and waited. "You can read. You tell me — if I'm eighty-some now, what was I at the freedom?"

Forrest calculated with his finger on the dark floor. "Forty-some, I guess."

"Seem like to me I was older than that — *feel* like it, anyhow. But maybe not. All my children were born after freedom, so I was still plenty good when it come. I never had married in slavery times. I waited it out. I knew I was waiting."

"For what?" Forrest said.

"A fair chance to see my way to the end. The Fittses was good but the Fittses was *people*. They didn't own many niggers, didn't need to — rich as they was, little as they farmed — so they sold they surplus off every year, or give them away to they children and kin. I had good eyes; I looked and saw; and when I got to twelve and they kept me on — twelve was when they weeded, before breeding time — I said to myself. 'You hold your own. Tend your own heart, else they break it to hell.' "

"Why did they keep you?" Forrest said.

"My mama fought for me. Some people say I was kin to the

Fittses, and they kept they own. I used to be brighter in the skin
than now; bright niggers darken — you notice that? I always
aimed, when I got grown, to ask Mama what was the truth of that;
but I never did and now I reckon it's past too late." It was nearly
full night.

"Her husband was Dolfus, lived some miles from here on another place; and when he come to see her once a month on a pass
from his master, she make me sleep in the yard if it's summer.
But that don't make me call him father, and I still ain't. The
thing I *know* is, Mama fought for me. I never heard her do it; but
Zack Fitts told me — they youngest boy, that I played with. He
say my mama come in one evening to where they all set talking
in the parlor and tell the master she need to talk. He rise up and
go to meet her in the hall and ask what's troubling — she they
head cook, they jewel — and she say, 'Banky.' 'What Bunky
done?' he say. 'Nothing,' she say, 'but you want to kill me, you
send him off. I dead in two months. My heart dry in me.' Any
nigger say that but Mama be beat — good as he was, he won't stand
that. But Zack tell me his papa say 'Julia, go home and sleep,'
and she know she won. So I had me two debts — to Mama and
Master — and I paid on them for all them years till freedom
come, a good blacksmith; I'm still strong as iron. And, like I tell
you, I had me a lesson — hold to your black heart, else they ruin
it. I ain't saying I turned into no steer — too many heifers
around for that, and they coming at me — but I tell you what's
truth, white man, once I done humped and groveled my way
through the two, three years I was getting my nature, I found out
that stuff won't all they claiming. You can buy it and sell it or get
it free; but it ain't going to cure one trouble you got, not the least
boil rising on your black ass."
    Forrest said, "Why?"
    "You tell me," he said. "I big a fool as you. By time freedom
come, my mama was crazy; had lost every bit of the sense she
had. Times was hard — niggers all turning wild, white folks
turning mean, white trash taking over, our master dead, Zack
killed in the war, Mistress and her two girls setting out here just
staring at the woods like the woods could help. So I'm at the age
you say I am — full-growed man — and leave her, leave Mama

with Dip her onliest sister and strike out north. Three reasons
why: no work round here, nothing I can do for Mama but watch
her eat dirt from the roadbank and pick at herself and some
Yankee pass through holding a paper saying ironworkers wanted
in Baltimore, a dollar a day. So I walk to Maryland, Baltimore.
No such thing. They ain't hiring niggers. I ought to come home;
but what I eat if I come here? old honeysuckle? So I walk down
on the map a little and penetrate all round the state of Virginia,
doing nigger jobs — a little blacksmithing, a whole lot of digging; everybody back then always digging holes."

"Were you still by yourself? Traveling alone?"

"I left that out. Well, to answer your question — yes, I traveled alone; light as rabbit fur. But a whole lot of time I was
standing still or laying down, and then I had company. Two or
three wives; three, four sets of children. All named for me."

"Where are they now?"

He looked round slowly, both sides and behind, as though
they all might have gathered while he talked, as though by speaking he had summoned not only their memory but their faces,
palpable bodies. "They ain't with me. I ain't with them."

"You've come here hunting them?"

"*No* indeed. They never heard of here. I never used to tell
present folks my past."

Forrest said, "Is the story you're telling me true?" He felt that
an answer was urgent to him now; he didn't know why.

"Pretty nearly, pretty nearly — the way I recall it."

"Then go on. Tell the rest, to now."

The Negro waited. "Nothing else," he said. "What you expect? Eighty years of getting up, working, laying down. You
want to hear all that, you need eighty years — which I ain't got."

"Please. Why are you here, in this old place?"

"Same reason as you — looking."

"For what?"

"My mama."

Forrest gave a little chuff through his nose — laugh, wonder.

"She be in her hundreds, if you counting right. Nothing but a
girl when I was born. She always say I parted her ways while
they still was green — I her live firstborn. I looking for her."

Forrest said, "Why?"

"To see her again, see do she know me, did she ever get her right mind back, let her blame me some."

"Blame for what?"

"Not fighting no harder for her, when I could."

Forrest said, "How could you?"

"Sat and watched her, talked to her, answered her questions. All the stuff I though was vain."

Forrest said, "Did you fight for anybody?"

"Me," he said quickly and struck at himself — palm on his chest, twice, dry hollow thumps. Then he waited and thought and said, "Who the hell you? all time doubting me, all time asking *why?* I'm telling you *what,* the *what* I recall, what I need to find. If you here to listen, you listen to *what.* It's all I giving."

Forrest also waited. Then he said, "Beg your pardon."

"I don't beg yours. Who you anyhow?"

Forrest told him again — his name, age, home, his work.

"And you killed your woman?"

"What she felt for me, yes."

"But she still living?"

Forrest nodded, in the dark.

"And you hunting her?"

The answer reached Forrest from wherever it had waited — or freshly burgeoned. In total dark it caused him no pain to give it to this rank old madman, powerless to use its news, powerless to hurt. "No, I'm not," he said. "I am heading home."

Banky said, "I'm there. And I'm ready to sleep. You welcome to sleep in my poor home." He waited, then cackled with laughter awhile, then bowed from the waist toward where Forrest sat, then entered the black house.

There were two large rooms on the front of the house, the old public rooms. When Forrest stood and followed Banky indoors, he found him waiting in the hall, hand extended — found him with his own hand in the unrelieved dark. The dry old skin gave a rustle at his touch — hide of a rattler, dragon, hermit; the skin of all Negroes he had ever touched, the tough loving cooks (spiteful and tender) of his own childhood — but he did not refuse it; and Banky said, "You ready?" Forrest gave a nod that no human eye could have seen, and felt himself drawn off to the right — the center of that room — till his toes were stumped by a low soft obstacle. "This your bed." Banky left him.

Forrest squatted and felt at the mass on the floor — it seemed a pallet made of carpets or draperies; *dirt, vermin,* he thought but didn't care. Again a huge weight, greater than fatigue, was pressing him earthward. So great even he did not struggle to see it — to name it, discern its need, its diet. He loosened his high shoes and lay and sank. No fear. Surrender.

After hours of pure sleep and lesser dreams, he came to this — he has walked for days, in familiar country, southern Virginia (pine woods, rolling pastures, the trees and the air one enormous bell ceaselessly rung by millions of thirteen-year cicadas); and now, tired but calm, he has come to a small town, a boarding-house. He has signed his name in the book which the lady keeps by the door (the house is her home, small but cool; she is beautiful, a widow in her early forties, well-spoken, fighting with lovely and effortless grace to feed her children, herself, her servants by the hard expedient of opening her doors to a streaming world — he feels that in the dream). She leads him to a room on the back of the house, far from noise; and once she has shown him the wardrobe and basin, she turns to go, then stops and says, "This bed is yours." There are two iron beds, one large, one small — she has shown him the small. He does not ask why, only sets down his grip (which by now he has rigged with rope, as a pack); but she smiles and says, "You have paid for a room that holds two people. Now we'll wait for the other." Then she turns and goes; and he does not see her, has in fact no life at all till evening, when from far at the other side of the house a bell rings supper and he washes and goes. And has eaten a full meal — steak, pan gravy, corn, snap beans, tomatoes — when the lady appears in the dining room door and, grave as a sibyl, searches the faces of his fellow feeders. It is him she wants. He knows that at once — there is someone behind her in the darkening hall — but he does not speak. A fellow guest — a young man at his right — is asking him the purpose of his journey. As he offers his face to the lady's search, he is also trying to answer the question, to remember the answer. Just when he knows and is ready to speak, the lady speaks also but not to him. She turns to the person waiting behind her and clearly says, "Mayfield — take the seat by Mr. Mayfield." An elderly man — white hair in clean long locks to his shoulders, the clothes of a wanderer (more nearly a tramp) — steps slowly forward. As he comes, he studies only the floor; his shuffling feet — a careful mover, forced into care by age and exhaustion. Forrest thinks he should rise to help the man; but the young man beside him again asks the purpose of his lengthy trip; so he turns and says, "My health — for my health," and by then the old man is seated beside him. Silently. Breathing hard from his effort, the latest leg of his own long journey, but no word of greeting and no look, no smile. The old man faces only his plate, empty and white; and when Forrest passes the cooling food to him, he serves himself in silence, staring down. The young man beside Forrest asks what is wrong — "You look quite well" — but Forrest is openly watching the old man and knows, though he cannot look up to check, that the lady stands on in the doorway, watching also. She is watching two — Forrest, the old man — and still she is grave, not from puzzlement but fear that something will not happen. It does. Then. The old man separates a biscuit into halves. He is Forrest's father. Forrest sees it; no question of doubt or error. He senses that the lady is also smiling. Forrest speaks the name — "Robinson. Father. Robinson Mayfield." The old man eats the biscuit slowly, still watching his plate. He does not seem hungry. He is eating because he has been led here where eating is expected. Yet when he has chewed it all and swallowed, he turns to Forrest, waiting with eyes from the morning which Forrest remembers; but with this crushing difference: their gaze is no longer needy or searching, merely polite. He is trying to think of an answer for this stranger smiling beside him. No one but Forrest is waiting now — all the others are eating blackberry roll (it is mid-July); the lady has gone. The old man — Robinson Mayfield undoubtedly, the father Forrest has not seen for twenty-seven years, for whom he now yearns — that old man carefully says, "Forgive me." He smiles. "Maybe so. You may very well be right. I am too tired to say. Too tired, too far." Forrest does not wonder *too far* from what or why his heart yearns so fiercely tonight for the simple sound of his own name spoken in that old voice. He says, "Forgiven," and turns to the food congealed on his plate.

In the midst of that (at the point where Forrest heard the dinner bell), black Banky came to the door of the room and stood —

no light. Since leaving Forrest here, he had been to the kitchen
to deposit their pan, then into the breezeway to wash his feet,
then back to the front room opposite Forrest's. He had sat in an
armchair and tried to sleep (he had not slept flat on his back for
years — danger of death) but had failed and succeeded only in
thinking: memory, faces he had hoped to see only in heaven (he
was certain of heaven, though afraid to go). So he'd crossed the
hall and listened for the sounds that would locate Forrest and,
more, tell his nature — the secret signals of kindness or cruelty
which, all his life, Banky had detected in darkness or light, near
or far. He stood and listened till the end of the dream. There
seemed to be sounds of quicker breath, two muffled blows of a
fist on the floor; but age had dulled the special keenness of his
organ of knowledge (that film of skin on his palms, in his nostrils,
across his eyes, that received from the world — or had for eight
decades — the urgent news: early warning or, rarely, confirma-
tion of clear path ahead, invitation to safety, pleasure, rest);
and silence had taken the room again. So Banky moved slowly
to enter the space, sliding each foot forward with fear and care
so as not to touch the body somewhere there asleep, afloat in its
secret life, cast away. Banky thought some of that — and felt it
all — and when he knew that his right foot had come to the
edge of the body, he stopped and waited a little, thinking. The
white man, covered in dark beneath him — in reach of all his
organs of touch, his harmful instruments — seemed quiet again,
entirely quiet. Banky slowly reached to his own hip pocket —
no fumbling now — and found his knife. He opened it silently
and in one move, fluid and quiet as a snake — no cracking of
joints — he knelt to the floor. His knees touched Forrest's warm
right hand where, abandoned in the dream, it lay open, empty.
The knife was in Banky's own right hand. He extended his left
and with perfect aim inserted his forefinger, dry, and touched
Forrest — lightly on the palm. Misery poured from the hand into
Banky like the jolting current he had known thirty years before
when lightning struck a mule he had just finished plowing —
fifty yards away — and slammed through the damp earth to burn
his feet. His finger moved on, still accurately, and stopped at the
crest of the sleeping wrist where a pulse thudded up to meet him
like cries, deep wide-spaced bellowing. He had not felt active
pity for years, maybe since his mother lost her mind and raved;

but he felt it now and knew its name — and also thought he knew its demand. He drew back his probing hand, extended the other — the right hand armed with the open knife — and with no need to gauge his force or feel for his target, he pulled the sharp edge once across the wrist. Lightly though, a dry rehearsal. He felt again. The wrist was dry and in that instant of touch Banky knew he could not help this man, not give him the peace that lay in his power to render now. He drew back his knife, folded it, and hid it in his pocket again. Then, knowing there was no chance that he would sleep and die unawares, he lay slowly back on the hard floor. Forrest was just beyond his reach — ten inches more than the length of his arm; and to ease the morning, the strange awakening, Banky's head was laid at Forrest's feet. At first light, Forrest would not have to wake to immediate sight of Banky's eyes, open and waiting.

He woke a good two hours past dawn, not from any external sound or movement or Banky's nearness or the light full on him through the tall east window, but from satiation, a rest so deep and venturesome as to give him the sense, as his eyes broke open, of lightness and cleanness, of a life unburdened by past or future, all an open *present* like a cleared field in sunlight. A sense of healing that bore in its heart no threat to end. His dream had sunk beneath conscious memory, and the turbulence that rose from its plummet was hope. He could live his life; he knew the way. And so he was happy — for twenty, thirty seconds. He had waked on his back and all he had seen till then was ceiling — the strangely intact, unstained white plaster twelve feet above.

But Banky had waited as long as he could. When he heard the final sounds of waking, he quickly rose to his knees again and was there over Forrest — "I'm going with you."

Forrest looked. All the causes of misery stood in him, large and genuine, his respite ended. "Where am I going?" he said.

Banky smiled — the first time. "You say. I'm following."

Forrest said, "Why?"

"You by yourself now. You need some help, need somebody. I'm free and ready."

Forrest said, "You're hunting your mother."

"Did I tell you that?" Banky said. "I was. When I came back down here, I thought I was — two, three weeks ago. First day, I come straight here, found this. I knew it was the place — somebody told me years ago the Fittses had sold out to some poor trash that had built this hotel and then gone broke. But before they left, they tore down all that was in my memory, except your springs and a tree or two I recognized. All the quarters was gone — my mama's house, Dip her sister's, the shop I forged in. Trees and foul water. So I walked on to Micro — I knew that good, ain't barely changed — and asked this old white man in the store if he heard of Julia Patterson. He told me, 'Sure. Old crazy Julia. Lived back yonder with all them dogs.' I ask was she live. He say he ain't seen her for twenty years; but he say, 'Don't trust me. Heap of folks I ain't seen ain't dead, and some of 'em come back and cheat me.' I ask him who must I trust; and he said, 'Won't she a Fitts nigger? Miss Caroline Fitts still living up the road.' He tell me where; so I go and there she — old as me, and meaner, and three-fourths blind; but she knew me the minute she` see my face. 'You're too late, Banky,' she say first thing. 'I'm poor as you.' It looked like she was, but she a big liar. I say to her I ain't here for money, but can she tell me where Mama is? She say to me, no, as quick as that. 'When she die?' I say. Miss Caroline say, 'Who say she dead? Maybe she living in the Washington White House, cooking angel food cakes for Teddy Roosevelt. Maybe she living in a shack near here with fourteen hounds, eating dirt and scratching. Either way, you're no good to her now. Too late, Banky — too late again.' She always been the bitch in the crowd, Miss Caroline; but she tell what her mouth think is so; so I didn't backtalk none at all. I say to her, 'True.' Then she say, 'Where you living?' and I ask her do she have a suggestion? She say no again; she quick as ever. I ask her, 'Who own that old piece of hotel where the house used to be?' She say, 'I do.' I told her I heard the Fittses lost it. 'Did,' she say, 'but the trash that bought it couldn't sit there and work long enough to pay the mortgage, so it's mine again.' Then she study me hard; then say, 'You want it?' I say yes — to see what she mean. 'Take it,' she say. 'It's mine to give. Take it, use it, and when you done, burn it. But don't come asking me for Julia again, or money or food. Don't bring me your face another time.' Then she shut the door. I swear to God — two weeks ago."

Forrest nodded. "I believe you. You've got a grand home."
He smiled, waved round at the big bright room.

Banky said, "This don't mean birdshit to me."

Forrest said, "It does to me." He had heard all that, half risen,
arms propped behind him. Now he reached for his shoes and
laced them on carefully. Then he stood and walked four steps
toward the door (nearer to the door than Banky, still kneeling);
then he turned and said, "I'm sorry, Banky, and I thank you for
kindness. I am going home myself — eventually, I hope." As
Forrest spoke, he knew he had said that last night; but it came
entirely differently now — like the mention of a gate, a goal, not
a terminus. "And the way I'll live, I cannot use you. I would be
no help on earth to you."

"Help won't what I needed," Banky said. "I helping myself"
He rose, faced Forrest, and extended his arms to demonstrate
his truthfulness — his strength well-tended for a man any age,
the knowledge of his years intact, unhardened, offered for use.

Though he did not know it, and never would, Forrest had
taken the thing he could use — the message imparted by Banky's
example, inserted in his sleep, the dream (still buried beneath
his memory) of his own lost father, burnt-out, abandoned. He
felt in his coat, withdrew his wallet, and extended a paper dollar
toward Banky. "For your trouble," he said.

Banky shook his head and held his place, his eyes full open,
unblinking on Forrest, who said again, "Thank you," and turned
and, finding his grip in the hall, went quickly out.

ABRAHAM ROTHBERG

Polonaise

(FROM THE MASSACHUSETTS REVIEW)

THAT WEEKEND I'd reserved to myself. My wife had been feeling tired and rundown and I'd arranged for her to take my sons to her sister's farm in Connecticut for a long weekend. The Torczyn invitation came in the mail days after the arrangements were completed, a typical Torczyn printed card that looked much like an invitation to a children's birthday party, and I saw Sally's relief plain on her face. It got her off the hook in two separate ways. Because she was always more than a little shamefaced when she left me to my own devices, even if it was only for a single night out at a professional meeting or for a shopping jaunt, and especially guilty when the housekeeper was to be off at the same time, Sally urged me to go to the Torczyn party.

"After all," she reminded me, "you'll be home alone for three whole days! Even Marthe will be off. What will you do with yourself?" In spite of my protestations that I liked being alone, or perhaps because of them, Sally behaved as if I could not get myself a meal or make a bed, and would perish of loneliness and boredom. If there was something genuine in her concern and something surreptitious in her sense of dereliction, real or fancied, there was also her sense of foreboding; as if after twenty-five years of marriage I should find that I could, in solitude, dispense with her person and presence, as if I might, somehow, somewhere — in her absence and as a result of it, discover that *femme fatale* whose passionate concern would once and for all put me beyond her reach.

If Sally was guilty and uncertain about leaving, she was also relieved, because she didn't like the Torczyn kind of party: too much drinking, too much food, too much noise, too much of the kind of emotional effusion and confusion which Sally found unappetizing and inelegant. Just as the fascinations of molecular biology, her field, and its mathematical abstractions were far more elegant than the grosser realities and disorders of the human body, so she preferred social encounters which did not call upon the deeper resources of her feeling or strain her self-control. It was a useful preference for the professional biologist, a preference she shared with Marek Torczyn, one of the less obvious reasons why both were so good at their jobs, why both had done such good research for the laboratories of the pharmaceutical corporation which paid their salaries. But such a trait, with all its elegant intellectuality, lacked the hearth-like quality for other human beings whose extremities might be cold and who might wish to warm at human fires.

When I came home from work on Friday evening, Sally and the boys were already gone and the house did, indeed, seem empty and echoing; but I soon had the Mozart playing and enjoyed the cold chicken and salad Sally had prepared and left me for dinner, that reminder of her role that she could not altogether forego, and the bottle of cold Soave I had shored up against the evening.

For the weekend I had jotted down a list of long-delayed household chores. The garden was its usual October shambles, crying out for raking, cleaning, pruning, fertilizing, liming, and all the rest of the necessary and time-consuming tasks which preparation for winter entails. We had had a gardener until a few years before when a couple of extra inches around the waist and Sally, impressed by what some of her knowing medical colleagues had written about physical exercise as a means of preventing heart attacks in the middle-aged, prevailed on me to do the gardening myself. Writers are, and have to be, sedentary creatures — they spend a large part of their lives sitting on their tails at a desk — so Sally always was urging me to play tennis or squash or go for a swim, none of which I did. So she had let the gardener go; she knew I wouldn't let things die, or wouldn't if I could help it.

By late Saturday afternoon I was able to check off most of the items on my list: the garden was, if only for a solitary hour, clear of red and yellow beech, maple and locust leaves; the roses were pruned and mulched, the grass and shrubs fed against the long winter ahead, the entire bucolic autumnal ritual indulged in and endured. Storm doors and windows had been hoisted to replace the screens and all the rest of the battening down for the cold had been completed. I sat in the living room, the curtains drawn against the wild orange anger of a setting sun, and permitted myself the cool luxury of a Mozart piano concerto and a quiet bourbon. No sooner had I leaned back into my favorite wing chair, with a half-groan, half-sigh of contentment, full of the spurious sense of achievement that completing such minor myriad tasks gives, when the telephone rang.

"Professor Wallace?"

I didn't recognize the voice and the *professor* put me off. It had been more than a dozen years since I had left teaching and I couldn't imagine what ghost had come to pay a call. "This is he," I replied hesitantly, the whisky abruptly cold in my stomach.

"Martin? I fooled you, hah?"

It was Leszek Stawinski, an old friend, a poet and translator of note, and if one must make such catalogues, my favorite Pole. "You fooled me all right, Leszek," I confessed, "but you know that's not very hard to do."

"But you answer to professor!" Mock outrage.

"Well, I was one, a professor that is."

"Yes, so you were, Martin," Leszek said, as if he'd forgotten, though I knew he hadn't. For Leszek, in spite of his own anti-academic tirades and rebellious anti-establishment posture, retained that European respect for the titles and honors of the academy. "You are coming to the Torczyn party? We'll stop off and you can drive us there. Anne and I will be at your place in one hour exactly. Okay?"

I remembered Leszek blind drunk at the last Torczyn party, what he had done then, and how much more anxious Anne would be this time. And how Leszek hated to drive, always got lost in the wilds of Long Island's suburbs once he got off the clearly marked parkways that brought him down from Nyack. They were two of the very few old friends I had left, so I felt called upon to say for them to come ahead: I knew I couldn't get away with not going to the Torczyn party.

Before he rang off Leszek told me that I'd particularly enjoy this party because Marek and Maria were giving it for the Polish novelist Stanislaw Danzig who was now visiting the States on one of the government cultural-exchange programs. Among the half-dozen best-known and most talented Polish writers, Danzig was an old Warsaw friend of the Torczyns and an intimate of Maria's sister Ursula for more than twenty years.

I had not seen the Stawinskis since early summer. Their faces had changed in those months but the greetings and embraces were warm as always. Only after I had taken their coats, given them chairs, and unthinkingly offered drinks, which Anne refused for both of them, did I see the new small red scar on Leszek's left cheek, over the bone which supported the horn rim of his glasses. The scar made his boyish ascetic face more wounded and wrathful looking than ever; it added to the rage of feeling and perception I knew pulsed behind his green eyes and that was fused with a flinty warmth that often became, unaccountably, sentimentality. My Slav soul, Leszek was wont to explain, half-boastfully, half-apologetically, flaying the Anglo-Saxon "coldness" he had never liked or understood; and in part paying a debt to his first wife who was a bona fide Anglo-Saxon. In spirit the man who had survived the Polish debacle of 1939 and the Soviet prison camps of Central Asia, the man who had endured a first marriage until his son was grown, and then endured the divorce which separated him from that only child he loved more than anyone in the world — except Anne — coexisted uneasily with the youth who still sang *Stenka Razin* or *Moscow Nights* in Russian in a tenor voice filled with tears, a voice that sometimes, especially when he was drinking, broke with the weight of his emotions. When deepest in his cups, he sometimes sang — in English — *Mein Yiddische Mama* in the heartrending was that only a boy orphaned from the age of eight who had spent most of his youth in a variety of rigid, harsh Polish Catholic orphanages could manage. But why *Mein Yiddische Mama,* I could never fathom. And who was to say which of his qualities, the "soft" or "flinty," had most helped him to survive the rigors of his life? Not I. Surely not I.

Leszek touched his fingertips to the new scar and told me that a surgeon had excised a cyst during the summer. He asked, for Leszek was vain about his lean good looks, if the scar was so noticeable. Obviously I had been staring. I adopted the rough style of our humor and told him it made the rebellious cast of his face more like that of the monstrous St. Just, that rebel he professed to admire extravagantly. "That scar's no revolutionary change," I remarked.

"Funny," he said, refusing to laugh.

Anne seemed more changed, although there were no visible scars. She wore a red velvet dress I remembered from at least ten years before, the tight bodice molding the fine shape of her shoulders and breasts, the skirt flaring away from her slender girl's waist; I could see where the skirt had been shortened to meet the fashions, showing more of her short yet exquisite legs. Her puritanical head was older and seemed out of place on that still young, still sensual body: her fine black hair swept back into a matronly pompadour proudly revealed the gray streaks; beneath, the small peregrine falcon's sharp nose and hooded eyes were weakened and softened by the disappointed mouth and uncertain chin. Her skin, lined and carelessly powdered, had the same pallor as the antique cameo that hung on a long chain between her breasts, face turned in, blank silver back out. More than anything Anne looked like the old Russian gentry of the postwar Tsarist emigration during its shabbier days in Berlin and Paris.

I wanted to lift the downturned ends of her mouth into a smile, but, already wreathed in cigarette smoke, she seemed a remote sibyl, tiny, regal, and lost-looking. Despairing of my own resources, no novelty for me in life in general and in human relations in particular, I excused myself and went upstairs to get the gift I had brought back from Japan for her. She took the damascene pin from the unfinished wooden box, held it in her cupped palm, as if the classical bamboo pattern spoke something only to her, and murmured, "Beautiful." The smoke brought tears to her eyes but no smile graced her lips and she didn't try the pin on. Leszek, glancing awkwardly at me, said, "You see, Anne, I told you Martin wouldn't forget you." Just what slight of the soul that unction was supposed to heal I didn't know, but the damascene pin did not seem quite the kind of remembrance Anne required.

On the way to the Torczyns, Leszek talked of how much he wanted to get the hell away from the cities. Nyack was too close, there wasn't enough space, the air and river were polluted, there were too many people, and it was too expensive. Over the summer, while I had been traveling in Japan, they had driven through New England, Leszek for the first time, and there he had discovered the setting in which he wished to live, a landscape with the bleak rockiness and dour pines which, he said, reminded him of his area of Poland. In great detail Leszek explained how, up in Maine, taxes, food, land and houses cost half of what they did in New York; and how, once they settled in there, he'd be able to give up translation, which he hated and did for a living, or at least give up a large part of it, so that he could devote himself to his own poetry.

"You know how Leszek is, Martin," Anne said, shrugging. "Now that we've got this house fixed up and comfortable, he wants to move. When we get the one in Maine in shape, he'll want to move farther north, to Nova Scotia."

"It's exile's foot," I said. "Worse than athlete's feet. Always itching."

They ignored me. "Now, honey," Leszek began, "you know that's not," but I cut off the long protest by announcing that we had arrived. I parked the car in bloody pools of leaves and we got out and walked up the drive. The Torczyns were always building new additions to their house, or taking pieces off, or rerouting the driveway, or reshaping the garden, so that I didn't even recognize the house. Leszek rang the bell and a woman I didn't know came to the door.

"Hello," I said, "you don't recognize us." It was clear that she didn't and was puzzled by our breezy manner.

"Come in," she said, hesitantly, "come in please." Leszek spoke to her in Polish but she seemed uncertain still.

"Aren't the Torczyns expecting us?" I inquired.

"Ahhah! the Torczyns," the woman exclaimed, her face relieved and smiling now. "Wrong house here. Torczyns live next door."

We apologized, Leszek taking the formal lead and, having kissed her hand gallantly, he led us out. Cutting across the lawn to the Torczyns' we laughed like children. "Did you see that?" Leszek whispered hoarsely, unable to control his guffaws. "She didn't even know who we were, but she greeted us like old friends and invited us in."

"Polish hospitality," Anne commented wryly.

"I didn't know Marek and Maria had any Polish neighbors," I said.

"That's because Maria's always complaining that she has no one to talk to, that she's sick of the little minds and conventions of suburbia, that Americans have acquaintances but no friends," Anne mocked Maria's histrionic manner.

"Something like that. Maria always manages to accuse us of not being good 'European' friends, though it's always *us* who call *them,* or we who drop by to see them. If we don't, months pass without our hearing from or seeing them." I laughed. "It makes Sally furious."

"It should," Anne remarked.

"*You* should be more sympathetic to Maria," Leszek advised. "She and Marek moved into this neighborhood so they could have some Poles around, and a Polish parish church. They wanted to see that the children wouldn't lose the language or the traditions altogether."

"Maria feels only her own loneliness," Anne retorted. A bitterness edged her voice that I had heard before and been moved by, as I was now, again.

This time it was the right house and Marek Torczyn greeted us with that formal manner and British-accented English which, with his own curious diffidence and disdain, was enough to make me feel slightly uncomfortable about being welcome. Always. Marek perennially seemed to be talking to people from some great height where he stood alone, and I was hard put to it to discover if that was because he spoke from some special sense of detachment twice removed or simply the illusion created by his height. One of the handsomest men I had ever seen, Marek was over six feet three inches tall, powerfully but gracefully built, with the lean aristocratic good looks which distinguishes Polish rulers from their peasantry, and makes them seem almost an altogether different race, which in fact they might well be. The differences were great but perhaps nowhere clearer than in Marek's nose — lean, acquiline, with slim slashes of nostril — and Leszek's ski-jump thicker nose, softer, with rounded nares:

they might have represented the two Polands, the two cultures, town and country, gentry and serf, which had struggled on that bleak plain for a thousand years and which were perhaps symbolized unwittingly by the two-headed Polish eagle — but the resemblances were only physical.

"We've just met your neighbors," I told Marek.

"Have you?"

"I led Leszek and Anne up the garden path to the wrong house," I added. "Didn't recognize yours. You've changed something again, haven't you?"

"No," Marek answered. "You just haven't been here for such a long time, you don't remember."

"Oh come on, Marek, don't talk like your wife," I said acerbly.

He laughed. "See what intimacy will do." Then, ruefully, added, "Well, proximity anyway."

Marek ushered us into the living room where Maria, in the rich linguistic mélange of an English full of accents and intonations which combined deep-throated Polish consonants and upper-palate French vowels, exclaimed, "Ahha, they are here!" She embraced Leszek even before he could manage to kiss her hand and I saw the tremor of lip beginning that Anne swiftly suppressed. "Leszek," Maria cried, "how I am missing you! I am happy you come already. And you are missing vodka. Four, five rounds already." She squeezed him audibly. "Is very good to see you." She only just touched Anne's shoulders and grazed her cheek. "Anne —" when Maria said the name it sounded like *on* "— how nice you can come." When she pulled me against her, holding her arms around my waist so tightly that I felt all her body against mine from chest to knees, she lowered her voice to husky provocative intimacy, whispering. "Martin" — *Maar* . . . *teen* — "my love. I am glad." She did not look behind me for Sally, and when I made a quick explanation of Sally's absence, Maria waved it away: it was clear that for her Sally's absence was not a thing of great moment.

We were the last guests to arrive. The others already sat around the room, glasses in hand, talking: Danzig, the Polish novelist, his wife, Helga, Maria's sister, Ursula, and an elderly white-haired American lady named Cartwright. Marek served drinks almost before we were seated and when he came to pouring the chilled vodka for me, his face dared me to say "when" sooner than he thought properly manly and befitting the occasion. I don't enjoy drinking much. I don't like the taste of alcohol and I don't like the way it always depresses me. People generally take that to mean that I get drunk easily, and nothing could be further from the truth. Perhaps it was because I had plenty of body weight to absorb the alcohol, perhaps because I didn't like drinking and had no intention of getting drunk, but whatever it was I didn't easily get pie-eyed. I had over the years tucked away as much and more than most men, though with the advancing years I had taken care not to drink on an empty stomach and even, before an evening of heavy drinking, to take the precaution of a tablespoon of mineral oil. All I want, an old friend of mine, now estranged, used to say, is a fair advantage; and that was all I took. But I never reached the point of enjoying it.

Drinking had always been a bone of contention between other people and me. Jews don't drink and are therefore less manly. Writers are supposed to drink; it invites the Muse. Look at Dylan or Scott or whomever. Publishers, editors and agents always softened you up for the negotiations or refusal to negotiate with the preliminary flatteries and martinis before the post-prandial brandy-and-coffee realities. So I had also learned to drink to survive, learned to handle alcohol as part of the reality of American life in which I was immersed. Yet I had not forgotten the domiciliary virtues and puritanism of the wine blessed at meals which was a blessing to conviviality, but nothing more. Because of that there was often working in me the half-triumphant, half-bitter pleasure of watching those who had set out to get me drunk, get drunk themselves, their eyes slowly glazing and going out of focus, their movements first becoming studied then uncontrolled, and finally their speech, that holy attribute of the human, turning thick-tongued and bestial. With Marek and Leszek, an evening could not be enjoyed without the protection? stimulation? lubrication? of alcohol, and when Anne and I were there, or when Sally joined us, there was that eyelinked understanding of those on the sidelines who did not dance the polka.

Marek handed me a glass so full of vodka that I had to sip it quickly to keep it from spilling over; and I had to keep myself from knocking it back in a single draught as a gesture of bravado.

I sat and listened uncomprehendingly to the rattle of Polish talk around me and thought how much the Torczyn house had changed. Maria and Marek had given it an almost European air that was a triumph, or at least a Parthian victory, over its Cape Cod, mass-produced boxiness. Besides the money spent, the house showed the signs of Maria's torrential energies and talents, and of Marek's taste and travels. And Maria *was* a torrent, a female geyser of energy and feeling, a marvelous housekeeper, a superlative European-style cook, a gardener whose thumb was so green that in the short space of a decade it had made her roses prizewinners at the local flower shows.

Everywhere there were traces of Marek's scientific peregrinations, the conventions that scientists now went to as casually as weekends to Atlantic City. A three-stringed *gusla* from Yugoslavia hung diagonally on one wall; a serpentine chunk of California driftwood made into a lamp sat on a small Louis Seize end table; a magnificent Caribbean conch shell lay open and clamoring on the cocktail table. A semi-abstract painting in the early style of Kandinsky showed two women in shifts, their backs turned and their heels dug into Kentucky blue grass as high as their thighs. They tried to hold back two leaping, dark-red Irish setters. Right next to the painting was an ancient cloth-of-gold tapestry with a woven battle motif arraying a Polish peasant on foot in battle against a Teutonic knight in armor on horseback. The Torczyn house held too many old things for the straight lines of the architecture: it gave me an uneasy sense of tension and misgiving that I could never quite master, as if I were being called upon by an act of imaginative will to join unbridgeable opposites, traditions that met, if anywhere, asymptotic to infinity.

Anne's eye caught mine, her face shaping that expression of seditious rebuke which every married writer knows as the disapproval of his wife's soul; it does *not* say stop looking, or stop listening, or stop paying attention: instead, it commands, cajoles, cries out, "Stop observing! Stop eavesdropping! Stop gathering material!" In short, stop being a writer. As much use as to say stop breathing. Once Sally's sister, when she thought she saw herself in a story I had written, had burst out, "Martin's a sponge, a lousy old sponge soaking up people's feelings and thoughts, trying to soak up their secret lives, so he can squeeze them out into his writing." She hadn't meant that as a compliment either; and Sally had taken great care to convey her sister's tone to me when she relayed the comment.

The dinner did Maria and us proud. Spanish melon and prosciutto, *boeuf bourguignon,* saffroned rice, a huge escarole salad with chickpeas and hot French garlic bread. Dessert was pear and boursin and port salut. All of it washed down with bottle after bottle of Valpolicella which Marek kept urging on everyone — no glass was ever more than half-empty before he refilled it to the brim. I enjoyed the food and wine and, seated as I was between Maria and her sister Ursula, both of whom did the serving, I was pretty much left out of the dinner conversation, though I listened.

Danzig, in slow, precise English, halting now and then to lapse into a Polish phrase which either Marek or Leszek translated almost without pause, told how he and his wife were going to see America, the *real* America, via Greyhound bus, making a great six-week loop through the country — Washington, D.C., New Orleans, the Southwest, Los Angeles and San Francisco, then back through the Middle Western "heartland" to Chicago and finally back to New York. Leszek rebuked him for not including New England on the itinerary. Although it had taken Leszek some twenty years of living in the States before getting to see New England, he told the Danzigs that New England was the real heart and mind of America, its source and conscience, the fulcrum of political power, and should, therefore, not be bypassed. I had, over the years, heard many such conversations and they always left me distressed. Listening to Leszek and many other foreigners, visitors and those who had lived in the country for many years, I wondered if I had learned anything about the countries I had traveled in and the several I had lived in other than my own, for foreigners seemed to me always to have missed the shape, the essence, the meaning of America and its spirit. Yet, when I despaired that the country would forever elude them, I remembered de Tocqueville and Bryce: it was at least possible, even for intellectuals, to penetrate to the heart, though I knew that the America those two had analyzed was a far simpler place than America was now. And in the quiet of the nights, when I thought about it, I wondered if anyone, even those American born and bred, had penetrated to the heart of the country.

Danzig's face was interesting, strong, regular features, intelligent, reluctant brown eyes, and an almost effeminately mobile mouth. He wore the conventional European writer's uniform: gray tweed jacket with black leather elbow patches, dark gray trousers, a black slipover and dark tie which contrasted with a soft-collared white shirt. Much later, when we left, I saw that he even had the rest of the uniform, the double-breasted tan trenchcoat, epaulets and all, à la Camus or Humphrey Bogart, as you chose. Of course, he went bareheaded though whether a navy beret was hidden in a capacious pocket I didn't know. The dark clothing gave Danzig a funereal air belied by the studied cheerfulness of his manner. He had the writer's watchfulness, of others and himself, but with Danzig it seemed the true writer's self-absorption: this was a man who lived with his finger forever on his own pulse. His wife, big, blonde, and Brunnhilde-like, with a thick, beer-barrel strength that contrasted with Danzig's sapling slenderness, was altogether another sort, outgoing and really gay, with the air of having so often seen and endured — perhaps even staved off — the very worst that nothing and no one could frighten her again. Danzig looked a dapper forty-five; his wife an unkempt decade older, but perhaps that was because she watched him with a maternal alertness simultaneously touching and nauseating. Helga spoke no English though she said she understood quite well; but she would occasionally address me in schoolgirl French that indicated she understood considerably less than she thought — in both languages.

It was Maria's sister Ursula I watched most attentively. If the loss of one's mother tongue wrought havoc with a writer, as it had even with Leszek who, in anguished transcendence that reminded me of Conrad's epic wrestling with the language, had learned to write English with a purity of style imbued with a bleak Polish-Russian poignance that, at the white heat of his inspiration, managed to fuse all three cultures, for an actress the loss of her native language was catastrophic. Leszek had come first to England and then to America as a youth in his twenties; Ursula had arrived in the United States only the year before, more than fifty, bereft of any way to practice her art. Acting required companies, players, stages, most of all an audience that spoke the same language and shared the same traditions; of this there was none in the United States for a Polish actress, however talented and skilled.

Maria and Marek had brought Ursula to the States from Poland the year before and, with characteristic generosity, supplied affidavits and passage money for her and for her twenty-year-old daughter, Wiktoria, and then taken the new arrivals into their house until they could find their footing. Wiktoria had picked up the language quickly, taken a job, made some friends — she was young, winsome and pretty — and was already expert at the frug and the monkey; but for Ursula things were more difficult. She read English fluently and spoke it in a careful, grammatical way; but it was not enough to find anything but the simplest of jobs at a firm where she had to stand all day on a line packaging cosmetics. She and Wiktoria did not want to be burdens, not even dependents, so they took what jobs they could get because they needed the money. I had later tried to find Ursula a job on a Polish-language radio station, then on a small Polish-language newspaper, but I'd failed at both. Though I saw that she had lost weight she could ill afford, her face grown drawn and paler, and it was apparent that she was terribly lonely, I never heard her complain. Staying with the Torczyns saved her from the worst isolation and deprivation of new immigrants, but it also impeded her, kept her from being forced to make new friends and to rely on English for communication.

I liked Ursula, respected her courage and dignity, and enjoyed seeing her. It was not merely that she had once been an exceptionally pretty woman, that she was still lovely, with a strange, birdlike quality, as if she might suddenly take flight, but for the fact that one of her wings was broken. She bore a remarkable resemblance to the Italian moving-picture star, Giuletta Massina, but a combination of the peasant girl Gelsomina of *La Strada* and the haute-bourgeoise lady of *Juliet of the Spirits*. Married to Matthias Maciek, one of Poland's foremost moving-picture directors and one of Danzig's oldest friends, Ursula had led a stormy life with him for more than twenty-five years until, four years before she left Poland, he had divorced her for a twenty-three-

year-old actress who was then his leading lady. Maria had told
me that this was the step which finally persuaded Ursula to consider emigrating. Before that she had insisted that if Poland was
for her a prison, she would not deprive Wiktoria of a father so
long as Maciek kept coming home — even as infrequently as he
did. The divorce was the watershed: after that, since Maciek
apparently felt only the most sporadic and brief desire to see his
daughter, Ursula saw no further reason for remaining in the Warsaw *cul de sac* and she had agreed to Maria's prompting to come
to the new world.

Brandy and coffee were served in a small sitting room that
adjoined the living room; it faced out on a garden and through
the floor-to-ceiling thermopane windows I saw the Turczyns'
bronze-leafed plum tree, its brown-barked arms raised as if to
pirouette. Slightly stupefied by the flood of food, liquor and conversation, I sat silent until Leszek commented that I was unduly
quiet and Marek, pouring another dollop of cognac into my glass,
said that I was drunk. When that failed to produce the appropriate
rise out of me, Marek invited me to see some guns he had
bought.

Marek's study was on the first floor of the house, a booklined
room I knew well, for I had visited it often enough when Marek's
back had gone out of kilter shortly after Ursula and Wiktoria had
arrived from Poland to stay with them. I remembered particularly a sweltering August day I had come to bring Marek some
books and help him pass the time of day. Naked, except for
white undershorts, he lay there like an Indian fakir flat out on a
board, hoping his disc would slip back into proper alignment, his
big frame gaunt, his face pinched with pain, the skin over his
bones an oil film that looked as if it might evaporate if a breeze
stirred. Before I could ask how he felt, he had burst out: "It's a
goddam harem, Martin! A harem, do you hear? Five women in
this house, and now" — a piercing groan — "my mother's coming to visit too!"

I made jokes about sultans and harems and some men having
all the luck, but he didn't even grin; and then, for the first time, I
noticed that his sideburns had gone completely white. It had
been a bad time all around and only after surgery and a back

brace had Marek been able to resume his daily round; by then he
was a different man.

"How do you like these?" he asked, pointing to where an
ancient musket, a flintlock fowling piece and a ball pistol hung
on the wall. I took each one down, as I was intended to, sighted
down the barrels, cocked them and went through the whole self-
conscious routine of appreciation while Marek told me about this
little London greengrocer who had been inveigled into buying a
truckload of such antique weapons and been unable to sell
them. As a result Marek had been able to buy those three beautiful old guns for a song. Yes, *for a song* — his very words. I
didn't ask what song they were designed to sing, because I knew,
a threnody that all of us in the 20th century knew well enough.

Abruptly, without transition, or so it seemed to me, Marek was
telling me about his father. On several occasions over the years I
had met Marek's mother, an old whitehaired woman, broad-
boned but thin, with an erect carriage and a face whose flesh had
been winnowed away to the fine stubborn bones. Always in
black, with little white lace ruffs at the throat that called attention to the wrinkled flesh rather than hid it, she had the manner
of a woman once beautiful and still proud. Marek had inherited
both her good looks and her pride, and he sometimes talked of
her, much less frequently of his sister, whose picture sat on his
desk and on the mantelpiece in the living room, forever young,
she having been killed in the Warsaw Uprising, but this was the
first time he had talked about his father to me.

Toying with the chased silver decorations of the ancient pistol,
Marek exclaimed, "*Absolutely without fear!* He was that kind of
man. A mad man." Marek looked up from the pistol. "Once we
went to the movies in one of the tougher sections of Warsaw. I
couldn't have been more than twelve then. We were sitting in
the theater, my father, my mother and I, when someone behind
us began to heckle my father about taking his hat off. And when
my father ignored the heckling, the man began to make some
abusive comments about that — toff? —" Marek looked at me
inquiringly, and when I nodded, went on, "— not taking his
goddam headgear off. My father stood up, turned around, calm
and slow as you please, and gave the man a whack across the
head with his walking stick, a heavy shaft of old walnut he
always carried — and a riot started. I thought we were going to

be lynched. The lights went on, the whole audience piled out into the street to get this toff, but my father simply led us out behind him, shielding us with his cloak and brandishing that stick, ready to do battle with all of them."

"Without taking his hat off?"

Marek nodded, grinning. "Without even considering it." He laughed. "Mad. Absolutely lunatic. I guess *they* thought he was crazy too. They couldn't believe that he meant it. What man in his right mind takes on a whole neighborhood — the man he had coshed had dozens of friends there in the audience — and so calmly? So they let him march my mother and me through the whole damn mob of them though my father had opened that man's scalp from his crown to his ear and his friends were clamoring for our blood."

"If you read enough books like *The Scarlet Pimpernel* when you're young," I remarked, "you begin to believe that's the way a man must behave."

Marek hesitated. "Is that bad?" he asked, but clearly he was not inquiring of me.

"Sometimes," I replied anyway.

Marek pulled the trigger of the pistol and the hammer clicked futilely. "Yet, if they had asked him politely, with the proper *Pan*, I'm sure he would have removed his hat without a murmur." He replaced the pistol on the wall hooks, "A gentlemen's code." An uneasy silence fell, airless, between us.

"What happened to him?" I asked, sensing his unspoken urgent desire to tell me about his father as if it were another presence in the room, a Banquo's ghost or *Doppelgänger*. To ask was very difficult for me: I had my own reluctance to ask Europeans of our generation that kind of question, especially Eastern Europeans.

"The Germans killed him," he said, slowly, taking a breath between each word. I had learned that expression well and long ago, not merely from having been in the war. It told of some brooks too broad for leaping. Ask an American such a question about relatives killed, even an American Jew, and he would usually say, "The *Nazis* killed him, or her, or them." But ask a European and invariably you hear instead, "The Germans," usually with a bitterly scatological adjective preceding. It said a great deal about their foreign policies and ours — and their histories.

I nodded. Recognition? Sympathy? Acquiescence? Sorrow?

Shared injury? All of my father's family had perished. I never knew what that nod meant when I made it, but I knew that it hurt my stiff-necked human pride to be forced to it.

"My father was one of the Poles," Marek continued, "who knew it was coming back in '36 and '37. He wasn't one of the ostriches. He didn't think Poland was a great power, the way the Colonels did. So he tried to persuade some of his richer friends to set up a military hospital. He got all kinds of contributions, wheedling, cajoling, God knows how! He even managed to get one of his Counts to lend him a castle! Then he started to put a military hospital together inside it. All by himself. By the time the Germans came in '39, beds, staff, surgery, almost all of it was ready, but they were desperately short of drugs. My father kept the hospital in medical supplies, scrounging things everywhere. Then one day he heard of someone on the outskirts of the city who was supposed to have a stock of morphine, a pharmacist, and off he went in the car to get it. By himself, of course. No one could be spared from the hospital, the wounded were flooding in, and he wouldn't listen to anyone's advice to take someone along with him, even a driver."

"And?"

"We found him three days later, in the car, dead. Germans were already in the suburbs. It was a German bullet that killed him, but it might have been one of our own *Volksdeutsch*. Nobody knew. No witnesses. Or at least none we could find."

"All that courage coming to that," I lamented, and not for the elder Torczyn alone.

"Everything comes to that," Marek said. He carefully realigned the guns on the wall. "Absolutely fearless man," he repeated.

"An epithet? Or a compliment?"

"Always both for me, Martin. More epithet than compliment, I suppose."

"How Jewish that sounds!" I said, trying to make a joke of it.

Marek smiled, took my arm and led me toward the landing. "My mother is always hinting darkly, and privately, that way back there somewhere there's some Jewish blood."

"Welcome to another persecuted elite!"

"Don't I have enough trouble being a Pole?" he retorted, and the sentence had a singularly American ring.

*

Downstairs, Stanislaw Danzig and Leszek were deep in a quarrel about the hopelessness of contemporary Polish life. Leszek was scathing on the monopoly of all aspects of life by the Party and the dreary fact that the alternative was the medievalism of the Church, the Cardinal and Our Lady of Czestochowa. Where, Leszek grumbled, could any man of good will, modern spirit and clear intelligence find a place in contemporary Polish life? No wonder Polish young people were disenchanted, interested only in out-landish clothing, hairdos and the wild irresponsibilities of rock-and-roll music and dancing when even the best of their elders had all been compromised by hypocrisy and cowardice, poisoned by gloom and lethargy and despair. As we sat down I caught Maria's raised eyebrow, but since Marek ignored it, I felt free to do so too: if explanations were forthcoming, they ought to come from him.

Sitting on the edge of his chair, Danzig patiently explained that geography was Poland's tragedy; forever caught in the nutcracker between Prussians and Russians, what else could Poland do? I saw that he was uncomfortable both because of the obvious political reasons — he was a guest from a Communist country, which re-quired twofold discretions — and because of the necessarily careful choice of English words. But for Anne, Mrs. Cartwright and me, and his own sensitive courtesy, Danzig would gratefully have lapsed into Polish. With a smile that was only slightly patronizing Danzig reminded Leszek that Leszek had been out of the country since 1940 and didn't know anything about the nation's postwar life, couldn't, in fact, understand it because he hadn't been obliged to endure it. In short, though Leszek was a Pole by birth and sensibility, he had forfeited his birthright by emigration, was now more American than European, more outlander than native, and could not therefore speak with authority and insight of the Polish predicament.

A few years earlier, when the dangers of arrest or imprisonment for emigrés had for a time dissolved in the first lukewarm East-West rapprochement, Leszek had visited Poland to attend an inter-national P.E.N. Club congress of translators. It had been his first trip since he had left the country with the Germans on his heels — and he had stayed for a month, traveling over most of the country. Until then he had sung the virtues of his homeland to us, romantically remembering Poland as superior to the crass refrig-

erator and corporation civilization of the States, proudly extolling
Polish courage and gaiety in the face of adversity. No wry comments of mine about Colonel Beck or Marshal Smigly-Rydz, no
minor recollections of their alliance with Hitler and the Third
Reich until they were themselves threatened, no realistic notice of
Polish living standards or political authoritarianism, had been able
to dispel his roseate vision. But the reality of Poland had. After his
visit Leszek was bitterly disillusioned, critical of what he called "Polish reality" in ways which made even my crabbed comments seem
generous and compassionate. "Truth," Leszek had said then, tears
in his eyes, "they don't even recognize it any more. They don't
know what the word means. My countrymen live under the lie,
with the lie, for the lie. And they've lived that way for so long,
tangled up with it like men entwined with a filthy whore, limb
locked with limb, that they can't tell prostitute from wife any
more." It was, for Leszek, an unusual image because, however
inconsistenly, he was extraordinarily prim and puritanical in his
language and in his notions of what was acceptable sexual behavior.

I reminded him of observations Orwell and Aldous Huxley had
made decades ago, and of his own Polish Czeslaw Milosz's more
recent notion of "controlled schizophrenia," particularly among
Polish intellectuals and Party members. What they wrote, Leszek
fulminated, was nonsense. All the Poles were simply cowards and
liars, and flattered themselves by thinking that they were being
political realists, detached and objective, when they were in fact
barely able to keep their proverbial stuck-up noses out of the ruck
of the big lie in which they were immersed. Where they were not
knaves and Soviet sycophants, Party hacks and fools, they were
naive and ignorant of the world as it was. Now, pointing his finger
at Danzig like a prosecuting attorney at a trial, Leszek insisted that
Poles no longer knew the truth, about their own or the outside
world, because even those who were in so-called opposition had
swallowed so much of the Party line, they didn't know fact from
fiction. "And that's why we have no literature, no novels, no stories,
no poems, no plays, that speak for Poland," Leszek concluded.
"Even the Russian writers and intellectuals have more courage."

"Yes," I murmured, hoping to smooth things over, yet maintain
the truth, "but so recently and so discreetly." No one seemed to
have heard me. "And much of that ugliness comes not simply from

cowardice or venality, but from being locked up there for two decades for Poland and more than four decades for the Russians. Having people like Mr. Danzig travel, letting him see the world with his own eyes, his own way, may help matters."

A slow flush rose up from Danzig's collar to his temples. He drew back in his chair, as if to hide in its recesses. "You cannot understand what it is like," he protested to Leszek.

"I saw. I was there. Warsaw. Cracow. Lublin. Gdansk. All alike," Leszek insisted, his hand chopping the air with each name like a guillotine. "Cut off! Provincial! Sunk in the muck and mire of pieties: Catholic, Marxist, nationalist."

"You cannot know," Danzig repeated, his mouth trembling, his head sad and shaking.

Marek tried to intervene then, to dissipate the heat of the argument, remarking that Polish writing was the best in Eastern Europe, and so were Polish films, paintings and sculpture. How much could one expect under the circumstances?

"*Under the circumstances!*" Leszek roared, incensed. "That pernicious phrase! The rotten apple in the garden. My God! Under the circumstances! You make art *out of* the circumstances, *because of* and *in spite of* the circumstances, not under the circumstances. That's why none of you have done anything important. Because you write *under* the circumstances. To hell with the circumstances!" He, for one, Leszek insisted, refused to demean Poland by comparing its achievements with those of its "Balkan" and "barbaric" neighbors. If Polish accomplishments could not be measured against France's, Russia's, England's, America's, yes, even Germany's, then the hell with it.

To divert the ferocity of Leszek's attack on Danzig, I tried to give — to impose? — some detachment and historical perspective on the discussion and in so doing, of course, made an error and committed a rudeness far more profound than Leszek's fierce concern. I said that writing under the circumstances, precisely because of what Danzig called Poland's tragic geography, had always been the tradition of Polish arts and letters, that as a result Polish writers and painters had always suffered from provincialism, from being cut off from the rest of Europe not only by their political misfortunes, their continual partition among more powerful neighbors, but by its nationalist consequences, so that even the heroic

Mickiewicz had not been able to transcend that provincialism, not been able to rise above the boundaries of his language and culture.

Poetry, Danzig almost spat, is what is left after a work of art is translated from one language to another. I knew the line; however unwittingly, I had struck him, I saw, a far more grievous blow than Leszek had. And I was *not* a Pole and consequently *not* forgiven. In a slow, bleak chant, Danzig keened his lament that only that literature lasted which was attached to and disseminated by great political power. The literature of England had reached its peak in the 16th century when England became a great power. The age of Elizabeth I had produced Shakespeare and Marlowe and the greatest burst of literary genius Europe had ever known. When Louis XIV made France the leading power on the Continent, Corneille, Racine, Molière, Pascal, La Fontaine and Rochefoucauld were the natural consequence. The same was true of 19th century Russia when, for the first time, the land of the Tsars became a power to be reckoned with in Europe; and it was also true of 19th century America, first come to great power and to great literature after the Civil War. No, Danzig mourned, his words a dirge, it was not the quality of the writing, nor even the genius of the artists, but the power of the guns, the network of foreign trade, the wealth of the mines, the fields, the factories and the banks, that brought the literature of a nation to the attention of the world and conferred greatness upon it. Though I saw some truth to what he said, I also saw no need at that point to put my finger on the flaw in his logic; that is, to remind him that perhaps part of the thrust that brought a nation to political and economic greatness was involved in bringing its arts to flower as well.

Danzig had had his nose rubbed in it in America already; I did not wish to add to his discomfiting. Leszek had taken Danzig to one of the leading American magazines to see if it would publish his translations of some of Danzig's best work. The editor, a man of worldwide reputation, had never heard of Stanislaw Danzig; and if he hadn't, then Danzig and his work couldn't be of much importance. His magazine, one of the redoubts of the so-called WASP Establishment, would therefore *not* be interested in publishing Mr. Danzig. The editor had spoken of Poles and Polish writing with that faintly supercilious Anglophile snobbery which made Poland sound like Outer Mongolia. Another editor, whose avant-garde magazine had pretensions to an international, multilingual and intellectual audience, had at least read two of Danzig's stories in French translations. But he said that no one in America gave a damn about Polish writing and refused outright even to look at Danzig's manuscripts. At the most illustrious Jewish literary magazine, Danzig, hopeful that there at last he would find a sympathetic ear, was brimming with stories of what it had been like to be a Jew and a writer in Poland during the long nightmare from 1939 to 1945, but the editor, bored and indifferent, had not even asked to look at any of Danzig's work.

Because of these findings, and though I had not intended it, I had struck Danzig a painful blow where he lived: I had said that his own work, that painful distillation of his time and place, his feeling and experience, had no pertinence outside of Poland; I had privately confirmed and sealed his public rejection. Now I was aware of what had happened, but the damage was done. Worse, I genuinely believed in what I said and in the logic of my position — that snare and delusion of intellectuals! — though it moved against the grain of my feeling and consideration for Danzig the man; it had carried me beyond the bounds of courtesy. I reminded Danzig that some writers did translate, did transcend time and place and language, that one could read Sophocles or Job or Dante with pleasure and pertinence without being able to read ancient Greek or Aramaic or medieval Italian; this was not true of Mickiewicz, for example, whom I had read in several English translations, verse and prose.

"The translations are all terrible," Leszek interjected. "Worse than terrible, banal."

Moreover, I added, the Bible, for one, had been written by a people without much political or economic power. In fact, the Israelites were nowhere as powerful as the empires among which they had lived and with whom they had contended — Egypt, Persia, Babylon, Rome — but their literature had outlived that of all those great kingdoms. It had even almost transcended the language of its original, being read and enjoyed and cherished in Latin, Greek and English, among many other languages, while only a tiny remnant still read the ancient Hebrew. The great empire, the true kingdom, I concluded sententiously, is of the spirit.

"Mickiewicz," Danzig said, so slowly he seemed to be gasping for air, "is a Goethe, a Shakespeare, an Isaiah — yes, *our* Goethe, *our* Shakespeare, *our* Isaiah. More, one cannot ask."

For an instant the Delacroix drawing of Mickiewicz stood before my eyes, the long hair, the acquiline nose and strong jaw, the heavy-lidded eyes and sensual mouth: it was almost as if I were in the act of insulting the man as well as the poet. "No, Mr. Danzig," I said, "the mournful truth is that for the great geniuses, for the great works of art, the truth of the human heart, not the truth of the nation or the state, is the essential truth, perhaps the only truth." To my astonishment, I saw that Leszek was nodding vigorously. "Because of that," I continued, "Sophocles and Dante are read everywhere, while Mickiewicz is read only in Poland; and because of that Dostoyevski and Balzac will be read wherever men continue to think and feel, when Sienkiewicz and Reymont are only footnotes in histories of European literature." I was sorry I'd been carried away and made a speech, carried away not only by my logic but by my rhetoric; and now I could have bitten my tongue.

"And the Bible," Danzig asked poisonously, "when the Jews have been forgotten?"

"That, too, I suppose," I answered, "because the single human voice speaks to the single human ear and heart over the centuries and the distances as nothing else does."

"Perhaps even the single human voice can't be heard now," Anne remarked, "perhaps it never could. Perhaps what survived survived only by accident, and what is considered great is great only by illusion." She spoke with her most sybilline expression, her pink tongue licking her dry lips where a fleck of cigarette paper was pasted, as if the words were too arid, too desert-like for her lips to speak unmoistened. Except for Mrs. Cartwright, whose bright, birdlike cheer remained unchanged, everyone turned grimly to Anne, hoping that her face would contradict with laughter, or even a grimace, the unrelieved aridity of her voice and words, but Anne's eyes were downcast, the eyelids dark, with the shadow of the future, or makeup.

Maria said too loudly that there was too much talk, too much brains, and called for more vodka and more dancing. She tuned the hi-fi up and ordered everyone to dance. The three married couples rose obediently, Ursula went to the kitchen, and I was left with Mrs. Cartwright. Politely, I asked how she was enjoying the party and in a high-pitched, Julie Andrews-like voice, she told me she was having a marvelous time. It was so much more interesting than the usual parties she went to. Foreigners, she smiled to take the sting out of the word — I knew what she meant, didn't I? — were just plain more fun than old Americans, weren't they? Her white, perfectly coiffured hair, her sparkling dentured smile and remote kindly brown eyes terrified me more than the black depths of Danzig's eyes or the bitter distances of Anne's: they were from another world altogether. She hadn't been to such a party for the longest time, she said. How good it was of the Torczyns to invite an old lady like her, a widow, to such a shindig. Yes, *shindig,* that was the word she used. How her husband, Malcolm, would have loved it! He'd been a lawyer, in real estate, you know, and he did so enjoy drinking and talking to people. I saw the tears start to her eyes and turned away, embarrassed, as much for myself as for her. Had she understood anything she'd heard that evening? Or had age and temperament simply removed her from the suffering and the struggle to the extent that the sound of human voices and the warm gurglings of digestion were enough to make the party perfect for her? Or did any party revive her feelings for a husband long dead and still mourned?

The records being played were fox trots, waltzes, tangos and rhumbas, all of which I danced well, but I surmised that as the evening wore on and the level of intoxication and despair rose, so would the tempo of the music quicken. Rock and roll would come soon enough, too soon for me; we could no more live in the terpsichorean past than in the historical. I asked Mrs. Cartwright to dance and as I held her at arm's length was not at all surprised to find that she smelled of lavender and danced a dainty, small-stepping fox trot. In the next hour I danced in succession with Mrs. Cartwright, with Helga Danzig, Anne, Ursula and Maria, and noted that each had her own particular style — and the style was the woman. Helga Danzig danced just the way she looked: big, clumsy, almost impossible to lead, dancing with her was like pushing a weight uphill, but the weight bore you no malice and was as good-natured about stepping on your toes as about your stepping on hers. She talked all the time we danced, telling me in her school-girl French how sorry she was that I had stumbled into such a discussion with "her Stash," because he was having such a bad time of it in the United States, the reality of the country having shocked into smithereens his preconceived notions of what America was like. Anne danced beautifully, with sinuous grace that was half-surrender, half-withdrawal, holding her body away from mine as if she understood and mistrusted its capacity to arouse, but wanting, crying out to be lifted off her feet, swept away. She danced with her eyes closed, permitting herself to be pervaded by the music and the movement, opening her eyes only when, as if by some inexplicable telepathic signal, she knew Leszek was heading for more vodka. And her eyes always opened at just the right time. Ursula danced as if she had no partner at all, belonged to no one and to no place, but was doomed to be the center of attraction for all eyes, yet a fey spirit never to be held in any single pair of arms. I did not dance with her so much as beside her, permitting her to express and display herself. Around her neck an old gold necklace with a strange modern pendant was hung; the pendant resembled a surrealist version of a crucifix and seemed both sacrilegious and appropriate as it whipped frenziedly against her breast, shoulders and back, as if she were being scourged, as if she were scourging herself, for dancing.

But for me Maria's dancing was the most disturbing. If Marek had been asked he would probably have said that he was one of the prime examples of the division of the two cultures — what Leszek called the great literary "snow job" — but he would have been excessively modest and perhaps talking about the wrong two cultures. Marek was an intelligent man, not quite an intellectual, for whatever good or evil that term portends, with an abiding interest in culture and politics. If he lacked Leszek's linguistic flare and poetic flame, he was nonetheless fluent in English, French and German besides his native Polish and had, I knew, only two years before taught himself Russian simply to keep pace with what Soviet biologists were doing in his field. Maria was different. If asked, she would have insisted that Marek was not interested in literary things; but as far as I could see she loved the literary chiefly for the *vie bohème* she thought went with it, the excitement, the drinking, the sex, the gossip, the gay life she had once known after Warsaw in Paris, Madrid and on the various seacoasts of France and Spain. It was a life she sorely missed, and the milieu was perhaps her natural element. If writers interested her, and they did, their books bored her; if the writer's life intrigued her, his work and his commitment to it exasperated her: she preferred parties of persistence, sex to creation.

And dancing with Maria was a sexual experience. She danced with her body as if by nature and art she should fit every curve of it into her partners' and so become part of them, make them a part of her. Insistently provocative, she was a landscape of desire, but difficult if not impossible to lead on the dance floor. Yet she was a graceful dancer. You saw when you watched her and felt when you danced with her that as a little girl Maria had gone to the right dancing masters, white gloves, dancing slippers of proper patent leather, frilly pink organdy dresses, and all; and there she learned the intricacies of the various dance steps as well as the regal posture that was so natural to her. The school had shaped her grace, framed it around a molten steel core that had little or nothing to do with it, and that core was neither graceful nor easily led. How she and Ursula could be sisters never ceased to astonish me and now, dancing with them one after the other made the battlement as unbearable in a tactile and kinesthetic way as it had been before psychologically: where Ursula melted away from the touch, Maria stood fast; where Maria threatened to prevail, Ursula seemed committed to doom.

While we danced Marek went around filling glasses and then stopped to talk to Danzig and Helga who sat, hands entwined, next to each other on the couch. Leszek, quite drunk now, held Anne close to him, both hands on her shoulders, his eyes shut behind his glasses. They moved only slightly, in a slow sensual two-step that fastened their bodies as close together as Maria had endeavored to fasten ours. "Look at them!" Maria exclaimed admiringly in my ear. As she spoke, Leszek opened his eyes, looked glassily down at Anne, and said loudly, "I love you, Anne." He noticed us then, saw us watching and listening, and proudly proclaimed, "You see, Martin, I love her. She's my honey." He hugged her to him in an embrace at once so Polish and unselfconscious that it was a joy to behold. Alcohol did have some salutary purposes for him. Anne, color on her pale cheeks, burrowed her nose into his shoulder, and they danced off.

Talking into my ear, Maria sent chills down my spine. "You know how is with Marek and me. I never want to marry with him. He wanted, never me. But he make me to marry. He write the papers, because we are in England and must have papers. The other way is all right with me. Because we don't have children, I don't care. You know the children is not mine, we are adopting."

Her shallow intense breathing, her quivering rib cage emphasized what she was telling me, though I had known it long ago and she had, over the years, told me herself several times. She had also forgotten that she had told Sally, who reported it to me, that if she did not want to marry Marek, she wanted to have him, live with him; and she had done everything to keep their liaison alive — even, at the last, marrying him. "See how they are!" she gestured at Anne and Leszek, still caught up in their slow, sensual music. "Is marvelous! A man have guts to say I love you. But must be able to say. Leszek has guts to say. Marek not . . . no guts."

For a few moments, the rhythm of the music and mood combined in a fugue of sympathy for Marek, knowing how difficult such demands, spoken or silent, were when made in a marriage and thinking, not without pain, of Sally. I knew Maria was wrong, that in such matters there were different courages and cowardices, as many as there were men and women, that diffidence was not always cowardice, that words were not always commitments nor silence the absence of feeling. It was not until I heard Maria say Sally that I realized she had continued to speak and was now talking about me. "You are disappointed man," she breathed into my ear, "and I know why you disappointed. You brilliant . . ." she sensed my reaction and reiterated ". . . yes, you brilliant man, but do not get what you expect, what you want in heart." I had not, she said, received the recognition of my talents as a writer, nor been given proper appreciation as a man; I had not managed to find what I wanted or merited in a woman. What Maria thought I wanted was a different woman from Sally, not one who sallied forth — the pun came to mind inevitable and unsummoned — to her laboratory and career, but one who remained at home and made me — *me!* — the center of her life. The responsibilities of a marriage in which I was the axis around which another human being's whole life rotated was stifling — and terrifying. I was a lover of more freedom, or at least of more tether — and too much of a coward to undertake such plunges into chaos. As my feet moved in the orderly foxtrot steps, they had to be kept from running away. I forced myself to listen and watched the play of feelings on Maria's face until gradually I saw that she thought she was talking about me and Sally but was simply, perhaps not so simply, talking about herself and Marek. With a sharp intake of breath, she said, briskly, and in what seemed to me a non sequitur, "I love you, Maar . . . teen. You know this," as if that explained and summed up everything.

I love you. Was that Maria's usual hyperbole — I *love* pilaf and Hermes scarves and Maserati cars and benedictine and brandy — the exaggeration of language that vodka and her limited English vocabulary imposed on her tumultuous temperament? Or was it simply the echo of the Costa Brava and the Costa del Sol, the *rive gauche* and the Côte Basque, Tangiers and Como, Soho and Greenwich Village, the you're a writer and interesting, and most of all you aren't my husband, so tonight, here, now, I love you, because you are strange, spare, different — *in*different? — and what it means is that I want you to make love to me? Or had she truly understood what she'd remarked on in Anne and Leszek and felt that she had missed that? Before I could ask, or she could answer, the record ended; the dance was done.

Mrs. Cartwright stood up, ladylike and still perfectly groomed, not a white hair out of place, though the rest of us showed the late-hour dishevelments of drinking and dancing and arguing; and Maria, the perfect hostess, hurried out of my arms to her side. Mrs. Cartwright murmured how late it was for her, how wonderful the party had been but she was an old lady and couldn't keep her eyes open after midnight even, a moue and a dentured smile, for the late, late show; but her eyes sparkled like rusty wet bolts and she seemed livelier and wider awake than any of us except the indefatigable Maria. Everyone rose and went through the ritual of trying to persuade her to stay, but Mrs. Cartwright would not permit herself to be persuaded. As she titteringly allowed it, the assembled Polish males each in turn bowed and kissed her hand; and then, having dismissed her, went back to the serious business of drinking, dancing, singing and quarreling while I accompanied Maria and Mrs. Cartwright to the door, not out of politeness but because I thought I might, before the moment passed entirely, get a word from Maria about what that *I love you* really meant. Only when we were in the vestibule helping Mrs. Cartwright into her coat did I realize that I was delighted we had been interrupted: I didn't really want to know. As I lifted the coat over her shoulder, Mrs. Cartwright turned her head to me, a quick coquettish swerve that smoothed the lines from her cheeks and throat, a gesture she had probably seen Vilma Banky perform for John Gilbert oh so long ago. "Your talk was so . . . stimulating, Mr. Wallace, so . . . exciting! How Malcolm would have enjoyed it!" Her eyes clouded with tears and her lips trembled. "To be killed playing polo! How simply stupid!" she grated, then gave my hand a fleeting kid-glove squeeze, and swirled out of the door.

While Maria closed the door I asked how long Malcolm Cartwright had been dead. "Is sixteen, seventeen years, maybe," she replied, abruptly cold and brusque. "Right after war."

"Did he really die playing polo?" I asked. Was that so unreal? so remote as I found it? And was Mrs. Cartwright herself?

Marie shrugged. "Maybe. Does not matter. He is dead."

Leszek stood in the classic posture of the orator, one hand pressing his vodka glass to his heart, the other arm outstretched, index finger pointing to the distance beyond the thermopane doors where the bronze tree outside elegantly raised its arms. As I sank down on the couch next to Anne I asked her softly what he was reciting. She had studied Russian and had, after all, lived with Leszek and his emigré Poles for half a dozen years. "Don't understand a bit of it, thank you," she said. "And I don't want to learn."

Marek, standing next to us, overheard. "Makes your life a bit more peaceful, eh?" he inquired. "You can turn us Poles off."

"No, only sometimes and only some Poles," Anne replied.

"Leszek's reciting a Mickiewicz poem, *At the Grace of the Countess Potocka*," Marek explained. In deliberately sing-song English, with baroque inflections, he translated:

> *O Polish beauty I too die in exile:*
> *Let kind hands strew this earth on me then,*
> *And when wayfarers stop and speak of you,*
> *I shall rise from my sleep to hear our own precious tongue:*
>
> *Let him who sings your sorrows once more to life,*
> *Seeing my grave nearby, make my sorrows a part of his song.*

Under her breath, in a reedy soprano, Anne mockingly sang, *"And I'll rise with my trumpet from out of my grave our own glorious Emperor defending."*

"*Your* grenadiers were traveling West, but defeated," Marek commented wryly.

"And these?" I asked.

"Stashu challenged Leszek's right to speak of Poles and the Polish way of life again," Marek said, "and Leszek is quoting Mickiewicz to give him the lie."

"Again?"

"Again," Anne interjected.

"Does Leszek really have to establish his *bona fides?*" I joked. "With appropriate verses from Poland's epic poet?"

"His Polish honor is at stake," Marek said, straightfaced.

"When he's drunk it is, anyway," Anne amended.

Anne and I went to the kitchen and left the Polish, flying thick and fast, the voices loud and emotion-charged. There, at the kitchen table, Anne poured two cups of coffee from the electric percolator, and we sat. The coffee was hot and strong and I drank it in grateful silence. "I'm irretrievably middle-aged," Anne said, not looking at me. "They can go on like that all night, night after night, eating and drinking, dancing and singing, talking, arguing, discussing. After midnight, I've had it."

"Middle-aged? Not you, Anne, you look the same as when we first met."

"Ah, Martin, gallantry will get you everywhere."

"It's been a long time, hasn't it?" I asked.

Anne smiled. "A very long time, Martin."

"After eleven o'clock at night, there are only three things I want to do: sleep, read, or . . ."

". . . yes, I know," she interjected, laughing. "I know you."

"I mean it."

"I know you do."

"What civilized person is different?"

"Only those 'barbarous' Poles." Anne inclined her head toward the other room.

We laughed together.

I asked if Leszek actually meant to move to Maine.

"He'd like to. In one way I can't really blame him. It *is* a lot cheaper up there. We could live on half of what it takes here, and that would take some of the strain off him. He could do a lot more writing and a lot less of the translations he has to do for money."

"And you?"

"I don't have much family left. My mother and my sisters are here, and my younger sister's going to have another child in a couple of months . . ."

". . . Congratulations!"

"Always an aunt and never . . ." her voice trailed off.

And then, because the hour was late, because I had had a great deal to drink, and because I saw the falcon and sparrow halves of Anne's face in bitter conflict over the coffee cup, I asked if Leszek had changed his mind about having children.

She shook her head.

I told her I had talked to Leszek about it during the spring when he and I had gone to see an exhibit of modern Polish painting. I had remarked, altogether too casually of course, that I'd come to the conclusion, properly belated, that I had been foolish not to have children earlier and not to have more than two.

"Returning the compliment, Martin?" Anne asked. Years before, when Leszek was still married to his first wife and I was still adamant against bringing another Jewish child into the world after Auschwitz, Anne had pleaded with me not to be a fool. Sensibly and eloquently pleaded. It was a long time before I listened and then not until I was listening to myself far more than to her. I remembered and I knew that she remembered too.

"Maybe, but I talked because I really think he's wrong. Oh, I know why he's reluctant, maybe more than most anyone, but I think he should change his mind not only for your sake, but for his."

"Too late," she said, "Altogether too late."

"You're not that old."

"No, but Leszek is."

I manufactured the leer I knew she expected and said, "I think he can make it."

She ignored me. "I don't even blame him, I suppose. Much as I'd like to. He's going to be fifty next year. And next year his son will be out of college, his last support payments finished at last. How can I ask him to start that whole thing all over again?"

"But *you* want a child?"

She nodded, dumbly.

"Then tell him so."

"Don't you think he knows?"

"Sure. Leszek's sensitive and perceptive, but he doesn't know how much."

"That's not something you communicate with words."

"You have other methods as well."

"Not with anything." There was iron in her voice. "If you have to, then it doesn't work, it won't help, it doesn't matter." She drank her coffee down to the dregs and made a face. "This is Leszek's last chance to write his own poetry, free of wars and imprisonment and alimony and child support. His last chance. I won't ask him to give it up."

"Yet *he* is asking you to give up having a child."

"My last chance too?" She smiled a self-deprecating grin. "Woman's role, you know. Sacrifice. Renunciation. Bowing the head."

"Borsht!"

"No, money."

"Is it only the money?"

"Only!" she exclaimed impatiently. "Don't be stupid, Martin. And don't play dumb either. You've lived through it. You know what it's like. Sure it's a matter of money, and strength, and time, and of not being so young any more, of not being able to start the whole damn cycle over again."

I thought she was going to cry, with anger and frustration, so I went around the table, put my hands on her shoulders, and was shaken off. Everyone, I thought, in politics as in marriage, buys his fulfillment with someone else's frustration; everyone buys his freedom with someone else's bondage. I left her alone there, as I knew she wanted to be left alone.

In the quiet of the upstairs bathroom, the voices below seemed the most distant muttering, like wind in the leaves, and I tried to put the same distance between me and the voices echoing in my head, but I couldn't. Not even the cold water on my face and wrists, or the wet comb through my thinning hair helped; and the dash of Marek's shaving lotion on my face only made me aware of the stubble of my beard and left me unrefreshed. As I was about to go down the stairs, Marek's and Maria's eight-year-old Irena came out of the bedroom in a blue nightgown, her eyes closed, and groped her way into the bathroom. When she emerged, one eye opened for a moment, stared at me and identified me. "Cover me," she commanded sleepily and then her eye closed and she stumbled back into the bedroom. I followed, tucked her in, then rearranged the blankets to cover her sister, Janina, in the next bed. For a long time I stood looking at their small flowering faces, listening to their breathing like music. All I could think of was how it would be for them when they grew up, if we left them any kind of world to grow up in. Knowing that I couldn't predict or probably even do anything about it, I turned on my heel and went back downstairs.

The living room shook with the tuned-up sound of rock-and-roll, the whine of electric guitars, the bleat of brass, the boom of drums and cymbals: Chopin had gone and the world was too much with us, late and soon. In the middle of the room, shaking to it, shaken by it, her skirt hiked high on her slender thighs, Ursula danced to that music, alone. Eyes closed, arms overhead surrendered her, arched body gave her away, hips gyrating debased her; yet, with all its naked desire and voluptuous longing her dance was curiously chaste, as if performed by a young girl before she was nubile, one of those Balinese children whose sensually expert dancing betrayed their innocence while mocking with their childhood the adults for whom they danced. In another sense, too, Ursula danced as if she were an old crone, past desire or fulfillment, who could still ape the essence: Ursula's desire no longer expected or even required gratification — there was no joy of man's desiring possible — it had turned in on itself; whipped, it had curdled to a thickness of loving fear and fearful love.

I don't know what the others felt as they watched — Leszek blinking nearsightedly behind his glasses, his face grim, his hands nervous; Anne's mouth tremulous and working, her face half-turned away as if she couldn't bear to watch nor bear not to; Helga Danzig's lips making silent words, frog-eyed — but no one moved to stop Ursula. The music rocked and rolled and everyone, hypnotized by the dance, the vodka, the fatigue, seemed old and beaten, like ancient savages squatting on the stony shores of some brackish lake in the shadow of blackened Polish pines, watching their shaman dance for them, plead for them into the face of the indifferent gods. *Totentanz.* Why did the only expression that came to mind come in German? Frenzied, the Gelsomina of the night turned and twisted, leaped and cavorted, on her own road of pain, and on ours, the Pan I knew had not panned out and wouldn't.

Afterwards, still breathless, Ursula sat on the couch in the sitting room with me, her eyes metallic, her upper lip beaded with sweat. She gripped my hand and I felt the spasms that convulsed her body as if they were my own. The others by then were drinking fresh coffee Maria had prepared, yet Ursula stubbornly would only drink vodka, tumblerful after tumblerful, swallowing that deceptive ichor of fermented potatoes that promised exaltation but only pounded people into the dark of earth like the blind roots of tubers from which it came: the Polish curse and comfort. At my side, her trembling became words, grammatically perfect English delivered with limping caution that belied the headlong reckless timbre of her voice. "I am afraid to die," she said, gasping as if death were upon her "Not of death, only to die. I cannot sleep. I cannot forget. I lie awake in the night, my flesh cold and wet, trembling that I will die."

All her life, she told me, had been a war, born in one, married and giving birth in another; even her marriage had been a war, to its death, yet in those days she never thought about dying. She had seen much death and many people die — Poland during the war was a veritable graveyard — but she was never afraid. Now suddenly she felt death near, like a garment she had left hanging in her closet and could not see or find though she knew it was there; the shroud in her wardrobe that would be her last cloak waited to envelop her and she could smell its stale fatal odor through the sachet and perfume with which she drenched her living clothes.

I tried humor, that weakest reed of the intelligence, and she looked at me perplexed. Her words and expression said — Ursula remained a skillful actress whose body communicated powerfully even without words — how can you be so unfeeling, how can your American insensitivity make a mockery of my naked terror? Her single sentence, "I am afraid to die," repeated now, was the sharpest rebuke. Ashamed, I told her that I was often forced to humor to guard my deepest feelings, that she was like all the rest of us in middle age: we had reached the stage where we knew death to be inevitable, knew ourselves not immune. If we had to live with that recognition constantly, if we were deprived of that magnificent and ignorant imperviousness of youth, it should — I almost said it must — make our lives more valuable, keener-edged to the touch, though I was not by any means sure that the conditional tense, that perpetual goad and tyranny of men and their language, could bear the weight of the logic any more than the reality could.

"And I shall die alone," Ursula said, as if she had not heard a single word of mine.

"You have Wiktoria," I reminded her.

"Not even divorce could take his claws out of me. Here." She let go of my hand and clutched her belly, her nails sibilant against the material of her dress. "I can still feel him . . . inside me." When she realized that what she had said was *double entendre,* her cheeks flamed and in a small voice she added, "And that only makes me more afraid."

Marriage, I thought, is a hand grenade with the pin out. You hold your breath waiting for the explosion. And when the grenade does, finally, go off, if it doesn't kill those close to it, it leaves them wounded or maimed and picking pieces of sharpnel from their flesh for the rest of their lives.

A story from my childhood came back and I told Ursula how the Biblical King David, having been apprised that he would die on a certain day, had on that day barricaded himself against death in the room where the altar and holy Ark where kept. Gripping the horns of the altar in the traditional posture of pleading for mercy, David had thrown himself on the Lord's compassion and prayed all day for deliverance from death. But the Angel of Death was cunning. Late in the afternoon, he knocked at the door of the room and spoke to the king with the voice of his beloved Bathsheba. When the king opened the door to speak to her, the Angel of Death struck the great David dead.

"I understand him, your King David," Ursula agreed. She pointed across the floor into the living room where Maria, gesticulating with her coffee cup, was holding forth. "But her I do *not* understand. My sister. My *younger* sister. She believes. She is good Catholic, maybe not in primitive way some priests would like, but she believes in God. Even during war she believed. And she was not afraid to die then. She is not afraid now."

I wondered about how Maria drank and danced and fought and raised roses and wouldn't let any party end before dawn, and sometimes not even then, and I said, "We're all afraid, Ursula, all. Maria too."

Ursula reached for her vodka glass, found it empty, and lit another cigarette instead. "All. Yes. I know. But doesn't help."

"To know that everyone else is afraid too, that everyone else must die, sooner or later, and die alone?"

"No consolation. Nothing. So what must I do for consolation?"

I gulped my vodka. "One must live. Every day. *Carpe diem.*"

Her laughter bordered on hysteria. "Americans! You are more old and cynical than all Europeans together. Even us Poles. And more naive." She began to sob. "One must live. Of course! Grasp?" she looked at me questioningly and I nodded her on, "the day. True! But how? Tell me that."

"I don't know that. I simply don't know."

Coughing smoke, the cigarette ash lengthening on her cigarette, she sat still except for her hand which crept back into mine and held it as if it were a life raft. The desperate always clutch at straws, I thought, with a bitterness and anger against myself I could not control or fathom. Abruptly she let go of me and in one swift graceful motion that spilled sparks and ashes from her cigarette into her lap, removed her necklace and dropped it into my palm. "Here," she said, "I want you to have for Sally. Is from Poland. Has been in my family for long time. It is, I think you call an heirloom." She pronounced it *hair*-loom.

The pile of gold links and pendant were cold in my palm. "You know I can't take it."

"Is gift for Sally because I like her. Maria doesn't like. When I first meet I thought too she was cold woman, then I know she is shy. Like me. Not like Maria. Sally is very kind with me. I appreciate and would like to give necklace for my appreciation."

"I can't take it, Ursula."

"Because is gold? That does not matter."

"Not because it's gold but because it's been in your family for a long time, because it's part of home and home is far away."

"You must take." She folded her hands over mine and pressed the necklace into the flesh of my fingers until they hurt.

"Ah, you are making love with *my* Martin," Maria said, suddenly looming over us. "My big sister always takes the boys away."

"You look like you've done well enough in spite of that," I said.

"Maar . . . teen," Maria said seriously, "never I can tell when you are gallant or giving insult."

"Being gallant to you would be an insult, Maria," I replied. Then, holding out my fist, I opened my fingers to show the necklace. "Please, Maria," I pleaded, "ask Ursula to take this back."

Eyes flashed between the sisters, then Maria replied, "If Ursula give, she want you to have."

Ursula, her voice perfectly controlled, said she wanted to give Sally a memento of Poland and a token of appreciation — and that settled the matter. To protest further would have been to be a boor or an ingrate, so I made an awkward European bow and kissed Ursula's hand, though I vowed to myself that I would find some way to have Sally return that necklace without hurting Ursula's feelings, or without hurting them too much. By then Ursula would be sober and presumably more rational. As I came up from kissing that cold pale hand, its blue veins standing out like stigmata, the others were all grouped around us, laughing and joking at my European gesture, saying they would make a good Pole out of me yet, in spite of myself.

Anne finally prevailed on Maria to let us all go home. The party was over. We put on our overcoats and after a typically prolonged conference about who would drive whom home decided that I'd take them all to my house and Leszek's car there and then Leszek would take the Danzigs back into the city on their way back to Nyack. I'd take Ursula home. We walked across the Torczyn front lawn while Leszek, drunkenly, in a raucous whisper suggested we go back to the next-door-neighbor Poles and start the evening all over again. Anne, as if she had read my mind, whispered in my ear that that was why she didn't want Leszek to take Ursula home, though she knew it was out of the way for me to do so, but once he got off the parkways, they'd be lost for the rest of the night and most of the morning. Anne finally managed to maneuver Leszek into the front seat of the car while the Danzigs and Ursula got into the rear seat. I heard Maria call something and turned to see her and Marek framed together in the doorway, the light from behind them leaving them completely in silhouette. I asked Leszek what she had said.

"Why don't we go back and have one more for the road," he explained, and began to try to open the car door.

"Oh, God, no!" Anne said, and held him back. "Get in, Martin, and get us out of here."

We drove to my house in silence, except for Leszek's occasional "Now, honey . . ." spoken as if in reply to some rebuke of Anne's, but he never finished the sentence and she had never spoken a word to him. As he got out of my car to switch to his own, I asked if he would like to have some coffee at my place. Anne and Helga agreed but Leszek was adamant. "Just lead me to the parkway, Martin, I'll be fine."

"You're drunk, Leszek," I said harshly, "so why don't you have a couple of cups of coffee first."

"You remember last New Year's eve?" he asked. "I was drunker, then, and I got home, didn't I? Tell him, honey," he appealed to Anne. When he saw that I was angry, he drew me aside, embraced me, kissing me on both cheeks as if he were a French general and I a *poilu* who had somehow survived the Marne and on whom he was bestowing a citation for valor. "Martin," he said in my ear, as if reading a decoration, "my friend, my good, my best American friend."

"Leszek," I responded, moved in spite of myself, "you reckless drunken idiot."

"No, Martin," he wagged his finger at me, "a saintly Dostoyevskian idiot. Alyosha. A divine fool. What can happen to me? I die? How many times have I risked that already?" He threw his arms out, widespread. "I owe a cock to Aesculapius."

We said goodnight. Danzig's handshake was a little gingerly when I said I hoped we'd meet again, but tightened and grateful when I told him, sincerely, how much I admired his writing. Anne's kiss was a quick butterfly on my cheek, her hiss goodnight a caress in my ear.

When I got back into my car, Ursula had already moved up to the front seat and we were alone. I led Leszek and his car on to the parkway, watching him in my rear mirror, and was relieved to see his slow, too-careful, 20-mile-an-hour pace until I had to turn off, on Ursula's instructions. Only then was I aware that she was crying, crying and smoking cigarettes, the lipsticked butts piled up in the dashboard ashtray. I drove under an elevated with pillars and old trolley tracks and cobblestones; to make matters worse hotrod kids were coming home from their Saturday-night dates so I had to concentrate on the driving. Besides, I could think of nothing comforting to say or do. Ursula moved closer to me, her shoulder transmitting to me that same inner quavering that her hand had earlier communicated, but when I made no response, she shrank away and leaned against the door, as far from me as she could get.

I wished I'd been able to put my arm around her to solace her, but that wasn't what she wanted or needed: and I couldn't provide what she did need. I'd tried that more than once in my lifetime and I knew how catastrophic it turned out: you didn't succeed in doing anything but making matters worse, much worse; some things could not be accomplished out of pity or compassion. More-over, nobody rebuilt anyone else's world; nobody could. Mostly nobody helped either — without love and often enough not even with love. But surely not with pity.

When I parked in front of her apartment house, Ursula asked me, reluctantly, to take her upstairs because she was afraid to ride the elevator alone. "You know I am afraid of so many things. Everything." She tried to smile but her eyes were frightened. I took her into the lobby and we waited for the elevator. It was an old-fashioned type with a grillwork door which had to be pushed shut before it would rise. When I succeeded in slamming it closed, the elevator began a slow, dignified ascent that would, in other circumstances, have been amusing. No sooner had it begun when Ursula once more wept convulsively until I said, "Don't be afraid. It's only a long sleep from which we don't wake up. That's it and that's all."

"It's not the death I am fearing," she sobbed, "it is the dying, the pain, the making myself dirty. Helpless. Feeble." She shuddered, gasping half-cries as if she were already stricken.

I grabbed her shoulder and shook her, gently, again and again, as if I were rocking a baby, until the cries died away and the elevator stopped at her floor. I took her key when her trembling hand could not find the lock with it, opened the door and held it open with my shoe while I gave her the key. "Is Wiktoria home?" I whispered.

Ursula nodded. "Thank you, Martin," she said huskily, speaking my name so shyly that I realized I'd never heard her use it before. It was as if we had just decided to call each other *du* or *tu*, of whatever the hell the intimate grammatical form for *you* was in

Polish; as if we'd sworn a *Bruderschaft* — again a German word! — that was somehow a reassertion of our common humanity.

On the parkway dawn was coming up, a wintry red-streaked morning with black-and-blue clouds low on the horizon. I drove fast, breaking the speed limit without even checking my side or rear mirrors, and I kept the car windows wide open to let in the night wind, hoping it would blow the evening clear out of my brain — but it didn't. By the time I reached home, the sun was up, low over the houses, an apocalyptic ball of flame that threatened to consume everything it outlined with morning fire.

In the living room, I took off my coat and shoes, threw them on a chair and then, because my feet were cold, went upstairs to find my slippers. As I stooped to pick them up, I saw a slip of paper on the floor beneath them and picked it up instead. It was the torn-off half of a schoolboy's notebook page, and between the widely spaced blue lines, in my younger son's erratic printing, was red-crayoned, "You Martians get off our Planet. You are green. We are white. Surrender or we'll attack. Bang. Bang. You're dead and so am I." I stared at it for a long time until I saw the paper shaking in my hand. Then I took it into my sons' room and put it back on his desk.

Downstairs, I poured another bourbon in the same glass I had left behind, what was it, twelve hours ago? and sank into my wing chair. It was cold and I realized that I'd left the thermostat on the nighttime setting but I was too exhausted to get up and change that. Instead I took the afghan Sally always left on the couch and covered myself. I must have fallen asleep then and what nightmares I dreamt I don't remember, but in what seemed like minutes I was wakened by the slamming of the front door. As I was about to get up, Sally strode in and with one withering look surveyed me and the room. "Look at you," she said disapprovingly, "just look at you! Sleeping in your clothes. In a chair." She bustled about, emptying ashtrays into the fireplace, picking up my glass and Anne's and Leszek's, refolding and replacing the afghan which had fallen at my feet, all the while muttering under her breath.

"You weren't due back until Monday morning," I growled.

"It's already late Sunday afternoon," Sally said, her apology a rebuke. I looked at my watch and out of the window, and plainly it was. "I wanted you to have one good meal this weekend so I thought I'd get back a little early and make us some Sunday dinner." She was defensive and evasive at once. "Besides the boys had some homework to do for tomorrow."

"Where are the boys?" I asked.

"Playing ball in the park with the Garrison kids," she replied. "They'll be home in about an hour." She went into the kitchen and I followed her.

"Well, how was the Torczyn party?" Sally asked over her shoulder, "or did you just stay home and get drunk?" She put on an apron, lit the oven and began to take food from the refrigerator.

Stretching sleepily I wondered if I ought to be cross, and then remembered Ursula's necklace in my pocket. I took it out and held it from my fingers. "Here," I offered, "a gift for you."

Sally turned, instantly suspicious, and looked quizzically at the gold links that glinted in the sunshine. "For me?" she asked.

"Yes. Maria's sister Ursula sent it."

"What in heaven's name for?"

For a painful moment I wanted to tell her, what in heaven and hell's name for, but the moment passed with some deep breathing and instead I reported, "She said you were kind to her, and she wanted you to have a memento of her homeland."

"Poland?"

"Where else?" I replied noncommittally, but I knew it was the wrong answer.

Sally took the necklace and held it up in front of her, examining it closely. "It's gold," she remarked, "and probably an heirloom. Why would she give such a thing away? And to someone she doesn't even know very well?"

"She was drunk," I said shortly.

"Do you think I ought to keep it?" Sally asked, visibly upset.

"No. I think you ought to return it. With a kind note thanking her."

"Thanks, but no thanks, is that it?"

I stared at her for a long time to see if I had missed an irony, then I simply nodded.

Sally looked relieved. She paused and now it was her turn to

peer carefully into my face and I, deliberately yawning and stretching sleepily, turned away. "I see," she said.

"What do you see now?" I asked sarcastically.

"I see that," her tone changed in mid-passage, "you'd better go
up and get washed and shaved and let me get some dinner. The
boys will be home soon and they'll be ravenous." She shooed me
out of the kitchen and because there was nothing more that could
profitably be said, or done, I went.

LESLIE SILKO

Lullaby

(FROM THE CHICAGO REVIEW)

THE SUN HAD GONE DOWN but the snow in the wind gave off its own light. It came in thick tufts like new wool — washed before the weaver spins it. Ayah reached out for it like her own babies had, and she smiled when she remembered how she had laughed at them. She was an old woman now, and her life had become memories. She sat down with her back against the wide cottonwood tree, feeling the rough bark on her back bones; she faced east and listened to the wind and snow sing a high-pitched Yeibechei song. Out of the wind she felt warmer, and she could watch the wide fluffy snow fill in her tracks, steadily, until the direction she had come from was gone. By the light of the snow she could see the dark outline of the big arroyo a few feet away. She was sitting on the edge of Cebolleta Creek, where in the springtime the thin cows would graze on grass already chewed flat to the ground. In the wide deep creek bed where only a trickle of water flowed in the summer, the skinny cows would wander, looking for new grass along winding paths splashed with manure.

Ayah pulled the old Army blanket over her head like a shawl. Jimmie's blanket — the one he had sent to her. That was a long time ago and the green wool was faded, and it was unraveling on the edges. She did not want to think about Jimmie. So she thought about the weaving and the way her mother had done it. On the tall wooden loom set into the sand under a tamarack tree for shade. She could see it clearly. She had been only a little girl when her grandma gave her the wooden combs to pull the twigs and burrs from the raw, freshly washed wool. And while she combed the wool, her grandma sat beside her, spinning a silvery strand of yarn around the smooth cedar spindle. Her mother worked at the loom with yarns dyed bright yellow and red and gold. She watched them dye the yarn in boiling black pots full of beeweed petals, juniper berries, and sage. The blankets her mother made were soft and woven so tight that rain rolled off them like birds' feathers. Ayah remembered sleeping warm on cold windy nights, wrapped in her mother's blankets on the hogan's sandy floor.

The snow drifted now, with the northwest wind hurling it in gusts. It drifted up around her black overshoes — old ones with little metal buckles. She smiled at the snow which was trying to cover her little by little. She could remember when they had no black rubber overshoes; only the high buckskin leggings that they wrapped over their elk-hide moccasins. If the snow was dry or frozen, a person could walk all day and not get wet; and in the evenings the beams of the ceiling would hang with lengths of pale buckskin leggings, drying out slowly.

She felt peaceful remembering. She didn't feel cold any more. Jimmie's blanket seemed warmer than it had ever been. And she could remember the morning he was born. She could remember whispering to her mother who was sleeping on the other side of the hogan, to tell her it was time now. She did not want to wake the others. The second time she called to her, her mother stood up and pulled on her shoes; she knew. They walked to the old stone hogan together, Ayah walking a step behind her mother. She waited alone, learning the rhythms of the pains while her mother went to call the old woman to help them. The morning was already warm even before dawn and Ayah smelled the bee flowers blooming and the young willow growing at the springs. She could remember that so clearly, but his birth merged into the births of the other children and to her it became all the same birth. They named him for the summer morning and in English they called him Jimmie.

It wasn't like Jimmie died. He just never came back, and one day a dark blue sedan with white writing on its doors pulled up in front of the boxcar shack where the rancher let the Indians live. A man in a khaki uniform trimmed in gold gave them a yellow piece of paper and told them that Jimmie was dead. He said the Army would try to get the body back and then it would be shipped to them; but it wasn't likely because the helicopter had burned after it crashed.

All of this was told to Chato because he could understand English. She stood inside the doorway holding the baby while Chato listened. Chato spoke English like a white man and he spoke Spanish too. He was taller than the white man and he stood straighter too. Chato didn't explain why; he just told the military man they could keep the body if they found it. The white man looked bewildered; he nodded his head and he left. Then Chato looked at her and shook his head. "Goddamn," he said in English, and then he told her "Jimmie isn't coming home anymore," and when he spoke, he used the words to speak of the dead. She didn't cry then, but she hurt inside with anger. And she mourned him as the years passed, when a horse fell with Chato and broke his leg, and the white rancher told them he wouldn't pay Chato until he could work again. She mourned Jimmie because he would have worked for his father then; he would have saddled the big bay horse and ridden the fence lines each day, with wire cutters and heavy gloves, fixing the breaks in the barbed wire and putting the stray cattle back inside again.

She mourned him after the white doctors came to take Danny and Ella away. She was at the shack alone that day when they came. It was back in the days before they hired Navajo women to go with them as interpreters. She recognized one of the doctors. She had seen him at the children's clinic at Cañoncito about a month ago. They were wearing khaki uniforms and they waved papers at her and a black ball point pen, trying to make her understand their English words. She was frightened by the way they looked at the children, like the lizard watches the fly. Danny was swinging on the tire swing in the elm tree behind the rancher's house, and Ella was toddling around the front door, dragging the broomstick horse Chato made for her. Ayah could see they wanted her to sign the papers, and Chato had taught her to sign her name. It was something she was proud of. She only wanted them to go, and to take their eyes away from her children.

She took the pen from the man without looking at his face and she signed the papers in three different places he pointed to. She stared at the ground by their feet and waited for them to leave. But they stood there and began to point and gesture at the children. Danny stopped swinging. Ayah could see his fear. She moved suddenly and grabbed Ella into her arms; the child squirmed, trying to get back to her toys. Ayah ran with the baby toward Danny; she screamed for him to run and then she grabbed him around his chest and carried him too. She ran south into the foothills of juniper trees and black lava rock. Behind her she heard the doctors running, but they had been taken by surprise, and as the hills became steeper and the cholla cactus were thicker, they stopped. When she reached the top of the hill, she stopped too to listen in case they were circling around her. But in a few minutes she heard a car engine start and they drove away. The children had been too surprised to cry while she ran with them. Danny was shaking and Ella's little fingers were gripping Ayah's blouse.

She stayed up in the hills for the rest of the day, sitting on a black lava boulder in the sunshine where she could see for miles all around her. The sky was light blue and cloudless, and it was warm for late April. The sun warmth relaxed her and took the fear and anger away. She lay back on the rock and watched the sky. It seemed to her that she could walk into the sky, stepping through clouds endlessly. Danny played with little pebbles and stones, pretending they were birds, eggs and then little rabbits. Ella sat at her feet and dropped fistfuls of dirt into the breeze, watching the dust and particles of sand intently. Ayah watched a hawk soar high above them, dark wings gliding; hunting or only watching, she did not know. The hawk was patient and he circled all afternoon before his disappeared around the high volcanic peak the Mexicans call Guadalupe.

Late in the afternoon, Ayah looked down at the gray boxcar shack with the paint all peeled from the wood; the stove pipe on the roof was rusted and crooked. The fire she had built that morning in the oil drum stove had burned out. Ella was asleep in her lap now and Danny sat close to her, complaining that he was hungry; he asked when they would go to the house. "We will stay up here until your father comes," she told him, "because those white men were chasing us." The boy remembered then and he nodded at her silently.

If Jimmie had been there he could have read those papers and explained to her what they said. Ayah would have known, then, never to sign them. The doctors came back the next day and they brought a BIA policeman with them. They told Chato they had her signature and that was all they needed. Except for the kids. She listened to Chato sullenly; she hated him when he told her it was the old woman who died in the winter, spitting blood; it was her old grandma who had given the children this disease. "They don't spit blood," she said coldly, "The whites lie." She held Ella and Danny close to her, ready to run to the hills again. "I want a medicine man first," she said to Chato, not looking at him. He shook his head. "It's too late now. The policeman is with them. You signed the paper." His voice was gentle.

It was worse than if they had died: to lose the children and to know that somewhere, in a place called Colorado, in a place full of sick and dying strangers, her children were without her. There had been babies that died soon after they were born, and one that died before he could walk. She had carried them herself, up to the boulders and great pieces of the cliff that long ago crashed down from Long Mesa; she laid them in the crevices of sandstone and buried them in fine brown sand with round quartz pebbles that washed down from the hills in the rain. She had endured it because they had been with her. But she could not bear this pain. She did not sleep for a long time after they took her children. She stayed on the hill where they had fled the first time, and she slept rolled up in the blanket Jimmie had sent her. She carried the pain in her belly and it was fed by everything she saw: the blue sky of their last day together and the dust and pebbles they played with; the swing in the elm tree and broomstick horse chocked life from her. The pain filled her stomach and there was no room for food or for her lungs to fill with air. The air and the food would have been theirs.

She hated Chato, not because he let the policeman and doctors put the screaming children in the government car, but because he had taught her to sign her name. Because it was like the old ones always told her about learning their language or any of their ways: it endangered you. She slept alone on the hill until the middle of November when the first snows came. Then she made a bed for herself where the children had slept. She did not lay down beside Chato again until many years later, when he was sick and shivering and only her body could keep him warm. The illness came after the white rancher told Chato he was too old to work for him any more, and Chato and his old woman should be out of the shack by the next afternoon because the rancher had hired new people to work there. That had satisfied her. To see how the white man repaid Chato's years of loyalty and work. All of Chato's fine-sounding English talk didn't change things.

II

It snowed steadily and the luminous light from the snow gradually diminished into the darkness. Somewhere in Cebolleta a dog barked and other village dogs joined with it. Ayah looked in the direction she had come, from the bar where Chato was buying the wine. Sometimes he told her to go on ahead and wait; and then he never came. And when she finally went back looking for him, she would find him passed out at the bottom of the wooden steps to Azzie's Bar. All the wine would be gone and most of the money too, from the pale blue check that came to them once a month in a government envelope. It was then that she would look at his face and his hands, scarred by ropes and the barbed wire of all those years, and she would think 'this man is a stranger'; for 40 years she had smiled at him and cooked his food, but he remained a stranger. She stood up again, with the snow almost to her knees, and she walked back to find Chato.

It was hard to walk in the deep snow and she felt the air burn in her lungs. She stopped a short distance from the bar to rest and readjust the blanket. But this time he wasn't waiting for her on the bottom step with his old Stetson hat pulled down and his shoulders hunched up in his long wool overcoat.

She was careful not to slip on the wooden steps. When she pushed the door open, warm air and cigarette smoke hit her face. She looked around slowly and deliberately, in every corner, in every dark place that the old man might find to sleep. The bar-owner didn't like Indians in there, especially Navajos, but he let Chato come in because he could talk Spanish like he was one of them. The men at the bar stared at her, and the bartender saw that she left the door open wide. Snow flakes were flying inside like moths and melting into a puddle on the oiled wood floor. He motioned at her to close the door, but she did not see him. She held herself straight and walked across the room slowly, searching the room with every step. The snow in her hair melted and she could feel it on her forehead. At the far corner of the room, she saw red flames at the mica window of the old stove door; she looked behind the stove just to make sure. The bar got quiet except for the Spanish polka music playing on the jukebox. She stood by the stove and shook the snow from her blanket and held it near the stove to dry. The wet wool smell reminded her of new-born goats in early March, brought inside to warm near the fire. She felt calm.

In past years they would have told her to get out. But her hair was white now and her face was wrinkled. They looked at her like she was a spider crawling slowly across the room. They were afraid; she could feel the fear. She looked at their faces steadily. They reminded her of the first time the white people brought her children back to her that winter. Danny had been shy and hid behind the thin white woman who brought them. And the baby had not known her until Ayah took her into her arms, and then Ella had nuzzled close to her as she had when she was nursing. The blonde woman was nervous and kept looking at a dainty gold watch on her wrist. She sat on the bench near the small window and watched the dark snow clouds gather around the mountains; she was worrying about the unpaved road. She was frightened by what she saw inside too: the strips of venison drying on a rope across the ceiling and the children jabbering excitedly in a language she did not know. So they stayed for only a few hours. Ayah watched the government car disappear down the road and she knew they were already being weaned from these lava hills and from this sky. The last time they came was in early June, and Ella stared at her the way the men in the bar were now staring. Ayah did not try to pick her up; she smiled at her instead and spoke cheerfully to Danny. When he tried to answer her, he could not seem to remember and he spoke English words with the Navajo. But he gave her a scrap of paper that he had found somewhere and carried in his pocket; it was folded in half, and he shyly looked up at her and said it was a bird. She asked Chato if they were home for good this time. He spoke to the white woman and she shook her head. "How much longer," he asked, and she said she didn't know; but Chato saw how she stared at the box car shack. Ayah turned away then. She did not say good-bye.

III

She felt satisfied that the men in the bar feared her. Maybe it was her face and the way she held her mouth with teeth clenched tight, like there was nothing anyone could do to her now. She walked north down the road, searching for the old man. She did this because she had the blanket, and there would be no place for him except with her and the blanket in the old adobe barn near the arroyo. They always slept there when they came to Cebolleta. If the money and the wine were gone, she would be relieved because then they could go home again; back to the old hogan with a dirt roof and rock walls where she herself had been born. And the next day the old man could go back to the few sheep they still had, to follow along behind them, guiding them into dry sandy arroyos where sparse grass grew. She knew he did not like walking behind old ewes when for so many years he rode big quarter horses and worked with cattle. But she wasn't sorry for him; he should have known all along what would happen.

There had not been enough rain for their garden in five years; and that was when Chato finally hitched a ride into the town and brought back brown boxes of rice and sugar and big tin cans of welfare peaches. After that, at the first of the month they went to Cebolleta to ask the postmaster for the check; and then Chato would go to the bar and cash it. They did this as they planted the garden every May, not because anything would survive the summer dust, but because it was time to do this. And the journey passed the days that smelled silent and dry like the caves above the canyon with yellow painted buffaloes on their walls.

IV

He was walking along the pavement when she found him. He did not stop or turn around when he heard her behind him. She walked beside him and she noticed how slowly he moved now. He smelled strong of woodsmoke and urine. Lately he had been forgetting. Sometimes he called her by his sister's name and she had been gone for a long time. Once she had found him wandering on the road to the white man's ranch, and she asked him why he was going that way; he laughed at her and said "you know they can't run that ranch without me," and he walked on determined, limping on the leg that had been crushed many years before. Now he looked at her curiously, as if for the first time, but he kept shuffling along, moving slowly along the side of the highway. His gray hair had grown long and spread out on the shoulders of the long overcoat. He wore the old felt hat pulled down over his ears. His boots were worn out at the toes and he had stuffed pieces of an old red shirt in the holes. The rags made his feet look like little animals up to their ears in snow. She laughed at his feet; the snow muffled the sound of her laugh. He stopped and looked at her again. The wind had quit blowing and the snow was falling straight down; the southeast sky was beginning to clear and Ayah could see a star.

"Let's rest awhile," she said to him. They walked away from the road and up the slope to the giant boulders that had tumbled down from the red sandrock mesa throughout the centuries of rainstorms and earth tremors. In a place where the boulders shut out the wind, they sat down with their backs against the rock. She offered half of the blanket to him and they sat wrapped together.

The storm passed swiftly. The clouds moved east. They were massive and full, crowding together across the sky. She watched them with the feeling of horses — steely blue-gray horses startled across the sky. The powerful haunches pushed into the distances and the tail hairs streamed white mist behind them. The sky cleared. Ayah saw that there was nothing between her and the stars. The sky cleared. Ayah saw that there was nothing between her and the stars. The light was crystalline. There was no shimmer, no distortion through earth haze. She breathed the clarity of the night sky; she smelled the purity of the half moon and the stars. He was lying on his side with his knees pulled up near his belly for warmth. His eyes were closed now, and in the light from the stars and the moon, he looked young again.

She could see it descend out of the night sky: an icy stillness from the edge of the thin moon. She recognized the freezing. It came gradually, sinking snow flake by snow flake until the crust was heavy and deep. It had the strength of the stars in Orion, and its journey was endless. Ayah knew that with the wine he would sleep. He would not feel it. She tucked the blanket around him, remembering how it was when Ella had been with her; and she felt the rush so big inside her heart for the babies. And she sang the only song she knew to sing for babies. She could not remember if she had ever sung it to her children, but she knew that her grandmother had sung it and her mother had sung it:

> The earth is your mother,
> she holds you.
> The sky is your father,
> he protects you.
> sleep,
> sleep,
> Rainbow is your sister,
> she loves you.
> The winds are your brothers,
> they sing to you.
> sleep,
> sleep,
> We are together always
> We are together always
> There never was a time
> when this
> was not so.

BARRY TARGAN

The Man Who Lived

(FROM THE SOUTHERN REVIEW)

*For as old age is that period of life most remote from infancy, who does
not see that old age in this universal man ought not to be sought in the
times nearest his birth, but in those most remote from it?*

BLAISE PASCAL

ON THE NIGHT General William Tecumseh Sherman burned At-
lanta (that was November 15, 1864), Frederick Kappel, junior, was
born. He was born in Pittsfield, Massachusetts, and his father,
Frederick Kappel, senior, who was with Sherman, would ever after
celebrate the two major events of his life with his yearly reflection
upon the ironies: that a city should die in part by the hand of him
whose son should come to live at the same moment. "It makes you
think that maybe there *are* reasons for it all," his father would say,
waving his hand out over the universe.

Frederick Kappel the elder did not believe in God — not after
Georgia. Only on November 15 he would come a little close. Then
he would stand on the ornate wooden scrolled porch of the substantial house his father had built on Nye Avenue in Pittsfield and
say to the autumn street, "It makes you think that maybe there *are*
reasons for it all."

But that yearly remission did not convince the son. And in the
years, all the years that came to him, he never thought that there
were reasons for any of it.

His own war came in 1898 when the U. S. S. *Maine* exploded in
Havana Harbor.

He was thirty-four but he enlisted, though out of no patriotic fervor or intent. Enlistment seemed to him as good a way as any of the others he had considered and subsided from to leave Pittsfield and the Berkshires, at least for a while, although he never came back. There was nothing to come back to even as there was nothing very much to leave from. But he thought that he was near to the middle of his life; he thought it to be half over, and although he was hardly a restless man, the idea that he had never been out of the state, not even across the near New York and Vermont borders, seemed to him improper. Enlistment had the simple urgency that could commit him to leaving, so he did it.

He spent this war in Florida watching railroad cars of meat cook themselves into seeping lakes of rancid grease widening under the cars while in a parallel siding, carloads of ice weathered unused back to vapor. In the end the ice and meat wasted, and so Frederick Kappel supposed, did he. But not for long. He was in and out of the army in about eight months altogether.

He was by craft and trade a bookbinder, a good skill to move about with as long as you stayed near a printer of books. Not that Frederick Kappel thought about that when, at fourteen, he had been put to apprenticeship in Pittsfield. That or anything else. In 1898, at war's end, at thirty-five years of age, he got as far back north as Philadelphia (to visit an acquaintance from the army) and settled down, taking a job on Race and 4th Street in the firm of Bauch and Brinker which he never left. Which he came to own.

And he took a wife, a cousin of one of the many Bauches, a heavy woman, near to thirty, who bore him four children — three girls and a male — in seven years, and died. He married a cousin of hers, who bore him two more children, both male, and then she died in the diphtheria epidemic of 1910. Kappel's third wife, a widow of a customer (Oswald, the founder of what became World Publishers), bore him no children and lasted until 1930 when she too died. His fourth and last wife, whom he married in 1932 when he was sixty-six, was fifty-seven, but he outlasted her too, healthy though she was and strong.

Frederick Kappel did not venture much beyond the bindery. His children grew up and had their children as he went on folding great creamy sheets of double crown or foolscap or royal into folios and octavos and sixteenmos and more. Wars came and went, the

Wright brothers flew and then Lindbergh flew the Atlantic and then men were on the moon. Nap Lajoie and Honus Wagner gave way to Babe Ruth and to Joe Dimaggio and to Willie Mays. He became a great-grandfather and a great-great-grandfather. Most of what little he knew of his world he found in newspapers (which he increasingly ignored), but mainly he learned from what he caught out of the books that passed into their rich clothing under his fingers. As he would sort and arrange the signatures to be sewn, his eyes would fix upon a paragraph or a stanza or a sentence but sometimes a page. He might never have read a book entire, but he was loyal to his fragments like a good Miscellany, and held them tightly, well bound in him.

When Frederick Kappel began his apprenticeship in 1879, all books were made by hand, everything even to the mixing of the pastes and glues; but his firm, under him, was one of the first to accept the rapidly developed bookbinding machinery — the stitching machines, the automatic folders, the jiggers, the conveyor belt pasters and casers, the still vinyl-impregnated fabrics, and even eventually the glue-backed papercovered books which Kappel could never think of as bound. But he did it, or rather Bauch and Brinker did it as the printers came with their demands.

Kappel himself kept at the art of his craft and specialized in the restoration of fine texts. He became well known for his skill, the authority to whom the rare and the beautiful were brought for his exquisite ministrations — the damaged first editions of the Nineteenth Century, Dr. Johnson's dictionary and his *Lives of the Poets,* a copy of Roger Ascham's *The Schoolemaster,* which was said to have been Queen Elizabeth's personal copy as well as a copy of Lord North's translation of *Plutarch's Lives* which he bound in a soft, floppy suede.

And once a nearly perfect conditoned but uncovered First Folio. The famous bibliophile Rosenbach had gotten it (in his ways) in mystery and had sold it enormously to Theodore Hyde who wanted it bound in leather. There had been argument. The Folger people had come up from Washington to protest and had marshaled pointless arguments from Shakespeareans all around. But there was nothing they could do and Kappel bound it in a leather so fine it made the senses ache from the sight of it, bound it in the old manner with cords rising through the leather of the spine.

It was about then and because of that that he became known beyond professional circles. About once a year thereafter someone would write a feature article on him and his business and personal workshop for one of the area newspapers, the Sunday sections. Mostly he bound expensively for those who could afford that last of elegances, whether they read or not.

Kappel stretched and dried his leathers and mixed his special pastes and glues and sharpened the blades for his cutters and waxed his linen threads, stitching and pressing together the world's history and its words, though he had none, history or words, of his own. Only in time, he did, as time which he had taken for granted for so long at last occurred to him.

In October of his eighty-fourth year — 1949 (in a month he would be eighty-five), Frederick Kappel sat in his private work-room and looked out of its one large window at the small square courtyard of garden that he had maintained in back of the bindery as it had grown up and outward and factory-ish over the decades. His workroom was as smooth and well rubbed as any of his other tools, abraded and formed into the fit of his hands and their own tasks: boxwood and pearwood folder ribs, light but firm as his own fingers; a mahogany sewing frame (a gift) swirlingly carved and turned in elaborate counterpoint to the simplicity of its stiff function; the trim paste pots stationed strategically along the workbench; pressure devices all about — nipping press, drying press, lying press, cutting press, pins and clips and pure sluggish steel ingot weights — until the warm-wooded, life-stained room became itself the mold and form of union, of boundness, the tight, secure domain of the artificer, order immanent.

He looked out at the trees which he had watched grow up from saplings and though he had seen them, the four maples, arch up to their mature height (as much as a city air would allow), he had not until the moment thought of what they measured, of the enormous tick of accumulation that they were, of fifty years. He sat gently looking out and thought back to a remarkable condition somewhere between the saplings and now, but he could not find any. That was when time occurred to Frederick Kappel, in the month before he would be eighty-five.

He looked out at October and the trees yellowing down into autumn, the day darkening into night. Neat plots of still-green grass surrounded each tree and between the green plots the right-angled walks were paved with faded, salt-stained red bricks in the old Philadelphia manner. Late purple asters bordered the walks and yellow chrysanthemums burst up at each corner. Behind him on his worktable desk lay Blaise Pascal's *Treatise on Vacuum.* He had finished the binding of it that afternoon and had finished just now his final approving inspection, and what he had read, as it was his nature to do, still was before him. He saw the trees through the elegance and dignity of the ten-point unmodified Baskerville type on the marvelous beige Amalfi paper, the paragraph super-imposed upon the trees, upon the season.

From the Preface:

For as old age is that period of life most remote from infancy, who does not see that old age in this universal man ought not to be sought in the times nearest his birth, but in those most remote from it?

He was not at all sure what that meant, but it would not go out of his head. The words hung there like odd, spiky fruit on the maples. Frederick Kappel eased back in his chair and waited. What came to him was this:

> *Oh would I were a boy again,*
> * When life seemed formed of sunny years,*
> *And all the heart knew of pain*
> * Was wept away in transient tears!*
> *When every tale Hope whispered then,*
> * My fancy deemed was only truth.*
> *Oh, would that I could know again,*
> * The happy visions of my youth.*
>   Oh Would I Were a Boy Again
> *Forth we went, a gallant band —*
> *Youth, Love, Gold and Pleasure.*

But he didn't know what that meant either. He knew what the words, the sentences, meant; he understood the idea of the poem. What he didn't know was what it meant to him. What happy visions were there in his youth? What hopes, disappointed or realized? Had there ever been pain or transient tears? How had he come to be here? Who was Gretta? Why, suddenly, this train of

thoughts? After eighty-five years? He turned in his mind the page
that the poem was on, a heavy Chatham buff-colored sheet with a
laid design on it. He had read the poem thirty years before, but his
fingers felt the stiffness of the paper and the granular surface.

Gretta was his first wife, the mother of Frederick III, Anna,
Elizabeth, and Clara. The light was going out of the garden
square, the maples silhouetting now, dark against darkness. He
sought for more of Gretta but that was all he could find. He could
not even see her face. He had last seen it thirty-nine years ago,
when he had buried her, when it was even then already too late in a
life to remember things.

It was hard to have memories when all there seemed to be was
future, when one wife came along to crowd out the other, when
entire structures came and went and with them whatever certainties and truths, calamities and triumphs attached. So that in
this October, in this strange moment, it seemed incredible to him
that he had grown up — smoked a first cigar, made love, learned a
trade — before Theodore Roosevelt was president, had married
and raised children while coal was still carried in sailing ships, and
had built as with other men a life. He had been — was still — a
voyager in time passing through galaxies of blurred existences.
But what had any of it meant to him? His second wife's name was
Martha. He rose up before the black night in his window.

A memory broke over him like the chill, thrilling cascade of wind
on the cutting edge of a summer storm. He and his brother and a
friend were climbing up through the almost dry river gorge of
October Mountain ten miles south of Pittsfield, where the frogs live
in their season by the tens of thousands, when the rain drove down
like a wedge into the rocky creek bed. The three of them had
scrambled up onto a ledge protected by an overhang. In thirty
minutes the water of the creek, now white and swift, slid onto their
platform. They crawled from under the ledge and up the muddy
bank to higher ground. Safe. A little adventure. Seventy years
ago. Now he shivered in the rainy clothes and in the bite of the
newly wetted green. Now.

He left his workroom office and then the building as a night shift
was entering. The men knew him and gestured soft greetings
which he nodded to. He went by cab to the apartment he lived in
in the Broadwood Hotel off of Rittenhouse Square since the death

of his final wife two years before. There he washed and changed
his clothing and went nearby to the Triangle, his club, where he
dined, as usual, in his place upon his Wednesday fare: braised
vegetables, cold sliced duck with apples, baked potatoes, and a half
bottle of an unknown Beaujolais which he seldom finished. He
read his Philadelphia *Bulletin* at supper, although the news and
the rest always seemed the same to him, always had. Tonight in a
feature section he saw

> *Much on earth is hidden from us, but to make up for that we have been*
> *given a precious mystic sense of our living bond with the other world, with*
> *the higher heavenly world,*

but before he had finished reading it, he knew what the rest would
say,

> *and the roots of our thoughts and feelings are not here but in other*
> *worlds. That is why the philosophers say that we cannot comprehend the*
> *reality of things on earth.*

He had bound that years ago in a stiff, heavy, hollowback fashion
with dazzling Bertini end papers. He read and remembered it now
in and from the newspaper. There was an exhibit of Dostoyevsky
memorabilia at the Art Alliance. The excerpt was from a letter
which later became part of the novel.
  That night, for the first time in twenty years, Frederick
Kappel dreamed — distinctly and clearly once again; what had
he had to dream to anyway? What he dreamed that night was paper,
typefaces, bindings, and fragments — the particles he had
cemented into whatever dimensions he possessed.

> *It has been a thousand times observed, and I must observe it once more,*
> *that the hours we pass with happy prospects in view, are more pleasing*
> *than those crowned with fruition.*

The words were in his head as sharp and glowing as the gilded and
embossed letters of the titles he had worked into leather with his
hot punches and roulettes.

It is notorious that the memory strengthens as you lay burdens upon it, and becomes trustworthy as you trust it.

But then:

A great memory does not make a philosopher, any more than a dictionary can be called a grammar.

He turned in his sleep; there was nothing but the words in his dreams.

> *In nature's infinite book of secrecy*
> *A little I can read.*

He twisted:

I have entered on a performance which is without precedent, and will have no imitator. I propose to show my fellow-mortals a man in all the integrity of nature; and this man shall be myself.

At last:

> *O Boys, the times I've seen!*
> *The things I've done and know!*
> *If you knew where I have been*
> *Or half the joys I've had,*
> *You never would leave me alone;*
> *But pester me to tell,*
> *Swearing to keep it dark,*
> *What . . . but I know quite well:*
> *Every solicitor's clerk*
> *Would break out and go mad;*
> *And all the dogs would bark!*
> *O Boys! O Boys!*

He awoke in the morning convinced that he had been mocked through the night — what times, indeed, had *he* seen? But by whom? By what agency?

He was in his workroom by nine o'clock, as ever. Whatever else he was starting, unbidden, to remember, he could not remember ever not being at his craft and task by nine o'clock. He speculated that perhaps he never missed a day. His son, Frederick Kappel III, Gretta's, came in. The business, Bauch and Brinker, was his to run though the ownership of it was divided into various parts among the other children. Where were they, the father thought as the son explained the meaning of some papers he was laying out before him.

"Where is William?"

"What, father? William? My brother?"

"Yes."

"In Chicago, I suppose." He looked at his watch. "Getting ready to drive to his office." William, though he had been taught the bookbinder's skills, had elected the law. "Why do you ask, father?" It was, after all, a strange question. Where, after all, should his second son, William, be? Where should his father expect him to be?

"Never mind," Frederick Kappel said. "It's nothing. Never mind." He turned to the business before him. "What is this?" And after Frederick had explained again, he nodded and signed at various places and was, again, alone for the day. As he preferred.

But that day he bound nothing. He sat before his window instead leafing through his fragments, as his fragments came before him. Dreaming or awake, it made no difference now, as though all that he had ever known, regardless of how little had determined to a last appearance, a summation.

For that was the construction that Frederick Kappel put upon what was happening to him. It was all, he accepted, the final consequence of age, of dying: this slow-motion spin of his life before his eyes. To the young swimmer caught beyond his depths and weakening, or to the old, drowning in years, it was the same. That is what it was, and perfect though his body and mind still were, or seemed to him to be at nearly eighty-five, death was not to be unexpected; and if that, death, was what was happening, then he was absolute.

But at what pace, for surely all men were dying:

> *To every man upon this earth*
> *Death cometh soon or late;*
> *And how can man die better*
> *Than facing fearful odds*

> *For the ashes of his father,*
> *And the temples of his gods?*

Soon or late, that was the question. But at eighty-five, how late was late? How late could be late? Not very, Frederick Kappel decided and settled down for it.

> *The years seem to rush by now, and I think of death as a fast approaching end of a journey — a double and treble reason for loving as well as working while it is day.*

But he did no work that day, nor the next nor the next. Not the old work anyway. If he worked at anything now it was on appraising the journey, or discovering it. If what he was fast approaching was the end of his, then where had he been? What had he traveled through?

He had been married longest to Hanna, twenty years, and though they had conceived no children, it was she who had been most mother to his progeny. Certainly for William and Martin, infants when Martha had died, Hanna was their mother. When she died in 1930, Frederick Kappel was sixty-six years old, all his children were out of the house or almost, the great depression was descending upon all, and the tremors of the war had not altogether concluded. He remembered now in this October that that was when he had first thought of death, thought that sixty-six was close to seventy, which was enough. He had had enough; all he could expect. Now, as then, he felt completed, or at least sufficient to his universal fate. He had begun, achieved, and now was ending: life's lucid parabola. But what had he achieved? Honor among book-binders? Wealth? Substantial sons? But when he came to the hard, squinting perusal of it, the craftsman's close attention to scrupulous detail, he could find little. He could not reach back easily for faces and Christmas parties or sharp pleasure or colors or triumph or occasions or failures. For a week now he had been looking at the maples, but all he could see was the striated bark and the burnishing leaves beginning to fall rapidly.

In the second week, close to November, his son asked after his health. And about his work. Without discussing it the father told him that he was well but that he would not accept new projects. He would complete what was at hand but no more. And he went back to his window and waiting.

By the end of November his trees were bare as too were the closets and bureau drawers of memories. He had waited for them like a host for guests; he had expected them soon to flood up and over him; and then he had nervously rummaged, and then he ransacked like a man running frantically through the empty house he has returned to, but too late. Gretta, Hanna, Martha, Betty, the children and grandchildren, his own parents, his bland war, Pittsfield and childhood, his century itself — all like tiny argent specks upon the broad black absorbing velvet of his past, tiny winking glints in the darkness. He stood on the needle point with nothing behind him and no time left for anything before. All that remained were the words that he had hooked out of the stream he had fished in; they were nearly all of whatever was of him. As the first snows of the winter began, he knew that. He added himself up.

Of Family:

> *It is not observed in history that families improve with time. It is rather discovered that the whole matter is like a comet, of which the brightest part is the head; and the tail, although long and luminous, is gradually shaded into obscurity.*

Children:

> *He that hath wife and children hath given hostages to fortune; for they are impediments to great enterprises, either of virtue or mischief.*

Of Fame:

> *Oh, who shall say that fame*
> *Is nothing but an empty name,*
> *When but for those, our mighty dead,*
> *All ages past a blank would be.*

Of Wives:

> *King David and King Solomon*
> *Led merry, merry, lives*

> *With many, many lady friends*
> *And many, many wives;*
> *But when old age crept over them —*
> *With many, many qualms,*
> *King Solomon wrote the Proverbs*
> *And King David wrote the Psalms.*

And even of death, all he had for it was

> *Is there beyond the silent night*
> *An endless day?*
> *Is death a door that leads to light?*
> *We cannot say,*

and other such remnants. Comets, hostages to fortune, great enterprises, mighty dead, David and Solomon, Proverbs and Psalms — what had he to do even with the flotsam of his reading? Through the winter he sat in his window and fingered the rags of his life.

On February 18 he woke up with a cold. Even as he dressed he knew it would worsen. By the time he got to the office he was slightly feverish, only enough so the flush beneath his white, smoothed flesh shone up through it, as sometimes pink will in the finest marble come up suffusingly out of depths. He sat in his chair and coughed and sneezed a little.

When his son saw him he wanted him to go home, to *his* home, so that he could be attended to.

"I've had colds before," Frederick Kappel told him. "Worse by far than this one." But you weren't eighty-five his son wanted to say but couldn't. Precisely, his father would have answered. At last he had his way. Of course death must have its agent. I approach my climacteric.

> *He had a startling genius, but somehow*
> *It didn't emerge;*
> *Always on the evolution of things*
> *That didn't evolve;*
> *Always verging toward some climax,*
> *But he never reached the verge;*

> *Always nearing the solution*
> *Of some theme he could not solve.*

Frederick Kappel laughed so hard at that, howled, that the secretary (for twenty years) in the outer office ran in to him; she had never heard him laugh, that way or any other. He laughed on, gasping and coughing and sneezing. Between his own tears squeezed out by the irony of the fragment, he saw her own tears, of pity, but what did she know? Then she ran for his son.

Still, after he had calmed down, he would not leave. He heard them mumbling in the outer office and soon Dr. Freed came. Dr. Freed examined him more thoroughly than for a cold, wrote two prescriptions, told him to go to his son's house till he recovered, and then told him to go to Florida for the rest of the winter and more. He thanked Dr. Freed and went back to looking out his window. Later he consented only to take the medicine. It wouldn't be long now, he thought. There isn't anything left to wait for. Death's predictive ambience of the past five months had turned assertive.

But he did not die. He did not even miss a day at his window.

> *Nature's first green is gold,*
> *Her hardest hue to hold.*
> *Her early leaf's a flower.*
> *But only so an hour.*

He watched as his maples blew out again, flinging their netting leaves out once more to entrap the sky. Birds came back. The tulips that he had ordered planted bloomed where the asters had been and would be. By the end of June he had never felt better, but different. He was lighter, as if his bones were hollowing; he felt himself floating, hardly feeling his own weight upon his foot when he stepped. And he *looked* lighter, more transluscent, like a thin parchment held against the light, like Moriki paper from Japan, like the spring leaf before it hardens against the summer heat. Thin and thinner he became until at the top of August, sitting now under his maples, he became like the subtlest of membrances, the thickness of a mere cell, so that he could not tell easily what was outside of him or inside. When a leaf fluttered; he fluttered; when a bird sang, he resonated; when the heavy summer raindrops pocked the dirt, he took the impress too.

There was no knowable joy to this, no express pleasure, only a great subsumptive neutrality, as though the long, nearly perfect vacuity which was his life had prepared him, or opened him, or by obliterating him had absorbed him. In mid-September, when the roses were coming back, he remembered a monument, the volumes of it he had bound, the veiny, calendered, burnt-umberish leather, the waxed threads, the sewing, the endsheets, the pressing, the carving, all of it. He had worked a long time on it a long time ago.

> *Only that day dawns to which we are awake*
> *There is more day to dawn   The sun is*
> *but a morning star.*

and

> *September 19, 1860: the temperature*
> *unseasonable. The foxes fur is thick.*
> *Birch buds seen longer than I remember.*

And then he was wholly clean.

And he lived on, lightening and lightening until at last he quavered in the particles of sound and pulsed along the frequencies of the photons in and out of the spectrum; until in his one hundred and sixth year, when it seemed to him increasingly, even against all of the reasonableness that he still possessed, that his life would not, would never leave him, he relinquished it.

JOSE YGLESIAS

The American Sickness

(FROM THE MASSACHUSETTS REVIEW)

THE FLIGHT TO MONTEVIDEO that Ellie's mother was taking left
from Kennedy Airport, and the drive down from Adams College
in Massachusetts provided the two of them with the opportunity of
passing on final instructions to one another. It was also one of the
two sure, annual occasions — coming from and going to Montevideo — when her mother felt the inclination to chat to no purpose. She had been flying up every spring and staying until school
opened in the fall before returning to her older daughter in
Uruguay. She had been doing this for five years, since Ellie and
her husband separated, but it was such a minor complication in her
life that Mercedes (Ellie had been taught to call her mother by her
first name during the Nazi occupation of France) was surprised
when Ellie said in Spanish, "You must wish sometimes that life
were simpler."

"My life or your life?" Mercedes said. "Or your son's?"

Ellie always listened to Mercedes from the stance of a detached,
friendly observer, and Mercedes' response made her laugh. "Let's
not talk about *my* life," she said. "And your grandson is a regular
American boy."

"Well, my life could not be simpler," Mercedes said, and reached
forward and pushed the ashtray on the dashboard closed. "I married one man and stayed with him."

Ellie laughed louder. "What a bitch you are!"

"This country has ruined your manners," Mercedes replied.
"Profanity is for men."

"You've never left Saragossa," Ellie said, "and yet we have
changed countries more often than our shoes."

"You exaggerate, as usual," Mercedes said. "It was two or three countries and no more."

Ellie said, "A German poet said that."

"German!" Mercedes said and smiled the austere smile that Ellie called her Castilian, aristocratic smile. "They traveled because they wanted to."

"A good German, Mercedes," Ellie said, and Mercedes sighed as if calling on some absent authority to confirm that her doubts about Germans were not unreasonable. "And it *was* four countries," Ellie insisted. "Spain, France, Uruguay, the United States."

"Speak for yourself," Mercedes said, and looked quickly at, and then away from, Hartford, which Ellie herself admitted was ridiculous. "I am only visiting this country."

"Mercedes!" Ellie exclaimed. "It is your grandchild's fatherland!"

"Ah yes," Mercedes said, and stroked her patent leather pocketbook as if she had won the argument.

Well, for me it's four countries, Ellie thought; and last year in Brazil, that's five.

"You cannot remember Spain," Mercedes said, pursuing her own argument. "You were two in 1937 when we crossed the International Bridge at Hendaye."

"How many times do I have to tell you, Mercedes, that I do remember!" Ellie said. "Irun was on fire."

"You remember your father's stories."

Ellie said, "May he rest in peace."

Mercedes hugged her before going on the plane, and got to the point Ellie had hoped to head off. "What do I tell them when I get there? Will you take the post at the university?"

"If I went back," Ellie said,, "I'd join the Tupamaros."

"Elvira, God forbid!" Mercedes exclaimed, using Ellie's Spanish name. "You know they are holding the position open for you. I shall tell them you accept and will come in June and the devil with these yearly trips of mine."

"No, no," Ellie said hurriedly. "Tell Don Diego that I shall write and give him my decision."

"It is an American sickness, this not making up one's mind," Mercedes said. "Don't kiss me if you do not mean to come."

"Mercedes, I shall kiss you no matter what." Once on each cheek, while Mercedes closed her eyes enduring her. "Give my sister my love."

Mercedes lifted her eyebrows to indicate she was exasperated.

Ellie said, "Maybe I shall come."

"You are still my same little chicken — with its head cut off," her mother replied, and turned quickly to the man waiting to check her ticket.

Going back, Ellie did not drive into New York City. Too tempting, and stopping at the lawyer's for the final papers might make her feel bad. She was half committed to a party at the Dawsons that night, and there was Jason — he was still only ten years old and he shouldn't be left to eat alone the very day his grandmother left. She drove over the Triborough Bridge without any trouble — it was two in the afternoon and traffic was manageable — but she had to slow down often and stop altogether a couple of times in the Bronx where, it seemed to her, the unfinished approach to the Connecticut Turnpike had been in a state of repair and indecision for years. "They don't know what they're doing," she said aloud. "Like me."

And she pondered again, now that Mercedes was out of the way, whether she should devote the school year to finishing her history of Brazil or to completing the translation of Clarin's *La Regenta*. Both projects were financed by grants — one from the Ford Foundation, the other from the National Translation Center — and she assuaged her guilt at accepting them simultaneously by recalling her Brazilian friends' encouragement last summer: "Take all you can get out of those Yankees — it will never be more than a tiny bit of what they have stolen from us."

"But I shall have to decide one of these days whether I am a literary historian or a political historian," she said brightly as she approached the first toll, where the man in the booth seeing her lips move asked, "What?"

"Lovely day," she said.

"Yeah?"

"Yes!" she insisted, and drove off laughing. They refuse to play their part, she thought; they do not have the Latins' sense that we must keep one another's spirits up. Such an insistently unhappy people. It was then she remembered the visiting lecturer two years ago who had told her she was like a Viennese torte.

"A Viennese torte!" she had said, delighted. "What kind — with fruit and nuts?"

"Oh, I guess I mean what we call a seven-layer cake here," he said. She nodded and he took heart to continue. "There's so much to one that you can lift a part of the cake from the rest and each section is a cake in itself."

The face of the lecturer blurred in her memory with those of men and women at cocktail parties looking puzzled when she was introduced as Ellie Smith. The faces cleared when she explained that until she married her name was Elvira Zaitegui. The puzzlement began again when they realized her accent was French. At that point she recited her résumé; it put them at ease and gave her something to talk about.

"The Zaitegui is Spanish Basque," she would begin. "At the age of two, when Franco took the north of Spain, I crossed over into France in my mother's arms. We lived there for nine years and then we went to Uruguay because Spain was out of the question. I went to school and college in Montevideo; married an American — therefore, Smith; and came to New York where I worked at my master's and also my doctorate at Columbia." She'd pause as if for questions, then add, "All very ordinary," and laugh with more pleasure than any Professor Smith would have.

Sometimes she was obliged to tell more. There was always more, for only fools thought her experience was ordinary — indeed, their response to her statement was a useful test — but she could never tell all. There were bits and pieces of her life that she forgot for months at a time or that friends didn't learn until long after they had become intimate. It was only after she divorced her husband that it occurred to her that he did not know why she called her mother Mercedes. Had she withheld it because of what it told about her? During the Nazi occupation, her father had been hid in a warehouse in Bordeaux, and she was taught to say Mercedes because the French family who had taken them in hoped that if her mother was sent away to a camp they could save Ellie by claiming her as their own. That was how Madame Paillard became — suddenly, as everything in her life — Maman. Yes, to have told her husband might have made her seem emotionally dependent, which she feared she was, and she had wanted to be helpful, no burden to him: therefore, the degrees and the teaching she undertook, which he considered competitive. Ay, ay, Americans, she thought, what are their hidden experiences?

There was only one experience she purposely kept to herself. The young graduate student in Brazil who stayed in her apartment for two weeks. One member of the five-men underground cell to which he belonged had been picked up by the police, and that meant that the other four had to disperse and stay under cover until they learned whether the one who was caught had talked. They usually talked. Pedro expected that his comrade would. He expected, too, that when it came time to leave her apartment he would have to lead a totally clandestine life in some other city, and he began to prepare for it by growing a mustache, reshaping his eyebrows, and shaving the hairline of his forehead to give himself a wide brow. "Goodbye to the College of Engineering," he said to her when the transformation was done. "Look at me, wouldn't you say I belong in Arts and Letters?"

She slept with him the day that she came home at midday from the National Archives, where she spent most days doing research, to give him the message, delivered to her there, that at seven that evening a car would be waiting for him on Copacabana. He was alone in the apartment when she told him. Mercedes had taken Jason to friends in Leblon to play on the beach and Ellie was to meet them for dinner there. "You thrive on all those old documents," her hostess announced when Ellie finally arrived that evening at Leblon, looking happy. "My, you're radiant!" And Ellie quickly greeted the others there.

"No, no," interrupted a young journalist with whom her friend had taken to pairing her. "It is Rio that does it — being away from that terrible country up north!"

Ellie's friend shook her head. "You are wrong — she is a Yankee and likes to work."

"I am three-quarters of an hour late," Ellie said. "How can you say I am a Yankee?"

Pedro had been simple and direct. Sleeping with him was akin to the care that Mercedes had taken of him for two weeks: his laundry was done at home, separately, to avoid suspicion; there was coffee on the stove for him at all hours. He hugged Ellie in excitement when she gave him the message, and then he asked her. Later, walking past the two doormen on duty in the lobby, she enjoyed the irony that only this once were they right about the divorced woman who went out alone so often. "When they see a woman and a man together," she said to Pedro in the car, "politics is the last thing on their minds. Like all you Brazilians. So be sure to kiss me goodbye when I drop you off."

But she kept her eyes on the rearview mirror as he leaned toward her and kissed her, and she noticed that the man in the car to which Pedro was transferring studied the sidewalk and the shop entrances. She waited until they drove away. Nothing happened that was not planned, and she arrived at her friends' in Leblon feeling so good because she felt supremely useful. Still, Pedro, who was twelve years younger than she, had his effect: the journalist, the naval officer, the librarian in the days that followed almost persuaded her in their different ways. It was her last month in Rio, but she held out: no, no, no, she had picked up the notion on the other side of Hendaye, an old Spanish prejudice nursed by Mercedes, that a divorced woman was a bad woman, and she was not going to live up to the part.

Behind the wheel now she shook her head at her summer's recollection, and saw in the disappointed face of the girl in dungarees, who stood by the last New Haven exit on the turnpike holding a placard that said ADAMS, that she had turned down a hiker. A girl too. She braked, moved into the graveled edge of the road and started to back up. In the rearview mirror she saw the dungareed figure sprint toward her car: it was a boy. She was tempted to take off again but remembered he was an Adams student. She'd be safe and, anyway, she needed a companion to keep her from reminiscing.

The boy looked in the window first, shook the long hair off his brows, and said, "Hi, Mrs. S.!"

"You!" she exclaimed, and quickly remembered his name. "Sandy Lands."

He settled into the seat next to hers, looked at her with a fair face that radiated wonder, and said, as she took off, "Wow, doesn't it blow your mind!"

"Gibberish," she replied. "Don't talk gibberish to me. If you mean that this is an extraordinary coincidence —"

"What else?"

"Then you shouldn't be so happy about it. I'm the last person you want to run into."

"Never, Mrs. S." He looked serene. "You're not one of the

deadies," he explained, and maneuvered two fingers into the pocket of his dungarees to extract a cigarette.

"You didn't register this fall, you didn't take my finals last spring —"

"I'm down on myself about that," he said, but didn't look unhappy. "I was going straight to your house to rap — to discuss it with you. You know, get the lay of the land."

"Oh, you want to be taken back?" she said, saw him begin the same search in his pockets for matches, and pointed to the lighter on the dashboard and pushed it in for him. "If that's a joint, I'm driving you straight to a police station."

"Ho, ho, I remember when you called them pigs," he said. "It's great to run into you like this. I was afraid you didn't come back from Brazil." He leaned back, relaxed, as if all his problems were solved. He held up the cigarette. "It's only a squashed Camel."

"I don't know why I did," she said, without thinking.

"Yeah," he said, and she knew that he must be looking at her with great seriousness. She glanced at him, to check. Third World, his innocent eyes said. "It's real down there," he said.

"Romantic nonsense," she replied. "You know I am a bourgeois liberal."

"God, Mrs. S., I apologized about that." His voice was small and aggrieved. "I was stoned that night, I never told you."

"Sandy!"

The snow had melted the day spring officially began when the students, Sandy prominently among them, occupied the administration building and the student center. Their first act was to paint "Ho Lives" on the token piece of marble above the wide glass doors of the center, a modern building; they couldn't bring themselves to deface the fake Gothic of the administration building, and there were many discussions later about that. Their second act was to issue, on the best paper in the president's office, their list of demands, all taken over from Berkeley and Columbia. Gayle Dawson, Ellie's department head, a man who had been expelled from the Communist Party in 1932 as a Trotskyist, was the first to show the mimeographed statement to her. "Workers and peasants of the Bronx, unite," he said.

She'd had to laugh but she didn't want to. She feared politics; it brought civil war, torture, exile; it was the cause of her father's

unhappy life. The last ten years he taught in a Catholic girls'
school in Montevideo, and when he died, an exile Republican newspaper carried an article about him. He died on a Wednesday, was
buried on Friday, was lauded in the weekly paper on Saturday, and
on Sunday afternoon the Jesuit head of the school came to visit
them. Was it true, he asked, that Sr. Zaitegui had been an atheist
and a Red? She was the youngest in the room and the question was
not directed at her. "He swallowed his pride to work for you," she
had volunteered, taking her stand on poltics. "To feed us he was
willing to forget about politics, which you people are not generous enough to do." In her mind she classed the Jesuit priest
with Gayle Dawson, and her father with the students. She felt
rather than perceived the connection, and all she could say to
Dawson when he showed her the demands of the strikers was,
"I'm worried about my students."

The students were in the buildings not quite forty-eight hours.
On the second evening came the bust. When news of it reached
her, she was meeting with some of the younger faculty members
who hoped to mediate between the students and the administration. They all rushed to the campus. Ellie sobbed when she saw
Sandy being dragged into a police van. This is madness, she
thought, I didn't feel this bad when my marriage broke up.

She brought herself under control and tried to think of a way to
be useful. She must get to the police station and see that they were
not mistreated. The police chief was her next-door neighbor,
and with mixed deference, fatherliness and self-importance,
he escorted her and a young Sinologist into the small town
jail. The cells were jammed and the noise let up enough when
they walked in for Ellie to hear Sandy clearly: "Here come
the bourgeois liberals expiating their guilt!" Followed by the
chanting, deafening in that confined corridor, "Pigs, pigs, pigs!"

"Everybody apologized to you, Mrs. S.," Sandy said. "Like we
didn't know then you don't go into action stoned."

"So what do you know now?" Ellie said.

"Hey, you're tough," he replied. "But I knew that."

She looked at him out of the corner of an eye, and he caught her
at it. They broke into laughter together.

"What if I told you I know how to put together a time-bomb?"
he said.

"I'd say you were crazy," she answered, and involuntarily accelerated the car. "But first of all, you wouldn't tell me, right?"

"No," he said, but he didn't sound convincing. She looked at him again, and again they laughed. "Why are you coming back to Adams?" she asked. "I thought all the activists were leaving the campuses."

"I want to become a doctor," he said. "I was up at a commune in Vermont all summer. What the Movement needs is doctors, lawyers, technicians."

"What?"

"Service skills," he explained.

"Technicians . . ." she began.

Sandy interrupted, "Electrical engineers who —"

"Don't tell me!" She took a hand off the wheel and waved it at him. "I don't want to know." They were approaching Hartford, and she kept up her warning hand. "Don't talk to me now anyway or I'll get into the wrong lane."

When she was on 91, she asked, "Did you go see the Mark Twain house?"

"Remember in your liberal arts days — I told you about it. Harriet Beecher Stowe also lived in Hartford. A center of radical abolitionists, then of the gilded age nouveaux riches," she explained and suppressed a smile because she sounded like the notes she kept on file cards.

"Oh yeah, yeah," he said.

"So?"

"I figured it was no log cabin."

"All right, half an hour and we'll be home," she said, in her classroom voice. "Are you willing to make some apologies?"

"Apologies?" he said.

"I'll do my best with the registrar and department heads," she explained, "but once I've felt them out you're going to have to come along with me and convince them you're serious. Dawson is on the disciplinary committee —"

"Oh God," he said.

"Sandy —"

"No, no, I'll say anything you want. I'll look as straight as the dean, I've got other duds up there . . ."

"You've got a place for tonight then?"

"Oh, I can crash a lot of pads," he replied.

"Good, I'll talk to Dawson tonight —" and chuckled to think this was what decided her to go to the party — "and you see me in my office tomorrow morning."

"When?" he asked.

"You just camp there early and wait — in fear and trembling."

"You Spaniards are really groovy," he said. His way of thanking her.

"Romantic nonsense," she replied.

The light was on in the foyer when Ellie picked up the mail at the table by the door. "Jason! Jason! she called.

His voice, ostentatiously well-modulated, answered from the living room, just a few steps away. "I'm here," he said. He was lying on his back on the floor, his legs up on the coffee table. The TV was on but the sound was not. "Waiting for the five o'clock news, Ellie," he added, letting her see the remote control in his hand.

"It's hardly sunset and you've got the lights on," she said. "All over the house too, I bet."

"I know what you're thinking," he said. "But I'm not scared. It's just a reflex — I turn them on automatically when I go into a room, honest."

"Don't you want to know about Mercedes?" she said, shuffling the letters she had gathered, and noticed there was one for her mother from her sister in Montevideo.

"What about Mercedes?" he asked. "There's a swell offer from *Time* magazine — nine cents an issue."

"She's your grandmother," Ellie replied. "Don't you want to know if she got off all right?"

"Well, obviously, for Christ's sakes," he said, and threw out his free hand and let it fall on the floor above his head.

Ellie perched on the arm of a chair and stopped looking through the letters. "Now listen, I want you, now that Mercedes isn't here to do it, to call me Elvira," she said. "Otherwise, I'll forget who I am."

"Okay, but none of that Javier stuff for me — you call me Jason," he replied. "I tell you what, you and I can switch to Spanish now and give the French a rest."

She didn't answer, instead cocked an ear toward the foyer and stairs. "Jason, I hear the radio in your room going."

Jason swung a leg off the coffee table and turned on the sound of the TV with the remote control gadget.

"Jason!" Ellie called.

"What! What!" he replied, louder than she.

"Go upstairs and turn it off."

"Why?"

"Because I'm going upstairs to lie down a moment before I prepare dinner and I don't want to have the radio blaring —"

Jason covered his eyes with one hand, in exasperation. "You're going upstairs — what's to prevent you from turning it off?"

"Because I'm not going into your filthy room!" She got up, the mail in one hand, her pocketbook in the other. "Besides it's a punishment. You go up and turn if off now before the five o'clock news —"

He dashed ahead of her and she met him again on the stairs coming down. "Stay out of my room," he said.

"A pleasure," she said.

She threw off her shoes without bending to ease them off, and then crossed to her bed. She put the mail on the night table and reminded herself that she should, as soon as she changed, take the mail to her study across the landing. Everything in its place. She pulled off her dress and lay in bed in her halfslip; she threw her arms out limply to relax. Now that Mercedes was gone, she must make sure to be neat — hang the clothes when she got up from this rest, find her shoes, straighten the bed — and not continue as the sloppy adolescent girl that she became when Mercedes visited. Her dependency. She smiled and pushed away the thought. "I'm not turning into an American," she said to the stain in the ceiling. "No worrier she." Then repeated this in French, Spanish, Italian, Portuguese, enjoying the effort it took her with each to find the equivalent for the American construction of no-worrier-she.

She thought of Mercedes' parting words, and rolled her head on the pillow from side to side: she did not want to think about leaving this country. No. New-term jitters, that's what her complaining had been. The letter from her sister Clara. She reached for it, opened it (messily, she chided herself) and learned, without warning, that Pedro was dead. Tortured to death by the secret police.

"Mom, Mom!" Jason called up the stairwell. "What do you want?"

She was sitting at the edge of the bed. She must have screamed. Her throat hurt and she heard the sound she'd made reverberating in her head now, like an echo. She tried to swallow, in order to answer Jason, and instead began to sob.

"Listen, Mom," Jason continued, "I'll clean it up later. Okay?"

"Okay," she called and crooked her arm over her face to stop the howl that threatened to follow. She remained on the edge of the bed hunched over, trying to remember Pedro's face, and watched her tears fall on her knees. The sound of the television reached her. She was used to watching the afternoon news with Jason and she straightened as reflex. "He's not news," she said to herself to explain why she didn't get up, and the thought helped her. She wiped her face with one hand and with the other took up her sister's letter again. "When I see you I'll tell you how we got the news from Brazil but meanwhile I thought Elvira would want to know," her sister ended. Along the margin she added, "His body has not been returned."

After a while she walked across the landing to the bathroom. She must think about dinner. As she walked into the bathroom she said, "And what am I doing in this miserable country?"

The only boy with short hair in her freshman class had said yesterday, "It seems to me, Mrs. Smith, that you always imply that we're responsible for every unfortunate thing that happens in Latin America."

"Miserable country," she repeated, and bent over the wash basin and threw water on her face to keep from crying again. There was no one she could talk to about Pedro. She would not go to the Dawsons' party. She would heat the chick pea potage her mother had cooked and make pepper steak with the leftover roast beef. If she went to the party she might talk about Pedro and she knew that later she would be sorry. What did they know about young men like him? She thought: he would not talk and that's why they tortured him to death. She sat on the edge of the bathtub while she absorbed that thought.

On the way to the kitchen, she passed the foyer and Jason said, "Okay if I have my dinner here?" She did not answer and he took it as a good sign. During a commercial he ran into the kitchen and told her there had been a call from Mrs. Dawson in the afternoon. "They've got a party at their house or something."

"I hope you weren't definite," Ellie said. "I don't know if I can go."

"Well, I told her it wouldn't be because of me," he replied. "I mean, you can't use that excuse anymore, Mom." He noticed the bottle of soy sauce on the stove, and added, "Wow, pepper steak!"

His exclamation reminded her of Sandy. If she didn't go to the party and talk to Dawson about him, she would not have much advice for Sandy when he came by her office in the morning. What had she planned to say to Dawson? How convince him of Sandy's seriousness now? Tell him that Sandy meant to work hard because the Movement needed doctors and lawyers and electrical engineers who could put together a bomb? She chuckled as she stirred the potage — this might be just the thing to tickle Dawson into helping Sandy. Then she thought of Pedro and was ashamed that she could so soon be distracted from mourning him. She lay down the spoon and checked that Jason had left the kitchen and quickly crossed herself, completing the gesture by bringing her closed hand to her mouth and kissing the thumbnail.

Biographical Notes

Biographical Notes

RUSSELL BANKS is the author of a novel, *Family Life,* and a collection of stories, *Searching for Survivors,* both published in the spring of 1975. His stories have appeared in numerous periodicals and anthologies. He is a member of the English Department faculty at the University of New Hampshire and is the Fiction-Writer-in-Residence at Emerson College in Boston for the year 1975–1976. At present he resides in Northwood Narrows, New Hampshire, and is finishing his second novel.

DONALD BARTHELME is the author of seven books, including *Come Back, Dr. Caligari, Snow White, City Life,* and *Guilty Pleasures,* a collection of parodies and political satire. His books have been translated into French, German, Italian, Spanish, Danish, Swedish, Finnish, Japanese, and other languages. His articles and stories have appeared in *The New Yorker, Esquire, Harper's, The Atlantic, Paris Review,* and other periodicals, and he is represented in more than seventy-five anthologies. He won a Guggenheim Fellowship in 1967, a National Institute of Arts and Letters Award in 1972, and a National Book Award for children's books in 1972. He has taught as Visiting Professor of English at Boston University and SUNY–Buffalo.

ROSELLEN BROWN began her career as a poet and her first book, *Some Deaths in the Delta and Other Poems,* was a National Council on the Arts selection for 1970. Her stories have appeared in many places, including *New American Review, Triquarterly,* and the *Hudson Review.* She has received grants from the National Endowment for the Arts, the Radcliffe Institute, and the Howard Foundation and has taught in Mississippi in the 1960s and the Bread Loaf Conference in the mid-seventies. She lives in Peterborough, New Hampshire, with her husband and two daughters.

JERRY BUMPUS was born in Mount Vernon, Illinios, in 1937, and is an M.F.A. from the Writers' Workshop in Iowa. He was included in *The*

Best American Short Stories 1974, and his stories have appeared in *Esquire, TriQuarterly, Transatlantic Review, Shenandoah,* and many other magazines. His novel *Anaconda* is available from *December* magazine, and a book of his stories, *Things in Place,* was recently published by the Fiction Collective. Mr. Bumpus teaches creative writing at San Diego University and is married to a genealogist who, in the summer, usually succeeds in luring him and their two daughters onto treks deep into the heartland and into the past.

FREDERICK BUSCH was born in Brooklyn in 1941 and now lives in Poolville, New York, with his wife Judith and their two sons. His books are *I Wanted a Year Without Fall, Breathing Trouble,* and *Hawkes: A Guide to His Fictions.* He is now working on a book of shorter fictions and teaching literature at Colgate University.

NANCY CHAIKIN graduated from the University of Michigan, where she won Avery Hopwood awards for short fiction and for critical essays. She has reviewed for *The Saturday Review* and her short stories have appeared in *Mademoiselle,* numerous quarterlies, two other *Best American* collections and *Fifty Modern Short Stories.* She writes a regularly published column for Long Island weeklies and has recently appeared in The Christian Science Monitor. She and her husband, a communications engineer, have three children and one grandchild. Mrs. Chaikin hopes, next year, to teach as well as write.

MARY CLEARMAN grew up in Montana and teaches English and drama at Northern Montana College. She has published numerous critical articles and short fiction in a number of journals. She has recently completed a novel entitled *The Jackalope.* Ms. Clearman has two children and enjoys flying a Cessna Skyhawk.

LYLL BECERRA DE JENKINS was born and raised in Colombia, South America, but has been living in the United States for the past eleven years. Before she took up writing she danced and taught flamenco. She has won a few prizes for her stories here and in South America. *Tyranny* is her second story published by *The New Yorker.* She resides in New Canaan, Connecticut, with her husband and five children.

ANDRE DUBUS was born in 1936, grew up in Louisiana, and served five and a half years as an officer in the peacetime Marine Corps before entering the Writers' Workshop at the University of Iowa. He now teaches at Bradford College in Bradford, Massachusetts. He has published a novel, *The Lieutenant* and has recently come out with a collection of stories, *Separate Flights.*

JESSE HILL FORD won *The Atlantic* 'First' award in 1959 for *The Surest Thing in Show Business.* More stories followed in *The Atlantic, The Paris Review, Playboy, Esquire,* and other magazines. A collection of his stories, *Fishes,*

Birds and Sons of Men appeared in 1969. Born in Troy, Alabama, in 1928, he attended Vanderbilt, the University of Florida, and the University of Oslo. A Fulbright Scholar, Guggenheim Fellow and Visiting Fellow at the Center for Advanced Study, Wesleyan, Connecticut, he was Visiting Professor at the University of Rochester during the spring semester.

WILLIAM HOFFMAN comes from West Virginia. He's been a newsman, a banker, and a teacher. He now works and lives with his wife and two daughters on a farm in Charlotte County, Virginia. He's had a play produced. He has published stories and seven novels.

EVAN HUNTER is the author of many novels, including *The Blackboard Jungle, Last Summer* and *Streets of Gold*. Under the pseudonym of Ed McBain, he is the author of thirty two novels in the 87th Precinct mystery series. He has written the screenplays for Alfred Hitchcock's *The Birds* and for his own novels *Strangers When We Meet* and *Fuzz*. His short stories have appeared in many American magazines, most frequently in *Playboy*. He makes his home in Sarasota with his wife and daughter.

PAUL KASER was born in Killbuck, Ohio, and received a B.A. in journalism from Kent State University in 1966. Shortly thereafter, he served in Vietnam in the Air Force and taught school there. He has an M.A. in English from California State University at Hayward where he is presently teaching. He has twice received grants for attendance at the Annual Squaw Valley Writers Conference from the California Arts Commission. He is married and lives in the San Francisco Bay area.

ALISTAIR MACLEOD is a native of Nova Scotia's Inverness County. He is presently on the staff of the Universiy of Windsor, Ontario, where he teaches English and Creative Writing and serves as fiction editor of the *University of Windsor Review*. His work has appeared in many magazines and anthologies including *Best American Short Stories 1969*. A collection of his fiction will be published by McClelland and Stewart in 1975.

JACK MATTHEWS is Professor of English at Ohio University, and spent the year 1974–1975 in Athens on a Guggenheim Fellowship. Married, with two grown daughters and a growing son, he is also the author of a volume of short stories, another of poetry, and five novels, along with many published essays, stories, poems, and reviews.

EUGENE McNAMARA was born in Oak Park, Illinois, but is now a Canadian citizen. Editor of the *University of Windsor Review*, he has had his stories and poems published in numerous journals and his book, *Interior Landscape: Selected Literary Criticism of Marshall McLuhan*, was published by McGraw Hill in 1969. Mr. McNamara teaches at the University of Windsor and is married with five children.

REYNOLDS PRICE was born in Macon, North Carolina, in 1933. He was educated at Duke and Oxford Universities, and since 1958 he has taught for a part of each year at Duke. His first novel, *A Long and Happy Life,* was published in 1962 and has been followed by three other novels, two volumes of short stories, and a volume of essays and scenes. The story in this collection appears, elaborated and in its full context, in his most recent novel, *The Surface of Earth,* published by Atheneum in 1975.

ABRAHAM ROTHBERG, a native New Yorker and World War II veteran, was educated at Brooklyn College, the University of Iowa, and Columbia University, where he received the B.A., M.A., and Ph.D. respectively. He is the author of six novels — *The Stalking Horse, The Sword of the Golem, The Other Man's Shoes, The Song of David Freed, The Heirs of Cain,* and *The Thousand Doors.* His other works include two books of history, two children's books, and a volume of literary criticism. A practicing novelist, journalist, editor, and college teacher, he is presently Associate Professor of English at St. John Fisher College in Rochester, New York.

LESLIE SILKO was born in Albuquerque, New Mexico. "I grew up at Laguna Pueblo," she writes. "I am of mixed-breed ancestry, but what I know is Laguna. This place I am from is everything I am as a writer and human being." At present she makes her home in Ketchikan, Alaska, where she is completing her first novel, as yet untitled, which will be published in 1976 by Richard Seaver/The Viking Press.

BARRY TARGAN was born in Atlantic City, New Jersey, in 1932. He was educated at Rutgers University, University of Chicago, and Brandeis University, from which he received a Ph.D. in English Literature. He has published short stories, poetry, and essays in such magazines and journals as *Esquire, The Southern Review, American Review, Salmagundi,* and *Quarterly Review of Literature.* Mr. Targan won the Iowa School of Letters Award for Short Fiction for 1975 and the University of Iowa Press published his collection of short stories in 1975. Mr. Targan lives with his wife and two sons in Schuylerville, New York.

JOSE YGLESIAS is one of three American novelists with his surname. The others are his wife Helen and his son Raphael. He lives in North Brooklin, Maine.

The Yearbook of the American Short Story

January 1 to December 31, 1974

Roll of Honor, 1974

I. *American Authors*

ABBOTT, LEE K., JR.
An Investment Never Stops Praying.
Epoch, Fall.

ADAMS, ALICE
Verlie, I Say Unto You. Atlantic, July.

BAKER, DONALD W.
The Cellar. New Letters, Fall.

BARBA, HARRY
Somewhere on the Moon's Moon.
Ararat, Spring.

BARTLETT, BRIAN
Women on Hill. Fiddlehead, Fall.

BELLOW, SAUL
Humboldt's Gift. Esquire.

CALDERAZZO, JOHN
The Wine Trick. Colorado Quarterly, Spring.

CLEARMAN, MARY
Monstero. North American Review, Winter.

CONROY, FRANK
Celestial Events. New Yorker, June 10.

CRUMLEY, JAMES
Daddy's Gone A-Hunting. Aspen Leaves, Vol. 1, No. 2.

CUMMINS, WALTER
Miss Wilcox' Ghost. St. Andrews Review, Summer.

CURLEY, DANIEL
In Northumberland Once. Massachusetts Review, Summer.

DE JENKINS, LYLL BECERRA
Pablo. New Yorker, January 7.

DISCH, THOMAS M.
Getting Into Death. Antaeus, Spring Summer.

DOLLARHIDE, LOUIS
A Monkey in a Magnolia Tree. Southern Review, Autumn.

DORIAN, MARGUERITE
Old Mezzotint. Response, Fall.

DRUM, CHARLES S.
El Gusano Duro de Xachtomel. Southwest Review, Summer.

ESSLINGER, PAT M.
The Puppet. Southern Review, Winter.

GALLANT, MAVIS
The Late Homecomer. New Yorker, July 8.

GARDNER, JOHN
The Music Lover. Antaeus, Spring-Summer.
GRIFFITH, JONATHAN
Sunday Silence. Carleton Miscellany, Spring-Summer.
GUGHIOTTA, BOBETTE
The Ghost — Blue Jeep. Virginia Quarterly Review, Autumn.

HARRIS, MacDONALD
Dr. Pettigott's Face. Iowa Review, Summer.
HASSLER, JON
The Undistinguished Poet. South Dakota Review, Spring.
HELPRIN, MARK
Leaving the Church. New Yorker, November 1.
HOFFMAN, ALLEN
Building Blocks. Commentary, May.
HOOD, HUGH
Going Out As a Ghost. Fiddlehead, Spring.

KAUFMAN, SUE
Under the Trees. Mademoiselle, February.
KITTREDGE, WILLIAM
The Man Who Loved Buzzards. Carolina Quarterly, Winter.
KRANES, DAVID
Little Sister. Western Humanities Review, Winter.

LAVIN, MARY
The Shrine. Sewanee Review, April-June.
The Mug of Water. Southern Review, Spring.
LEAHY, PATRICK
Dream of the Man Who Wouldn't Die. Backy 4.

MAI, WILLIAM
The Implement Man. Antaeus, Spring-Summer.

MATTHEWS, F. X.
The Winter Garden. Virginia Quarterly Review, Spring.
MAXWELL, WILLIAM
Over by the River. New Yorker, July 1.
MAYER, TOM
The Top of the World. Playboy, December.
METCALF, JOHN
Beryl. Canadian Fiction Magazine, Spring.
MINOT, STEPHEN
Phang Song. North American Review, Spring.
A Sometimes Memory. Sewanee Review, Fall.
Estuaries. Virginia Quarterly Review, Winter.
MOULTON, ELIZABETH
All We Like Sheep. Virginia Quarterly Review, Summer.
MOUNTZOURIS, H. L.
An American at the Movies. New Yorker, January 21.
Milkman's Boy. New Yorker, April 29.

OZICK, CYNTHIA
Usurpation. Esquire, May.

PACKER, NANCY HUDDLESTON
Second Wind. Southwest Review, Summer.
PETER, JOHN
Make a Joyful Noise. Malahat Review, July.
PROSE, FRANCINE
The Bandit Was My Neighbor. Atlantic, September.

RABE, DAVID
Ben Schmidt's Old Shoes. Mademoiselle, April.
ROTH, HENRY H.
To Grace, Love Alan. Perspective, Winter.

ROTH, RUSSELL
For Those Who Have No More to Give. South Dakota Review, Winter.

SANDBERG, PETER L.
The Death of the Snowy Egret. Literary Review, Spring.
SAROYAN, WILLIAM
Cowards. Harper's Magazine, June.
SINGER, ISAAC BASHEVIS
The Fatalist. Harper's Magazine, April.
SMITH, INGRID
Immortality to Jinotega. Southern Review, Autumn.
STAPLES, GEORGE
Mohammed from the Djebel. Antaeus, Spring-Summer.
SWEET, ROBERT BURDETTE
Of Golf and Disparate Love. Cimarron Review, April.

UPDIKE, JOHN
Nevada. Esquire, January.
Nakedness. Atlantic, June.

VALGARDSON, W. D.
A Private Comedy. University of Windsor Review, Spring.
VIVANTE, ARTURO
The Park. New Yorker, August 5.
VLIET, R. G.
Solitude. Southwest Review, Summer.

WILLIAMS, SHIRLEY
"The Lord Don't Like Ugly." New Letters, Winter

YATES, RICHARD
Evening on the Cote d'Azur—1952. Ploughshares, Vol. 2, No. 2.
YGLESIAS, HELEN
Kaddish and Other Matters. New Yorker, May 6.

II. *Foreign Authors*

BECKETT, SAMUEL
Mercier and Camier. Partisan Review, Vol. XLI, No. 3.
BERGELSON, DOVID
When All Is Said and Done. Trans. by Joachim Newgroschel. Antaeus, Autumn.
BORCHERT, WOLFGANG
The Sad Geraniums. Antaeus, Spring-Summer.

CHOUKRI, MOHAMMED
The Prophet's Slipper. Trans. by Paul Bowles. Harper's Magazine, February.
Bachir Alive and Dead. Trans. by Paul Bowles and the Author. Antaeus, Autumn.

GILLIATT, PENELOPE
Splendid Lives. New Yorker, August 5.
Autumn of a Dormouse. Atlantic, November.

HABTE-MARIAM, MESFIN
The Missing Grey. Prism International, Autumn.
HEJMADI, PADMA
Eknath. Southern Review, Summer.

KIELY, BENEDICT
There Are Meadows in Lanark. New Yorker, July 22.

LIMBOUR, GEORGES
The White Dog. Trans. by Donald Heiney. Iowa Review, Spring.

McWhirter, George
Why No Familiar Tune? Colorado Quarterly, Spring.

Oz, Amos
Stefa and Pomeranz. Commentary, August.

Rhys, Jean
La Grosse Fifi. Mademoiselle, October.

Sanchez, Luis Rafael
A Taste of Paradise. Trans. by Charles M. Cutler. Massachusetts Review, Winter-Spring.

Sarabhai, Miralirri
Kan. Aspen Leaves, Vol. 1, No. 2.

Sillitoe, Alan
Before Snow Comes. Prairie Schooner, Spring.

Stead, Christina
A View of the Homestead. Paris Review, Spring.

Von Doderer, Heimito
The Trumpets of Jericho. Trans. by Vincent Kling. Chicago Review, Vol. 26, No. 2.
Under Black Stars. Trans. by Vincent Kling. Chicago Review, Vol. 26, No. 2.

Walker, Ted
A Hill In Southern England. New Yorker, March 4.

Distinctive Short Stories, 1974

BRONER, E. M.
Habibi. Florida Quarterly, Spring.
BROWN, BRUCE BENNETT
Gilead Is Mine, Manasseh Is Mine. Wind, Spring.
BROWN, ROSELLEN
Why I Quit the Gowanus Liberation Front. Fiction International ⅔.
BRYAN, J. Y.
Frontier Vigil. Southwest Review, Winter.
BUMPUS, JERRY
Mr. Spoon's Visit. Prism International, Spring.
Our Golf Balls. Shenandoah, Spring.
BURR, ELAINE
Where the Woods Are. Cimarron Review, April.

CAMERON, DONALD
Snapshot: The Third Drunk. Atlantic, June.
CARLSON, ROY
A Problem of the Aged. Kansas Quarterly, Summer.
CARRINGTON, HAROLD
An Untitled Work. Gallimaufry, Fall.
CARVER, RAYMOND
The Fling. Perspective, Winter.
CASEY, JANE
Bloodlust. Shenandoah, Spring.
CHEEVER, JOHN
The Leaves, The Lion-Fish and The Bear. Esquire, November.
CHING, LAUREEN
Down by the River, Down by the Sea. South Dakota Review, Summer.
CIOFFARI, PHILIP
Self-Defense. Michigan Quarterly Review, Fall.
CLEARMAN, MARY
On the Hellgate. Four Quarters, Spring.
COLE, TOM
The Immense Walk of the Late Season Traveler. Esquire, September.

CULLINAN, ELIZABETH
An Accident. New Yorker, May 27.
CURLEY, DANIEL
Power Line. Four Quarters, Spring.

DASH, JOAN
A Slow Boat to Piraeus. Virginia Quarterly Review, Spring.
DEAL, BABS H.
Sailing to Byzantium. Southwest Review, Spring.
DEMARINIS, RICK
Under the Wheat. Iowa Review, Spring.
DUBUS, ANDRE
Going Under. North American Review, Spring.
DYBEK, STUART
The Long Thoughts. Iowa Review, Spring.

EATON, CHARLES EDWARD
The Secret of Aaron Blood. Southwest Review, Spring.
Madame Recamier's Last Farewell. Four Quarters, Winter.
EDWARDS, MARGARET
A Victory Garden in Search of a War. Greensboro Review, Spring.

FARRELL, JAMES
Joshua. Southern Review, Summer.
FELD, BERNARD
A Winter Story. Shenandoah, Spring.
FORSYTH, MALCOLM
The Promised Land. Southern Review, Summer.
FRANCIS, H. E.
Parts. Aphra, Winter.
FRIEDMAN, B. H.
Moving in Place. Hudson Review, Winter.

GALLANT, MAVIS
Irina. New Yorker, December 2.

GINGHER, MARIANNE
  No News. North American Review, Spring.
GOLDBERG, LESTER
  Joshua in the Rice Paddy. Colorado Quarterly, Spring.
GORDON, ROBERT
  Interregnum. Western Humanities Review, Summer.
GRAUBART, ROSE
  In A Mirror. Perspective, Winter.
GREENBERG, JOANNE
  You Asked Me About My Skates. Mademoiselle, June.
GREENE, GEORGE
  The Open University. Colorado Quarterly, Winter.
GREER, MARY ZETTLEMAN
  Sloan. Western Humanities Review, Fall.
GRIFFITH, PATRICIA
  Dust. Paris Review, Summer.

HALL, JAMES B.
  Young Marrieds. Shenandoah, Winter.
HARGRAVE, HARRY A.
  Brief December Day. Southern Humanities Review, Winter.
HARRINGTON, JOYCE
  The Cabin in the Hollow. Ellery Queen's Mystery Magazine, October.
HARTER, EVELYN
  A Drift of Incense. Kansas Quarterly, Winter.
HARTMAN, MATT
  Renee. Prism International, Autumn.
HAWKES, JOHN
  The Animal Eros. Antaeus, Spring-Summer.
HEMENWAY, ROBERT
  The Earthly Paradise. New Yorker, October 7.
HEMSCHEMEYER, JUDITH
  The Plastic Hip. Hudson Review, Summer.

HENDERSON, BILL
  Pop. Ontario Review, Fall.
HENDRIE, DON, JR.
  Ivory Soap. Iowa Review, Spring.
HERRIN, LAMAR
  The Rio Loja Ringmaster. Paris Review, Fall.
HOFFMAN, ALLEN
  Beggar Moon. Commentary, November.
HOSKINS, KATHERINE
  The Summer Time of Walter Thomas. Michigan Quarterly Review, Fall.
HOYER, GRACE
  Primal Therapy New Yorker, August 26.
HUGHES, MARY GRAY
  Don't Ever Cry in the A & P. Re: Artes Liberales, Fall.
HUMASON, S. M. W.
  Signs and Portents. Woman's Day, November.
HYDE, ELEANOR
  All Is Not Piroshki and Roses. Arizona Quarterly, Winter.

ICE, RUTH
  You Have to Pay. Kansas Quarterly, Winter.
IRSFELD, JOHN
  Stop, Rewind and Play. South Dakota Review, Spring.

JACKSON, JON
  Juggernaut. Ploughshares, Vol. 2, No. 1.
JACOBS, M. G.
  Bacon. Prairie Schooner, Summer.
JENNINGS, MICHAEL
  Sand So White. Carolina Quarterly, Fall.
JOHNSON, CANDACE
  Creak. Greensboro Review, Winter.

KALECHOFSKY, ROBERTA
  My Mother's Story. Forum, Winter.

KARATHEODORIS, J. J.
  Memorandum for a Rainy Night.
  South Dakota Review, Spring.
KEMPTON, MIKE
  Long Green. Paris Review, Fall.
KIRBY-SMITH, H. T.
  Herbie. Graffitti, Spring.
KRAFT, EUGENE
  Agnes' Quilt. Prairie Schooner, Summer.

LANGDON, JAMES
  The True Chameleon Is an Old
  World Lizard. Chicago Review,
  Vol. 26, No. 1.
LEFCOURT, PETER
  The Hangover Gambit. The Malahat
  Review, April.
LERMAN, LOUIS
  You Think God Is Jewish. Epoch,
  Winter.
LEWIS, CLAYTON W.
  Movie Times. Carolina Quarterly,
  Winter.
LOESER, KATINKA
  Honey-Moon. New Yorker, July 29.
LOWRY, BEVERLY
  Mama's Turn. Falcon, Vol. 5, No. 9.

McCARTIN, JAMES T.
  The Crazy Aunt. Arizona Quarterly,
  Winter.
MCLATCHY, J. D.
  The Dying Fall. Four Quarters, Autumn.
MAYER, DEBBIE
  Edcelina Baby Come Back Home.
  Redbook, November.
MAZUR, MARCIA LEVINE
  Tante Reba. National Jewish
  Monthly, April.
MENAKER, DANIEL
  Grief. New Yorker, January 28.
MERWIN, W. S.
  Two Stories. New Yorker, November
  18.

MONK, ELIZABETH GRAHAM
  A Mother. Yale Review, Summer.
MONTGOMERY, MARION
  The Front Porch. Georgia Review,
  Spring.
MOSHER, HOWARD FRANK
  First Snow. Four Quarters, Autumn.
MOSS, ROSE
  Siria. Cimarron Review, January.
MURDIE, DONNA HAGERTY
  Dark Place. Canadian Fiction, Summer.

NELSON, KENT
  The Clay Urn. Michigan Quarterly
  Review, Spring.
  To Go Unknowing. Sewanee Review,
  Winter.
NEWMAN, C. J.
  Your Green Coast. Malahat Review,
  July.
  Falling in Love, Again. Fiddlehead,
  Fall.

OATES, JOYCE CAROL
  The Golden Madonna. Playboy,
  March.
  Customs. Fiddlehead, Summer.
  Help. . . . Southern Review, Summer.
  The Snow Storm. Mademoiselle, September.
  The Transfiguration of Vincent Scoville. Canadian Fiction Magazine,
  Autumn.
  On the Gulf. South Carolina Review,
  November.
  Angst. University of Windsor Review, Fall-Winter.
OTT, STEPHEN DAVIS
  Divertimento. Western Humanities
  Review, Spring.

PAPENHAUSEN, CAROL
  The Unguarded Door. Prairie Schooner, Summer.
PETESCH, N. M.
  A Brief Biography of Ellie Brume.
  Kansas Quarterly, Winter.

PHILLIPS, LOUIS
   The Black Messiah Cape. South Dakota Review, Summer.

RAMSEY, JANE
   The Green Scent of Flowers. Literary Review, Spring.
RICE, MAGGIE
   Friday. Falcon, Vol. 5, No. 9.
RIPSTRA, STEVEN
   Wise Beyond My Years. Graffitti, Spring.
ROGERS, MICHAEL
   Do Not Worry About the Bear. Esquire, August.
ROOKE, LEON
   If You Love Me Meet Me There. University of Windsor Review, Spring.
   For Love of Eleanor. Southern Review, Summer.
ROGIN, GILBERT
   Night Thoughts. New Yorker, September 2.
ROSENSTEIN, HARRIET
   The Fraychie Story. Ms., March.

SADOFF, IRA
   An Enemy of the People. Carleton Miscellany, Spring-Summer.
SCHNEIDER, PHILIP
   The Pine. Nantucket Review, Summer-Fall.
SCHWARTZ, LYNNE SHARON
   Strategy. Aphra, Summer.
   Lucca. Ontario Review, Fall.
SHELBY, SUSAN
   Where Is Belinda? St. Andrews Review, Summer.
SHELNUTT, EVE
   The Apprentice. Virginia Quarterly Review, Summer.
SILVER, GARY
   A Fish Story. Colorado Quarterly, Spring.

SINGER, ISAAC BASHEVIS
   Three Encounters. New Yorker, February 25.
   A Tale of Two Sisters. Playboy, December.
SKEEN, P. PAINTER
   Winter Evenings: Spring Night. Epoch, Fall.
SMITH, C. W.
   Fearful Wishes. Mademoiselle, July.
SPENCER, ELIZABETH
   A Christian Education. Atlantic, March.
SPOHN, TERRY
   There Is a Hole in the Bottom of the Sea. Mississippi Review, Vol. III, No. 2.
STALLINGS, GARY
   Love. Kansas Quarterly, Summer.
STENFIELD, LARRY
   The Photographer and the Pony. Cimarron Review, July.
STERN, DANIEL
   Speak to Stone. Midstream, February.
STEVENS, AGNES SCOTT
   Sweet, Sweet Sorrow. Cimarron Review, October.
STOUT, ROBERT JOE
   The Hourglass. Kansas Quarterly, Summer.
STUART, JESSE
   Uncle Jeff Had a Fault. Southwest Review, Summer.
SUTHERLAND, FRASER
   Wilderness Wild — A Sexual Saga of the Canadian North. Canadian Fiction Magazine, Autumn.

TAAFE, GERALD
   The Assassination. Canadian Fiction Magazine, Autumn.
Taylor, DAVID C.
   Angel. Southern Review, Spring.
THOMAS, ANNABEL
   Twister. Forum, Winter.

THOMPSON, JEAN
Birds in Air. Fiction International ⅔.
TURNER, BLAIR PIERCE
Carla Boatwright. St. Andrews Review, Fall and Winter.

VAUDRIN, BILL
Hamushka. South Dakota Review, Summer.
VIVANTE, ARTURO
At the Dinner Table. New Yorker, December 30.
VEYIC, VLADIMIR
Wasting Time. Mademoiselle, January.

WAMPLER, MARTIN
Everything in the World. Southwest Review, Winter.
WEAVER, GORDON
At Otto Pfaff's Inn. Fiction International ⅔.

Granger Hunting. Southern Review, Summer.
WEST, PAUL
Tan Salaam. Paris Review, Spring.
WHEATCROFT, JOHN
The Appeal. Ohio Review, Winter.
WHITE, DORI
The Fence Is Down. McCall's, March.
WISER, WILLIAM
The Late Miss America. Georgia Review, Fall.
WOODS, WILLIAM CRAWFORD
Mayday. Atlantic, March.

ZACHARIA, DON
J. Partisan Review, Vol. XLI, No. 2.
ZELVER, PATRICIA
Norwegians. Esquire, January.
ZILLER, EUGENE
Moving. Literary Review, Spring.
ZVI, AVRAHAM BEN YITZHAK
Three Stories From a Labor Camp. National Jewish Monthly, October.

II. *Foreign Authors*

AKINAII, UEDA
Chrysanthemum Tryst. Trans. by Leon M. Zolbrod. Arizona Quarterly, Autumn.
ALI, SABAHATTIN
The Cart. Trans. by Fred Stark. New Letters, Summer.
ANDERSEN, BENNY
Layer Cake. Trans. by Hanne Gliese-Lee. Malahat Review, October.

BÖLL, HEINRICH
A Rare Breed of Man. Trans. by Dan and Barbara Perlmutter. Antaeus, Autumn.

DESNOES, EDMUNDO
An Adventure in the Tropics. Trans. by Eduardo Zayas Bazán. Paris Review, Spring.

DRABBLE, MARGARET
A Success Story. Ms., December.

GARSHIN, VSEVOLOD
The Signal. Trans. by Eugene M. Kayden. Colorado Quarterly, Summer.

HAWKES, JOHN
The Animal Eros. Antaeus, Spring-Summer.
HAZZARD, SHIRLEY
Sir Cecil's Ride. New Yorker, June 17.
HIDAYAT, SADIQ
The Man Who Killed His Passions. Trans. by Jerome W. Clinton. Literary Review, Fall.

KARASU, BILGE
A Wandering Monk. Trans. by Fred
Stark. New Letters, Summer.
KUNDERA, MILAN
The Hitchhiking Game. Let the Old
Dead Make Room for the New
Dead. The Golden Apple of Eter-
nal Desire. Esquire, April.

LENZ, SIEGFRIED
The House of Love. Trans. by Dan
Latimer. The Literary Review,
Summer.

MARQUIS, RENÉ
Three Men by the River. Massachu-
setts Review, Winter-Spring.
MENESES, GUILLERMO
Destiny Is a Forgotten God. Trans.
by Charles M. Sphar. Prism Inter-
national, Autumn.
MORTIMER, PENELOPE
A Love Story. New Yorker, July.

NESVISKY, MATTHEW
Immigrant Soldier. Response, Fall.

O'FAOLAIN, SEAN
Dürling or the Faithless Wife. Playboy, January.

PERERA, PADMA
Afternoon of the House. New
Yorker, June 24.

SÁNCHEZ, LUIS RAFAEL
A Taste of Paradise. Massachusetts
Review, Winter-Spring.

VON DODERER, HEIMITS
A Person Made of Porcelain. Trans.
by Vincent Kling. Chicago Review
Vol. 20, No. 2.

WALKER, TED
The Bedroom. New Yorker, November 25.

Addresses of American and Canadian Magazines Publishing Short Stories

American Review (formerly New American Review), 661 Fifth Avenue, New York, New York 10019

Americas, Organization of American States, Washington, D.C. 20006

Ampersand Magazine, Ltd., 816 South Hancock Street, Philadelphia, Pennsylvania 19147

Antaeus, 1 West 30th Street, New York, New York 10001

Antioch Review, 212 Xenia Avenue, Yellow Springs, Ohio 45387

Aphra, RFD, Box 355, Springtown, Pennsylvania 18081

Ararat, 109 East 40th Street, New York, New York 10016

Argosy, 205 East 42nd Street, New York, New York 10017

Arizona Quarterly, University of Arizona, Tucson, Arizona 85721

Arlington Quarterly, Box 366, University Station, Arlington, Texas 76010

Atlantic Monthly, 8 Arlington Street, Boston, Massachusetts 02116

Bachy, 11317 Santa Monica Boulevard, West Los Angeles, California 90025

Boston University Journal, Box 357, Boston University Station, Boston, Massachusetts 02215

Brushfire, Box 9012 University Station, Reno, Nevada

Canadian Fiction, 4248 Weisbrod Street, Prince George, British Columbia, Canada

Canadian Forum, 30 Front Street West, Toronto, Ontario, Canada

Capilano Review, 2055 Purcell Way, North Vancouver, British Columbia, Canada

Carleton Miscellany, Carleton College, Northfield, Minnesota 55057

Carolina Quarterly, P.O. Box 1117, Chapel Hill, North Carolina 27514

Chicago Review, University of Chicago, Chicago, Illinois 60637

Cimmaron Review, 203B Morrill Hall, Oklahoma State University, Stillwater, Oklahoma 74074

Colorado Quarterly, University of Colorado, Boulder, Colorado 80303